HEART ⊕F ST⊕NE

LUNA™
www.LUNA-Books.com

LUNA™

First trade printing November 2007

HEART OF STONE

ISBN-13: 978-0-373-80292-0
ISBN-10: 0-373-80292-7

www.LUNA-Books.com

Printed in U.S.A.

For my dad, Thomas Allen Murphy,
who likes this one best so far.

ACKNOWLEDGMENTS

Normally it doesn't take an army for me to write a book. This one, though, required a rather absurd amount of feedback. To wit:

My agent, Jennifer Jackson, made me do a major rewrite on the original manuscript, then said, "This is *much* better! Now cut another thirty pages from the first hundred and we'll really have something here!" You were right. Thank you.

My editor, Mary-Theresa Hussey, made me push the book in ways I wouldn't have on my own, ways that gave the story more depth and richness than I'd ever imagined it to have. Thank you, too. It would be okay if neither of you ever made me work that hard again....

The art department has once more outdone itself, giving me yet another cover I'm thrilled to have my work judged by. Glowing thanks are due to art director Kathleen Oudit and to artist Chris McGrath. You guys help build careers, and I cannot thank you enough.

Dor and Lisa helped me with New York details, so anything I got wrong is either their fault (!) or I made it up wholesale to fit the world. :)

Tara, Mary Anne and Janne gave me feedback on the third draft, by which time I could no longer see the book for the words, so their comments were invaluable. I believe Silkie and Jai, my usual suspects, read *every draft* without their enthusiasm flagging, and Trent read it at least three times. Their fortitude astounds me. Rob, Deborah, Lisa (again!), Lydia and Morgan listened to me whine interminably about revisions. Rob, in particular, offered some critical brainstorming sessions that did huge amounts to help me develop the mythology of this world; so, too, did Sarah. Thank you all.

And all I can say to Ted is that I literally could not have written this book without you. I'll give you a copy with the bits you helped with highlighted, and you'll see how true that is. Thank you so much, hon. I love you.

AUTHOR'S NOTE

Over the last couple of years I've had a lot of people comment on my discipline, a mysterious thing that they see as being more self-evident than I do. In most ways, writing is a job like any other: you have deadlines for projects and people get cranky if you don't turn them in on time. It's true that if you're writing without a contract or a publisher (which I was, when I wrote the first draft of *Heart of Stone*), it does take a lot of discipline. It also takes a lot of dreaming, because when you're writing on spec and hoping for that first sale, the only thing that keeps you going is faith and determination and the willingness to sit down in the chair and apply fingers to keyboard.

This book is the result of more butt-in-chair, fingers-to-keyboard work than I want to think about, and a massive chunk of it was done during an international move. I'm utterly astonished at how that kind of thing focuses the ol' mind: it's really easy to be a writer and discover you've whiled away your day, effectively creating a situation where you don't have time to work. (Notice how people with 9–5 jobs very, very rarely find themselves with a day where they just don't have time to go to work? I certainly never did.) It would have been extremely easy to not have time to work in the midst of moving across the world. In my case, I found out I can work through just about anything, if I really *have* to, and I suppose that's what people mean when they say they admire my discipline.

Me, I believe pretty much anyone can do the same thing, if they want to. I'd like to think some of that comes through in my stories—not much is actually impossible, if we not only *dream,* but *do.* The book you're holding is the result of both dreaming and doing. I hope you enjoy it!

Catie

SHE RAN, L⊕NG strides that ate the pavement despite her diminutive height. Her hair, full of corkscrew curls, was pulled back from her face, bunches jouncing as her feet impacted the asphalt surface. The words *feminine* and *female,* less interchangeable than they might seem, both described her well. *Feminine,* as he understood it, suggested a sort of delicacy, though not without strength. *Female* encompassed power as blunt and raw as sex. Watching her, neither descriptor would suffice without the other.

Lithe and athletic, she ran nearly every night, usually not long after sundown. Tonight she was late; midnight was barely an hour off, closer by far than the late-January sunset. He watched from his arboreal refuge, hunched high above the concrete paths, protective and possessive of the slender woman taking her exercise in a dangerous city.

There were safer places to run, safer times; he thought she must know that. The park was notorious for nighttime crime, but she threw away caution for something greater. For defiance against an ordered world, and perhaps for the thrill of knowing the danger she put herself in. There was confidence in her action, too; her size very likely precluded fighting off attackers, but the muscles that powered her run would help her outpace any enemy that might approach. It was a gambit, and he liked her for it. It reminded him of other women he'd known, sometimes braver than wise, always willing to risk themselves for others. Such demonstrations made him remember there was life outside the confines he'd created for himself.

So he watched from high in the treetops, protecting her whether she knew it or not. Choosing to make her safe despite the independent streak that sent her running after dark, without taking away her illusion of bold solitude. She would never see him, he reasoned. Her people were predators, and they'd come from the trees. In the primitive part of the mind that spoke of caution, *they* were the danger that came from above.

Humans never looked up.

He shook himself as she took a corner, careening out of sight. Then he leaped gracefully over the treetops, following.

Air burned in her lungs, every breath of cold searing deep and threatening to make her cough with its dryness. Each footfall on the asphalt was the jolt of a syllable through her body: *Ir. Ir. Ir. Ra. Shun. Al.* There were slick patches on the trail, thin sheets of black ice that didn't reflect until she was on them. She slid ten inches, keeping her center as if she wore ice skates, stomach tightening to make her core solid. Keeping control in an out-of-control moment. The action stung her body as vividly as a man's touch might, heat sweeping through her without regard for sense or sensibility. Then the ice was gone and she was running again.

Eyes up, watching the trail and the woods. The air was brisk and as clear as it ever got in New York. Pathways were lit by lamps that buzzed and flickered at whim. Patches of dark were to be wary of, making her heart beat faster with excitement. No headset. Taking risks was one thing. Outright stupidity was another, and even she knew she ran a thin line between the two already. Her own labored breathing and the pounding of her footsteps were enough to drown out more nearby noise than was safe. That was part of it, too, part of the irresistible draw of the park. She was not safe. Nothing she did would ever make her wholly safe.

It was almost like being able to fly.

"Irrational," Margrit whispered under her breath. The word seemed to give her feet wings like Hermes, sending her down the path with a new surge of speed. Feet jolting against the ground made echoes in her hips and breasts, every impact stinging her feet and reminding her of sex and laughter and the things that made life worth living.

Risking everything made it worth living. Friends, only half joking, wondered if she was suicidal, never quite understanding the adventure that drew Margrit to the park at night.

The Central Park rapist had confessed when she was in her first year of law school and still wondering if she should have chosen to follow in her parents' footsteps—either her mother's MBA or her father's medical degree—but the headlines that morning had solidified her belief in her own decision. Even now, seven years later, she knew her parents wished she'd chosen one of their professions, or at least a more profitable arm of law than the one she pursued, but thinking back to that day always rebuilt her confidence. Buoyed by the memory, she stretched her legs further and reached again for the feeling of freedom running in the park gave her.

Minutes later, she skidded to a halt under a light and leaned a hip against a battered bench, putting her hands on her knees. Her ponytail flipped upside down, nearly brushing the ground as she heaved in air. Thirty seconds and she would start running again. Twenty-nine. Twenty-eight.

"Good evening."

Margrit spasmed upward, whipping around to face the speaker. A man with pale hair and lifted eyebrows stood in the puddle of lamplight, several feet away. He was wearing a suit, and had his hands tucked in the pockets of the slacks. "I'm sorry," he said. "I didn't mean to frighten you."

"Jesus Christ." She backed away a step or two, putting even more distance between herself and the man. Caution knotted her stomach, sending chills of adrenaline through her. "Get the hell away from me." Every muscle in her body was bunched, ready to sprint, but her heart pounded harder with the thrill of the encounter than with the impulse to run. She wore running shoes, as opposed to his smooth-soled leather slip-ons, and had a head start. Caution hadn't flared into panic or even true fear yet; her confidence in her own abilities was greater than the evident danger.

That degree of cockiness was going to get her killed someday.

Not today, Margrit whispered to herself, and aloud warned, "I have a gun."

His eyebrows rose higher. "I don't." He took his hands

out of his pockets and lifted them slowly, so she could see more of his torso. His shirt was lilac in the lamplight, almost glowing against the jacket lining. There was no gun in evidence. "I was just out for a walk." He made a small, careful gesture to one side. "I didn't mean to startle you."

"Yeah, well, you freaking well did." Margrit edged back another step or two, balancing her weight on her toes. "This is Central Park, asshole. You don't start up conversations with people here. Especially in the middle of the night."

He spread his fingers. "Do you normally carry on conversations with people in Central Park in the middle of the night?"

"No." The excitement of the moment was passing, and so was the high from running. The sense of fun, if that was the right word for the encounter, faded with it. Margrit took one more step back. "I'm going now. Don't follow me." He had at least ten inches of height on her, but she had faith in her own speed. *Faith* warred with *confidence,* and both lost out to an unspoken admission of *arrogance* that almost brought an undermining smile to Margrit's lips.

"I won't, but—may I ask you one question?"

"You just did." Margrit curled her lip in irritation. She hated that particular piece of tomfoolery and resented it coming out of her own mouth. "What?"

"Where are you hiding your gun?" The man looked her up and down, more critically than lasciviously. Margrit glanced down at herself.

Tennies. Socks. Running tights with hot pink stripes that picked up the blue in the streetlamp and radiated neon purple. A snug white-and-green sweatshirt that covered her midriff only if she didn't move; otherwise, her belly flashed between hems.

There wasn't really anywhere for a gun.

Margrit looked up again. "None of your goddamn business." Her breath puffed in the cool air, reminding her that she was dressed for the late January weather only if she was running to keep herself warm. She bounced on her toes, muscle tightening in her calves. "Don't follow me," she warned again.

"I wouldn't dream of it," he murmured.

Margrit raced down the path, putting a dozen yards between herself and the man in a few seconds. When she looked back a moment later, he was gone.

"You're going to get yourself killed, Margrit."

Margrit leaned against the open door, doubled over to pull at her laces. Her breath still came in little puffs, and she counted out syllables with each one. *Ir. Ra. Shun. Al.* The encounter in the park had her repeating the word more often than usual. Irrationally safe. Irrationally foolish. Irrationally defensive.

"Hello, nice to see you, too, my day was fine, thanks, how about yours? What are you doing up this late, anyway? Where's Cam?" Margrit closed the door and locked it, leaning against the knob with both hands behind her. Her roommate stood down the hall, filling the kitchen door frame. "Cole, I'm fine, really." She straightened and came down the corridor, brushing past him. His sweater, thick cable knit, touched her arm as she did so, and she added, "Nice sweater," in hopes of distracting him, before she breathed, "I'm fine," a final time.

"She went to bed already. Five a.m. client. Thank you,"

he added automatically. "Irish wool. Cam gave it to me for Christmas."

Margrit shuddered. "Five a.m. Better her than me. Oh yeah, I remember. I said I was going to borrow it and she threatened to tie my legs in a knot. It's a nice sweater. She has good taste."

"Of course she does. She's dating me." Cole offered a brief smile that fell away again as he visibly realized Margrit had succeeded in distracting him. "You're fine this time, Grit. I'm afraid you're going to get hurt." He scowled across the kitchen, more in concern than anger. "You shouldn't run after dark."

"I know, but I didn't get out of work until late."

"You never do."

"Cole, what are you, my housemate or my big brother?"

"I'm your friend, and I worry about you when you go out running in Central Park in the middle of the night. You're going to get yourself killed."

"Maybe, but not tonight." The words lifted hairs on her arms, a reminder that she'd thought something similar facing the pale-haired man in the park. She should have heard him, Margrit thought. Even over the sound of her own breathing, she should have heard his approach and departure. Being careless enough to allow someone to sneak up on her was alarming.

But there'd been nothing of the predator in the man, despite his height. Margrit had defended enough criminals to know when she was being sized up as bait. The man in the park had moved with graceful, slow motions, as if aware his very bulk bespoke danger, and he mitigated as best he could with calming actions. As if she might be an easily startled animal—which she supposed she was. The idea brought a brief smile to her lips.

Margrit leaned on the counter and pulled the refrigerator door open. The appliance was an orange behemoth from the fifties, too stubborn to break down, energy inefficient and with a silver handle that could double as a club in a pinch. Margrit was unconscionably fond of it. She grabbed a cup of yogurt and bumped the door closed, turning to lean against it instead of the counter. "I didn't mean to worry you. I just really needed to go for a run."

"There's this crazy new invention, Grit. It's called a treadmill. They have them at gyms. Gyms that are open twenty-four hours a day, no less. Like the one Cam works at. She keeps offering you a membership."

"Bah." Margrit stuck her spoon in her mouth and turned to open the fridge again, looking for more food. "I don' like thredmillth. Y'don' go anywhrr."

"No, but there aren't random lunatics in the gym, either."

"Speaking of random lunatics, there was this guy in the park. Said hello to me." The memory of the man wouldn't leave her, lingering around the edges of her mind. His light eyes had been colorless in the park lamps, and he'd had a good mouth. Well shaped without being feminine, even pursed that way as he'd looked her over.

God. She had friends she'd known for years whose features she couldn't remember that clearly. Margrit shook her head, exiting the fridge with a plate of meatloaf in hand, using its mundanity to push away thoughts of the stranger. "You made dinner. I worship you."

Cole folded his arms over his chest, frowning. "Flattery will get you nowhere. What guy in the park? Dammit, Grit—"

"He was just some guy in a business suit." He hadn't looked cold. Despite thirty-degree weather and no winter coat, he'd seemed comfortable. The silk shirt beneath his suit jacket couldn't have afforded much warmth, but there'd been no shiver of cold flesh when he'd opened his jacket to show he was unarmed. Maybe the jacket had been so well cut as to hide padding, but Margrit doubted it. The breadth of shoulder and chest had looked to be all his own.

"And that what, renders him harmless?"

"I don't know. He looked like a lawyer or something. Speaking of which." Margrit cast a look of mock despair across the kitchen, at the same time feeling relief to have work that would take her mind off the blond man.

The kitchen expanded into the dining room, a solid-wood, double-door frame making the rooms nominally separate. Legal briefs and somber-colored binders were piled precariously on the dining room table, over which hung an enameled black birdcage instead of a light fixture. Two desk lamps fought for space on the edges of the table, bordering a laptop-size clearing. "I should get to work. Two hundred grand in student loans won't go away if I end up unemployed."

Cole snorted. "I know better, Margrit. You got through school on scholarships and help from your mom and dad."

Margrit pulled her lips back from her teeth in a false snarl. "You've known me too long. Let me tell myself little white lies, Cole. I like to pretend I'm not spoiled rotten. 'Mom and Dad paid for school' sounds so snotty. Anyway, I still won't have a job if I don't get my work done, and this place needs rent paid on it just like everywhere else."

"Did it ever occur to you working for somebody who paid better than Legal Aid might help with that?"

"Only every time I talk to Mom, so don't you start. That's what they get for sending me to Townsend. Oaths to make the world a better place stick with you. Legal Aid needs all the help they can get. And I'm good at it."

"You have an overdeveloped sense of responsibility, you know that?" Cole sighed, giving up the argument. "You should cook some kind of vegetable to go with the meatloaf. And go to bed so you can get to work early enough to leave at a decent hour so you're not running around Central damned Park in the middle of the night."

"I will," Margrit promised. "Swear to God. As soon as I've finished going over these papers." She gestured at the dining room table. "I'll be in bed by midnight."

"Margrit, it *is* midnight."

Margrit cast a guilty look toward the clock. "It's only a few minutes after eleven!"

Cole eyed the clock, then Margrit. "You know that going over papers doesn't mean going into the living room and turning on the TV?"

"Yeah. I'll be good. You can go to bed."

Cole drew his chin in and scrutinized her. "Promise?"

"I promise. Scout's honor." Margrit held up three fingers.

"Okay. Should I wake you up on my way out?"

"At four-thirty?" Margrit couldn't keep the horror out of her voice.

Cole shook his head. "I don't start until seven. Chef Vern's got a catering event tomorrow night and wants me to do the pastries for it, so somebody else gets to make the doughnuts."

"No wonder you're up so late." Margrit frowned. "When was the last time you made a doughnut, Cole?"

"Christmas," he said placidly. "You remember. Cam asked me to make them for breakfast."

"I meant for work."

"Oh. Probably in culinary school. Don't be difficult. Do you want me to get you up?"

Margrit pulled her hair out of its ponytail and scrubbed her hand through it, fingers catching in springy curls. "Yeah."

"Okay. Get your work done and go to bed. Night, Grit." Cole smiled at her and disappeared down the hall.

"Night, Cole," she called, and waited. When his door clicked shut, she grabbed the plate of meatloaf, a carton of double-swirl chocolate fudge chunk ice cream, a legal brief from the table and a pen from the birdcage, and sauntered into the living room to plunk down on the couch. Soft cushions grabbed her hips, sucking her in with the confidence of an old lover. Margrit spilled her armload onto the cushion next to her and switched on the TV, flipping to the news as she rescued the meatloaf before it stained her paperwork.

She elbowed open her binder and twisted her neck to read it as she ate. The television droned on in the background: a dockworker had drowned and the union was striking; two murder victims had been found in Queens. A note of local interest news was wedged between sound bites of doom and gloom: a 1920s speakeasy, recently discovered hidden behind a collapsed subway tunnel, was being opened to the public on a limited basis. Lest the site opening be considered too cheery, the reporter continued on to solemnly report a Park Avenue suicide. Margrit smiled ruefully at the endless bad news, its dismaying litany unable to deflate the good cheer she felt from her run.

"Irrational creature," she mumbled, then frowned at the ice cream carton. "Spoon." She fought her way out of the couch and brought the meat loaf plate into the kitchen, the binder still in her free hand.

She'd spent enough late nights on the case—a plea for clemency for a woman convicted of murdering a viciously abusive boyfriend—that she could see the annotated pages and carefully printed facts when she closed her eyes. Luka Johnson had served four years of a twenty-year sentence, only allowed to meet with her daughters once a week under highly supervised conditions. The case had been dropped in Margrit's lap literally weeks out of law school. She'd been Luka's advocate for the entire length of her incarceration.

Four years. It didn't seem so long, but Margrit had watched Luka's youngest daughter grow from a squalling babe in arms to a thoughtful, talkative little girl in that time. The children lived with a foster mother who cared for them very much, but every week that they left Luka behind in prison was a little harder for everyone. The trial judge was sympathetic to their cause; the state coalition against domestic violence had given its support. The governor was expected to hear and make a decision on the clemency within the week. Margrit couldn't stay away from the paperwork, grooming it for the hundredth time, wondering if she'd missed anything that might cost Luka and her children more years of their shared lives.

Ir-ra-shun-al, a corner of her brain chanted. Margrit smacked her head with the spoon. As if doing so turned up the reception, the TV in the other room suddenly got louder, a female reporter's voice cutting through the quiet apartment: "...park improvements will have to be delayed...." The sound cut out again. Spoon in her mouth, Margrit went back to the living room and dropped into the couch, juggling ice cream and the remote to turn up the volume as she watched the pink-cheeked reporter.

"This area of the park, scheduled for renovation, is tonight the scene of a crime the likes of which has not been witnessed in over a decade," the woman said earnestly. Locks of hair blew into her eyes and she tucked them behind an ear with a gloved hand. Margrit sat up straighter, clutching the ice cream carton. "A young woman was brutally murdered here tonight, just beyond where I'm standing now, Jim. I have with me Nereida Holmes, who witnessed the attack."

The reporter turned, angling her microphone under the mouth of a petite woman with large eyes and carefully arranged, flat shining curls. She wore a chocolate-brown coat, the collar lined with darker fur. In the hard white light of the TV camera, the fur looked stiff and unyielding, as if it would prick the woman's chin.

"It looked like he hit her, no?" Nereida Holmes's words were tinged with a faint Spanish accent. "He was crouched over her, like he was some kinda animal. Growling. There was blood on his hands. And then he saw me and ran away."

The reporter pulled the mike back, demanded, "Can you tell us what he looked like?" and thrust it toward Nereida again.

"Um, yes, he was a white guy, maybe so tall?" she lifted a hand well above her head, some inches beyond the top of the reporter's head, too. "He had long legs—you could see that even when he was down low. And he had light hair, real light, and good shoulders. I couldn't see nothing else, 'cept he was wearing a business suit, but no winter jacket." She shook her head. "He musta been cold."

C.E. MURPHY

"Anything else you can tell us?"

Nereida blanched even more. "I heard that girl screaming. It was terrible. I hope they catch that bastard."

"Thank you, Ms. Holmes." The reporter turned back to the camera. "Anyone wishing to report seeing a man of this description in Central Park between the hours of 10:45 and 11:15 p.m. this evening, please contact the police immediately. This is Holly Perry, reporting for Channel Three. Back to you, Jim."

Ice cream slid off Margrit's spoon and plopped onto her running tights, the chill immediate and sharp against her thigh. She startled, stuffing the spoon back into the carton, and reached for the remote. She turned the television off and sat, silent, staring at the blank screen.

TWO

THE BELLS OF the nearby cathedral counted out the small hours of the morning, warning of the need to retreat before sunlight found him. He watched her window from his high perch across the street, safe on an apartment building rooftop. It would be such a little thing to stand on her balcony, such an easy thing to do. To make himself just that much more a part of her life. A glance inside her world, a moment of intimacy beyond anything he'd shared in more years than he cared to recall....

Such a risk.

Logic dictated he wouldn't be noticed, not at this hour, when so many lights were off, implying slumber behind curtained windows. It was nothing: half a block, a few floors down. He stretched and flexed as if he might make good the thought.

The danger was that, of all the windows in that row of apartments, hers was the only one with the lights still on. He shifted his weight forward, then settled back again, rumbling with indecision. Surely she slept. There'd been no movement since minutes after he'd followed her home. Surely she slept, and the amber light bathing the balcony wouldn't reveal him to prying eyes.

Centuries of habit left him hanging back, unable to make the leap. He'd chanced it once already that evening, in speaking to her. Getting close enough to see that her curling hair was browner than he'd thought, that her petite form was even smaller than he'd expected. Close enough to see the strength in her legs and the muscle in her stomach as her shirt shifted against her skin. Soft fabric; softer-looking skin, made sallow by park lights until he couldn't be sure of its color. He'd never seen her in daylight. He never would.

Close enough to see emotion in her dark eyes. Anger at being startled, defensiveness and caution, but not the fear he'd expected from a woman accosted, no matter how politely, in Central Park after dark. It was the lack of fear that had prompted him to follow her home.

He hadn't done that in a long time, not in three years. He'd wondered and imagined, but never dared. She lived much closer to the park than he'd thought, west of the unfinished cathedral. He knew from signs posted on the streets that students lived there, paying prices for their postage-stamp apartments that would have bought whole townships in his youth.

There was a man in the apartment with her. His tenor voice had been by turns cajoling and concerned, while she—*Margrit*. Leaning back, he savored the name, baring a slow, toothy smile. "Margrit," the man in the apartment had called her, while they'd argued over her safety and her job at something called Legal Aid.

So she was a lawyer. He had no personal experience with

lawyers; he tended to think of them as white knights in pursuit of justice, though even he knew from television that the idea bordered on absurd. But still, she was a lawyer, and her name was Margrit. The information was a priceless gift, stolen from the air as their voices carried out through the glass balcony doors. It was more detail about a woman he watched than he'd learned in decades.

He curled his fingers, feeling the heavy scrape of nails against his palms, and dropped deeper into a crouch, his shoulders slumped. Consequences could not be damned. There would be no silent leap through the city night to look in Margrit's window, not tonight and not any night henceforth.

Winter chill had little effect on his kind, but cold seemed to penetrate his bones as he accepted the truth. He drew warmth around him in a winged cloak, and put a hand down on icy cement, bracing himself on three points as he watched Margrit's window and waited for dawn to come.

She ran across the Rockefeller Center skating rink, skidding on the ice more dramatically than she'd ever done racing the paths of Central Park. Hundreds of people surrounded her, small and dark-haired, black-eyed and smooth-skinned. None of them reached to help as she slid, but stood apart, watching her with calm wide eyes.

Heat followed her, melting the ice and turning it to water. When she lifted her gaze, the watchers wore soft fur cloaks that repelled the rising flood, while she swam against a current that came from nowhere. Nothing seemed to move them, even her stretched-out fingers pleading for help.

Hot fingers wrapped around hers, a slight man's solid

grasp. He pulled her up with surprising ease, then bowed gallantly. A white silk cravat as long as Doctor Who's fluttered around him, catching in wind created by burgeoning heat. He whispered something indecipherable, then arched his eyebrows and nodded behind her. Margrit whipped around in a hiss of skirts, her practical running clothes replaced by a gown that she knew, instinctively, suggested a height her petite frame had never seen.

Dancers surrounded her in a ballroom filled with golden light, the small dark people at the skating rink now gliding across the floor with such grace she could only gape, admiration mixed with despair. No one could move so beautifully. Surrounded by them, she felt cloddish and slow, like a lump of earth trying to emulate a star.

Something changed. With a rustle of warning, the crowd parted to allow a tall man entrance. He wore silver, more striking than simple white, and it made him a ghost among the small dark people, eminently dangerous. His pale hair was long and loose, no longer tied back as it had been when she'd seen him in the park. A few strands fell in slashes across his cheekbones, emphasizing a brief and deadly smile.

A weapon pressed against the inside of Margrit's wrist: a pencil. She acted without considering, leaping forward and slamming the wooden spike into the vampire's breast.

He brought his hand up, to catch the pieces as the pencil shattered against his chest. Confusion lit colorless eyes as he lifted his gaze to Margrit's, and she felt fury color hers.

"But it worked on *Buffy!*"

The last word broke, her voice cracking, and someone shook her shoulder. "Margrit. Wake up, Grit. You fell asleep on the couch. Again!" The voice was fondly impatient. "Wake up. You're having a nightmare."

She sat up with a gasp, then fell back on the couch, groaning. Papers crinkled under her shoulder. She put the heel of her hand to her eye, rubbing to waken herself, and swung her head to stare blearily at Cole, who crouched beside the couch.

He reached out and pulled the DVD player's remote control device from under her hair. "You've got a bright red impression of this on your face," he said. "I thought you said you were going to bed."

"Whutimeissih?" Margrit groaned again and sat up, running her fingers over her cheek. Small indentations marred it, her jaw marked with the recognizable curve of the remote's oversized play button. She pushed at it without focus, half expecting the TV to come on and a DVD to start running.

"It's six thirty." Cole hung his arms over his knees like a gorilla. "What time did you fall asleep?"

Margrit grunted. "Two? Sunfin like that. Dyhaffalookso awake?" She glared at Cole.

"Yeah, I do have to look so awake." He gave her a fond, if exasperated, smile. "I got up half an hour ago and I've showered. Cam's already gone. I thought you were going to go to bed, Grit."

"I was." Memory cleared her mind and she scrunched her eyes shut. "I was, but I turned on the TV—" Cole growled disapprovingly and she raised her voice, ignoring him "—and the guy I told you about seeing last night probably butchered a girl in the park after I came in. I didn't feel like sleeping after that." She suddenly recalled her dream, remembering the pale man's gentle movements and the strength evident in his hands. Neighbors would say he seemed like such a nice man. She shivered, bringing her attention back to Cole's dismayed question: "Did you call Tony?"

Margrit shifted her gaze away. "No. I didn't even think of it. It was the middle of the night."

She could almost hear her housemate grind his teeth. "You're on the outs again, aren't you? It can't be that bad. Come on, Margrit. You met a murderer and didn't think to call your own personal homicide detective?"

She hunched her shoulders. "He's not my own personal anything, Cole. You know how things are."

"Call him, Grit. And promise me you're not going into the park again after dark. Margrit, promise me." He forced a little humor into his voice. "How're we going to pay rent on this place if you get yourself killed? We need you."

Margrit turned her head to the side, birdlike, to eye him. "Cam'd beat the landlord up if he threatened to throw you out. What's the point in having a fiancée who's a physical trainer if you can't sic her on the bad guys?"

"She can bench-press a Mini, not defeat Chuck Norris in hand-to-hand combat," Cole said. "So you need to not get killed, okay?"

Margrit leaned to the left, looking over Cole's shoulder at the VCR clock. "I won't get killed, and you'd better get going. You're gonna be late."

He put his palms on his thighs and levered himself up with a sigh. "Just be careful, Grit, okay?"

"I'm always careful. Go, you're gonna be late."

"Yeah." Cole gave her a brief smile and left. Margrit nearly sank back down into the couch, then growled at herself and shuffled through the apartment and into the bathroom. Cole had left the medicine cabinet door open, and her reflection caught her unawares as she switched the light on.

Dark brown corkscrew curls stood out from her face, deliberate highlights of red and gold catching the light. Her hair had too much body to be ruined by a night's sleep, but café latte skin was a mishmash of red marks from cheekbone to jaw on the right side. Margrit groaned and ran her palm over them again, serving to redden her face more without having a noticeable effect on the imprint.

"They'll run you out on a rail, girl." She skimmed her shirt and bra off, making a pile on the floor. Her legs had narrow lines down the sides from the seams on the running tights, and there were wrinkles on her torso from her shirt crumpling against it. Her toenails glittered gold as she climbed into the shower and stood in the water collecting in the bottom of the tub. Every three weeks she poured a bottle of clog remover down the drain, starting anew the battle against shedding hair. It was almost time to do it again.

Sunday, she promised. Sunday, she would clean the bathroom.

Twenty minutes later, wrapped in a towel and scowling at the uninspiring contents of her closet, she amended Sunday's plans to include laundry.

"What are you doing here?"

Margrit ducked her head at the greeting, looking up again with a hint of humor dancing in her eyes. "Hi, Tony." She'd lingered at the Homicide doorway, waiting to be noticed before entering; more than one semifamiliar face had given her a quick smile of greeting while she watched the detective who was, as Cole had surmised, her off-again lover. After weeks apart, as usual, Margrit found his warm Italian coloring and strong features surprising. Rather than making the heart grow fonder, distance made it forgetful, blurring the edges of good looks into something more white bread and bland.

Humor infused the thought. If anything, the man she'd met in the park the night before should be the white bread one, with his pale skin and paler hair, his bone structure so well shaped it might have been carved by a sculptor. Tony, by comparison, was vivacious and alive, especially now, with anger drawing his eyebrows down and bringing more color to his cheeks.

"No." The detective got to his feet and leaned his weight on his desk, making it less a barrier and more a tool of aggravation. "You don't get to walk in with a cheerful 'Hi, Tony' when you haven't called for three weeks and I don't even know what I've done wrong this time." His hair was shorter than the last time Margrit'd seen him, clipped just the wrong length and making his ears look too big for his head. Margrit threaded through gray desks and patches of winter sunlight as he spoke. She reached him and leaned across his desk until their heads were only inches apart, answering quietly.

"You didn't call, either, Tony. All right? Are we even?"

"No, we're not." His knuckles turned white from pressure before he dropped his chin to his chest and muttered, "This isn't the place to talk about it." A Brooklyn accent came through strong in the last words, spoken so fast Margrit leaned in another few centimeters to make sure she caught every word. "What are you doing here, Margrit?"

"Official business, actually. I wasn't just dropping by." Too late she realized the impact of her phrasing, but the words were spoken. He looked up, only a hint of injury visible in his brown eyes. "Tony—"

"Forget about it. What is it now, another hardened criminal to get off?"

Margrit felt her own knuckles turning white as she leaned too hard against the desk, afraid to allow herself to speak for several long seconds. "This is why it never works, Tony," she said, all but under her breath. The argument was as old as their relationship, two people separated by the same justice system. "Can we not do this right now? It's not going to change anything. I'm still going to go down to my job at the Legal Aid offices when we're done talking, just like I do every day. But right now I need to talk to you."

"You know, if you want a low-paying lawyer job, you could go work for the D.A.'s office prosecuting these bastards instead of getting them off."

"Tony!" Margrit brought his gaze up with the sharpness of her tone, then held her breath until she trusted her voice again. "I talked with the guy you want to bring in for the Central Park murder last night."

Personal insult and injury bled out of Tony's face, replaced by professional interest tinged with anger and concern. "When?"

"Last night. Right before the murder. I was out running." Margrit lifted a hand to stop the lecture before it began. "Shut up, Tony, and just let me finish, okay?" She watched him set his teeth together, holding the pose a moment before he gestured for her to take a seat. Margrit did, crossing her legs at the knee and brushing invisible lint off the slacks she'd finally selected. "The park lights bleached enough that I don't know what color his eyes were. Light colored, blue or green, but they could've been yellow. Same with his hair. Pale, practically white under the lights. We talked for about thirty seconds. I can probably give a good enough description for an artist."

Tony sighed explosively. "I'll get one. Does Russell know you're going to be late?" At Margrit's nod he sighed again and picked up his phone, punching in a four-digit number and requesting a sketch artist before hanging up and turning a dark expression on Margrit again. "Why didn't you call me last night, Grit?"

She pressed her fingertips against her eyelids, trying not to disturb the makeup she'd applied to hide signs of the nightmare she'd had. "Because I hadn't called in three weeks," she muttered into her palms. "Because our conversations always turn into fights. Because I didn't know what to say. I don't know, Tony. I didn't know how to call."

"Picking up the phone and dialing the number is a good start, Grit, and 'I just met a murderer' would have been one hell of an icebreaker. A guy'll forgive a lot for that."

"Especially when he's a homicide detective." Margrit took her hands away from her eyes, looking at the spots of soft brown eye shadow left on her fingers. "Cole'd already lectured me on running in the park, and I didn't want more of it. I hadn't talked to you in weeks. I didn't know what to say. A bunch of stupid reasons. I guess it was easier to face you in sunlight."

Tony cast a wry look at dirty, glazed windows and the thin morning light struggling through them. "In that case I'm surprised I saw you before March."

"Tony…"

"Over lunch," he said quietly. "Can we talk over lunch?"

Margrit lifted her eyebrows. "Are you going to be able to take lunch?"

Chagrin crossed the detective's face and he let a shoulder rise and fall in a shrug. "I didn't say it'd be lunch today. Look—dammit." The last word came out softly before he stood and gestured past Margrit to a bald man approaching his desk. "Margrit Knight, this is Jason Webster, our sketch artist. You'll be working with him on describing our suspect. Later," he added sotto voce to Margrit. "I'll call you later."

She'd ducked out of the police station at ten-thirty, well before the promise of "in after lunch" she'd made her boss. Enough time to hurry home and change into workout clothes and take a daytime run in the park. It'd make everyone happy: she would get to run, and neither Cole nor Tony would have to worry.

A compulsive check of her cell phone told her Tony hadn't called. Not that a couple hours with the sketch artist properly qualified as *later,* but Margrit checked a second time. As if she'd misread, she teased herself, but the mockery had more sting to it than she liked to admit to. She pushed the phone back into a zip-top pocket on her hip and lengthened her stride again, trying to capture the sense of freedom running in the park usually brought her.

It escaped her for once, her sneakers pounding out the

syllables: *ir-rah-shun-al*. Irrational to expect him to have called already; irrational to hope it.

She went around a corner and splashed through a puddle that would be ice after dark. The whole relationship was irrational, always bordering on disaster, always coming back together. It wasn't just the sex that kept them coming back for more, although that didn't hurt. There was some inherent challenge they saw in one another, something unnamed that Margrit wasn't sure she wanted to label.

What drove them apart was easier to quantify. They stood on opposite sides of a flawed legal system. It made for an endless bone of contention, but never quite enough to keep them apart for good. Some days that seemed important. Today, abruptly, it didn't. Margrit pulled her phone out again and dialed the detective's number.

"How about dinner tomorrow?" she asked his voice mail. "I'm sorry I haven't called, Tony. I want to talk about it, okay?" She hung up, good humor restoring itself, as she darted around other joggers, feeling lithe and quick. Within moments, she was in a flat-out run, focusing on the horizon, nothing in the world but her harsh breathing and the ricochet of her feet against the pavement. Her blood felt hot, burning in her hands and cheeks, as tears brought on by speed blurred the corners of her vision.

Reaching the end of her route brought her to a violent stop, skidding and tripping over her own feet in the spasms of muscles pushed hard enough that they no longer knew how to do anything but continue forward. Margrit walked it off, stopping to flip her ponytail upside down and gasp for air after the numbness faded from her thighs. When she straightened it was with a clear expectation formed. Genuine surprise swept her as the blond murderer proved to be nowhere in sight.

Murderer. That wasn't fair. He was wanted for questioning, not necessarily guilty. And he hadn't hurt her. She was sure he wouldn't hurt her, given a second chance.

She let out a quick blast of hot breath that steamed in the cold afternoon air. That sort of dubious logic would get her killed, if not by the blond man, then by Cole or Tony, whose concern might drive them to frustrated homicide. The sense of expectation lingered, and she frowned into winter browns and greens, searching.

New joggers, the women running in pairs or groups, made their way around people talking on their cell phones and children hauling their parents across paths. Weak light from the low sun glinted through the trees, making empty branches into shimmering sticks. An ordinary morning at the park. The dead girl hardly mattered. The blond man was nowhere to be seen.

Margrit waited, then twisted her wrist to look at her watch, shrugged, and jogged home to change clothes for work.

Something was wrong.

Sunset had come and gone, and there was no sign of his ward. His dark-haired, fearless runner. *Margrit*. He savored the name even as he glided from one tree to another, searching the routes she ran. She changed them regularly, a sensible self-defensive measure, but he had watched her for years. He knew the paths she preferred, the stretches of park that she defaulted to.

Did her scent linger in the air or was it his imagination? His own hope, prodding him to belief where none belonged? He had wanted to speak with her again. To hear her voice, even colored with caution. Her accusing irritation the night before had woken in him a spark of life so long dampened he was surprised to discover it still existed.

He'd hunched in the cold atop the building across the street until dawn had driven him away. Wondering, from that distance, if he might ever step past the threshold into the warmth of her life, and dismissing the possibility in the same moment.

The kitchen window had been open, wind shifting a curtain enough to allow him to see that the table in the dining room was covered with paper, used as a workspace rather than for sharing meals. Changing light flickered from the room beyond it, a television droning on. His ears had pricked, preternatural hearing picking out words even from across a street filled with city noises. He was unaccustomed to bothering with such focused listening, but last night, having learned her name, having dared as much as he already had, he'd heard stories of trouble in the park. Hardly unusual, but the man described—

He had lost his focus then, catching his breath as he wrapped his mind around the idea that someone had described *him* as the murderer. Shudders had taken him, despite the fact that he didn't feel the night's cold. It was impossible; he only needed to explain.

Explain to Margrit. She was a lawyer. She could defend him when he couldn't possibly defend himself. And there was no one else. He closed his eyes briefly, trying to remember the last time he might have turned to a human for help. A moment later his eyes came open again and he chuckled under his breath. Over a century and a half ago. Since then he'd had even less contact with mortals than he'd had with his own kind, and he went to some lengths to avoid his own. A faint smile curled his mouth, then faded once more.

To miss her tonight. That, he hadn't counted on. A chill slid through him, making him flex his shoulders in discomfort. Had she recognized him from the news report? How could she not? But he hadn't anticipated it keeping her out of the park.

He curled his hands into loose fists and spread his wings, feeling wind catch under them as he launched into the sky. He had to find a way to speak to her.

THREE

"YOU EVER FEEL like you're being watched?" Margrit's question came with a laugh and an uncomfortable shift of her shoulders.

Cole, a few yards ahead and escorting Cameron over an icy patch, glanced back with an elevated eyebrow. "Everybody feels like they're being watched, Grit. Paranoia is part of a healthy New York City lifestyle."

Margrit laughed again and hurried the few steps to catch up, avoiding the slick stretch. "Yeah, I guess you're right."

"It's because you're a lawyer," Cameron said easily. "You think everybody's out to get you, because they are. First we hang all the lawyers. Cole, I told you we should've gotten here earlier. Look at the line."

"Dinner took longer than I expected," he answered patiently. "We'll be inside in five minutes, Cam. It's fine."

"Says you," she retorted. "You're not wearing heels and a short skirt in twenty-nine-degree weather."

Cole took a judicious step back, looking Cameron up and down before sighing happily. "Yeah. I know. But you are."

She laughed out loud and reached for his hand, tugging him over to steal a kiss. "I guess that's why I keep doing it, too. Charmer."

"You mean you're not dressing up for the other girls? I thought that's what women did."

"Only if they don't have you," Cam said, then widened her eyes and snapped her fingers. "And gosh, I guess they don't."

"You two are disgusting." Margrit tossed off the accusation in a light voice, turning in line to scan the street. There was an itch between her shoulder blades that hadn't lessened since her run in the park, making her uncomfortable. She was accustomed to feeling wary and watching out for herself, but the lingering sense of actually being followed and watched was new. There was no particular reason or way the blond man from the park might find her a second night in a row, but the idea that he would rode her like a bad dream.

The image of him as a vampire in her dream made Margrit shudder again and turn back to Cole and Cameron. "Cute," she said with a quick smile, trying to reassert her place in a normal evening with friends, "but disgusting. I'm glad you asked me to come out with you."

An innocent man wanted for murder would— She let the thought break off, knowing better. Might well *not* go to the police, for a dozen reasons. Innocent until proven guilty carried little weight, with a brutally murdered woman in the park and an eyewitness stepping forward. Still, there was no reason to expect to see him, and no good reason to want to. One chance encounter did not a relationship make.

Relationship. She wondered at herself for the word, goose bumps crawling over her skin. Cameron, oblivious to Margrit's mental gymnastics, smiled back. "You haven't been out with us since Christmas. It's about time you said yes."

"It's about time you were home early enough in the evening to be invited." Cole wrapped his arms around Cameron's waist from behind, standing on his toes to rest his chin on her shoulder, and playing up the difference in their height. "I thought I was seeing things when I got home and you were there."

Margrit laughed. "I told you, I just ended up working from home after talking to Tony. Russell okayed it."

"Maybe you should see if he'd okay it more often," Cameron suggested. "Hey, we're moving." She nodded at the line. "We might even get in." They squeaked through the club doors seconds before the bouncer held up his hand and prevented the next wave of hopefuls from entering.

Music washed through Margrit's veins, as if her heart was driving it. She stopped just inside the club, taking a breath so deep she seemed to be inhaling the sound. She could all but taste it, the throb of life coppery at the back of her throat. It was a welcome distraction from thought, letting her push away images of the blond man, of Tony and of her job with equal ease.

She laughed, soundless under the pervasive beat, and tilted her head back, letting the rhythm prickle her skin. Cameron stopped at her elbow to yell, "You haven't been out in way too long, Margrit. You look like you just tasted chocolate for the first time!"

"Maybe you're right," she shouted back. "You guys want a drink?" She mimed tipping back a bottle. Cam and Cole both nodded. "I'll meet you in the Blue Room!"

Cole gave her a thumbs-up and, hand in hand with Cameron, slid through the crowd toward the dance floors. Margrit watched them go, grinning, then went the other way, jostling for a position in line at the nearest bar. The club was busier than she expected for midweek, and she cast a wry grin at the crowd. Cameron was right: she needed to get out a little more. At least once a week, she promised herself abruptly. There had to be one night a week when she could get out of work early enough to spend time with friends and in the company of sensually impersonal strangers. All work and no play led to obsessions over apparently murderous strangers in Central Park. There were less dangerous pastimes to pursue.

"Hey," said a voice at her elbow. Margrit half turned, looking up a few inches at a dark-eyed guy with a bright smile. "You want to dance?"

"Later!" She nodded toward the bar, and he nodded in turn, stepping back. Margrit glanced over her shoulder a few minutes later as she maneuvered through the crowd, two beers and a ginger ale in hand, to find him following at a discreet distance. She grinned and ducked through a doorway.

The Blue Room was the club's main space and its namesake. Two stories of strobes and spotlights changed the color of the air every few moments, cycling through blue every third change, to emphasize the name. Fog-machine smoke rolled through, the air dry and faintly tangy as dancers made swirls in the haze.

Cameron and Cole leaned against one another and against the metal railing of a landing halfway up to the second-floor balcony. Cam was scouting the room's entrances, watching for Margrit, and raised a hand when they made eye contact. She lifted the bottles in response and scurried up the grate stairs, handing Cam the ginger ale. Cam accepted, teasing, "Thought you got lost."

"Just people watching." Margrit turned to look down into the crowd. "Somebody even asked me to dance."

"Did you?"

"Nope, I was on a mission. Deliver drinks. He was following me a minute ago."

"Ooh, creepy," Cam pronounced. "Maybe he's your stalker."

Margrit laughed. "What happened to a healthy city paranoia? I think I just needed to get out and remember what it's like to have fun."

Cam chuckled and clinked her bottle against Margrit's. Cole bonked his against the other two, nodding approvingly. "Do you mind playing drink hawk and saving our spot here while Cam wears me out? Then you can spell me down on the dance floor."

"Sure." Margrit collected bottles again and waved her friends down the stairs, then leaned over the railing with her bottle dangling from her fingertips and the other two safely tucked against her arm.

"Is it later enough yet?" The dark-eyed man appeared at her elbow again, smiling. Margrit laughed and shook her head.

"Not now, sorry. Gotta watch my friends' drinks. One of them'll be back soon, so why don't you catch me on the floor?"

He spread his hands, disappointed, then shrugged in agreement as he jogged down the stairs. Strobe lighting made sharp shadows in the muscles of his shoulders. Margrit watched approvingly, then searched out Cole and Cameron on the dance floor. Cole was more graceful than Cam, flowing from one movement to another with elegance.

Cameron exuded the raw power of pure joy in letting go, like a drummer in a rock band. They made a nice contrast. Margrit drank her beer, smiling down at them.

Cole had exaggerated his lack of stamina. They stayed on the floor through half a dozen songs, until Margrit's beer was gone and the music drove her to dance on the stairwell, still holding two bottles. She waved, trying to get Cole's attention, then squeaked air out through compressed lips, waiting with growing impatience for one of them to tire. As revenge for having to wait, she drank half of Cole's beer.

Someone tapped her on the shoulder. Margrit rolled her eyes and turned. "Look, I said—"

The blond man from the park looked down at her quizzically.

"Son of a bitch!" The appeal of encountering him again turned to sour panic in Margrit's belly, reality of dancing with a devil slaughtering a half-formed fantasy of taming the beast. Margrit threw Cole's beer upward, foam and alcohol spraying into the blond man's face. He yowled, hands flung up to protect his eyes. Margrit abandoned the remaining bottle, sending it careening over the metal railing and into the dancers below as she scrambled down the stairs. Her heel caught in the metal grating, snapping and pitching her forward.

An instant later she was on her feet at the bottom with no clear idea of how she'd gotten there. Her broken heel was poking out of the grate of one step at a rakish angle, a lone monument to her presence there.

Cole and Cameron appeared at her side, alarm and

concern on their faces. "Margrit? What the hell happened?" Cole took her arm, as if her balance might be questionable.

"It was—he was—didn't you see? Up there?" She jerked her chin up, staring at the landing above.

He wasn't there.

Margrit shook her head hard, trying to clear it as she gazed in disbelief. "I swear to God," she said. "He was there. Just a second ago. I swear."

"Who, Grit?" Cole's voice was coaxing, as if he was talking to a small child or a puppy.

"The—the guy from the park!"

"Jesus, are you sure?" Cameron bolted up a couple steps, as if to go charging after the man. "Are you sure?"

"Of course I'm sure! He was there, just a second ago. Then he vanished! He disappeared last night, too."

"What do you mean, he disappeared last night?" Cole frowned down at her, eyebrows pinched together.

"He disappeared! I ran about ten feet, looked back, and he was gone, poof, no sign of him. Just like now!"

Cole and Cameron exchanged glances. Frustration born from knowing how absurd she sounded sent a childish wave of anger through Margrit. "I'm not kidding! Guys, I'm serious! Why would I make something like this up, dammit?"

"It's one way to get back together with Tony," Cole muttered. Margrit glared at him as Cameron bent to work the broken heel out of the grating, then lifted it between her fingers to waggle it.

"'Cause you really didn't like those shoes?"

Margrit's lip curled, her irritation disproportionate to the gently teasing question. "They were ninety dollar shoes,

Cameron. I liked them." When a hurt expression flashed across her friend's face, Margrit gritted her teeth, trying to rein in her temper. "Security cameras. The club's got security cameras."

Cam and Cole exchanged glances again, Cam's lower lip protruding as she tilted her head in acknowledgment. "Think they'll let us look at them?"

"They'll let the cops, if they won't let us," Margrit said.

"How did you get involved in this, Margrit?" The question was delivered through Anthony Pulcella's teeth, an aside she wasn't meant to answer. He'd been off duty long enough to arrive at the club in a Knicks jacket and jeans, less formal than the on-duty suit he usually wore. "I got your message. Sorry I haven't called. They put me on point for this investigation."

"Congratulations," Margrit said without irony. "It's okay."

"Dinner tomorrow," Tony continued. "If I can make it, I'd like that."

Margrit pulled a brief smile. "Another reason we're always on and off. Incompatible schedules."

"We'll talk about that, too," he said under his breath.

"As soon as we get a chance," Margrit agreed. "Look, they wouldn't let me watch the security videos without you."

"Of course they wouldn't. You're not an authority." The conversation took them from the Blue Room's front door into brightly lit back corridors, following the club's tension-ridden manager, a woman in her fifties who clearly wanted to be elsewhere. A reedy, pimply-faced kid scrambled to his feet as she pushed the door open and gestured them into a small room filled with video screens.

"This is Detective Pulcella, Ira, and the woman who saw

the suspect. Go ahead and play the tapes for them. Do you need me here, Detective?"

Tony gave the woman an apologetic smile. "I'm afraid I might, if it's clear he hasn't left the premises. We may need to close the club down, and I'll need your cooperation and expertise to make that happen smoothly." The woman's expression loosened a little at the flattery, and Tony turned his smile on Ira. "Can you cue the tapes?"

The kid gave Tony a superior look. "Already done, man. You think I been coolin' my heels all this time? Over there." He pointed with a pencil toward a small set of four screens shoved into a corner. "Top corner's the front door. Other three are all angles of the Blue Room." He jabbed at the bottom of one screen with his pencil. "There's the landing she was on. Got it?"

"Got it." Tony shanghaied Ira's chair and offered it to Margrit, then leaned over her as the videos began to play. Ira stalked out, clearly offended at the dismissive treatment.

"Okay, that's us getting into the Blue Room. Do we need to watch this? I don't know how to fast-forward this thing." Margrit prodded a button, then pulled her hand back. Tony reached around her and hit the fast-forward, sending the video people into convulsive, jerky motion. On screen, Margrit finished her beer and drank Cole's in epileptic spasms.

"How much have you had to drink tonight, Grit?"

"A couple of bee— Oh, come on, Tony."

The detective glanced at her. "Nothing personal. Two beers?"

"One beer, and half of Cole's," she muttered.

"Um-hmm."

Margrit scowled, then straightened in Ira's chair. "There."

The blond man edged through the dance crowd on the upper level, the video blurring and leaving a trail of dark pixels behind him as he moved. He rounded the corner to the stairs, head lowered to watch his feet, and disappeared from one screen, reappearing in the next. His head was still lowered, hair glowing white in the grainy black-and-white video, face foreshortened and features indefinable. The third camera, facing Margrit, caught him in profile as he trotted down the stairs, stretched-out pixels still following him like mist-obscured wings. "Goddammit," Tony muttered. "Look up, you son of a bitch."

The cameras swiveled as if responding to Tony's command, their sweep of the room offering new angles. The second screen showed the man in profile, the third catching him full-on as he reached out to tap Margrit's shoulder. He was still looking down; she stood at least half a foot shorter than he was. Tony paused the tape, studying the differences in height. "He's what, about six foot, or six one?"

"He's taller than that," Margrit said with a hint of impatience. "I told you this morning. He's six-three or four."

"Grit, you're short, and I can see he's not that much taller than you."

"I was wearing three-inch heels."

Tony glanced at her bare feet. "What happened to them?"

"You'll see."

He sucked his cheeks in, staring at her a moment, then hit Play again. The video Margrit turned, shrieked silently and flung the beer into the blonde's face. His head reared back, his features visible for barely an instant before his hands covered them and he doubled over in obvious pain.

Tony paused the tape again and looked at Margrit,

amused and admiring. "You never did that to me when I tapped your shoulder."

"You've never been suspected of murder."

Tony flashed a grin and resumed playing the tape. On screen, Margrit ran two steps down the staircase before her heel snapped. She lurched, executing a roll she hadn't known she was capable of. Her chin tucked neatly against her chest, her body compacting itself into a ball, while her skirt rode up high enough that the curve of her bottom was revealed. Watching herself, she was perversely glad she'd been wearing lace undies instead of granny panties.

Her spine barely hit the stairs, as far as she could see, and after two complete somersaults she landed, crouched, on her toes, hands spread and balance forward. Tony took his attention from the screen to stare at her. "How in hell did you do that?"

"Pure blind luck," Margrit said, gaping at her image. The recorded Margrit whipped around and looked up the stairs, reminding them both what they were supposed to be watching.

The man was gone.

"Well, goddammit," Tony said mildly, and leaned closer to study the other screens briefly. "I don't see him. Rewind it." He reached past her and punched the button himself.

In the rewind, as Margrit tumbled up the stairs, there was nothing, then a blur of blackness, and then the man in the space he'd occupied. "What the hell was that?" Tony played it forward, this time both of them watching the suspect.

Margrit threw the beer in his face. He doubled over again, falling into a crouch as he wiped his eyes frantically. His head wrenched to the side as Margrit stumbled, and he made one quick, aborted attempt to catch her, the movement so fast his image blurred again—white this time, the color of his shirt. He missed by a finger's breadth, frustration contorting his features as he fell back into his crouched position.

Then all his energy seemed to rechannel. He uncoiled like a striking snake, the blur of black pixels that followed him expanding, curving around his body and shadowing him. A streak of brightness—the white of his shirt—etched a line through the blackness as it shot upward, off the top of the screen and out of sight.

"WHAT THE HELL was that? Rewind it! Rewind it!" Tony jabbed the rewind button hard enough to bruise his finger, swearing again as the tape zipped backward. The scene replayed itself while he leaned in, nose nearly touching the screen. "Where'd he go? Where'd he go?! Kid! Where's the camera kid? What's his name? Ira!"

"Boy," Margrit said to the screen, all but under her breath. "And I thought my little acrobatic trick was showy."

"That was impossible," Tony snapped. "I don't know what the hell happened there, but the video musta gotten screwed up. That just wasn't possible. He couldn't have jumped out of the viewing area, and where the hell'd he leap to? None of the other cameras show him landing anywhere. He's gotta still be in the building. Gotta be." His words fell over themselves even faster than usual, rising and falling nasal tones. Margrit found herself smiling at him. "What?" he demanded. "What're you grinning at?"

"You're cute when you're upset," she said. His jaw

clamped shut and color scalded his cheekbones. The door opened with a bang and a sullen-looking Ira came in, dragging another chair.

"You've got lousy timing, Grit," Tony muttered, before rounding on the security technician. "Where were you? Never mind. I need to look at every video in that room at—" He broke off to glower at the time stamp on the frozen video frame. "At 10:19 p.m. I gotta be able to see everything. Margrit." Spoken with Brooklyn intensity, it came out *Mahgrit*. "I was gonna ask if I could give you a ride home, but there's somethin' weird goin' on here. I donno how long this's gonna take, and, well—" he forced a smile and slowed down his speech, accent thinning "—I don't think there's much you can do here."

"Does that mean I'm dismissed, Detective?" Margrit ducked her head, feeling a faint smile of frustration pull at her mouth. The demarcation between her job and his had never seemed more vivid. Rationally, she understood, but emotion was more slippery. "Just when things are getting interesting."

"Don't be a pain in the ass, Grit. Not right now, okay?"

"Yeah. Whatever." She heard the snappishness in her words and laughed, a sound of irritation rather than humor. She knotted her hand, trying to release ire before speaking again. "Look, I'm going to find Cole and Cam, and maybe we'll keep hanging out. You'll be able to find me if you need me to ID somebody, or something, all right?"

"Yeah." Tony was already turning back to the video screens, forgetting Margrit was there. "Go have a good evening. I've got work to do."

* * *

Rhythm pushed Margrit around the dance floor, until she was drifting like a leaf on a river's surface. Strobe lights flashed and she lifted her hands into the air, weaving her arms together as sinuously as she could. The strobe chopped the motions into gorgeously inhuman pulses of motion, impossible to achieve in reality. Fog swirled above her, lit brilliant blue-white by the bursts of light. Steel girders threw soft-edged shadows against the dark paint of the ceiling high above. *Stars,* Margrit thought. The club needed to put tiny Christmas lights up there, to make stars against the ceiling. Buoyed by the music, she thought she might be able to break away and fly, if there were stars up above.

Dancers jostled around her. Margrit let herself be moved by them, feeling only distantly attached to her own body. Cole and Cameron had gone to the swing-dance room. Margrit, content to stay with the ever-changing music in the Blue Room, had waved them off with a smile, knowing they'd find her when they were ready to leave. To her surprise, the dark-eyed man located her and claimed a dance or two. He vanished when she forgot she was dancing with him, and turned away.

An arm encircled her waist, sliding possessively across the silk of her camisole. Margrit returned to her body with a jolt that shot electricity through her fingers and toes. It made a cold knot in her belly that melted to warmth, spilling down to pulse between her thighs, making her laugh with desire. She closed her eyes and wound a hand up and backward, to wrap her fingers around the nape of her partner's neck. His hands slid to her hips, rucking up the hem of her top, to settle against her suede skirt. He could be anyone. He could be the killer; he could be the dark-eyed man who'd asked her to dance earlier. Not knowing was half the fun.

Irrational, she whispered to the beat of the music, and let herself go again.

He was a strong dancer, very sure of himself, his hands intimate without being obtrusive. The two of them fit together well, despite his height, and Margrit tucked her hips back with a purring smile. She felt the curve of his body as he lowered his head, felt the warmth of his breath against her shoulder, making her shiver. He moved a palm to her waist, then pulled her closer, protectively, as if he could warm her with his own body heat.

Margrit relaxed back into him, grinning lazily, eyes still closed. His breath spilled over her shoulder again, against her neck, and she tilted her chin up, exposing more throat. He hesitated, close enough that she could feel the heat of his mouth against her skin before he murmured, "I didn't kill that girl."

Adrenaline crashed through Margrit, leaving her fingertips cold and a twist of sickness under her sternum. She straightened abruptly, the sensation of flight and freedom lost. As if in response, the strobe lighting cut out. Spotlights swept the crowd instead, dancers standing out in brilliant purples and oranges. Sweat and alcohol and perfumes mingled in the air, giving it a too-sweet scent, like over-sugared candy. Margrit could hear individual voices, as if the cacophony of music had suddenly died, leaving everyone shouting into silence. She clenched down on the panic in her belly, feeling heavy when an instant ago she'd been soaring weightless among the stars.

"I didn't kill her." Beyond the urgency in his voice, Margrit detected a hint of an Eastern European accent that hadn't been noticeable the night before. She latched onto the detail; it would be something to report to Tony.

A deep breath calmed the fear boiling in her stomach and left behind nervous excitement. If Tony was watching the screens, she might be able to delay the blond man until he arrived. It was a risk worth taking.

She turned in the man's arms.

Every ounce of intimacy between them was lost. The man stood rigidly, his head shoved forward as he hunched over her. Margrit leaned back from his arms, the muscles of her legs bunched, ready to run. If she were an outside observer, she would judge their relationship a dangerous one, she decided—built on passion and anger rather than romance. Her heart knocked against her ribs even as she studied his face, trying to memorize his features so she could offer a better description to the police.

A spotlight washed over them, turning his eyes vivid violet, then moved away, leaving them green in the predominantly blue lighting of the club. "I didn't," he said for the third time, "kill her. Please believe me."

"Then talk to the cops. You'll be fine if you're innocent." Margrit felt her biceps contracting, tension bleeding out of her body any way it could.

"I can't. I truly can't. But I haven't hurt anyone."

"I don't suppose you'd like to tell me who did," Margrit snapped.

"I would like that very much, but I don't *know*."

"Yeah." She stepped back. "Right." The man touched his fingers to her lips, so quickly and gently her exhalation turned into a bewildered laugh instead of the scream she intended.

"Please," he said. "Don't scream. My name is Alban Korund."

"*Maagh.*" Margrit swallowed the sound, surprised at how automatic the impulse to respond in kind with her name was. Alban smiled, a flicker of understanding and dismay.

"Please. You have no reason to trust me, I know, but I need your help."

"My help." She stared up at him. They stood only a few inches apart, unmoving among the sea of bodies, like a couple so lost in one another they'd forgotten to keep dancing. Only the tension between them gave lie to that illusion. "Why would I help you?" she asked. "And why me?"

"Because I'm innocent," Alban whispered, "and because you're not easily frightened."

Margrit's heart skipped a beat, hanging painfully in her chest a moment too long. A jolt of stress angled through the empty place where the heartbeat should have been, and she gasped, stumbling a step. Alban caught her, a hand around her elbow to steady her, then let go again almost before she knew he'd touched her. "Please," he repeated. "I don't have much time. Will you help me?"

"I—"

The attitude of the dancers changed, a sudden switch from casual to disturbed. Heads turned, bodies straightening, as if in response to a silent warning that not all was right with the world. Margrit and Alban looked toward the DJ's table, the direction the alteration had come from.

Tony pushed his way through the crowd. His clothes didn't set him apart from a dancer who wanted onto the floor, but the brusque way he moved, full of purpose, did. There was no acknowledgment of the music in his movements.

"Dammit!" Alban cast one desperate look down at Margrit, then disappeared from her side. In almost the same moment Tony grabbed her shoulders, examining her with a critical glare, then released her to continue after his prey. A cobalt spotlight lit Alban's hair to a fiery blue. Then the strobes popped back on, and Margrit lost them both in the crowd.

He hadn't kissed anyone in nearly two hundred years.

She was almost as surprised as he was, looking him up and down. "Goin' slumming or something, buddy?" She was tall and plump, with kohl-rimmed eyes, her hair dyed an unnatural black. In his slacks and button-down shirt, hair pulled back in a long ponytail, he no more fit into the Anne Rice Victoriana Room than anywhere else in the club.

Still, there'd been no choice. Margrit had swept the street with her gaze that evening, watching for someone who wasn't there. Searching in shadows between alleys and cracks in buildings, not looking up, where he hid among rooftops. He'd followed her from her building after night had fallen, boldness driving him to linger across the street, high in the sky, to wait for her evening run. Instead, she'd left with friends, dressed as he'd never seen her: in a short trench coat thrown on over a skirt no longer than a promise, showing off slender strong legs. Tall heels shaped her calves, her stride as certain in them as it was in running shoes. He'd caught only a glimpse of the camisole she wore, clinging to her ribs and hugging her waist, when she'd slipped her coat off just inside a restaurant door.

He'd quashed the desire to follow her in, an impulse stronger than anything he could remember in decades. He'd protected her in the beginning because her daring nighttime runs woke fondness in him. But a few moments' stolen conversation had lit embers so long banked he'd never have imagined they might still bear heat. Even that he might have ignored, had the news not borne whispers of impossible things to his ears. *Need* had arisen in him: a need to prove himself innocent to Margrit; a need to avoid becoming even more of a fugitive from the human world than his people were by their very nature.

With that need came awareness of his own limitations. Margrit's indignation at being accosted had reflected back the shallowness of his own existence. In all his centuries, he had never found himself or his enduring path to be wanting, but now he was reminded of a vitality so long forgotten he almost wondered if it had ever been. He had not—not!—let himself brush his hands over her arms to feel the softness of her skin, or his mouth over her shoulder before he'd spoken, for all that she'd seemed to invite it. The closeness they'd shared had been heady enough, so extraordinary as to make him risk uncharacteristic things.

Such as kissing this woman now standing before him. "Flirting with a beautiful woman is never slumming."

A sly smile of disbelief stained her mouth as surely as her lipstick stained his own. A pang of guilt laced through him, already too late. Authorities knew he was in the building, and he could not afford to be caught in their presence come sunrise. The chance to get Margrit away and speak with her had come and gone. The only thing left was his own survival. Nothing else would have driven him to the measure he'd already taken, much less the one he was about to.

He lifted his gaze, examining the room briefly. It was littered with carved vampires and gargoyles, their stone forms making drink holders and seats for the dancers. The walls held mock gaslights and candles, giving off flickering yellow light usually overwhelmed by the dance floor light show. The bar was dark polished wood, the seats covered in red velvet with worn spots, and the dancers were pale and beautiful in their dramatic dark clothing. "I have an idea," he murmured to the girl. "There are three security cameras…"

"An' she comes over an' he goes over an'—"

"We can see it, Ira." Tony waved his hand, silencing him. On the security screens, the kohl-eyed girl grinned at the camera in the corner and reached up. The picture cut out. In the opposite corner, Alban was recorded doing the same thing, except he kept his eyes and head lowered so the camera recorded only the top of his blond head.

The detective swore and hit the security-room desk with the heel of his hand. The Goth girl had been detained in the hall; Margrit could hear her talking to another cop.

"Man, I thought he wanted to, y'know, like, make out. Get a little down and dirty in the club, y'know? I thought it was cool." She was pale-faced and sullen, her lipstick so dark red it bordered on black. "That's all. I'll pay for the wire, Jesus. But then he was fuckin' gone, man. Bailed and left me to take the blame. Bastard."

An air vent at the top of the wall opposite the camera was

found with its grate dangling from just one screw. The third camera in the Goth Room had caught Alban frantically un-twisting screws after the other two cameras had been disabled.

Tony pounded the desk again. "A full-grown man couldn't have fit into that vent, goddammit. Especially not in forty-five seconds. He didn't have time. And nobody saw it happen!" The third camera—hidden behind a bubble in the Goth Room ceiling—hadn't filmed Alban's scramble into the vent, but had focused instead on its sweep around the room. "Goddammit. Westing! Anybody find anything in the furnace room yet?"

"No, sir. They're searching the perimeter of the building, too." The cop talking to the Goth girl leaned into the security-room door, frowning at Margrit. She lifted an eyebrow brazenly, challenging him to question her presence there. He spread the fingers of one hand in appeasement and focused on Tony instead.

"Keep looking," Detective Pulcella muttered.

"Yes, sir. What do you want me to do with her?" The cop gestured at the Goth girl. Tony scowled at her, scowled at Margrit and scowled at his coworker.

"Arrest her for vandalism and get all her information. She might end up as an accessory to murder."

"Murder! Jesus fucking Christ! What the fuck are you talkin' about? I clipped a couple wires and I said I'd pay for the fuckin' things! C'mon, they're not really fuckin' press-ing charges, are they? C'mon! C'mon! Gimme a fuckin' break here!"

Westing sighed. "Sorry. Come on. I'll check up on the air-conditioning vents when I'm done." The last was directed at Pulcella as he escorted the livid girl out of Margrit's sight. Tony

C.E. MURPHY

watched the tape one more time, swearing, and stomped out of the security office. Margrit followed in his wake.

"He told me he didn't do it." It was the first thing she'd said since they'd finished ushering everyone out of the club, one at a time, past her. Margrit had stood there, shaking her head, unable to identify Alban among the hundreds of club-goers.

"Of course he said he didn't do it." The detective stalked into the Blue Room, his movements deliberate. "If everybody would just come on in to the police and say, 'Yeah, I did it,' my job would be a lot easier. Of course he said he didn't do it. How the hell did I lose him?"

"Desperation makes people do weird things." Margrit sat on the stairs she'd fallen down earlier, closing her eyes briefly. There'd been no threat in Alban's touch as he'd danced with her. Even when he'd spoken, soft words lifting hairs at her nape, she hadn't felt menace. Intensity, yes; enough that the memory made breathing harder, cold and warm shivering through her in equal parts. If he'd meant her harm, he might have taken her from the dance floor, using fear to cow her into behaving. "You watched the tape ten times, Tony. The vent was the only way out. Where else could he have gone?"

"I don't know. I don't know!" Tony puffed out his cheeks and glanced over at her. "Look, Grit, it's three in the morning. There's really nothing else you can do here. Let one of my men drive you home, okay?"

She mimicked him unintentionally, pursing her own lips, then nodded and dragged herself to her feet, using the stair railing as leverage. "Yeah, all right. I'm sorry I didn't grab him when he took off, Tony."

"That wouldn't have been a good idea. Apprehending

criminals isn't your job." A faint smile washed over his mouth. "Getting them off is."

Weariness swept Margrit's own smile away. "The joke's old, Tony," she said quietly. "It was old the first time. Are we ever going to get past that?" She exhaled, looking away to make it clear she didn't want to pursue the topic just then, and lifted her eyebrows, bringing the conversation back to where it had begun. "The whole heroic citizen's arrest thing would've been nice, anyway."

"Margrit…" Tony let her name trail off as acknowledgment of the dropped discussion, then sighed. "I don't need you to be a hero, Grit. I need you to keep yourself safe." He crossed to her, putting his hands on her waist and his forehead against hers, just briefly. "Go on home, okay?" His voice was quieter. "Take care of yourself. I'll call tomorrow if I can make it to dinner. It'll be a last-minute thing if I can. You know how the first forty-eight hours go."

"Yeah," she said again. "I know. Just call if you can." She echoed his sigh and stood on her toes to steal a brief kiss. "Look, I'll grab a cab. You guys have enough to do without somebody driving me home."

"Thanks." Tony let her go and she felt his gaze on her all the way out the door.

FIVE

THE CH⊕RUS IN her head had changed. Feet slapping against the concrete now rang out in time with *worse-than-use-less, worse-than-use-less*. Margrit collapsed onto a park bench and stared up at the weak noonday sun, heaving for air. She'd slept badly, her dreams haunted by Alban's strong hands and the blur of pixels that had followed his disappearance from the Blue Room.

Cam's alarm in the other bedroom had awakened her at four in the morning. After twenty minutes of tossing, she'd gotten up and gone to the office. It was hours before her coworkers began to arrive, the time productive to the point of absurdity. If practicality didn't demand she be available until five o'clock more or less daily, Margrit thought she might petition her boss to allow her to work the same kind of early morning hours Cole did, just for the joy of getting things done. Practicality, she reminded herself, and the unlikelihood of wanting to get up at four in the morning regularly. As it was, it'd taken a rare cup of coffee to get her through until an early lunch, when she'd pulled on running gear in hopes of shaking off exhaustion with endorphins.

Children ran rampant over the playground equipment across the path from her, as their parents watched. Gleeful shrieks split the air, sounds so sharp they seemed to press the color from the sky. So sharp, too, as to be easily heard over Margrit's headset. Daytime running allowed her the luxury of exercising to music, a noisy rock beat that helped set her pace.

She pulled one of the earphones out and slid down the bench, eyes almost crossing with fatigue. Children in brightly colored jackets made blurry shapes as her focus wandered. Beyond the jungle gym, kids on swing sets created gaudy arches against the brown grass, Margrit's imagination turning the scene into surrealist artwork.

Just across from her, a ponytailed girl of about four tried with great determination to crawl up the underside of dome-shaped monkey bars. A bigger kid gave her a boost onto the first rung, and she scrambled up jubilantly, hands and knees hooked over the bars from beneath. She crawled to the top of the dome and hung there, upside down, her breath steaming in the chilly air and a broad grin of satisfaction smeared across her face. Margrit laughed and applauded quietly.

The little girl curled up and wrapped her hands around the bars again, and continued down the other side of the dome, inverting herself entirely. Margrit squinched one eye shut, afraid the child would fall on her head. Instead, when she could reach the ground with her outstretched hands, she unfolded her knees from the lowest bars, executing a brief handstand before she rolled onto her back and climbed to her feet, incredibly pleased with herself.

Margrit grinned again and turned her face back to the sky, imagining a set of monkey bars big enough for her to do that on. The strobe-lit girders in the club flashed through her mind, the spans stretching and meeting at corners like the monkey bars did. Margrit snickered and made claws with her hands, trying to imagine hanging on to bars that big. She'd have to wrap her whole arms around them, and her legs. It'd be no good for acrobatics like the child had performed. What a sense of superiority one would have, though, looking upside down at all the dancers below, spying on them without their knowledge.

The pixilated blur of Alban jumping made a bright line behind her eyelids. Margrit jolted upright, grabbing the bench's slats. "Holy shit!"

A handful of disapproving parents turned to glare at her. Margrit clapped a palm over her mouth, wide-eyed with guilt, then moved her hand to whisper, "Sorry," as if a quiet apology made up for blurting a curse at a noticeable volume. "Holy shit," she repeated, this time in a whisper all to herself.

"He hid in the rafters." Margrit flung herself into the seat by Tony's desk with an air of triumph. Tony stared at her, first blankly, then in disbelief. Dark circles shadowed his eyes and lines creased the skin at the corners of his mouth, giving a hint of what aging would bring. On a man twenty years his senior the lines would be distinguishing, giving a handsome face with character and strength. But for the moment, Margrit said, "You look terrible," without thinking.

He snorted a laugh. "Thanks. You look like *you* got enough sleep." He gestured to her running gear. "Enough to exercise, anyway."

"I'm faking it. Runner's high. I ran here from work."

He glanced at a clock. "Early lunch?"

"I got to work at five this morning. Anyway, I told Russell I'd remembered something else about the guy in the park and I had to talk to you. I think he figures getting bent out of shape when I'm trying to help another public service agency is counterproductive. He'll take it out in blood later. But listen, Tony." She leaned forward to seize his hand, enthusiasm overtaking her. "He hid in the rafters. In the Blue Room girders. No cameras look up there."

Tony chuckled, a rough low sound. "I'm sure there's a nicer way to say this, but you're out of your fucking mind."

"I'm not!" She let go of his hand and thumped her fist on a stack of paperwork on his desk. "We saw him jump, right? In the video."

He tilted his head back and blew out a noisy breath. "The ceiling in there's thirty feet high, Margrit. Even where you were, it's gotta be twenty, twenty-two feet." He lowered his head, eyeing her. "You really trying to tell me you think he jumped twenty feet straight in the air?"

Margrit folded her arms. "You got a better suggestion?"

"No," he said after long moments. "But it's just not possible."

"What if he was on something?" she demanded.

"He didn't act like he was."

"Well, maybe it's something you don't know about. Maybe he's an Olympic athlete. I don't know, but look. We can at least find out if somebody was in the rafters."

Tony's eyebrows shot up, challenging. Margrit tossed her ponytail, grinning at him. "Betcha nobody dusts up there."

His eyebrows drew down, then slowly rose again, his expression clearing. A smile crept across his face and then he laughed. "All right. All right. I think you're crazy, but he went somewhere, and that's not a half-bad idea. If you're right, I might even be able to get prints." He clapped his hands together and stood up, weariness swept away.

"Do I get to come?" Margrit asked. "C'mon, Tony." She stood, bouncing on her toes. "It was my idea. I promise I won't touch anything. Swear to God. I just want to know if I was right."

He looked at her, still grinning. "How about if I tell you over dinner tonight?"

"How about I go with you and we discuss what we find over dinner tonight?"

Tony laughed. "That wasn't supposed to be an opening for negotiation."

"I'm a lawyer, Tony. Everything is negotiation."

He swung his jacket on, eyeing her sideways. "You won't touch anything. And if any trouble crops up you'll do what I say, and get out of there."

"Scout's honor," Margrit promised, holding up three fingers.

He held up two fingers. "I was a Cub Scout," he told her dryly. "You got it wrong."

"I was a Girl Scout, Tony, and it's three fingers for them." Margrit arched an eyebrow, then tipped her head toward the door. "C'mon. Let's go."

Margrit stood to one side of the Blue Room, arms folded under her breasts as she watched a young officer scramble up an aluminum ladder. Tony shuddered faintly and she smiled, edging toward him. "What was it you were doing when you found out how thin air is and how hard the ground is?"

"Playing tag," he answered in a low voice. "On the roof. You know that."

Margrit's smile broadened. "Yeah, but I really like reminding you."

"Watching McLaughlin is reminder enough."

"She's right, sir," the officer in question called down. "Somebody was up here."

Tony shot Margrit an incredulous look, growling, "I still don't see how it's possible," before tipping his head back to shout up the ladder. "Think we can lift any prints?"

"We can try." McLaughlin came skidding down the ladder with a reckless heed for his own mortality. Margrit moved to the side, remembering her promise to not be a nuisance. There were three officers, including Tony, although one was searching the rest of the club in case something had been missed the night before.

The club looked uncomfortably different during the day. Round white fluorescent lights, the bulbs protected by wire frames, had been turned on last night while the building was being emptied, but they seemed uglier during daylight hours. The rooms no longer echoed with remembered music, but stood empty and bare, mirrored walls reflecting a mundane existence that the night pushed away. Footsteps were audible against the hard floors. Margrit could hear water burbling in the pipes.

McLaughlin scaled the ladder again and Pulcella ambled over to Margrit's side. "It was a good call," he said. "I still don't know how he got out of here without us seeing him, and I sure as hell don't know how he made that jump, but it was a good call. You should turn away from the dark side and become a cop."

Tension tightened Margrit's shoulders and she let out a long sigh. "I like to think I'm one of the good guys, Tony. Sometimes I even get to defend innocent people." Her cell phone rang from the depths of her jacket pocket. Margrit dug it out with more force than necessary, the distraction annoying and welcome all at once. There was never a good time to talk about it, she thought. Part of the nature of their relationship, and why it was off as much as it was on. "Besides," she muttered, "it was just a hunch." She wandered away from the detective, holding the phone to her ear.

"Hi, this is Margrit."

"This is Russell. Are you finished with your business with Tony?" Her boss's voice was hurried, urgency clipping his words. "The governor's announcing his decision on the Johnson case this afternoon."

"What? Sh—!" Margrit swallowed the curse, remembering just in time to be professional. "What time?" She aborted another curse, stalking in a small, agitated circle.

"One o'clock. During a luncheon with the Women's City Club."

Margrit clenched her hand in a fist. "God, I hope that's good news. All right. I'll be there as fast as I can. Damn!" She twisted her wrist, looking at the bangle gold watch she wore. It was eleven-thirty, and she cast up a prayer of thanks that she'd gotten to work early. "I've got to take a shower, Russell. I ran to the police station. I'll be there in an hour. The office, or are we meeting him somewhere?"

"Office. You and I will be going over together. Just get back here, Counselor."

"On my way." Margrit snapped her phone shut and turned, all but running into Tony, whose eyebrows were lifted.

"Hot date?"

"Yeah. My clemency case is about to be decided."

Tony's eyebrows shot up higher. "The Luka Johnson case?"

"Yeah. I've—"

"And there you were claiming just a second ago that you were one of the good guys. The good guys don't get murderers out of jail, Grit." He was only half kidding, his smile not reaching his eyes.

Margrit pressed her lips together, giving her head one short shake. "It was self-defense, Tony, and I don't want to get into it right now. I've got to go."

"All right, fine. Look, Margrit, we never would've seen him without your hunch." Tony squinted against the lights, which hung a few feet below the girders, rendering them effectively invisible. "You did good. Thanks."

She nodded, stepping around him. "You're welcome."

"I think I got something, sir," McLaughlin called down. The detective tilted his head up, squinting at the lights and McLaughlin's shadow among them. Margrit took two steps toward the door, then turned back, curiosity impelling her to linger.

"Be careful with it," Tony called, then lifted his eyebrows at her again. "Thought you had to run."

"Yeah. Yeah, I just…" Margrit's calves knotted up and she bounced in anxiety.

"I know. You've just got to know." He gave her a faint, comprehending smile.

"I'm being careful," McLaughlin said, "but there's something weird." He looked down over his shoulder.

"Weird," Tony echoed. "Is that your clinical diagnosis, Officer?"

"Yes, sir, it is," he replied without a hint of sarcasm. "I'll be down in a minute and you can see for yourself." He grinned then, a note of humor in his voice. "Unless you want to come up here, sir."

"Watch it, Officer," Tony said good-naturedly. The man on the ladder laughed. His descent this time was much more cautious, and he spoke as he came down the last few rungs.

"I got an index through ring finger on the left hand and a partial thumb and pinky," he announced. "And I dusted a partial of his shoes. We'll let the guys in forensics do their magic."

"His shoes?" Margrit peered up into the lights, remembering the little girl hanging from the monkey bars, and envisioning herself grasping onto the girders with her arms wrapped around them. "How'd he get his shoes up there?" She glanced at her watch again. She could spare another minute. Two, tops.

"Honestly, it looks like somebody perched up there for a while, ma'am. Like he just dropped down from on top and crouched there. I'm guessing he's left-handed," McLaughlin said to Tony. "Judging from the fact that his left hand was his third balance point." He laid the prints out on the DJ's table, sweeping a finger over the film-covered dusting paper. "He kept most of his weight on the middle three fingers, only brushed the surface with pinky and thumb. But look at the prints, sir."

Pulcella leaned over the paper, holding his breath as an unnecessary caution. After several long seconds he straightened up, letting his breath out in an explosion. "He must've been wearing gloves."

"He was *not* wearing gloves," Margrit said with absolute certainty. Both cops turned to look at her and color flooded her cheeks. "Well, he wasn't," she mumbled. "We were dancing. I had my hands over his. He wasn't wearing gloves."

Tony's expression darkened, one part concern and one part jealousy that not even McLaughlin could miss. He looked from his boss to Margrit, then let out an intended-to-be-nonchalant whistle and deliberately turned back to the prints. Margrit thrust her jaw out and met Tony's eyes forthrightly. After a few moments he lifted his chin and turned his head away, a gesture of defeat Margrit wouldn't have expected from him.

"Alright," he grunted. "So tell me how you explain this." He made a short, sharp movement, indicating the prints. Margrit walked forward warily, not quite trusting the invitation to intrude. Neither cop spoke again, preventing her, and she leaned over the prints.

"He wasn't wearing gloves," she repeated, less certainly, nearly a full minute later. Tony stood behind her left shoulder; she twisted her head to look back at him. "I mean, what I don't know about fingerprints could fill a library, but—" She broke off and frowned down at the prints again. "But I'm sure he wasn't wearing gloves."

Ridges and swirls of fine black dust marked the paper. Margrit turned her own hand up, examining her fingerprints closely and comparing them to the prints on the paper. The ridges on her fingertips were much closer together than Alban's, with nearly twice as many swirls.

There was a peculiar consistency to Alban's, as if tiny streams of water had carved them into oxbows. In the spaces between the ridges, there were porous marks, suggesting pumice. "Acid burns...?" Margrit suggested.

"You're sure he wasn't wearing gloves," Tony growled.

Ir-rah-shun-al pounded out in her temples, better than counting to ten. Margrit inhaled and spoke carefully. "I'm sure he wasn't when we were dancing. I didn't look at his hands on the stairs, though."

"I can't *believe* you danced with him." The detective scowled at her abruptly. "What were you, out of your mind?"

"I didn't know who he was!" Margrit yelled. McLaughlin took two judicious steps backward and found a mote of dust on his shirt to become concerned with.

"Didn't you?" Tony demanded. "You've been very cozy with this whole investigation since minute one, Grit."

Margrit's jaw fell open. "What?"

"You're the best eyewitness we've got, someone who actually spoke with him the night of the murders. He just 'happens' to show up at the club you're at last night? You just 'happen' to think he might have been hiding in the rafters? Is this some kind of sick game, Margrit?" Anger and suspicion flooded his voice, as well as jealousy. "It's not an uncommon pattern for an accomplice to provide just enough information to drag an investigation out. Are you pulling some sort of shit like that, Grit? It's a federal offense!"

Margrit thinned her lips, deliberately spreading her fingers as if she could release tension through them. When she trusted herself to speak, she said, "I'm well aware of the penalties of interfering in a murder investigation, Anthony. If you intend to arrest me, I invite you to do it now. Otherwise, I suggest you put some more thought behind your spurious claims."

"Or what," Tony sneered, "you'll sue me for libel?"

"It's slander," Margrit said through her teeth. "Libel is if it's in print. If you'll excuse me, I have somewhere to be." She turned and stalked toward the door, so tense with anger she could scarcely walk in a straight line.

"Margrit! *Margrit!*" Tony's shout followed her down the street.

She ignored him, still walking with great precision, afraid if she began to run she would mow somebody down. The detective caught up to her and grabbed her arm, turning her around. Margrit dropped her gaze to his hand and then lifted it to his eyes.

He let go as if she'd screamed, tucking his hands behind his back, then bringing them forward again to twist together. "I'm sorry. Look, I'm sorry, okay? I don't have an excuse. I haven't had enough sleep, but that's not an excuse, and I'm sorry. I don't know what got into me."

"Apparently what got into you was the idea that I'm a co-conspirator in a murder case. A suspect, if that word was too big, Detective." Margrit's voice found its courtroom tones, polite and mocking to mask outrage.

Tony blanched. "I don't think you're a suspect. It's just—"

"Just a remarkable series of coincidences," she said with a pointed smile. "I'm so glad you don't think I'm a suspect, Tony. There's something we agree on. If you'll excuse me," she said again, and turned away.

Tony grabbed her arm once more and spun her around. He lifted both hands to her face and caught her cheeks, bringing his mouth down to hers for a desperate, intense kiss.

For a few seconds Margrit was too stunned to react. His mouth was warm, hands gentle against her face, despite the ardor of the kiss. Someone walking by wolf-whistled with approval.

Margrit shoved Tony away with all her strength, balled up a fist and threw a punch that cracked her knuckles when it hit.

He yowled in pain and surprise, clutching his nose as he staggered back, tears springing to his eyes and spilling down his cheeks. Pure astonishment mingled with hurt in his expression, half-hidden behind his hands.

Margrit shook her fingers, loosening the injured knuckles as she trembled with fury, staring up at him. "This isn't the movies, Tony," she spat. "That kind of bullshit doesn't work in real life."

Vibrating with angry energy, she turned on her heel and stalked down the street, leaving the detective behind.

A quick shower and change of clothes before a seven-minute subway ride calmed her temper enough that Margrit managed to not stomp as she came back into the office. Her boss met her a few steps inside the door, giving her a brief, approving once-over.

"I didn't think you were going to make it." Russell Lomax was thirty years Margrit's elder and usually dressed in better-quality suits than most public employees could afford. "The governor's aide just called. They'd like you to meet them at the City Club. You look good, Counselor."

"Is Luka going to be there?" Margrit glanced at herself—burgundy skirt suit, cream-colored blouse—and scowled at her right hand, where the knuckles were swollen and the skin broken.

"She is. You'll be meeting her in the back room and you'll all three go out to talk to the press together." Russell frowned at her hand. "What happened?"

"Nothing." Margrit shook her head. "It's fine. I hope the governor meeting with us is a good sign. He wouldn't be such a bastard to pull this kind of big stunt for denying the case, would he?" She scowled at her hand again.

"I don't know. We can hope not," Russell said with an easy shrug, then lifted his eyebrows at something behind her. "Someone's lucky day."

"Luka's, I hope." Margrit looked over her shoulder. A delivery boy with a vase full of yellow roses peered at her.

"Margrit Knight? These are for you. Sign here, please." The boy thrust the vase at her, and Margrit blinked, taking it and fumbling as she tried to comply without dropping it. Russell, looking amused, came to her rescue, scooping up the vase.

"Secret admirer, Margrit?"

"Not that I know about." She signed and the delivery boy departed as she pushed aside a bundle of baby's breath to find the card. A quiet laugh, still tinged with anger, escaped as she read it: "I'm a jerk. Forgive me and keep our dinner date? Call me.—Tony"

Margrit curled the card in her fist and shook her head as Russell looked on curiously. "Tony," she said. "We had a fight." Her boss's expression invited further explanation, but she shook her head again. "We've got more important things to focus on. Let's go see how this thing turns out."

SIX

"IT'LL BE ALL right." Margrit offered a reassuring smile, squeezing Luka Johnson's hand and letting calm suffuse her voice. It was an act, a show of composure that hid the fact that her heart was lodged in her throat. Luka's dark complexion was ashy, her brown eyes flat from worry; she needed Margrit's confident manner even more than Margrit herself did. There was a discreet police escort outside the room, keeping the bustle of the hall away from the prisoner and her lawyer.

. "But what if it ain't—isn't?"

Margrit exhaled shakily and lifted a foot to display her shoe. "These are very pointy heels. I'll step on his toes if it isn't." The door whooshed open as she spoke, and Luka's eyes widened. "He heard that, didn't he," Margrit mouthed, before turning to face the governor.

"I heard that, Ms. Knight." Amusement colored the man's voice, no concern for the state of his feet evident. He was tall, with features too heavy for handsomeness, but strong enough to give him presence. He offered a hand first to Margrit, then stepped past her to say, "Mrs. Johnson. I apologize. I should have called you both earlier today, but my planned luncheon was canceled and the City Club asked me to step in when their speaker canceled, as well. It's been a hectic morning."

"You could say that, sir." The words came automatically, despite Margrit's churning stomach and fluttering heart. Law school had taught her to schmooze through stress, if nothing else. "It's an honor to meet you."

He grinned down at her. "You, too. You've got a hell of an advocate here, Mrs. Johnson." He turned back to Luka, the grin tempering into a compassionate smile. "I imagine I've got you both sick with worry, so let me go ahead and make myself clear before we go in to the lunch."

Luka's hand grasped Margrit's in a white-knuckled grip.

"Even on my worst day, I wouldn't pull off this kind of spectacle to break a family's heart, Mrs. Johnson. Clemency is granted," the governor said. "You're free to go."

He stepped forward to help Margrit catch Luka as her legs went out from under her.

The afternoon passed not in a blur, Margrit thought later, but a roar. Anything the governor said as he helped Luka back to her feet was lost in the pounding of blood in Margrit's ears and the unprofessionally brilliant grin as she pumped his hand in gratitude. Her eyes stung with tears that overflowed without warning, turning into gasping laughs and hiccups of relief and pride and delight. The members of the City Club literally stood and cheered, their applause cutting through the ringing in Margrit's ears in quick staccato bursts. She stood with her arm around Luka's waist, the two of them supporting one another, and when the governor beckoned her forward to speak to the club, she tugged Luka with her.

"Today is the hard-won culmination of three years work," she said into the microphone, to a hundred beaming faces. "Luka and I are both so very pleased and very relieved. So very grateful, Governor, thank you so very much. This is not the first case in which clemency has been granted to a woman acting in self-defense, but it is still a landmark. There are so many small steps we must take in order to assure the safety of everyone in this great city of ours. I hope that someday cases like Luka Johnson's won't be necessary anymore, but today's decision reinforces our determination to take those steps, to continue moving in the right direction. There is so much I could say to all of you—even if I'm preaching to the choir!—but if you'll excuse us, I think there are a couple of little girls waiting to see their mother." Arm still wrapped around Luka's waist, both of them beaming, Margrit withdrew from the luncheon to the sounds of cheers.

Outside the hall was chaos, the press bunched together like a murder of crows. Flash photography blinded them both as microphones were thrust under their noses, and Margrit shouted out the same words she'd spoken in the hall. Hands lifted, she brought the volume of shouts and questions down as they edged forward, nodding encouragement to Luka when she answered a handful of questions herself. It was difficult to pick any one voice out of the din, and Margrit kept losing her determined expression to a grin as she elbowed reporters aside. Russell waited at the bottom of the steps, vehicle idling. Even when the door closed and cut off the reporters' voices, the pounding of the ocean stayed in Margrit's ears.

"…which nobody can deny!"

The roar was still with her, this time in her colleagues' voices as they lifted toasts to her for… Margrit had lost track of the rounds, which probably accounted for some of the roar, she admitted to herself. It wasn't nearly late enough in the day to be… "Tipsy," she said out loud, firmly. Russell, on the bar stool beside her, laughed.

"You passed tipsy an hour ago, Margrit. You passed tipsy when you climbed up on the bar to start giving speeches."

She laughed with him. "At least I'm not standing on it anymore!"

"Just sitting," Russell agreed with a nod. "You're tanked."

"I am not." Margrit allowed herself a tiny grin and a shrug. "Okay, maybe a little."

"Although I wouldn't normally encourage someone to get drunk in front of her boss, I think this time you've earned it. Congratulations, Margrit." Russell shook her hand for the third time, making her grin yet again.

"Thank you, sir. You should've seen the kids," she added to anybody who would listen. "When Luka came in with me the older girl got so excited she burst into tears, so the little girl did, and then we all did." Luka had embraced the girls' foster mother fiercely, promising she'd remain a part of their lives. When Margrit had finally excused herself, the four of them, women and girls alike, had been sitting together in a tight bundle, catching up and holding on. Margrit left feeling like she was walking on clouds.

"So you decided on no dinner date?" Russell asked.

Margrit squinted at him, eyebrows drawn down in furrows before they suddenly shot up. "Oh, shit. No! Crap!" She slid off the counter to the bar stool, then to the floor, dismayed at how it wobbled.

Russell laughed. "You okay? You've had a lot to drink."

"We all have," Margrit said with a quick grin. "But I haven't drunk enough to drown my career in alcohol, sir. I'm all right. I'll be back in a bit."

The silence outside the bar was deafening. Margrit leaned against the building, still smiling broadly as she auto-dialed Tony. There was no answer, but voice mail picked up and she said, "I won my case. You're forgiven. Sorry I didn't get back to you earlier. Um, dinner tomorrow night, maybe? If we can both make it, anyway. Call me back, Tony. I miss you."

Margrit heard the note of wryness in her own voice as she ended the call. She missed him when times were good more than when they were bad. Another reason, probably, that they rarely stayed together more than a few months before taking a break. It'd been going on for years now, with too much time invested to walk away, yet too many down moments to consider it a successful relationship.

Alban Korund's pale gaze, colorless in the strange club lighting, flashed in her memory, a startling counterpart to thoughts of Tony Pulcella and his warm Italian coloring. Margrit shook the image off, muttering "Bah" under her breath as she pushed away from the building wall. Men wanted for murder had no business lingering in her imagination, even when the erratic bond with Tony seemed to be a little more strained than usual.

"Miss Knight?" A woman—a girl, really—appeared out of nowhere, as suddenly as Alban departed. Margrit straightened her shoulders, irritated at the stubborn focus of her thoughts.

"I'm sorry," she said brusquely. "I don't have any spare change." She turned her back, reaching for the bar door.

The girl blurted, "No!" and caught her elbow. Margrit jerked away, turning back in outraged astonishment that made the stranger cringe, though it didn't stop her tongue.

"I need your help, please. Please, I saw you on the news and I don't know where else to go." She shifted a bundle under a gray blanket wrapped around her thin shoulders, the whole motion as smooth and choreographed as a dance, then looked up pleadingly. "They're going to tear our building down and we don't have anywhere else to go. Please, Ms. Knight."

"We?" Margrit asked warily. The girl nodded and slipped the blanket away to show Margrit a contented, tiny baby who blinked sleepily and waved a little fist at her.

"My daughter and I. Please. Can you help us?"

Margrit groaned and let the bar door swing shut again.

Alban stepped back, letting the shadows of an alley swallow him. His hair was too bright, too noticeable, to risk moving farther into the light. The police might see him, but more to the point, the *girl* might see him. What was she doing there? What were *they* doing here?

A human couldn't recognize the slightly too fluid movements. Humans saw inexpressible grace if they noticed anything at all. It took another of the Old Races to see one of their own. The girl moved as if she'd been born to live in water, as if the natural substance around her supported her weight, and gravity had no effect. He'd thought there were none of her people left, the selkies whose attempt at saving themselves had driven them out of the sight and minds of the other remaining Old Races.

Alban folded his arms over his chest, watching the girl, watching Margrit. She'd missed her evening run, but others had been out, stretching their legs and jogging, talking about the day's news. Talking about Margrit—*his* Margrit, the lawyer for Legal Aid. He'd leaped from one tree to another, following the conversation. Margrit Knight. She was as he'd imagined a lawyer should be: a warrior, fighting the good fight.

He came downtown over the rooftops, finding her offices on Water Street. Early nights were in his favor for once, allowing him to watch from above as a herd of proud, laughing lawyers swept Margrit out of the building as evening fell. It was the second time he'd seen her in something other than running outfits, and as much poise and taste were reflected in her professional clothes as the soft camisole and skirt he'd touched the night before. He curled his hand, feeling none of that delicacy in his own form.

One of a dozen reasons he ought never to have spoken to her at all. Ironically, it was the same reason that made him want to clear his name with her, though he could hardly imagine explaining that reason to her.

What, then, he wondered, did he intend to do? Without explanations, there could be nothing between them, not even the trust needed for a lawyer to fight for her client. With explanations—

With explanations there could be nothing at all. It was

the reality of her people and his. Alban lowered his head, folding his fingers into a loose fist. He'd listened to voices below calling congratulations, until the air around him rang with them. Good-natured arguments over who had the honor of buying the first drink lingered even after Margrit and her compatriots entered the upscale pub they'd chosen.

Half a dozen times he'd thought of following them in, wisdom overcoming the impulse every time. He was wanted for questioning about a murder. Walking into a room filled with lawyers would hardly keep him out of the public eye, and he didn't dare be detained past sunrise. And now too many years of deliberately staying apart had cost him. Margrit had been alone for a few moments, leaning against the building as she spoke into her phone. There had been time to approach. Two centuries of caution made him too slow, and now the girl had joined her.

The girl. Legend had it that the selkie race had tried to save itself by breeding with humans. The other Old Races abhorred the tactic, and no one had wept when the selkies had faded away, drowned in the cold seas they'd come from. A few, it seemed, survived. Alban shook his head and hunched his shoulders as he stood in the shadows. For all their attempts to preserve themselves, it appeared the selkies were left hiding in the darkness with the rest of the Old Races.

Alban strained to hear the conversation, but the wind carried their words the wrong direction, his sensitive hearing unable to compensate. Moving closer was out of the question, the chances of revealing himself too high.

He missed the weight of wings as he shifted his shoulders, the motion too slight without them. Ironic, to counsel himself to patience now, when it was that forbearance that had lost him the chance to speak with Margrit. He sighed and settled deeper into the shadows, watching the two women. He would take the next chance. He had to.

It would explain everything, Margrit thought, if this girl had been following her since yesterday, working up her nerve to come forward. It would explain her own vague uneasiness and sense of being followed. But she'd said she'd heard Margrit's name only that evening, and Alban had been at the Blue Room the night before. The idea crystallized briefly before fading away again: he'd found her at the club, too unlikely to be coincidence. There had been something to her paranoia.

Warmth flushed through Margrit, a blush of color that had no business belonging to the idea of being followed. Keeping a dangerous habit was bad enough. Not-so-vicarious thrills at having her own stalker was considerably worse.

Though still, even with the peculiar fingerprints, even with the impossibility of Alban's leap, what remained was the confidence of his hands on her hips, and the curiosity in his eyes as they'd spoken.

Margrit stifled another groan, this time of impatience at herself, and wrenched her attention back to the young woman asking for her help.

She was pretty in a mournful way, with brown eyes so dark they seemed to have no boundary between iris and pupil. Her cheeks were hollow and the knees of her jeans were pale with wear and age. The hems were ratty and the sneakers had seen better days. She was a picture of betrayed innocence, a good witness, Margrit thought clinically, and dropped her chin in a nod. "What's your name?"

"Cara. Cara Delaney. Thank you. Thank you for listening."

Margrit shook her head. "I haven't done anything yet. You're not twenty-one, are you."

"No."

"So much for a shot to warm you up. It's fine. Let's get back to my office, though. It's warmer there and it's just around the block." She touched the girl's shoulder, encouraging her into motion. "You understand this kind of thing doesn't just happen overnight?" she asked as they walked. "It takes permits and notices and hearings to tear down buildings, even old ones."

"There weren't any. I swear, Ms. Knight—"

"I believe that you haven't seen any. It's just that it may be a place to start an injunction against the squatters being thrown out." Margrit glanced at her. "Squatters, right?"

Cara nodded. Margrit followed suit, studying her again. The right clothes would make her the perfect witness: nothing too good, but clearly the best a homeless girl could afford. With her fragile loveliness and large eyes, and a helpless baby on her hip, she'd be a poster child for the poor displaced by the whims of the wealthy. "How old's your daughter?"

"Three months. Her name's Deirdre." The name was gently drawn out, much the way Cara had said her own name.

"That's pretty. So's she."

Cara smiled. "Thank you. It means sorrowful."

Margrit blinked. "Why would you give her a sad name?"

"My people think a name should do many things. Reflect your circumstances, maybe give you something to stand up for, or fight against."

Margrit's eyebrows shot up. "Your people?"

Cara's cheeks darkened in a flush and she fixed her gaze on her feet. "The Irish," she said after a few seconds. Margrit pulled her eyebrows back down where they belonged and smiled.

"I don't think I've ever heard anybody say it quite that way before. Are you from Ireland? You don't sound like it."

"I was born there."

"Are you—"

"My father was an American citizen," Cara interrupted. "I'm not illegal, if that's what you're thinking."

Margrit exhaled, slowing as she nodded at the Legal Aid Society building. "My office is in here. I'm glad you're legal. That makes things less complicated." The guard at the door straightened as Margrit led Cara up the steps and smiled at him. "Evening, Mark."

"Thought you were out celebrating, Ms. Knight."

"Margrit!" she reminded him for the hundredth time. He was well over six feet tall, and thick-shouldered as a wall, relying on intimidation rather than an inclination to hurt people to get his job done. He'd worked there longer than Margrit had and still refused to call her by her first name. "This is Cara. She's with me."

"Miss." Mark ducked his head politely as he unkeyed the security alarm and unlocked the door. "Call down when you're leaving, Ms. Knight, so I can turn off the alarm."

"We will," Margrit promised. "Thanks, Mark. Come on, Cara. I can at least make a pot of coffee while we talk."

* * *

The security guard keyed the pad again as Margrit and the selkie girl disappeared into the lobby. Alban walked to the other side of the street, casting quick glances at the building as he ducked his head over a cup of coffee that was more for show than to quench thirst. A light came on in an office on the second floor and he let out a sigh that steamed in the chilly air. The guard watched him, caution in his eyes. Alban inclined his head and picked up his pace, letting his feet take him around the corner and out of sight.

Habit made him check the street even as he gathered himself. There were always stragglers in the city, drunks or homeless or late businessmen who might catch a glimpse of him if he allowed himself to become careless. A few times he'd been noticed, springing upward as he did now, a blur of strength and power hesitating on window ledges only long enough to pounce to the next. Fortunately, drunks and homeless were rarely considered reliable, and businessmen wouldn't risk their reputations with stories of creatures scaling building walls in a single bound.

The ledge he found suited him, close enough to the street to watch easily, but far enough up that he would go unnoticed. Even if someone did see him, they would only be surprised, and uncertain if they'd ever noticed the stonework on the building before. There were risks, and then there were the constants of human nature.

Alban crouched, three points on the ledge and his right elbow draped over his knee. Wings settled around his shoulders, falling like a heavy cloak, and he waited, still as stone, for Margrit or the dawn.

SEVEN

THE LIGHT CLICKED off, sudden darkness across the street briefly incomprehensible. Alban blinked without understanding, then pushed back, hands on his knees as he straightened his spine. Bells from a nearby church had rung the first small hour of the morning long enough ago that he'd begun to think dawn would make an entrance before Margrit Knight took her leave from work, even if wintertime bought him more hours than a summer night would. Sunrise might come late, but he still preferred to be safely ensconced in his home well before it broke. Perching on building ledges during daylight hours made discovery far more likely.

The patient security guard, whose rounds had kept him within Alban's line of sight all night, pressed a code into the numerical safety box on the building's side, and a moment later held the door for a tired-looking Margrit. She gave him a weary smile, pulling her coat around herself more tightly against wind coming up from the water. It carried her words and a quiet laugh as she shook her head: "I've already called one, but I wouldn't mind company until it gets here. Thanks, Mark. Did Cara get out safely?"

"Paid for her cab," Mark replied. "She didn't want me to, but it's bad, walking around with a baby that late."

Margrit flashed a smile and turned her gaze up to the skyline. Hope and fear swept Alban, an unexpected combination of emotion that left a chill behind. For a moment her eyes lighted on him, then went on without recognition or notice. *Of course,* he thought, though disappointment replaced hope.

"Did you get a receipt?" Margrit asked. "Let me pay you back, anyway. I think Russell will assign somebody to the case, so I can get reimbursed." She dug into her purse as Mark shook his head.

"Don't need to, Miss Knight. Didn't do it just to get my money back. She needed a ride, that's all."

Margrit's smile deepened. "You're a good man, Mark. Thanks. I didn't even think of it." She tugged something out of her purse anyway, palm-size and oddly textured, silver over metallic red, then slid it in her pocket. Alban tipped his head, watching her actions, which were easy enough to be ritual, then brought his attention back to the conversation.

"Been a long day," the security guard said. "You can't remember everything."

"Don't tell me that." Margrit walked down the steps, peering up the street for her taxi. "Next thing I know you'll be telling me I can't save the world."

"Wouldn't bet against you, Miss Knight."

Margrit grinned over her shoulder at the guard, then

looked back up at the sky. "That's what I like to hear. Thanks." Her smile faded to a frown. "Mark, was that there before?" She lifted a hand, pointing a gloved finger directly at Alban.

So much for humans never looking up. Stillness was a way of being—not flinching, not moving, requiring no more thought than breathing did. Alban's heart thudded with the panic of discovery regardless, even as a part of him wanted to laugh at his own fears. His intention was to bring himself to Margrit's notice. Being found out shouldn't be alarming, especially when she couldn't possibly recognize him.

The guard came down the stairs to follow her extended arm. "Musta been, Miss Knight. Don't remember seeing it, though."

Margrit dropped her hand slowly and nodded. "I swear I've looked out my window a million times at that building and never saw it before."

"Funny what we notice," Mark agreed. "Here's your cab, Miss Knight." He stepped past her as the vehicle pulled up, and opened the door for her. Margrit gave him a grateful smile and ducked into the car.

A grin, full of unusual wickedness, broke through Alban's stony expression. He leaped upward, leaving his perch behind, and paused long enough on the rooftop to catch Mark's bewildered expression when he looked up to find the statue on the ledge gone.

A matter of steps between the taxi and her apartment building's front door was all the time he had. There'd be no room for prevarication, no chance to back out. He waited on a balcony a few stories up, not wanting the cab driver to catch sight of him and perhaps identify him. Trusting Margrit wouldn't turn him in was enough of a gamble, though at least it would be difficult for her to catch him, if she was so inclined. The cab pulled away as she scurried up the steps to unlock the front door.

Alban dropped from the balcony, landing in a crouch on the sidewalk a few yards behind her, and pushed to his feet before murmuring, "Margrit."

She twisted the lock open and stepped inside without looking back. Silver wire glinted at her ear, suddenly resolving: headphones attached to the palm-size metallic-red MP3 player that swung from her wrist. "Mar—!"

The door clicked shut. Alban stepped back with a gasp of disbelieving laughter. No light came on in the front of her apartment. He'd have no chance of catching her in the kitchen without breaking in. He stood staring up at the building, then spread his hands helplessly. "Margrit?"

There was no answer, nor had he expected one. Time held him in its slow grip, watching her window until even he began to feel cold settling onto his skin. Then he shook himself and took to rooftops and sky, returning home in befuddlement.

"You wanted to see me?" Margrit leaned into her boss's office, trying to look wide-awake and perky. She was getting old. A few days of an upset sleep schedule wasn't as easy to get by on as it'd been in college.

Russell glanced up and gestured her in. "Yes, come in, Margrit, please. Have a seat. I've been looking over the notes you took on last night's petitioner." He tapped the pile of paperwork she had left, information about Cara and data regarding building codes and wrecking protocols. Looking at it, Margrit felt a surge of satisfaction; squatters rights weren't in her field of expertise, but she thought she'd put together a good preliminary package. "How late were you here?"

She dropped into one of the visitor's chairs. "I don't know. One or two. I sent Cara home earlier than that, but I wanted to get some information together for you to look at. It was almost eight when we got here," she added to herself. Tony should have answered his phone at that hour. It wasn't too late to call. Work may have caught him, but she wished he'd returned the call. Even a late night would have been nice to share after a triumphant day.

Margrit pulled her mind back to the topic at hand, shrugging. "I asked her everything I could think of and told her I'd try to get you to assign someone to help her. It's—"

"You."

Margrit straightened in the chair, enough adrenaline washing through her to wake her up fully. "I appreciate the offer, sir, but I'm really not any sort of an expert on housing situations. I was thinking Nichole—"

"If you need her help, I'll ask her to do what she can. I spent a while on the phone this morning." He glanced at the clock, which read a little after ten.

Margrit shifted her shoulders guiltily. "I would've been in earlier, sir, but—" she cleared her throat and offered a lame smile along with the unvarnished truth "…but I was still sleeping."

Russell smiled. "It's all right. None of us were here bright and early. Maybe a little too much celebrating." He shook his head. "I didn't mean to reprimand you. You've done a fine job here the last few years. You're exactly the sort of person we need in Legal Aid. Young, dedicated, enthusiastic."

Pretty, Margrit thought. There were other words, too, that Russell avoided, as her boss and as a male. Descriptors that would be inappropriate to point out as being among her strengths as a lawyer. She nodded slightly, acknowledging his compliments without speaking.

"You make a good public face." Russell leaned forward. "Which is part of why I want you on this case. As I was saying, I made some phone calls this morning. This building," he said, nodding toward the stack of papers Margrit had left, "is owned by Eliseo Daisani."

The air abruptly weighed heavier on Margrit's shoulders. "*The* Eliseo Daisani?" As if there might be more than one, she teased herself, trying to deflate a spurt of panic that ballooned in her stomach. "Then it's even more imperative, sir, that you have someone experienced in this field—"

"I want you. You're high profile right now, Margrit, and that'll only help us. This girl, this Cara, approached you directly. It's a good story for the press." He sat back, gesturing at her. "You'll make a good face as an adversary against Daisani's corporation. We need that, too. And it doesn't hurt that—"

He broke off, waiting for her to finish his sentence for him. Margrit studied him silently, her gaze level. It took so little time for him to complete it that only someone who knew he expected the defendant to speak for herself would have heard the hesitation. "—you're black."

Margrit thinned her lips, then said coolly, "I'm also white and probably American Indian, Russell. Nobody's going to be fooled by sending me into the Projects. I grew up in Flushing, for God's sake. Dad's a surgeon." She propped her fingers in a steeple in front of her chest, a posture learned from her father. "Mother is a corporate finance manager. I'm not a Cinderella story."

"Nor am I going to try to sell you as one. Nonetheless, it's a card to play and I intend to use it to our benefit."

"Sir." Margrit could hear the anger in the clipped way she spoke the word. She folded her hands out of their steeple and found them re-forming it above her lap, her fingertips now pointed accusingly at her boss. "By putting me as lead counsel on this you're trying to make people think, 'Look, a black girl who's done well. Now she's giving back to the little people she came from. Good for her!' You're using me to lie by way of public perception." A shred of guilt whipped through her as she remembered how she'd sized up Cara's physical appearance as a potential benefit when she climbed on the witness stand. But Margrit pushed the memory away, meeting Russell's gaze with her own forthright anger.

"Does that mean you're refusing the case, Counselor?"

Goddammit. Margrit bit back the words, staring at him. "It means I'd like some time to think about it, sir."

"I'll expect a decision by this afternoon. Margrit," he added, as she stood and stalked toward the door. She turned back, lips compressed. "Your name is already in the news right now. If Cara Delaney or anyone at her building mentions talking to you about this, you may find yourself on Eliseo Daisani's radar. He's a powerful man, and information has a way of making its way to the ears of the powerful. Think carefully, but think quickly. If there's a compelling enough reason behind him wanting this building to come down, you may find yourself with a dangerous enemy."

"Thank you, sir." Margrit left his office with her fists clenched, and snatched up her coat on the way out of the building. There was no thinking about her destination; thought might send her in the other direction. She hailed a cab rather than give in to the desire to run her anger out. A dockworker might reasonably show up to an impromptu meeting sweaty and disheveled. A lawyer for Legal Aid couldn't afford that as a first impression.

Particularly not with the target she had in mind.

Daisani's personal assistant made heroin chic look like a healthy lifestyle choice. Everything about the woman was thin: her hair, scraped back against her skull into a bun so tight it looked like it must give her a headache; her eyes, behind rectangle-framed tortoiseshell glasses; her nose, which was pinched enough that Margrit thought she must have a hard time breathing. She was excruciatingly well dressed, but the linen and silk of her suit somehow managed to play up the sharpness of her shoulders and the vicious angles of her collarbones. Margrit, in an ivory suit she'd rescued from the dry cleaners, felt unexpectedly lush in comparison.

"Do you have an appointment?"

Margrit startled, trying not to stare. She'd expected a voice as thin and nasal as the woman, a piercing soprano. Instead she spoke in a warm contralto with bright notes to it, like rich liqueur poured over ice. The tone was professional enough to border on unfriendly, but it couldn't hide the depth of music in her voice. Margrit's planned arguments to win an appointment with Daisani were abandoned in favor of a heartfelt, "You have a beautiful voice."

The thin woman went still for a moment, then flickered a smile that did nothing to relax her features. "Thank you. Do you have an appointment?"

Impatience, Margrit told herself, would get her nowhere. They both knew she didn't have an appointment, but form had to be met. She proffered a wry smile and shook her head. "I'm afraid not. I was hoping—"

"Mr. Daisani," the narrow woman said, "is a very busy man."

"I understand." Margrit kept the rueful smile, and gestured to one of the lobby chairs. "I'd be glad to wait. I only need a few minutes of his time."

The woman opened an appointment book of rich, embossed brown leather that complemented the pale wood of the enormous curved desk Eliseo Daisani's personal assistant was barricaded behind. There was nothing in the office that wasn't sumptuous. The lobby chairs were antiques, some covered in pale leather, others in rich red velvet that looked so soft Margrit had forced herself not to stop and brush her fingers across it as she entered. The hardwood floors gleamed as if they were polished every night, scuffs removed with prejudice. The walls were paneled wood, as polished as the floors, all of it harkening back to an era decades before Margrit's own.

Paintings on the walls dated from the twenties, art deco at its finest, with the exception of one discreet portrait of a slim, dusky man behind the assistant's desk. A woman bearing a striking resemblance to the assistant herself was also in the portrait, her hair cut in a sharp bob that did much more for her thin features than the tense bun this woman wore. Margrit dared a nod at the portrait, asking, "Your grandmother?"

As if she might be surprised by what lay there, the assistant turned to look at the painting. "Vanessa Gray," she said. "And Dominic Daisani, Mr. Daisani's father." The second showing of interest in her, rather than Eliseo Daisani, seemed to thaw a very slender thread within the woman. A note of pride entered her rich voice as she turned back to Margrit. "I was named for her. My family has worked with Mr. Daisani's family for a long time." With the slight relaxation, she looked like the before picture of a makeover: there was beauty in her, tightly restrained. Margrit wondered what had made her decide to go the sourpuss route instead of playing up the glamour within.

"She was lovely. You look like her." The compliments were honest, and Margrit offered another smile along with them, stepping back from the desk. "I really don't mind waiting. Just a few minutes of his time, maybe?"

Vanessa Gray the younger pursed her thin lips and nodded very subtly toward a chair. Margrit took the victory, smiled again and retreated to await her chance.

"Miss Knight. What a pleasure to meet you." Eliseo Daisani came around a marble desk that would fill Margrit's bedroom, and offered her a hand, clasping hers in both of his when she took it. He was barely taller than she was, wiry in build, and his hands were disconcertingly hot.

"The pleasure is mine, Mr. Daisani." Margrit spoke with a degree of reservation. "I appreciate you sharing a few minutes of your time."

C.E. MURPHY

"When the rising star of the city's Legal Aid Society comes knocking on my door, I am of course predisposed to discover her mission." Daisani winked, making fun of himself. He was too thin for good looks, but his grin was disarming and he clearly knew it. Despite herself, Margrit smiled.

"I think you probably know why I'm here, Mr. Daisani."

"Of course I do. It's the price of being me. Someone has to be aware of all these details, and I was the best man for the job. Please, won't you sit down?" He ushered her to a love seat coupled with a couch in front of floor-to-ceiling windows that overlooked the city. "Isn't the view tremendous?" he asked, sounding as if he'd called it up especially for her. "Some days I don't get any work done at all, just looking down at the city. Well, between that and the books." He gestured easily at the far end of the office, which was walled to the ceiling with pale wooden shelves filled with hundreds of books, interspersed with decorative objects. "May I get you some water?"

"Yes, please. Do you mind?" She gestured toward the bookshelves in turn, taking a step or two in their direction. Daisani made a generous, expansive hand wave, inviting her to look as he went to a wet bar at the other end of the enormous office. "I don't have that problem," Margrit added as she approached the shelves. "My office is a cubicle in the middle of a building. Is that a Rodin?"

"It is." Daisani sounded pleased as he joined her, offering a glass that gave a low, subtle ring of sound as Margrit took it. *Crystal,* she thought, trying not to look as startled as she felt. Of course it would be crystal. Nothing in Daisani's office was of a halfway measure. "You have an excellent eye, Miss Knight."

"I've never even seen photos of this before. It looks like an early sculpture of *The Secret*." Margrit reached out to touch the marble hands, clasped together in silent eternity. "I didn't know he'd done more than one version. I should be so lucky as to have knickknacks like yours, Mr. Daisani." She turned her head, studying a pair of soft-looking furs pinned to the wall at the end of the shelves. One was much smaller than the other, and a thread of cool wariness slipped through Margrit. Daisani was a hunter, and apparently didn't care if his prey was a mother with child. She turned her gaze back to him, keeping her expression neutral.

Daisani beamed at her. "An excellent eye," he repeated. "I'll be certain to arrange for a much better view." Margrit blinked at him and his eyebrows—dark, inquisitive—rose. "In your new office."

"My what?"

"Your new office." Daisani's eyebrows went higher, as if he was surprised it was necessary to explain. "As counsel for Daisani Incorporated, of course. You didn't think I'd put you in a cubicle, did you? In *this* building?" He twirled a finger, making it clear the whole building was at his disposal.

"Counsel for what?" Margrit could feel heat building in her cheeks, a distressing indicator that she'd been outplayed and was too startled to react quickly. "I'm sorry, what?"

Daisani smiled beatifically, leaning on his desk as he reached for his own water. He crossed one ankle over the other, his polished leather shoes so bright that they caught Margrit's attention as easily as they bounced the light. "It's an excellent, excellent time to make a play for moving up in the world. I absolutely approve. It's been, what, three, going on four years now, of Legal Aid? A number of minor victories and a few setbacks, though those are to be expected. But now with the Johnson case making headlines, you've paid your dues. You may, of course, want to take on one more case, just so it's not quite so obvious that it's time to pay off the bills now. Wouldn't you say? As it happens, I'm delighted to tell you that I have an opening extraordinarily well suited for your skills."

He leaned forward from the waist, flashing a conspiratorial grin. "And to your temperament, Miss Knight. It's a noble pursuit, wanting to help those less fortunate than you are, but you needn't live in near poverty yourself to do it. In fact, your address may be a touch unfashionable. After an appropriate amount of time we'll certainly want to discuss moving you to, oh, say, the Upper East Side?" He came upright again, his shoulders back and spine straight, the posture of a confident man.

Margrit swallowed, folding her hands around the crystal glass carefully. "I'm a far cry from living in poverty, Mr. Daisani. I'm not here about a job."

"Of course you are. This is an audition. You just don't realize it yet, Miss Knight. The idealists rarely do." Daisani lifted a finger, then laid it alongside his nose, like a swarthy Santa Claus. "It's all right. I won't hold it against you."

A little bubble of anger heated up inside Margrit's belly. It stiffened her spine and shut her expression down into something neutral. Daisani saw it, too, and laughed, leaning toward her again. "I've offended you."

"Not at all." Margrit worked to keep emotion out of her voice. "But I think I've learned what I needed to know."

"Oh, no." Daisani's voice dropped, smoothing out like

cream and sugar. "No, Miss Knight, I don't think you have at all." Magnanimity suddenly splashed back into him and he spread his hands, a welcoming gesture. "But you will, and I'm positively fascinated to see how that turns out. The job offer still stands, Miss Knight. For a little while, at least."

"At least until I've taken that one more case?" Margrit asked, the words coming out thin. "The one that's for show, so I don't look like I'm abandoning the cause too easily?"

"At least that long," Daisani agreed. "Think how pleased your parents will be, Miss Knight. Moving up in the world. Focusing on problems that are really more suited for your intelligence and passion, rather than taking on hard-luck cases for a fraction of what you're worth. Please," he added, "do tell your mother hello the next time you speak with her. Delightful woman. Uncanny insight into the fluctuations of the stock market. If she were a shade less ethical you'd be absurdly wealthy." Daisani tapped the end of his nose, winking again. "And I know from absurdly wealthy, Miss Knight. It's been a delight meeting you. Let me escort you out."

"That's all right." Margrit put on a quick smile and hoped it warmed her eyes. "I can find my own way, and I think your assistant would take umbrage at the personal attention."

Daisani laughed and gave a half bow, then waved his hand toward the door. "As you wish, Miss Knight. Good afternoon."

EIGHT

"I'LL TAKE THE case." Margrit stood in Russell's doorway again, clenching her fists into knots and loosening them again. Eliseo Daisani's cool assumption of her reason for being at his offices rankled, driving her to take a stance she wasn't wholly convinced she should. Still, the decision was made, and Margrit hated second-guessing herself. "I'm going to need help, Russell. This isn't my area of expertise."

"You've mentioned that several times today." Her boss put his elbows on his desk and leaned forward, smiling. "I knew you'd come around. I've talked to Nichole about being second counsel, and she's fine with that."

"Is she? Or is she putting on a good show?"

"Either way." Russell shrugged. "You're going to be very short on time with this project, Margrit. Eliseo Daisani is used to getting his own way, and his pockets run deep."

"So I've seen," Margrit said under her breath, feeling a fresh wash of insult and irritation. "I'll get started this afternoon, but I'm leaving on time, Russell. I've got a date tonight." Her phone was still in hand, the call from Tony having caught her on the stairs as she'd reentered the Legal Aid Society building. Still bubbling with outrage over Daisani's offer, Margrit had had to rein herself in to keep from snapping at the detective and refusing his offer of dinner out that evening. It was dismaying that her comfort with him made him the easiest target to lash out at when frustration took her. They'd gotten back together often enough that she must think it safe, but it wasn't the way to have a peaceful relationship.

Peaceful. The word made her cringe. It suggested no challenges, which was both unrealistic and inappropriate. But certainly there had to be a degree of peacefulness, to let them continue forward. The danger was in only being a couple when there was peace between them, and that seemed too close to what they had.

"Tony?" At Margrit's nod, Russell smiled. "Glad things are working out."

She lifted a shoulder and let it fall, dismissing the question of whether things were working out, then sighed. "I'll be here twenty-four-seven after tonight."

"Promise me you'll at least go home to shower," Russell said. "Please. For all our sakes." He tipped his chin toward the hall behind her. "Go on. You've got a lot of work to do, and I expect brilliance, Counselor."

"He actually had the balls to say it, Cole. Russell said I was good for the case because I'm black. He actually said that. And then. *Then.*" Outrage had her in its grasp again, Cole the unwary mark who'd asked how her day had gone. Margrit stood before her closet, eyebrows knit together so hard her head ached. "Dammit, I don't have anything to wear!"

Cole leaned in her bedroom doorway, watching her warily as he thumped a wooden spoon against his shoulder. "You could go like that. I'm sure Tony would appreciate it."

Margrit scowled at him. "I am not going on a date in a sports bra and running tights."

"You going to take all this moodiness out on Tony? I thought you two were trying to patch it up." Her housemate pushed away from her door and stepped across the piles of clothes that littered the floor. "I don't understand how someone with a mind as orderly as yours can live in a room as messy as this one. And then what?"

"A clean desk is a sign of a cluttered mind," Margrit muttered. She sat down on her bed, surrounded by lumps of discarded clothing, and put her face in her hands. "Then I went to see Eliseo Daisani."

"You what?" Cole turned away from her closet, spoon lifted like a ceremonial spear. "You *what?*"

"I went to see Eliseo Daisani," Margrit repeated. "He knows my mother."

"How?"

"I have no idea! He offered me a job!"

Cole put his spoon hand against the closet as if he needed the physical support. "Eliseo Daisani offered you a job?"

Margrit looked up through her fingers. "Yeah."

"Did you say yes?"

"Of course not!"

"Margrit! He'd pay you half a million dollars a year! What'd you say?"

She snorted and flopped violently onto her back. "And move me to the upper East Side. What do you *think* I said?"

Cole shook his head and turned his attention back to her closet, rifling through it. "I think you went back to work and said to your racist boss you'd take the case against Daisani, despite it not being your area of expertise, and despite your fears about how it'll play to the media. Grit, you've got more clothes than Cameron and me put together. How can you have nothing to wear?"

"Those ones are all dirty!" Margrit pointed accusingly at her closet without looking at it. "And those ones are all—*wrong!*" She smacked the pile beside her, then shoved it away as she scowled. "And that's exactly what I did. He's not racist," she added in another mutter. "He's playing the advantages he has, and it pisses me off."

"All wrong…" Cole sounded exasperated, ignoring her defense of Russell. "Where are you going for dinner?"

"I don't know. Moroccan, I think. He knows I like it. So not dressy." Margrit picked up a handful of clothes from the bed and discarded them again with an overwrought sigh.

Cole snorted. "You've been totally played, Grit. Are you aware of that?"

Margrit frowned at his shoulders. "What are you talking about?"

"'Eliseo Daisani is a dangerous man. You might make an enemy.' Russell might as well have painted a bull's-eye on the case and loosed you at it like an arrow, Grit. Either he knows you incredibly well or he's astonishingly lucky. Here, wear this." Cole pulled out a gold camisole and a red cashmere sweater, tossing them on top of her. "And jeans. It's not like you have to make a stellar first impression."

"Maybe I should try. This whole thing with Tony... Do you really think he played me?"

"Tony?" Cole blinked at her. "You two play each other like violins, Grit. That's why you keep getting back together."

"Russell, Cole. Do you think Russell played me?"

"Oh. I think anybody who knows anything about you knows that waving a red flag in front of you will get you to charge the target. You're the world's most stereotypical Taurus."

"I am not." Margrit sat up with the camisole and sweater clutched against her chest. "What'm I going to do when you and Cam get married and move to the boonies and I don't have my favorite metrosexual to clothe and feed me?"

"You'll go on dates naked. What time's he picking you up?"

The doorbell rang. Margrit started guiltily and hugged the sweater harder. Cole laughed, wagging his spoon as he left her room. "I'll distract him. You owe me, Grit."

Shouts of laughter greeted Margrit when she emerged from the bedroom a few minutes later. She followed the sound through the apartment, finding Cole and Tony relaxed in the living room and drinking beer. Tony climbed to his feet, holding the bottle behind his back as he glowered good-naturedly at Cole. "You promised she'd be half an hour."

"Well, she usually is. You gave him that shiner, Grit?"

The skin around Tony's left eye, along the nose and under the socket, shone deep blue and purple. The inner corner of his eye was red and weepy, fluttering as if it could neither stay open nor close comfortably. Margrit put a hand over her mouth, staring in surprise. "Wow." She flexed her other hand, glancing down at the swollen, reddish knuckles, then looked back up at the bruised man before her. "I think you lost that fight."

He touched the area gingerly. "Ya think?" He dropped his hand and looked her up and down, a smile crooking his mouth. "You look fantastic. I like the red. We ready?"

"Almost. I just have one question."

Tony exchanged a glance with Cole. "This can't be good." He looked back at Margrit. "Shoot."

"How on earth did you get those roses to the office so fast? It didn't take me that long to get back to work."

Laughter crinkled Tony's eyes, and then he winced, touching his fingers to the bruise again. "I called Anita and begged her for a favor."

"I thought her flower shop wasn't open yet."

"It opens officially on the first, but this was an emergency. I threw myself on her big-sisterly mercies."

"Did you tell her what you'd done?"

"She wouldn't send the flowers until I did. She said men pulling that sort of shit was exactly what keeps her from getting married again." Tony made a face. "Despite Mama and Papa nagging."

"Or maybe because of their nagging. Your mom puts mine to shame. Well, tell her thank-you for the flowers. They were beautiful."

"I don't get thanked? My sister does?"

"Life isn't fair, is it?" Margrit sat down on the couch to pull her shoes on, then stood again, smiling.

Tony cast a despairing look at Cole. "Why do I keep trying to make this work?"

"Because she's beautiful, intelligent and challenging?" Cole suggested.

Margrit dimpled. "Careful, or I'll try stealing you from Cam. Do we have reservations, Tony?"

"Yeah. We should go. Anaconda says hi, by the way. She wants to know if you're all coming over for the Superbowl on Sunday. It's tradition."

Margrit laughed. "We've only done it twice!"

"Tradition gets set fast in my family. Besides, Ana's thirteen. You wouldn't want to break her heart."

"Okay, but I'm telling her you're calling her Anaconda out of her hearing."

"I'm going to have to marry her," Tony said under his breath to Cole. "Out of self-defense, if nothing else."

"Marrying me means I couldn't be *forced* to testify against you, Tony, not that I wouldn't volunteer to."

Tony clutched his heart. "Ow. All right, let's go before I get stung by any more slings and arrows. They're holding a table for us."

"So." They spoke the word at the same time and let laughter take them, Tony reaching across the table to curl his fingers over Margrit's before releasing her hand. "I did my best," he said, gesturing to the restaurant. Booths were set around its outer perimeter, crimson velvet curtains separating one from another. A lightweight gauze net fell over the entrance to their own booth, making the lighting hazy and friendly and offering an illusion of solitude. Sound was surprisingly muffled, giving them more privacy than Margrit expected in a busy restaurant.

"You did good," she acknowledged. "I'm amazed we both got the night off. Tony, I'm sorry I hadn't called. In the last few weeks, I mean."

He held up a hand, cutting off the apology. "This is how we do it every time, Grit. Can we try something different?"

Margrit leaned back and gave him a dubious smile. "I don't know. That sounds like a chick line. Have you been reading relationship books?"

Something between embarrassment and smugness crossed Tony's face. "Worse. I've been talking to Anne-Marie."

"Oh, God. Professionally?"

"Are you kidding? I'm a cop. I can't afford a therapist. No, just more of that big-sisterly advice. I get flowers from the one and relationship advice from the other."

"How's her son doing?"

"Still in trouble. You know how boys are at sixteen. Sometimes I think Amie got a psychotherapy degree so she could understand her kid. You're changing the subject, Grit."

"I still don't get how you got *Amie* out of *Anne-Marie*. Anyway. Sorry, I didn't mean to change the subject." Shivers crept up Margrit's spine, making her wonder how true the statement was. She leaned forward again, suddenly and uncomfortably aware she was using what Anne-Marie would call open body language. "Okay. I'm listening."

"I just want to skip all the recriminations, Grit. No more of this my fault your fault, I'm sorry you're sorry thing. We've been doing that for years."

"Are you sure you haven't been reading relationship books?"

"Margrit. Come on. I'm being serious."

"Yeah." She ducked her head, chin against her chest before she looked up. "Yeah, I can tell. Sorr—mmm." She closed her mouth on the apology and studied the man across the table from her. His eyes were dark and serious, his mouth held as if he wasn't sure if he should be smiling or frowning. "So this is the fish or cut bait conversation," she said after a moment.

Tony exhaled a semiexplosive laugh. "Not how I would've phrased it, but yeah, I guess so. I mean, what I said back at the apartment—"

Cold slipped through Margrit's belly as if she'd been drinking ice water. "Tony…"

"I'm not proposing." His smile went thin and a little flat. "We've spent as much time off in the last three or four years as on. I don't think that's a good place to start suggesting marriage from. But the thing is we keep getting back together, Grit. So maybe that says something."

"Yeah." She dropped her head again, more a nod this time. "I've been thinking that a lot the last few days, too. I've also been thinking we're good together when things are good, and we fall apart whenever there's a bump, person-ally or professionally. Doesn't that say something, too?"

"Maybe it says we're not trying very hard." Tony fell silent as the waiter appeared, bringing a bowl of enormous pro-portions with a dozen different foodstuffs in it. He settled it into the middle of the table, murmured after their well-being and disappeared again, leaving them to their conver-sation. Margrit reached out to snag a strip of meat and crunchy onions, dangling them over her plate without eating.

"We can't keep doing the whose-side-are-you-on thing if there's any chance of making it succeed, Tony. I work for Legal Aid and I'm not planning on quitting, even if—" She broke off, unwilling to get into the discussion of Eliseo Daisani just then. "Even if you don't like it. And that's the one that sends us skittering in opposite directions most often. That and our schedules."

"We both work too much," Tony agreed—his translation of the last statement. "And I'm not sure either of us can do much about that. Maybe you could."

Margrit's smile thinned. "Let's not turn this into the woman sacrificing her career for the sake of the relationship, Tony. We might as well walk away right now if that's where you're going with it."

"No." He hesitated. "I don't know. Maybe it was. It just seems more like a lawyer could work fewer hours than a cop, more predictably than a cop. Emergencies," he added, with an explanatory spread of his hands.

"And what am I supposed to do with this reduced work schedule of mine? Sit at home waiting for my man to come back from the war? I don't think so, Anthony. We make this work around the way we really are, or we don't make it work at all."

"You have no romance in you at all, Grit." Tony pulled a wry smile into place and Margrit cut off a disbelieving snort.

"There's nothing romantic about subsuming my personality and ambitions in favor of a man's. What would you say if I said the only way to make this happen was for you to be home at six o'clock every day and to never put yourself in any danger?"

"I'd take a good hard look at business school," Tony answered softly.

The words hit Margrit in the stomach with the force of a wrecking ball, obliterating any appetite she had. The meat and onions dropped to her plate and she wiped her fingers on a napkin, belly churning too much to even consider licking her fingers.

"Tony…"

He managed another faint smile. "Look, Margrit, my dad's a cop, too. I know how hard it is to be an officer's wife. My mom's good at it, but you know, that's a choice she makes every day of her life. I like my job and I'm good at it. Quitting wouldn't be my preference, but if there's got to be a line drawn somewhere—" He allowed himself a shrug "Then I'm willing to look around for ways to cross it."

"You're serious." Margrit's heart fluttered in her chest, beating too fast and bringing washes of color to her cheeks that café latte skin wasn't dark enough to hide. "Jesus, Tony, you're serious?"

"Yeah. That was the point of this conversation, Grit. I'm serious. Or I want to be serious, anyway. About you. Come on, Margrit," he added after a few seconds, taking in her expression. "Is it that surprising? Is it that bad?"

"No!" She blurted the word, wiping her hand compulsively on her napkin again. "No, it's just…I just wasn't expecting it. We've been through this whole thing so many times I didn't expect…" She trailed off again, then managed a quiet laugh. "I didn't expect anything to change." She lifted a palm to stop his words before he spoke. "I'm not putting any blame on either of us for not trying to change before now. It's not that important anymore. Not if we're trying to look forward."

Tony nodded and she let out a breath, glad to be understood, though she fell silent for a few long minutes as they studied one another. "Look," she finally said. "There's got to be some middle ground here. Neither of us should have to give up our careers to make this work. If you can keep me updated on when you've got to work late, I can at least try to make my late nights the same as yours. That'd be a good place to start, right? And when you have emergencies, I won't get pissed and stop calling."

"And I'll stop riding you about your job," Tony agreed quietly. "It's a place to start." He looked at the table. "Are you hungry?"

"Honestly?" She looked over the bowl of food and shook her head. "Not at all."

"Want to go back to my place?"

Margrit's grin broadened. "Yeah." She poked her head through the gauze curtains, waving down their waiter, and asked for their dinner to be packed up to go.

"Call a cab or walk?" Margrit leaned heavily against Tony's side, fighting off giggles as she wrapped an arm around his ribs and grinned up at him. He slung his arm around her shoulders, swinging the bag of food from his other hand.

"Probably better take a cab. It's a long walk."

Margrit slipped away and jogged ahead a few steps, turning to bounce on her toes in mockery. "C'mon, slowpoke. You can make it. Can't catch me, I'm the ginger-bread man!"

"You're the gingerbread nut." He stepped toward the street, waving the bag to hail a cab. "You can run home. I'll be there waiting when you arrive all sweaty and smelly."

"Then you'll just have to wash my back in the shower." Margrit glanced down the street before dancing into it, jabbing fists at the air. "Float like a butterfly, sting like a bee!"

"You already stung me once this week," Tony said. "I'd rather not have a repeat performance. The shower, though…"

Margrit laughed and spun in the street as he stepped off the curb. "How about we skip the running, take a cab and just get right to the back-scrubbing?"

"Now that's my idea of a da—*Margrit!*"

Tires squealed and blinding headlights flashed. Margrit flung a hand up to protect her eyes, and an incredible weight and strength slammed into her belly. Her forehead smashed against something hard and solid.

The world went black.

NINE

AN ACRID SMELL woke her. Margrit gagged and coughed, trying to wave the scent away. Her hand slapped against cool flesh that barely gave with the impact; someone moved as she opened her eyes. Blue neon lights swam in her vision and she shut her eyes again, clenching her teeth against nausea.

"How do you feel?" The male voice, deep and gravelly, was vaguely familiar. Margrit pried her eyes open once more and sat up.

The world did a sharp plunge and twist to the left, taking her stomach with it. She rolled to her side and vomited. A minute later, tears dripping from her eyes, she saw there was a stainless steel bowl settled on the floor, clearly meant for the purpose for which it had just been used.

"Your aim is excellent," the voice said wryly. "Lie down. I believe you have a concussion."

"Where am I?" Margrit curled into a ball, unable to do anything but lie down even if she wanted to. The room spun every time she opened her eyes, so she kept them closed, her forehead wrinkled with pain and concentration.

"In a safe place," he murmured.

"A hospital? Am I in a hospital? There was a…a car."

"Not in a hospital. The car didn't hit you."

Margrit let out a feeble laugh. "Then did you get the number of the Mack truck that did?"

"I'm afraid that was me." Some of the gravel left his voice, making it more familiar still. Margrit's eyes popped open and she regretted it when the room lurched precariously.

"Alban?" She pressed her eyes shut again as she asked the question, unwilling to risk another bout of sickness.

"Yes." His weight squashed the mattress and he put a cold cloth against her forehead. "You have a concussion," he repeated. "Mild, but you should stay still awhile, and shouldn't fall asleep."

Sleep. An overwhelming exhaustion swept over Margrit. "Sleep sounds nice," she whispered.

"No." Alban slid fingers beneath her chin, turning her head slowly and gently. Margrit clenched her teeth.

"Don't do that," she said hoarsely. "I'll puke again."

"Better that than sleeping. I apologize for the concussion."

"What'd you hit me with? And what's wrong with the lights?" Margrit kept her eyes closed and tried swallowing to clear the rasp in her voice.

She heard, rather than saw, Alban shift and look upward. "The lights?"

"They're neon. Or is it just my eyes?" She was afraid to open them again to find out.

"Oh." Alban was silent a moment or two. "They are neon.

We're in…" Wryness filled his voice again. "Not the best part of town. I apologize."

"You dress well for somebody who can't afford a decent place to live." Margrit lifted a hand to her forehead, still without opening her eyes, and prodded the swollen goose egg there. "You're also very polite for a murderer."

Some of the politeness left his voice, surprise replacing it. "You're personally acquainted with a lot of murderers?"

"You'd be surprised who you meet in my line of work."

A droll note infused his response. "I suppose I would be. I'm not a murderer, Margrit. If I wanted you dead, the car would have done a fine job of it."

"Except it wouldn't be personal. They say serial killers like to make things personal." Margrit's eyes opened again against her will. "Wait." The neon lights lunged toward her and she moaned. "You were driving that car?"

"Of course not. I was trying to save your life."

She frowned faintly and pressed her fingertips against her eyes. Squealing tires. Blinding lights. An impact of colossal proportions. "Are you sure the car didn't hit me?"

Alban chuckled and moved from the edge of the bed. "Yes."

"It *felt* like a car hit me."

There was another silence. "That, too, would be easier to explain later. When you're well."

Even with her eyes closed, the lights seemed to pulse and wobble, making bright, sickening sparks behind her eyelids. There was something wrong with the way she felt, more than the pain and nausea of the concussion. Margrit swallowed, trying to pinpoint the source of discomfort. "Why am I not in a hospital?"

"I wouldn't be able to talk to you in a hospital, and I need to talk to you." He sounded patient but tired.

"Why can't you talk to me in a hospital?"

"For one," Alban said, "I seem to be wanted for murder."

Margrit thought she might blush, if her head didn't hurt so badly that the idea make her temples throb.

"For another," Alban said more slowly, "hospital visiting hours tend to be during the day."

"So, what?" Margrit wished she dared open her eyes, even just to stare at the ceiling. "You're a vampire?"

He sounded a bit startled as he answered, "No. Not at all."

"So I don't see the problem, then."

Alban went quiet again, except for small clinking sounds, as if coffee was being prepared. Water boiled, a kettle whistling, high-pitched enough to set Margrit's teeth on edge. The screech cut off after a few seconds and she slumped in the cot, relief as palpable as discomfort. "I'll help you sit up," he said, his voice at her side. "I have a tea for you to drink. It'll help the pain and the swelling."

"They seem to be doing fine on their own," Margrit said groggily.

Alban chuckled again and slid an arm behind her shoulders, enveloping one of her hands in his. The touch was gentle, his hands dwarfing hers in strength and size. Her heart hammered harder, making her temples pound, but it cleared her mind a little. She knew the thrill of feeling in danger: that was what was missing. She wasn't afraid. In pain, yes, but not in distress for her life.

"I must've hit my head harder than I thought," she mumbled.

Worry came into Alban's voice. "Can you not sit?"

"No, I can sit. I'm just—" She stopped abruptly, unwilling to give up the only advantage she might have. A kidnapper didn't need to know his victim wasn't afraid of him. "I can sit," she repeated instead.

Alban helped her upright. "There's a wall to your left if you need something to lean on."

She put her hand out, finding it, and shifted against it before Alban folded her hands around a sturdy mug. Margrit smiled without opening her eyes. "Nice cup."

"Thank you," he said with mild surprise. "I made it."

"Really?" She opened her eyes, looking at neon lights reflected in yellow tea. The mug was stoneware, glazed a pale seaweed-green and had a chip in the handle. Spiderweb cracks lined the glazing at the bottom of the cup. "It looks old."

"I was young when I made it."

Margrit looked up cautiously, the room swimming and dipping alarmingly behind Alban. He appeared to be around thirty-five. "Yeah. 'Cause you're so old now."

He smiled. "Drink your tea."

She lifted the cup, inhaling the scents of honey and lemon, then hesitated. "You said you were innocent. At the club you said you were innocent but you couldn't go to the cops. Why? Are you here illegally? You said you needed to talk to someone who wasn't easily frightened, and that's why you wanted to speak to me. How do you know if I'm easily frightened or not? Why do you need someone who's not?" She threw the questions out as if they were barriers to any harm that might come to her, words being her only weapons. They helped her focus through the throbbing in her skull, though the pain didn't ease any.

Alban's smile came again, sorrow touching it. "You could say I was an illegal immigrant, though it's an oversimplification of gross proportions. The reasons I can't go to the authorities are very much tied to the reasons I need to talk to someone who isn't easily frightened, Margrit. I know a little about you. What I know gives me the irrational hope you can help me. Please." He nodded at the mug she held. "Drink the tea, and we can talk."

Ir. Rah. Shun. Al.

Margrit met his eyes, then drank the tea.

He hadn't intended to lie to her.

The tea had been brewed to clear her head, not put her to sleep, though he doubted she would believe him when she awoke a second time. Alban dropped into a crouch, watching her, then lifted his own hand to stare at it dispassionately. She might believe him, he amended silently, if she would listen at all. In retrospect, he'd realized he'd never made the healing tea for a human woman before, and that the potency should probably have been halved for someone her size. He was unaccustomed to thinking in terms of how his people differed from hers, except the most obvious.

The way she slept, for example. Color flushed her cheeks, her breathing deep and even. He breathed imperceptibly when he slept, with no restless flutters of eyelashes or twisting in the covers. Margrit knotted and loosened a hand around the mug she still held, revealing bruises on her knuckles. He reached out to touch the injuries, then stopped, the gesture seeming an intrusion. Even slipping the mug from her fingers seemed rude, so he'd left it in her grasp. He would have to wonder, or ask, how she'd hurt herself.

He gave a snort of disbelief, skeptical that they might ever hold such an ordinary conversation.

But why not? For a woman seized by a stranger—a man wanted for questioning about a murder, no less—Margrit retained her equanimity wonderfully well. The head injury may have helped with that, pain giving her something internal to focus on rather than her situation, but her questions had not been those of a woman befuddled. She wasn't presenting a bold face; there was no scent of fear about her at all. If she could face so much with such ease, perhaps the rest might be less insurmountable than he'd always imagined.

Margrit stirred and whimpered, lifting her hand toward her head. Alban reached to comfort her, then stopped again. Better to go out and get an ordinary drug like aspirin than to offer her another dosage of the tea that had always helped him. He pushed himself erect, hesitating a moment longer as she fell into a deeper sleep. She would be all right for the brief time he'd be gone.

A flash of humor creased his face. She would have to be. He couldn't carry her unconscious body to the nearest convenience store. He brushed his fingers over her hair, not quite touching the tangle of curls, then was gone.

A nasal buzz erupted; Margrit flinched awake, hefting the mug she still clutched. The room's shadows were blue, the only light the garish color from the neon sign outside. It hummed incessantly, making her wonder how she'd slept at all.

The answer came to her easily, and she tightened her fingers around the mug. Alban had drugged her, despite his assurances of wanting to talk. Anger rose, then dissipated as she realized the pain was largely gone, reduced to a dull throb in her forehead. For a moment Margrit counted out the pulses, *ir-rah-shun-al*. There was still no hollow fear in her belly. There hadn't been since the flash of headlights and Tony's panicked shout.

Tony. He would be worried sick. Margrit sat up, holding her head as she groaned. Her cell phone. Her purse. She fumbled on the table by the cot, searching for the purse without looking. Her fingers closed around a strap just as the window slid open, a hush of sound that let in a shaft of cold air. Margrit jerked around.

A monster perched in the window. Winged and clawed, it overflowed the frame. Neon lights backlit it, red and blue that cast demonic shadows across sharp, harsh features. Its eyes were wide and colorless in the gloom.

Margrit screamed, instinct driving her to fling her purse at the thing. The monster batted it away easily, then hopped forward, landing on the cot. The bed sagged and creaked, then collapsed. Margrit snatched Alban's mug up and swung it as hard as she could into the monster's temple. Shards exploded everywhere. The creature roared in pain, rolling sideways off the collapsed cot, and disappeared into the jumble of shadows and clutter. Margrit staggered to her feet, panting, and lurched out the window.

Metal bit into her feet as she scrambled onto the fire escape. She stared down, wondering where her shoes had gone, then swayed as the ground, twenty feet below, rippled and spun. She took another step forward, running a hip into the safety railing, and felt her balance give way entirely. Her feet scraped against the metal grating as she fell forward, grabbing feebly at the rail in an attempt to stop her fall. The alley floor below zoomed close, like a movie camera rushing in to examine a detail.

What a stupid way to die, she thought, and closed her eyes.

An arm, solid and muscular, snagged her around the waist and hauled her backward. Margrit spun upright again, her head snapping back and cracking against…something too hard to be Alban's chest. A hollow sound popped in her ears, and she doubled over, vomiting through the fire escape grate. Bile spattered on the walkway below. The arm around her waist held her steady, then pulled her back in the window she'd made her escape through. Once on the shambles of the cot again, Margrit whimpered and slid out of the embrace, into the blankets.

"Are you all right?" Alban, standing above her, looked down with concern in his eyes and blood trickling from a crescent-shaped cut on his temple. Margrit scrambled into the corner, using the walls for support as she shoved herself to her feet.

Someone from the bar below pounded savagely on the little apartment's door, cursing them both for the vomit. Neither of them moved, staring at one another. After several minutes, the pounding ceased and the irate bartender stomped away.

Only then did Margrit trust herself to so much as swallow, a hard raw gulp. "What," she rasped, "the *fuck*. Are you?"

Alban hesitated. "That would be easier to—"

She shot a hand up, stopping the words with her palm. Her heartbeat pounded in her throat, thickening her voice with anger that overrode fear. "Not later. Now. Tell me now."

Her fingertips tingled as adrenaline rushed through her body, buoying her up despite the redoubled pain in her head.

"Easier to show you than explain," Alban murmured. Margrit stared at him, her nostrils flared and her jaw thrust out in fury and distrust. She nodded once, shaking with too much flight-or-fight energy to speak.

Alban stepped backward, as if to give her space, and inside that step, transformed.

Margrit saw it, yet couldn't see it, all at once. Space contracted around him, and he grew to fill it, like a sudden deep breath that strained the lungs. The blue light that had bleached fair skin to a sickly white now corroded pockets of gray with purple shadows. He dropped into a crouch, his weight on three points, right hand resting on his knee.

The harsh neon light made hard planes of his face. He shifted one shoulder, changing his weight, and spread wings with long narrow tarsals at peak and edge, like elongated fingers with paper-thin skin stretched between them. Slender blood vessels made black lines through fragile-looking skin, like etchings in silver. For a few seconds he held the pose, breathlessly larger than life, so very still it seemed there could be no life in him. Impossibility blurred into aching beauty, a sculptor's Pygmalion dream made real by the gods as he settled into place, wings folding down so smoothly Margrit had to look twice to see them, even knowing they were there.

His shoulders were massive, his skin almost white. Not human white, but pure and rich, like carved alabaster. *Literally,* Margrit thought with a twinge of hysteria. This wasn't the mock thrill of a late-night run through Central Park. Alien fear clenched her heart, making her feel every beat slamming through her lungs and chasing air away. She laughed, the sound high-pitched and frightened. Alban's head came up, his lips pressed together. The wide mouth was beautifully shaped, even in the incredible new form he wore.

He looked like himself and he didn't. The narrow line of his nose had broadened, as had his cheekbones and the set of his eyes. Pale hair fell loose and long over his shoulders, color bleached from it until it was unmistakably white, even in the garish neon lights. When he shook his hair back, his ears swept into distinct points, so fine and delicate Margrit thought a good thump with a fingertip might shatter them. His eyes were colorless, pupils large and swallowing all the available light. It was unquestionably the man Margrit had seen in the park.

It was incontestably *not*.

She backed up a step. "What the hell are you?"

Alban didn't move, though light played on muscle as if he had, breaking shadow into points and curves. The width of his shoulders clearly tapered to a slender waist. The hand that rested on one thigh was overlarge and the nails taloned; the thigh beneath it was muscle so solid it could have been carved of—

"What the *fuck* are you?" Margrit's voice shot up, almost a shriek.

"My family name is Korund," Alban rumbled. It was the granite-on-granite voice she'd heard before, the one that seemed familiar and strange all at once. Margrit put her palm against her concussed forehead and closed her eyes for a moment. "It means stone," he added. The sound lifted goose bumps on her arms, and she shivered as she looked down at him again. Even crouched, he was easily four feet tall. "I am—your people would call me—a gargoyle."

Margrit stared at him in silence, then shook her head violently. "That's impossible."

Alban's mouth curved in a smile. "Merely improbable."

"No!" The word came out too sharply, and Margrit found herself backing up. "No, it's just impossible. I don't know what the *hell* kind of hallucinogenic was in that tea, but you're going to regret it, I swear to God you're going to regret it—"

Alban stood up. Margrit's throat went dry as she raked in seven feet of gargoyle with one look.

Seven feet of naked gargoyle.

"Jesus Christ." Color scalded her cheeks, banishing terror in one embarrassed swoop.

Alban's wings stretched again, tips bumping against the ceiling only half unfurled, his bulk added to immeasurably. "I'm out of the habit of clothes in this form," he said dryly, stepping past her to pull open a drawer and drag a pair of jeans out, and on. "My apologies."

Margrit swallowed and averted her eyes. "What happened to them? Your clothes."

"A gargoyle transforms in front of you, and you wonder about his clothes?" Alban turned back to her, safely clad in jeans that were no less distracting than the nakedness of a moment before. Margrit stared at his hips, where ivory skin slid into dark denim, and swallowed again. There were no telltale curls, no chest hair of any color running in a V down his abdomen to be hidden by the jeans. Her fingers curled as she fought the urge to step forward and touch his stomach and see if it was as absurdly smooth to touch as it was to look at. She wondered if stony skin would be cool under her hand, or warm as human flesh.

"Margrit?"

She yanked her gaze back up to his face. Her head ached, bright pulses of pain behind her eyes. "What the hell was in that tea?" she asked again, voice hoarse.

"Willow bark," Alban said, puzzled. "A little...oh. No drugs, no hallucinogens. I'm afraid I'm real. And the clothes stay with the form."

"So you, what, don't need them in this one?" Margrit asked faintly. His feet were enormously wide, as if his weight was meant to stand forward on them, though he didn't. The nails there were taloned, too, just like his hands. Margrit's gaze drifted to the jeans again, this time at the hems. They were undamaged, belying the breadth of his feet. "That must get chilly. Shrinkage and everything. Embarrassing." Her voice was shrill and thin, a barrier against accepting the impossible as it stood before her.

A whisper of humor entered Alban's tone. "Stone doesn't react like flesh. I don't suffer—" more amusement flooded the word "—shrinkage. In this form I don't usually need clothes. Having them change with me would be inconvenient, don't you think? I would destroy my outfit at dawn each day."

"Dawn?" Margrit looked back up at him. Her mind was addled, she thought distantly. It was the only possible explanation for standing there holding a near normal conversation with a gargoyle. She shivered hard and wrapped her arms around herself, still staring at him. Fear, no longer distracted by the extraordinarily pragmatic question of his clothing, swept back over her, taking the strength from her muscles and leaving her shaking.

"The sunlight holds power over my kind." Alban dropped into a crouch again, both hands folded over his knees now. He looked comfortable, as if it was his natural stance. "Rather like your people's tales of vampires, although we're not destroyed. Only transformed."

"Into…stone?" Margrit put her fingertips against her forehead again, testing the injury there. It throbbed badly enough to make her dizzy once more. She was hallucinating. The thought gave her comfort even as she swayed and shivered.

"Or very nearly," Alban agreed, and offered her a hand, his palm up. Margrit stared at it as if it might bite her. Alban closed his fingers against his palm, loosely, then let his hand fall. "I'm not your enemy, Margrit. I won't hurt you."

"You can't possibly exist." She closed her eyes. "I want to go home."

"Will you hear me out?"

"No!" Her eyes flew open. "No, I just want to go *home*. My friends will be worried sick about me."

"Call them," Alban urged. Margrit snorted, then whimpered as the inhalation seemed to drive spikes through her nose and into her brain.

"Call them and say what?" she demanded, cradling her head in both hands. "'Don't worry, I'm fine, a lunatic with a special effects machine has got me'?" She turned and dropped to her hands and knees, looking for her purse in the tawdry neon light. The impact with the floor sent a jolt of agony through her head, but she scrounged around until she found the bag.

"I'm leaving now." She climbed to her feet. "I'm leaving now, and you're not going to stop me." Weaving her way to the door took fierce concentration, one careful step after another.

Alban dropped his head. "Margrit. Please."

"*No.*" She hesitated with her hand on the knob, expecting a word from him, a movement to stop her. It didn't come.

She yanked the door open and stumbled out.

TEN

THE FR⊕N✝ D⊕⊕R swung open as Margrit fumbled with the lock, which doubled and swam together again no matter how hard she concentrated. Cole swept her into his arms, incoherent with relief. Margrit's knees stopped working and she clung to him. Cam enveloped both of them in a hug.

"See, I said she was okay, Cole. You're okay, aren't you, Grit?" Cameron unfolded Margrit from Cole's arms, wrapping her own arm around her waist to keep her steady. "Good God, what happened to your head? How many fingers am I holding up?"

"Two?" Margrit hazarded.

Cam clucked her tongue. "No, sweetheart, just one. God, we've been worried sick. Cole, call Tony. Oh, you are, good man. He told us you'd been hit by a car," Cam said to Margrit, who looked at her blankly. "He said you went flying and he couldn't find you. You've been gone for hours, Grit. Where've you been? Sit down. Let me get a compress for your head."

Somehow, Margrit had been shuffled into the living room

during the barrage of words. Cam sat her down on the couch, and Margrit sank back into it, shutting her eyes. "Don't fall asleep, Grit!"

Cole, a cell phone pressed against his ear, knelt by the couch to take her hand. "Cam's right, Grit. Don't fall asleep, okay?"

"Pssh," Margrit said. "You always tell me to sleep more."

Cole smiled lopsidedly. "Not right now. Where've you been, Grit? What happened? Tony!" His voice sharpened and he turned his attention to the phone. "Grit's back. I don't know. She just staggered in. A knot the size of Texas on her head, but she's okay. Maybe a concussion. All right. We won't. Okay. See you soon." He hung up the phone and dropped it on the coffee table. "Tony'll be here in a few minutes."

"Tony? Oh good. We were going to have sex," Margrit said gravely, then winced.

Cameron choked on a laugh. "Too much information, Grit. TMI."

"No kidding," Margrit muttered. "My head hurts."

"We've been frantic, hon. I called your parents. Everyone was afraid—" Cole broke off, pale as Margrit straightened up.

"When'd you phone them? Call back. Tell them I'm fine. They don't have to come in." That, if nothing else, was clear in her mind. "I'm not dead, and if they come they'll be here for days, Cole. I swear, I'm fine. I'm fine. I'm fine," she promised.

Cole's lopsided smile flashed again. "So fine you're announcing your sex life to anybody who wants to listen. Maybe you're right. Maybe your parents shouldn't hear that.

I called them right after Tony phoned here, but your mom's a practical woman, Grit. She just got very calm and said she'd contact some of her network to see whether anyone could help find you. She thought she could do it better from there than here. Panic feeds on itself, she said."

Margrit slid down in the couch, feeling it grab her hips. Alban had been more polite, she thought, when they'd danced. The couch was pushy. Not a nice date. She wanted to snort at her own absurdity, but was afraid it would hurt her head. "Go Mom," she whispered. "She's probably got half of Queens awake. What time is it?"

"About two. You've been gone six hours."

"Six hours. It didn't seem that long. I slept more than I thought. Please call them. Tell Mom I'll phone her as soon as my head stops hurting. Tomorrow." Margrit closed her eyes, the pounding in her temples fading a little. "Thanks for worrying. I'm okay."

"Of course you are," Cam said with a briskness reserved for emotional emergencies. "Take this." She folded something into Margrit's hand, then moved it to her head. Cold pierced through the throbbing and Margrit yelped, straightening up again and jerking the ice away. "It's good for you," Cam said.

"I can tell you're a physical trainer. Work through the pain, right?" She pulled her feet up onto the couch and leaned on the arm, holding the ice pack against her head gingerly.

"You got it, babe. God, I'm so glad you're okay, Margrit."

"Me, too. Can somebody call my parents?"

She felt Cameron and Cole exchange wordless glances before Cam said, "All right. You sure you don't want me to ask them to come in?"

Margrit squinted her eyes open and frowned at Cameron, who lifted her hands in defeat. "Okay. Rest for a while. We'll wake you up every twenty minutes or so. I don't want you sleeping through that concussion."

"Hey." Cam's murmur made Margrit catch her breath and whimper. "You've got a visitor, Grit. Wake up."

"Go 'way," Margrit said sulkily. Cameron laughed quietly and did. Tony sat down on the edge of the couch, the shifting weight making Margrit squint again before she pushed herself upright, frowning. "What happened?"

"I was going to ask you the same question. Where have you been? It's two in the morning, Margrit." Tony's eyebrows drew into a frown.

Margrit shook her head carefully. The room spun, but not as dramatically as before. She looked around for the ice pack. "I don't know. What happened?"

"The car came out of nowhere. I got the license number, but it's stolen. Belonged to somebody in Connecticut."

"And it hit me?"

Tony hesitated. "It had to have. It happened so fast. I saw you fly into the air." He broke off again, scowling. "And then you were gone. I looked, but—where did you *go?*"

"I don't know. I woke up in an apartment somewhere. Alban was there."

"You got away from him?" Tony's voice rose an octave.

"He let me go. He didn't hurt me." Margrit pressed her eyes shut again, watching Alban's impossible transformation replay behind her eyelids.

"Can you describe the apartment? The part of town?

Any landmarks?" Concern and professionalism mixed in Tony's voice, the cop struggling briefly with the man.

No, Margrit thought, the cop *was* the man. As much as the lawyer was the woman, with her. "We're gonna have to work on that," she mumbled. "Redefining ourselves outside of the job."

"What?"

She shook her head again, another small, careful motion. "Nothing. There was a bar," she said fuzzily, then closed her eyes. "I don't know. I really don't. I got a cab outside the bar, but I just don't remember, Tony. I'm sorry. Everything's blurry."

Clarity snapped through her, bright enough that pain spiked behind her eyes. The car's headlights blinded her again, this time in memory. Something hit her, slamming into her ribs, bruising them: Alban's broad shoulder. She doubled over, smashing her forehead not against the car, but against the improbable solidity of his back.

Like smashing her head against stone.

There was nothing after that, no memory of flight, nothing until the smelling salts in the apartment and the explosive pain in her head.

"I don't remember." It was true enough. The waking moments in the apartment were clear, but the time surrounding it stretched and pulled thin, unfocused and difficult to hold in memory. Almost a blessing. She wasn't sure what she might do if she could direct Tony to Alban's hideaway. Wasn't at all sure what Tony would do if faced with Alban's incredible secret.

Wasn't sure what *she* wanted to do with the knowledge she now had, or if she could do anything about it at all.

She heard Tony inhale slowly, deliberately, and then let the breath out again. "It's okay," he said, keeping his voice steady. "Concussions screw with people's memories. The important thing is that you're okay. Thank God you're okay."

"I'm all right," Margrit agreed without opening her eyes. "Just tired. Really tired."

"They haven't been letting you sleep, have they?"

"Just naps," Margrit mumbled. "That's all Alban would let me have, either. He gave me some kind of tea and I got better. But then I hit my head again."

"On what?" Tony asked. Margrit pried her eyes open and frowned at him.

"On Alban." She watched his expression crumble with dismay and let her eyes close again. "Maybe I'm still a little out of it. I just need rest."

"All right." Cam appeared from the kitchen, clapping her hands together as if knocking off eraser dust. "I'll stay up with her. You—"

Margrit was asleep before the arrangements were finished.

She popped awake ten seconds before Cameron's alarm went off. Twin spots reflected on the television screen gave her a moment's pause, the headache receded but the double vision remaining. She frowned at the screen as the alarm went off and Cam sat up with a groan. A quarter-size circle of light shone on her forehead, a second one shining past her onto the TV screen. Margrit squinted over her shoulder, then breathed in relieved recognition at the slats of the dining room birdcage, which broke the morning sun into columns of light. "I think I'm better."

"Oh good. I can get some sleep." Cameron stretched and climbed to her feet, padding across the living room and through the dining room to the kitchen. "Want some yogurt?"

Margrit's stomach rumbled and she clapped a hand over it. "Yeah. I feel like I haven't eaten in a week. Yogurt. Eggs." She stood up cautiously. The room didn't sway, and she grinned again. "Yeah, I'm better. Oh! Oh hell. Where's Tony? I thought of something while I was sleeping."

Cameron looked around the fridge door and peered through her bangs at Margrit. "He got a call around three and went to work. Did you remember where you were?"

"What? No, but I want to look at the club tapes again. I need to check something."

"Well, it's after ten. You could give him a call."

"Oh, God. My work." Margrit bolted for the phone.

"I already called them." Cam held up a carton of strawberry yogurt. "You're good for a couple of days. They said take the rest of the week off."

Margrit took the yogurt, then frowned. "Isn't it Friday?"

"Well." Cam ate a spoonful of her own yogurt. "Yeah."

"Generous of them. No, I've got to at least call Russell. I have to talk to him about the Delaney case." Margrit pulled the top off the yogurt cup and licked the foil, fumbling with the phone. "Crap." She put the yogurt down so she could dial, then wedged the phone against her ear and stole bites of yogurt between speaking. "Voice mail," she reported a minute later. "I need to go in. I'm gonna take a shower and head over there, okay?"

"Breakfast first," Cam said equitably.

"Shower, then breakfast, and I swear, you and Cole are like my parents. Did somebody call them?"

"Yes." The following silence spoke volumes about what they'd had to say. Cam shook her head, then stepped over to Margrit to give her a brief, hard hug. "Call your mom tonight, okay? She's worried. I'm really glad you're all right, Grit."

"Me, too," Margrit mumbled back. "Okay."

Cam smiled and let her go. "Go shower. I'll make you eggs and toast."

"Thank you. You're the best. Man, I feel better."

"Good. Now go." Cam shooed at her, grinning. "Go, or you'll be standing here babbling until the sun goes down."

Blood rushed through Margrit's ears, suddenly pounding like the sea. Sunset was only hours away.

Only hours until she could see Alban.

She shook herself and went to shower.

Margrit rapped on Russell's door, announcing her presence. He glanced up and gestured her in, the shirt and tie he wore making her self-conscious as she stopped inside the door and leaned on it, clad in her running tights and sweatshirt. Russell took in her closed-off stance, arms folded around her ribs, and tilted his head. "All the way in, Margrit."

She shook her head, staying where she was. "I'm fine, thanks. I just wanted to stop by and see if there was anything I needed to take home for the weekend."

Russell got up, frowning, and came around his desk to

put a hand on her shoulder. "Are you sure you're all right? Everyone's very concerned. I didn't expect to see you today."

"I've been better," Margrit admitted. "No, but I'm okay. I'm not hurt." She unwrapped an arm to touch the bruise at her hairline. "Despite appearances, maybe. And I'm not here for work," she added, flicking her fingers at her clothes. "But you said we were going to have a lot of fast work to do, and I don't think I can afford a three-day delay if that's the case. I thought I'd come in tomorrow to start doing groundwork."

"After being hit by a car and disappearing for half a night?" Russell sounded caught between admiration and dismay. "You have an overdeveloped sense of responsibility, Margrit."

"It's what makes me a good lawyer. Besides, I've got the whole day off today. That's practically a vacation."

"Obviously I'm doing something wrong," Russell said dryly. "I thought vacations involved white sand beaches and cerulean skies, not concussions and working over the weekend. Still."

Margrit grinned at the floor.

"Still," Russell added, "I appreciate your dedication. Nichole's been looking over what Daisani's corporation has pulled together. They've got most of the permits necessary to bring the building down."

"How many of them did they buy?" Margrit asked under her breath.

Her boss acknowledged the barb with a helpless shrug. "I imagine they'll have the rest of them bought and paid for soon enough. We're going to have to move very fast to make a difference."

Margrit's smile got bigger and she stretched her legs out, showing off her running tights. "Hey, moving fast is my specialty. As of tomorrow, I'm all about the case."

"And until then?"

"Rest. I promise." Margrit lifted her hands, protesting her innocence. "I'll get some rest."

She just hadn't said *when* she'd get some rest. Margrit threaded her way past desks and chairs, hesitating a few yards from Tony's workstation. He was wearing last night's clothes, a department jacket thrown over his shoulders for warmth, and his movements were slower than she was used to seeing from him, exhaustion in every motion. "Tony?"

He glanced up, then did a double take and came to his feet. "Margrit. Jesus." She pushed the chair by his desk aside and grunted quietly as he pulled her into his arms, trying not to knock her forehead against his chin. He hugged her hard for a few seconds, then set her back, hands on her shoulders as he examined her. "You're all right?"

"Yeah." Her smile felt watery. "My head still hurts, but I'm not seeing double anymore. Cam said you didn't leave until you got called in for work. Thanks." She stood on her toes to steal a kiss, garnering a catcall from one of his coworkers. "What'd you get dragged in for?"

He ignored the question momentarily, brushing his thumb over her hairline, not touching the bruise. "That looks terrible."

Margrit smiled and traced a circle around the bruise on his eye, also without touching it. "We're a matched pair now. It—*sss!* Ow. Hurts! Don't touch it!"

Tony pulled his hands back. "Sorry. I didn't mean to."

"It hurts," Margrit repeated, probing at the tender flesh despite having just scolded Tony for doing so. "But it's just a bruise now, not a concussion. I'm okay. I came by because I think I thought of something. Do you have the Blue Room security tapes?"

His expression flattened, wariness battling the hope. "Yeah."

"Can I watch them again?"

"What're you looking for?"

"I'll know if I see it. Just let me watch them."

"Margrit…" He grimaced, turning the flesh around his mouth white. "Another woman was murdered last night."

Nausea that had faded with the concussion's symptoms slammed back into Margrit's belly, making her cold all over. "When?"

"Between eleven and one. While you were missing."

"I was…" She closed her eyes, shivering. "I was unconscious most of the night, Tony. He was gone when I woke up the second time. But he didn't seem dangerous."

"If he's not dangerous and not guilty he's got no reason to not come talk to the police. Just because he didn't hurt you doesn't mean anything, Margrit. He could regard you as a prize. Guys like this do." Tony's voice was grim. "It was the same M.O., same time frame, same location."

"The *same* location?" Margrit's voice rose. Tony winced at the pitch and shook his head.

"In the park. Not the exact same place. Up on the north end. Anything you've remembered might be important. Come on." A tilt of his head invited her through the station and into a media room, where she waited several minutes for him to sign out evidence before returning with the videos. He primed them while she watched, tapping her finger against her pursed mouth.

"That one. The Goth Room." She leaned forward on the TV table, watching the screen from the center dome camera's point of view.

"What're you looking for?" he asked again. Margrit shook her head, holding up a hand to gain his silence. The video rolled from Alban's entrance. The corner camera wires were snipped, and before the next rotation of the center camera, the grating was wrenched from the wall, dangling as evidence of Alban's escape route. "That's it." Tony reached for the off button, but Margrit thwacked his fingers.

"Don't! I want to watch for another minute."

"There's nothing else to see. Getting hit on the head was bad for you." Tony sat back, waiting. The camera made its rotation, recording the carved statues and the dancers in the club. Margrit shot a finger out and pressed the pause button. The picture froze and Tony sat up. "What? What?"

Along the crowded wall of seats was a new statue, wedged into a narrow space near a carved vampire. Someone's long coat was flung over its shoulder, making it easy to miss along the busy partition. Its snarling face was turned away from the camera, but the line of its jaw was visible, both broad and delicate, carefully chiseled. Long white hair fell over its shoulder, beneath the coat. The camera's quality was too low to pick them up, but Margrit knew the hair would be carved into individual strands, a masterwork of sculpture. Upswept, pointed ears poked through the stone-work hair.

"It's just another statue," Tony said impatiently. "What's the big deal?"

"It—" Margrit broke off, staring at the gargoyle on the screen, then sighed. "It wasn't there before."

"Of course it was." He rewound the tape, scowling.

A minute earlier, the gargoyle wasn't there. Tony snapped upright, scowling with disbelief at the screen. "No way. No fucking way." He fast-forwarded the tape again, watching the gargoyle appear. "Christ, but this guy's good."

"Good?" Margrit glanced away from the screen. "What do you mean?"

"Look at him." Tony shook his head, grudging admiration in his voice. "Cool as a cucumber. Must've had that costume with him. Knew just where to hide. How the hell did he get out of there without us seeing him?"

"A costume?" Margrit asked faintly.

Tony chuckled. "It's damned clever. He must've lit out of there while the camera was facing the other direction, same way he got into place." Tony slipped an arm around her shoulders, tugging her against his chest murmuring, "Good eyes. Good thought," into her hair. "Memory's crazy, isn't it? You don't even know you've seen something wrong until it hits you. Good job. Thanks, Margrit. It gives me something to work with."

She cleared her throat, turning her head under Tony's chin to look back at the screen. "A costume," she repeated. But it hadn't been a costume. She remembered, all too clearly, the way the space seemed to shift around Alban as he became something both greater and lesser than a man.

"We'll go back to the club and see if we can find any traces of the wig, anything he might've left behind. I wonder how he got out of there." Tony loosened his arms enough to inch back and smile down at her. "Thanks, Grit. I don't know what we'll get out of it, but it's more than we had before." The smile faded into concern. "Go home and get some rest, okay? I'll call you as soon as I can."

She nodded slowly, studying the video screen a moment longer. "Okay." She turned a brief smile up at the detective. "All right. Good luck."

"Be careful, Grit." He nodded a goodbye and turned back to the screen as Margrit left, glancing at her watch.

It wouldn't be sunset for hours. Making good on her promise to rest sounded like a wise idea.

The sky went dusky blue, the sun disappearing behind the horizon, followed by a noticeable drop in temperature. Margrit tightened her arms around herself, still half-asleep. The walk from her apartment to the park hadn't quite woken her up, despite the chill. She'd slept five hours, which would wreak havoc on her sleep schedule later, but the lingering headache had faded to almost nothing. A phone call to her doctor had assured her exercise after a mild concussion wasn't a problem unless she was planning on joining a football game, in which case he advised against it. Margrit had promised not to play any contact sports, and went to the park, confident a run would take care of the rest of the head blow's aftereffects.

She stretched against a park bench, shaking herself out before starting a slow jog. A mounted policeman rode past her, nodding a concerned greeting. Margrit waved, feeling guilty. It was barely past sunset, she rationalized. People were still out, cops patrolling the pathways. The hour she'd be out running wasn't long enough or late enough to put her in danger.

And the gargoyle wouldn't dare come out tonight, anyway. He might be seen and arrested.

Margrit's gaze went to the sky a dozen times regardless, looking for shapes that couldn't be. Park lights flickered on, casting new shadows that warred briefly with the last of the light from the horizon, then triumphed. The darkness held no broad-shouldered, winged creatures. Wry disappointment churned in Margrit's stomach and she shook her head, smiling at herself. No rational person would want a gargoyle—an utterly impossible being—haunting her, anyway.

She lengthened her stride, watching the sky, and ran.

ELEVEN

HE HADN'T COME.

The knowledge left an empty place in Margrit's heart, unexplainable disappointment. She stood beneath the canopy over her building's front door, looking back toward the park. Not that it was visible: streetlights illuminated the lower reaches of the cathedral nearby, its towers gray and ghostly in the night air. The park lay on the other side, well enough hidden that she couldn't see it even if she wasn't at ground level. Alban wasn't going to glide out of the trees like some fairy-tale creature, ready to sweep her up and carry her away from all this.

A little shiver ran over her. All this. What was *all this* that she wanted escape from? She had the life she'd built, one deliberate step after another. A good school, a successful career, a relationship that looked as if it might be deciding on a sensible adult path. There was nothing to escape. There was no place for a stony-skinned…

Margrit found herself hesitating over the word *monster.* She'd met monsters, men whose humanity was far more removed than Alban's seemed to be. *Creature,* perhaps, or *being. Being* lacked the pejorative implications the other words carried. There was no place for an extraordinary being like Alban in the ordered life she'd built.

She'd decided that herself, by refusing to help him. Despite his size and strength, his obviously inhuman capabilities, he'd let her go. He hadn't stopped her with a word, as he might have. Margrit lifted her eyes to the buildings around her own, searching the shadows. Didn't he know he might have stopped her with a word? With her name? It was how it worked in the stories. She walks away and he stops her with a single desperate plea, her name. It was classic.

And it was the stuff of films and storybooks. In the real world, men didn't stop a woman with the utterance of one word, no more than a matter could be settled by an angry John Wayne kiss. By all rights, Alban's behavior had been gentlemanly, no untoward pressure or embarrassing displays. That was the end of it. Margrit shook her head and turned away from the street, jogging into her building and up to her apartment.

"What's wrong with your cell phone?" Cole called as she came in the door. "I needed cinnamon, too, but I couldn't get ahold of you."

She padded to the kitchen. "What?"

"What?" Cole blinked over his shoulder at her. "Oh, Grit. I thought you were Cam."

"Not unless she's really been working on her tan." Margrit came to peer around his arm at the stove. "What's for dinner? Where's Cam?"

"She went to get some evaporated milk. We're out. Did you make something with it?"

"I don't even know what evaporated milk is, Cole. Wouldn't it be gone by default? I did use the last of the cinnamon, though."

Cole turned an astonished look on her. Margrit shrugged. "Cinnamon toast. What, you think I was making cinnamon cheesecake or something?"

"No, but now that you mention it, that sounds like a great idea. Why don't you?"

Margrit gaped at him in horror. Cole laughed. "Someday you're going to have to explain your great fear of cooking to me, Grit."

She climbed onto the counter, ignoring his scowl as she locked her elbows and leaned. "You really want to know?"

"The curiosity is killing me."

"The truth is that I'm a pretty good cook, but if I admit that, you'll stop cooking for me."

Cole cast her such a dubious look that she laughed aloud. "I'm serious. I'm hideously lazy and I work too much, so left to my own devices I just fry eggs and make toast. If I let on I can do more, you might start expecting me to pull my weight."

"What are you going to do when Cam and I get married?"

"Go on dates naked," Margrit said promptly, then arched her eyebrows. "I don't know. Move in as your live-in maid?"

"I've seen your bedroom, Grit. It doesn't make a convincing argument for your housecleaning skills."

"I guess I'm going to have to find a boyfriend who can cook, then." Margrit grinned.

"Speaking of which, what's the story with Tony? He's Italian. Don't good Italian boys learn how to cook at about the same time they start breathing?"

Margrit felt her grin slide into uncertainty as she stared at her feet. Three years of dating, and Tony's image slipped away from her when they'd been apart for a few weeks. A handful of days, and Alban's wouldn't leave her. She felt as if her mind had been cross-wired, bringing up the wrong intensities for each man. "So I hear. What's for dinner?"

Cole gave her a searching look, then turned back to his preparations. "Chicken in cream sauce. That's why I needed the evaporated milk. You avoided the question, Grit. What's up with you two?"

She studied her toes. "I guess we're going to really try to make it work," she answered quietly. "We talked about it at dinner last night. We're going to try to work through things instead of shrugging it off when circumstances get a little rough." Which was part of why she'd told Alban no, Margrit reminded herself fiercely. She was making a commitment to something real, not a fantasy. Involving herself in Alban's world would only create a wall between herself and Tony that might never be breached.

If that wall hadn't already been built.

"Congratulations." Cole glanced at her again, and modified his tone. "Congratulations?"

"Yeah." Margrit put doubts away and looked up with a smile. "We've just got a lot of talking to do, and these murders are his case, so things are still pretty shaky. Shouldn't you be using cream for the chicken in cream sauce?"

Cole turned and leveled a wooden spoon at her. "Speak not of that which you do not understand, young Jedi."

Margrit laughed. "Yes, Master." The door swung open and Cam strode in, a paper bag of groceries tucked in the crook of her elbow. "Hey, Cam."

"Hey, Grit." Cameron slung the sack onto the counter and Cole rooted through it, coming out with the evaporated milk and a bag of carrots, which he looked at quizzically. Cam shrugged. "I like carrots. I thought you could steam some to go with the chicken. You feeling better, Grit?"

"Much, thanks."

"Carrots? With my chicken in cream sauce?"

"They'll be pretty!"

Margrit laughed. "Look, I've got some work to do. I'm going to let you two fight over whether there'll be carrots with dinner or not. Is there anything I can do first, Cole?"

He looked around the kitchen. "No," he said thoughtfully. "No, I think I can handle it by myself, or with Cameron's capable help. It'll be a strain," he added. "Getting it all done without you, I mean. Which is to say, I don't know how I'll get through it without you standing here asking me what a strainer is for."

"I know what a strainer is for." Margrit stuck her chin out. "It's for getting rid of the pulp in lemonade. Ick."

"Ick," Cam repeated. "That's one of those professional lawyer terms. I thought you had the day off, Margrit."

She looked guiltily toward the pile of papers on the dining room table. "Day off is relative."

"Speaking of relatives." Cole eyed her sternly. "Your mother called twice while you were out."

Margrit slid off the counter, wrinkling her nose. "Okay. Call me for dinner. It's the only way I'll get off the phone with her." She pulled the phone from the kitchen wall and stepped out onto the balcony, then went back inside for a coat and two blankets before calling home. Nestled beneath them in a corner of the tiny balcony, she watched the sky, waiting for her mother to pick up, and found herself smiling at her worried "Margrit?"

"Hi, Mom. I'm good. Don't worry, okay? I'm sorry I didn't call earlier," she added hastily. "I slept most of the day."

"You're sure you're all right? Daddy could look at you—"

"I'm fine, Mom," Margrit repeated. "I don't need Daddy to check my head. He'd only say I was addled, anyway." It was his eternal diagnosis of his daughter's state of being, spoken in a deep solemn baritone that did nothing to hide the spark of humor in his brown eyes. "He'd be right for once, too," she added with a laugh. "Honestly, I'm fine."

Her mother sighed, a quiet sound full of concern. "I wish you'd consider moving out here, sweetheart. It's so much safer than where you are. The condo next to us—"

"Mom! I'm not going to move in next door, okay? And I'm not in a bad part of town. Even if I was, I wasn't here when I got hit. I know you worry, but this is a great place for me, not that far from work—"

"And ridiculously expensive," her mother interjected.

Margrit grimaced, unable to argue. "That's why I've got housemates, Mom."

"And what are you going to do when they get married?"

"Maybe I'll ask Tony to move in," Margrit said, then bit her tongue. Her mother's astounded silence filled the line.

"Margrit?"

"Nothing, Mom." Margrit started to bump her head against the wall and remembered her injury in the nick of time. "We're just kind of talking about getting serious."

"That would be wonderful," her mother said after a pause. "If you're sure it's what you want." Margrit cast her gaze to the top of the building across the street, trying not to laugh with frustration.

"I thought you liked Tony, Mom."

"I do. It's just…"

"That he's Italian-American? He can't help being white, Mom, and besides, he's really more of a nice golden-brown color all over," Margrit said, straight-faced.

"Margrit!"

Laughter won, breaking free briefly before Margrit rested her head gently against the wall. "Mom, this is a relationship, not a political statement."

"Everything's a political statement, sweetheart."

"Then my politics in this case are that I like the guy, all right?" The laughter fled, leaving frustration in its place again. "It shouldn't matter."

"It shouldn't," her mother agreed, a follow-up *but it does* left unspoken.

Margrit sighed. "Mama, what do you want me to do? I like Tony. He's a good guy. If I end up with him it doesn't mean I don't appreciate my heritage, you know? And it's not like there's only one branch to our background. I mean, I hate to break it to you, but we're not exactly the products of a hundred generations of pure African breeding. There's plenty of cream in the coffee."

"Margrit, this isn't an appropriate discussion."

Margrit bit her teeth together to keep from pointing out that her mother had begun it. Then she exhaled slowly, letting frustration go. "Okay. New topic. I met Eliseo Daisani yesterday, and he said to tell you hello. You know him?"

She could all but hear her mother's inhalation. "Why did you meet with Eliseo?" The name was spoken carefully, as if it hadn't passed her lips in a long time, but she was afraid speaking it might betray something.

"I'm taking a case against him. Where do you know him from, Mom? I can't believe you know the richest guy on the East Coast and never told me."

"I knew him a long time ago, sweetheart. Back when he was only the richest man in New York. Margrit, be very careful. Eliseo is accustomed to getting what he wants. I know you're very capable, but he's a bad enemy to make."

"People keep telling me that. Mom, if you know him you could give me all kinds of insight into his psyche. It could be really helpfu—"

"Not tonight, Margrit. If you're certain you're all right, I'll let you go. Don't work too hard, sweetheart."

Margrit pulled the phone from her ear to look at it in disbelief before bringing it back, a grin staining her face. "Okay, Mom. I love you and I'll try to come see you next weekend. Tell Daddy I love him, too, and that I'm *fine,* really." They hung up, and Margrit shed blankets to return to the kitchen, still grinning.

Cole looked up from his dinner preparations in surprise. "No rescue necessary tonight?"

"I've found the magic phrase to get her off the phone. It turns out to be 'Eliseo Daisani said hi.'"

"Seriously?" Cam's attention focused like a bloodhound on the scent. "Your mom knows Eliseo Daisani? The Eliseo Daisani? Do you think they had a thing?"

"Oh, my God. I don't even want to think that." Margrit laughed and shucked her coat. "It'd take all the wind out of her sails about Tony, that's for sure. The way she talks you'd think she never thought a white guy was cute in her life."

"Wait. How'd we get from Daisani to Tony?"

"We got—" The phone in Margrit's hand shrilled, making her start. "We got a phone call, apparently," she muttered, and thumbed it on. "Hello?" Cole turned to watch her, eyebrows elevated as he waited to see who it was for.

"Margrit?"

Her stomach felt suddenly empty, and an unexpected wave of cold washed over her forearms and calves. Trusting her poker face to have not betrayed her, she waved the phone at Cole. "It's for me." She pulled her coat back on and stepped onto the balcony again, closing the door behind her and crouching against it, her gaze fixed on the ground five stories below. "Alban?"

He exhaled. "Do you know how many M. Knights there are in the phone book?"

"No." She could feel her shoulders pulling back with tension, as if a dagger had been stuffed between them.

"Thirty-four. And none of them with your address listed. This was not an easy number to find," he said with a plaintive note.

"You know my *address*?" Margrit's voice shot up.

Alban was silent a few moments. "I apologize. I've been watching you."

"Jesus motherfucking Christ." Margrit hung up the phone and stared at the receiver in her hand. Disappointment at not seeing Alban in the park didn't, it seemed, equate to being delighted at him calling or knowing her address. Consistency was the hobgoblin of small minds.

The phone rang again. Margrit let it ring, staring at it, until Cole called, "Grit? You gonna get that?" from the kitchen.

"No." She thumbed the receiver on anyway, willing her heartbeat to slow down. It stuck in her throat instead, making the emptiness in her stomach bubble.

"I'm sorry," Alban said.

"*Sorry?* You're creepy! How long have you been watching me?"

He was silent again, long enough to make Margrit shiver with discomfort and fear. "Perhaps three years," he finally said. "I've watched you running in the park. I…am concerned for your safety."

"Oh good." Margrit's voice rose to a high register. "So to protect me from stalkers you thought you'd stalk me a little? For years? Jesus Christ!"

"Not stalk." Alban spoke in a low, apologetic rumble. "Protect, Margrit. It's in my nature."

"Yeah, well, calling the freaking *cops* on you is in mine!"

There was another silence, even longer, before he murmured, "You haven't hung up."

Margrit closed her eyes. She couldn't quite bring herself to do it. Her stomach churned with nerves, but a buzz of excitement made her hands cold and her breathing short. Even if the gargoyle knew where she lived, she felt safe here. Continuing the conversation felt like walking a tightrope, the safety net far below, but still in place.

"Margrit?" he asked after a few moments. "Are you there?"

"Yeah, I'm here." *Stupid,* she whispered to herself, but she didn't hang up. "I didn't think you knew how to use a phone."

There was a perplexed silence. "Why wouldn't I?"

Margrit glanced back toward the kitchen, where Cole and

Cameron bantered, then dropped her chin to her chest, closing her eyes. "I don't know. It doesn't seem like your style."

"You know so much about my style?" Alban sounded amused.

"No! Look, what do you want? Why'd you come up to me in the park? If you didn't kill that girl—those girls, more than one is dead now—then just go talk to the cops. You're wanted for questioning, not murder." *Not yet, anyway,* she amended silently. "Who did kill them?" Anger and determination prodded her even more than the pulse-racing stimulation of fear.

"I cannot go to the police." Alban's voice dropped, quiet determination filling it. "My...condition," he said carefully, "forbids it. If I should be kept in custody past dawn—no."

"Your *condition*," Margrit mimicked. "Why are you even worried about—about what people like us think, anyway?"

"My life is already lived in shadows," he said. "To spend every night hiding my face until these murders are solved or until those who would pursue it die is too much. Margrit, listen to me. Talking to you in the park the same night that girl died was an unspeakably bad coincidence. It was the first time I had the nerve to do it. I never intended to speak to you again. I only wanted to hear your voice."

Margrit shuddered. "That's incredibly freaky."

"I suppose it is. I hadn't thought of it like that. I...wouldn't. But I'd intended to leave you alone after that." He fell silent a moment or two. "You might be glad circumstances forced me to act otherwise. That car would have killed you."

"So, what, you just follow me around town every night making sure I'm safe? Oh, Christ." She lifted her gaze, focusing across the street without seeing. "The gargoyle on the building across my street at work. The one Mark and I couldn't remember seeing before. That was you. Oh, my God."

"It was, yes. I've been seeking another opportunity to speak to you. Could we continue this conversation in person? I don't like talking about myself over the phone."

"Gee, I wonder why. My roommates are home," Margrit said. "They're not going to take kindly to you knocking on the door."

"I believe I can avoid that," Alban said into the phone and in her other ear. Margrit jerked her head up at the echo, and scrambled to her feet as Alban, wings spread, glided down to her balcony, landing with a gentle clatter on the grated floor.

He seemed larger outside the confines of a room. Broad shoulders shifted easily in the city lights, wings folding behind him into near invisibility. The alien lines of his face were still handsome, and his body language spoke of confidence. He still wore the jeans, disconcerting on a creature who looked like he was best suited to guarding cathedrals. By comparison, her memory of him seemed like a dream, half remembered and hazy. His presence was as palpable as a mountainside, so solid Margrit wanted to step forward and put her hands against his chest and push, to see if she could move him. To see if the broad expanse of bare skin would be warm and soft under her touch, or if it would be as still and cool as the stone it resembled.

To see if his breath would catch at her small hands on him, as hers wanted to, simply at the sight of him. To revel in astonished pleasure at the difference in their coloring, her mocha fingers a splash across his alabaster skin.

"Jesus Christ," Margrit said into the phone. Alban quirked heavy white eyebrows and clipped his cell phone shut, turning his palm up to show her the instrument, dwarfed by his hand. Margrit swallowed and lowered her own phone, thumbing it off. "My roommates are inside," she repeated thickly. "If I scream—"

"I'll be gone before they can get here," Alban promised. "Margrit, I don't want to hurt you. I need your help." Space inverted around him, and he shrank, changing from the gargoyle to the man. His voice changed register, still recognizably Alban, without the granite. "Is this less distressing?" he asked. Margrit thought she detected a note of wistfulness in the smooth tone. She closed her eyes.

"Look." Her own voice was too high, and she couldn't bring it down again. "Look, whoever, whatever you are, I can't help you. I can't even believe you exist."

"Even though you see me standing before you?"

Margrit's eyes opened involuntarily. "I hit my head," she said without conviction. "I'm suffering aftereffects."

"No," Alban said. "I am a gargoyle, one of the last of the Old Races. And I—"

"Need my help, yeah, I got that part."

"Please." He rumbled the word, though the man was smaller than the stone beast, had less breadth of chest to deepen speech. Margrit closed her hand around the balcony railing, inhaling to speak.

The phone rang.

She flinched violently, nearly dropping the device. It shrilled again and she set her jaw, watching Alban, daring him to move as she lifted the phone and thumbed it on.

"I see you," Tony said.

TWELVE

MARGRIT FOUGHT THE impulse to crouch again, to make herself as small a target as possible, an irrational reaction born of pure fear and guilt. Her whole body wanted to flee, as if the act of being discovered with the gargoyle somehow made her a fugitive, too. She locked her knees, fingers clenched around the phone. "Tony?"

"I can see you," he repeated. "Two of my men will be at your door in about twenty seconds."

"Tony, what the hell are you doing here? What—?"

"I was on my way over when somebody called in a tip, saying they'd seen a man meeting your pal's description in the area." His tones were a shade too clipped to be conversational. "Imagine my surprise."

"Margrit?" Alban asked softly.

She shook her head, knotting her fingers around the railing as she peered down at the street. Tony leaned on the hood of his car, phone at his ear, watching her from five stories below.

"Tony, I swear to God this isn't what it seems. Jesus, I barely even know what it does look like."

"It looks like you've invited a suspected murderer into your house, Grit. Or are you going to tell me he flew onto your balcony?"

Margrit ground her teeth, shooting Alban a black look. He offered her a wan smile in return, more humor infusing it than she thought appropriate. Then, unexpectedly, sympathetic laughter bloomed inside her. "Would you believe me if I did?"

"Oh, I'm all ears, Grit. I'd just love to hear this story. Wait, don't tell me. You were just about to call me, right?" Tony's anger took the amusement back out of the situation, and an equally profound sympathy for the cop flooded Margrit.

She cast one more desperate glance at Alban, then shrugged. "He flew onto the balcony. I'd just said I was going to call the cops." Alban's eyes widened and Margrit closed hers, shrugging, then moved her thumb over the phone's mouthpiece so she could speak to the gargoyle. "He'd be more likely to believe space aliens beamed you down than the truth, Alban. It doesn't matter. I could tell him the truth from now until Judgment Day and it'd fall on deaf ears."

"You're very confident," Alban whispered.

Margrit opened her eyes and flashed him a smile. "Sure. It's not my life I'm defending."

Tony swore, loudly enough to echo up from the street below. Margrit flinched, uncovering the receiver again. "You wouldn't believe me, Tony. Nothing I say is going to help you understand. I'm sorry." Her knuckles ached, her hand wrapped so tightly around the railing she could feel iron digging marks into her palm.

She flinched again as a solid knock rattled the front door.

Alban's gaze shot upward, examining the four stories to the top of the apartment building. "Margrit, do you trust me?"

"Cole, don't answer that!" Margrit turned away from the gargoyle to bellow through the door as her roommate yanked it open.

"Grit? What's wr—Jesus Christ!"

"Cole, this isn't—this is isn't what it looks like," Margrit blurted again. Alban took his eyes from the rooftops and sketched a brief bow in Cole's direction, elegant formality in the midst of descending chaos. A touch of delight brimmed and burst in Margrit at the gargoyle's peculiarly consummate grace. The knocking on the front door intensified. Cam ran for the door, calling, "What the hell's going on?"

"Don't open the door, Cameron!" Margrit's shout stopped her in her tracks, and she whipped back around to look at the group on the balcony. Confused astonishment filled her face and she froze for a few precious seconds. "Alban, *go.*" Margrit spun to face him, catching surprise brightening his eyes, though he didn't move. "Go!"

"Margrit," he breathed.

At the same time Cole was saying, in bewilderment, "I don't even know what it looks like. That's the guy—Jesus *Christ,* Grit, call the cops!"

He snatched the phone from her hand, and Margrit heard Tony say, "They're already here, Cole."

Cole stepped onto the balcony between Alban and Margrit. "You're not going to hurt her," he growled.

Alban moved back, retreating as far as he could on the tiny balcony. "I have no intention of hurting her."

"Margrit," Cole said, "get out of here."

"Alban, *go!*"

"This is the police!" a voice bellowed through the front door "Open up or we'll break the door!"

"Cam, answer the door! Margrit, you've got to—"

"What?" Margrit demanded. "I've got to what, Cole? You think I can explain this? You wouldn't believe me if I tried," she repeated under her breath.

"Open up!"

"Goddammit, Margrit!"

The pounding on the door receded, leaving only the sound of her heartbeat crashing in her ears. Cameron bolted for the door again. Margrit wet her lips, looking beyond Cole at the tall gargoyle. There was a peculiar mix of hope and determination in his eyes, a look she knew startlingly well. Not because of him, but because of the men and women she'd worked with. It was an expression of desperation, the open, raw acknowledgment that he was playing his last card. If she didn't take his hand now, he would be lost.

"Do you trust me, Margrit?"

The words echoed in her mind, bringing chills. She hadn't heard him ask the first time, though now, with them repeated, it was as if they'd been tattooed on her skin, waiting for her to notice their strength. The question cut through the shouting and the too-loud drumming of her heart, making a place of silent stillness inside her, the world around her fading away. Margrit licked her lips again, painfully aware on a courtroom-lawyer level that it was a tell, revealing her fear and uncertainty to anyone who wanted to read it. Alban held himself terribly still, a step beyond Cole, letting her study the fine lines of his human face and the desperate hope in his eyes.

He had let her go, more than once. Had saved her from the speeding car and had let her walk away from him despite her refusal to help. His hands, when they'd danced, had been sensual, not threatening.

And he had watched her for years, maybe keeping her safe. A jolt of curiosity shot through her. Was Alban the reason she felt inexplicably safe in the park every night? She was wary, even frightened, but beneath caution lay a certainty as solid as her heartbeat. *Idiot,* she thought, but she met Alban's eyes. "I—"

Cameron yanked the front door open, flinging herself out of the way as two armed police officers crashed through, taking in the narrow hallway and the layout of the apartment with a glance. One of them sighted the trio on the balcony and barked, "This way!"

Cole spun to face the officers, hands lifted, the phone still clasped in one. Margrit heard Tony shout, "Surrender!" both from the phone and in an echo from below.

Alban's lips curled in a snarl, his humanity suddenly lost. "Tomorrow," he growled.

The word was almost lost beneath cops shouting, "Put your hands up!" Margrit threw a panicked glance at the police officers and lifted her arms, her gaze snapping back to Alban.

"Who's on first," he said. "After sunset."

Then he leaped, an astonishing burst of motion that flung him from Margrit's balcony to the next one up, kitty-corner. Another leap brought him to the seventh floor, then to the eighth, as Margrit gaped after him. The cops burst onto her balcony, weapons cupped, but Alban disappeared over the rooftop, and Tony barked an order against shooting. One of the cops lowered his weapon, staring toward the empty sky. "What the fuck was that?"

"Margrit?" Cole's voice was filled with fear and confusion. "What…"

She looked at him helplessly, spreading her fingers. One of the cops grabbed her arm, twisting it down behind her back. Margrit let him turn her without struggling, wincing at the cold bite of metal snapping around her wrist. "You're coming down to the station to answer some questions about some murders, lady."

The ride to the station was conducted in infuriated silence, Margrit's only statement being that she wanted her lawyer. Tony, swearing, made the call from the station, while she was herded unceremoniously to an interrogation cell. She sat down in the chair provided, fully aware that its front legs were subtly shorter than its back legs. Just enough to keep her off balance, literally, her thighs forced to keep her aligned. It was one of a hundred tricks to make suspects uncomfortable and on edge. Margrit pressed her cold fingers against her eyes, the cuffs gone now that she was confined in the cell. The minutes stretched out, her thighs trembling slightly with the effort of keeping herself level, but she disregarded the temptation to get up and pace. She wanted to project tired impatience and a willingness to cooperate, not the image of a caged animal.

Tony finally stalked in and slammed the door, frustration and anger radiating with every move he made. Margrit watched the muscles in his tense shoulders bunch and release, adding to their breadth. If it weren't for the anger and agitation, he would be beautiful in motion, but instead he paced as if it were he who'd been arrested.

Not like Alban, Margrit thought wearily. The gargoyle's movements were graceful. Inhumanly graceful. She huffed a breath of semiamused dismay and slid down in the chair.

It seemed to trigger a reaction. "What the fuck is going on, Margrit? What are you doing with this guy? Is it some kind of—what *is* it?"

"Counsel would advise me not to answer that, Tony, and I'm not going to."

"Come on, Margrit, this is me and you, not—"

"No." Her voice was sharp. "Me and you happen outside of interrogation cells, Tony. Right now anything I say can and will be held against me."

"I don't really believe—"

"Good. I mean, the worst you could get me for is co-conspirator…" Worst. As if that didn't carry a twenty-to-life sentence itself. "But you obviously know that's patently ridiculous, because you haven't arrested me for anything. What do you want?"

Tony stopped pacing and leaned across the table, hands planted like concrete struts against the metal. "I want you to tell me what you know about this guy."

"I don't know anything." She couldn't tell him what little she did know, couldn't possibly. It wouldn't be Ryker's Island, if she did; it would be Bedlam. "His name is Alban Korund. He says he hasn't killed anyone. He also said he's been stalking me for three years. If anything, I'm more like a potential victim than a helper in this case. That's all I know." *Who's on first after sunset,* Alban had said. What the hell did that mean? "Are you going to arrest me?"

"Don't tempt me." Tony straightened again. Margrit

pushed back in her chair, feeling the faint strain in her thighs from keeping steady in the slanted seat.

"If you don't arrest me, Tony, there's nothing stopping me from walking out of here."

"Except the fact that you yourself just said you're a likely victim in this case."

"Oh, for God's sake." Margrit stood up. "You don't believe I'm your murderer, Tony, or even that I'm in cahoots with him. I swear to God, I never saw the guy before three days ago—"

"Sit!" Tony swung back to her, barking the order. Margrit set her teeth together and stayed on her feet. "How'd he get on your balcony?"

"The same damn way he got off it! He's got pogo sticks in his shoes, I don't know! Jesus, Tony! I didn't invite him into the fucking house! Ask Cole and Cameron!"

"Your answers don't match up, Margrit."

"Yes, they fucking do." Exhaustion swept over her, taking away the last adrenaline brought on by the near arrest, and leaving her tone flat and tired. "You watched him go bouncing over the goddamn building like some kind of blond Spider-Man, just like the rest of us did. I don't know how the hell he did it, but if I was in it with him, wouldn't I have gone with him? He keeps coming after me because he says he thinks I can help him. I swear to God I don't know why he thinks that. I haven't encouraged him. Who the hell tipped you off, anyway?"

Tony gave her a sullen look. "An anonymous caller, not that it matters, since I was three blocks away, anyway."

"An anonymous caller. What a lucky break for you. You got to show up with the troops in tow instead of all alone to find your girlfriend two-timing you with a murderer. *Jesus,* Tony, is *that* what you think?"

He stared at her. "Is it what I should think?"

Margrit stared back, then flung her hands up. "For God's sake. Yes, Tony. I've had two dozen boyfriends in the time we've been off. Why do you think we never stay together for more than a couple months? I get bored and start looking for new meat." She dropped her arms, staring at him. "Is that what you want to hear? Does that make it all better somehow?"

Disbelief and betrayal warred for dominance in Tony's eyes, and his color was high from emotion. Margrit groaned. "Don't be an idiot, Anthony. Are you sure you want to try to make it work, if that's how much you trust me?" So much for *them* not happening inside a police station. On the other hand, arguing about their personal lives was better than trying to explain the beautiful gargoyle who'd invaded Margrit's world.

"I thought we weren't talking about this here," Tony said through gritted teeth.

Margrit flung her hands up again and threw herself into the chair with furious disregard, sending it scraping across the floor. As if the action were a cue, a tap sounded on the door and a cop looked in. "Her lawyer's here."

"Yeah, whatever." Tony gestured and Russell entered, still dressed in the suit he'd worn that morning.

"Is Ms. Knight under arrest?"

Tony sighed, his expression unfriendly as he looked back and forth between Margrit and her boss. "No."

"Then I think we have nothing more to do here. Margrit?"

She pushed her hair back and climbed to her feet again, making the motions as smooth and controlled as she could. "Thanks, Russell. Sorry about this."

"It's all right. Detective, excuse us." Russell gestured to the still-open door, indicating that Margrit should precede him.

"I think she should be under police protection." Tony's voice was jagged with the same weariness Margrit felt. She looked over her shoulder at Russell, who lifted his eyebrows, then turned to Tony when she shook her head fractionally.

"Ms. Knight doesn't feel that's necessary at this juncture. Thank you for your concern, Detective. Margrit," he repeated. She nodded wearily, knocking her shoulder on the door frame as she cut too close.

"Margrit." It was Tony this time. She exhaled slowly, wrapping her hand around her abused shoulder. His expression was neutral, but his words were testy. "Who's Janx?"

Margrit's shoulders sagged. "I have absolutely no fucking idea, Tony." Russell's hand at the small of her back guided her out of the station.

"Do you want to talk about what's going on?" Russell didn't speak until they got to the corner, well beyond the station. He lifted a hand to hail a cab, watching Margrit out of the corner of his eye.

"I barely know what's going on. Thank you for coming down, Russell. I hope it's not too awkward a position for you."

"No, it was a good choice. But if this kind of thing is going to happen a lot…" He shot her a smile, causing a gurgle of laughter in Margrit's throat.

"God, I hope not. I've just got this—this guy. My own personal stalker." She sighed, then dragged in a deep breath, trying to rid herself of the impulse to sigh again. "The guy the cops think is killing people in the park."

Russell lowered his hand and turned to face her, arms folded across his chest. "The cops think."

"Yeah." Margrit stared down the street, then shook her head. "Can we walk?" She started off down the sidewalk without waiting for an answer. "The cops think. I don't think I buy it. Tony… This guy, his name's Alban, showed up on my balcony, and Tony saw him there. He was threatening to stick me with being a co-conspirator, which is just bullshit, and I don't know where it came from, except, I don't know, jealousy. Which is bullshit, too. Excuse my French."

"If this Alban needs a lawyer, Margrit…"

"It's more complicated than that." She glanced at her boss, shoving her hands into her jeans pockets. "More complicated than I can explain."

Delicately, Russell said, "Are you involved with him?"

She barked laughter. "No. No, not at all." The memory of Alban's gaze, quiet and hopeful, rose in her mind and lingered. Margrit closed her eyes, trying to push it away, and thought instead of ivory skin sliding into dark denim. "It's more like he's an illegal immigrant and can't trust anybody in authority," she said through gritted teeth, and forced her eyes open to cut off the visual memory. "It's complicated," she repeated. "Look, I should just go home. Tony's not going to pick me up again. If he really thinks I'm involved in something with Alban, he let me go so he could tail me and find out what I do. I cannot believe he'd think I'd be—" she struggled for a word and only came up with the one Russell had just used "—involved. With something like this."

"Then cover your ass, Margrit." Russell's voice became darkened, his eyebrows drawing down. "Don't see this Alban again. Stay with your friends and coworkers, with people who can provide alibis. Don't throw your career away over this. We'll be lucky if the papers don't pick it up."

Margrit groaned and tilted her head back, looking at the few visible stars that forced their way through the city lights. "I know. And what great timing, right when I'm on top of my game. I'll watch myself, Russell. And I swear—" she held up her fingers in an oath "—if anything hinky happens I'll call you immediately. I won't let this get any worse."

"Hinky." Russell allowed himself a grin. "Did you really just say hinky?"

"I've had a traumatizing night. Give me a break." She lifted her arm to hail a taxi as he nodded. A yellow cab careened toward her, and she felt her stomach tighten, trying not to leap backward.

Russell noticed the flinch and frowned.

"You'll be all right getting home?"

"Yeah." Margrit flashed a quick smile. "Got to get back on the horse sometime, right? I'll be fine. You need a ride?"

"I'll take the subway. Take care of yourself, Margrit."

"Yeah." She climbed into the cab, Russell thumping the top as he closed the door behind her. She slid down in the seat, grateful for the relative comfort of the cushions and the warmth of the vehicle. "Who's on first after sunset. Janx. Jesus Christ, everybody's lost their freaking minds."

"You got it, lady." The cab pulled away from the curb.

Margrit opened her eyes, frowning. "Got what?"

"Huo's On First." The cab driver cut a glance at her in the rearview mirror. "Ain't that whatcha said?"

"Who's on—what? What?" Margrit sat up straighter, goose bumps rising on her arms.

The cabbie eyed her. "Huo's On First. It's a bookstore down on First." It was clear he wanted to add, "You dumb broad," but he held his tongue, watching her in the mirror. "You wanna go there or not?"

"Yeah." Her weariness slipped away and she leaned forward, gazing out the window. "Yeah, I do."

tried not to elbow another stack of books to the floor. Used bookstores—at least the best of them—always seemed to be as crowded as this one was, as if walking around ran a distant second to the importance of the bound and printed pages.

"Insomniacs." The voice came from above, making Margrit glance up, startled. A very small woman with black hair and blacker eyes peeped down from the top of a shelving unit. The set of her face was purposeful, fine lines carved around her eyes and the corners of her mouth. Margrit took two steps back to better see her as she clambered over the top of the shelves and down the ladder, knocking off a stack of books as she passed them. Margrit snatched two out of the air, the other three raining to the floor with finality.

"Thank you." The woman hopped down from the ladder, rescuing the fallen books and brushing dust off their covers with definitive motions. "You're new here, aren't you? Welcome to Huo's On First. I'm Chelsea." She offered her hand. "Chelsea Huo." Her eyes crinkled with pleasure, and Margrit smiled as she shook it.

"It's nice to meet you, Ms. Huo. I'm Margrit Knight."

"Chelsea."

"Chelsea," Margrit echoed obediently. Chelsea's eyes crinkled again, her smile making wizened apple wrinkles in her round face. "Nice to meet you," she repeated. "Insomniacs?"

"Are why the store is open so late. I get all sorts of sleepless customers, looking for the comfort of books, or sometimes for one dull enough to send them into slumber. They're constants, aren't they?" Chelsea asked cheerfully.

THE D⊕⊕RBELL JANGLED pleasantly when Margrit stopped inside the door, taking in a tiny, crowded store with towering shelves overloaded with books. The space had a sense of serenity that seemed impossible to dislodge, with the scent of old books mixing with the sweetness of tea. She turned back to look over her shoulder at the reversed letters on the door, proclaiming Huo's On First: An Eclectic Bookshop, with hours that seemed extraordinarily late for a bookstore. A feeling of contentment settled over her, making her smile. The aura of bookstores, so calm and quiet, had the power to soothe her even after a day like the one that had passed. It was the same aura of sanctuary provided by churches, albeit with more reading material and considerably more comfortable chairs.

She ducked between stacks, hunching her shoulders to keep from brushing against shelves. A ladder leaned against a wall, its wide steps stacked precariously with paperbacks. Margrit picked one up, flipping through the pages as she

"Books are. That's why we like them so much. They seem immutable. They're not, of course, not from the author's first draft to the tenth printing, but they seem like it." She leaned in confidentially. "And used bookstores like this one are always crowded because the books breed, you see."

Margrit laughed, looking up at shelves tilting toward one another with the weight of volumes, and grinned. "I didn't even know I'd said that out loud. It explains a lot, though."

"Doesn't it? Now, what can I do for you, Margrit? What are you looking for tonight?"

"I'm looking for—" Margrit cut the words off with a hard swallow. "I'm supposed to meet someone here. Tomorrow."

Chelsea's feather-fine eyebrows rose. "You're a little early, then, aren't you? Who are you meeting?"

"His name is Alban." Margrit folded her arms around herself, glancing down an aisle between shelves. She felt, more than saw, stillness settle over Chelsea, and looked back at her curiously.

"Of course," the tiny woman murmured. "You're the runner in the park. The young lawyer. Peculiar that he should contact you, but—mmm. Well. How interesting."

"You know him?" Margrit's voice broke as she reached for Chelsea's arm, at the last instant stopping herself from grabbing the other woman. "You actually know him? I mean, do you really know *about* him?" She almost laughed with frustration, trying to rein in frantic words. She sounded as if she was bordering on lunacy, even to herself. It took a moment to deliberately flex her fingers and move her hand back from Chelsea's arm, pulling in a discreet breath as she did so. "Please," she said in a calmer voice, "if you really know Alban, it'd be nice to have somebody tell me I'm not losing my mind."

Chelsea Huo reached up and grabbed Margrit's chin, pulling her down for examination. Margrit bit back a growl of protest at the proprietary action and let the tiny woman study her. Chelsea turned her face this way and that, as if inspecting her for flaws, and Margrit felt a growing sense of indignation rising in her. She wasn't chattel to be declared worthy or inspected for salability.

On the other hand, the imperious little woman knew Alban. It was the first chance to validate what he'd told her, and putting Chelsea off might close the only avenue of information available to her. Margrit bit her teeth together, feeling her jaw clench under Chelsea's fingers, and strove for a polite tone. "Please. I really don't know what I'm up against here."

The bookstore owner let her go with a critical click of her tongue. "Well, then, I suppose you'd better come in back and have a cup of tea."

"…I mean, it's not possible." Margrit ducked her head over the teacup, hands wrapped around it as if she was cold. "It just isn't possible. But I saw it. I saw him turn into a gargoyle. So either I'm losing my mind or…what did you put into this tea, anyway?" She squinted at the pale liquid semisuspiciously, then looked up at Chelsea with a crooked smile. "I've been not telling people." She could hear herself imbuing the words with capitals, Not Telling People, as if every waking moment had been focused on not sharing the new facet of the world she'd learned about. "All day. Every time I think about it I want to blurt something out, but who would believe me? So here I am with you." She lifted her eyes, half apologizing with the glance. "Spilling my guts. So

I hope to God you're one of the good guys, or I've totally screwed Alban."

"I'm not one of the bad guys." The bookseller's eyebrows fluttered up again. "Though I suppose one of the bad guys would say that, too. So you explain it—why are you telling me?"

Margrit ducked her head over the tea again, all but putting her nose in it. "Because Alban chose this place to meet, I guess. Because if I don't talk to someone I'm going to go insane." She glanced up again. "And because I don't really think I'm on the good drugs and imagining all this. I really need to understand what's going on. This is *awfully* good tea."

Chelsea's pure laugh rang up to the ceiling and bounced down again. "So you've said three times. Any more and I'll think you're full of blarney."

"But it's true!" Margrit protested, then bit her tongue.

Chelsea smiled delightedly at her. "Thank you. I grow it myself. All right, Margrit Knight. Much of this is not my story to tell, but I will tell you what I can. I'll tell you enough."

"Who gets to decide what enough is?"

"I do," Chelsea said with a simple shrug. "Because it's not my story."

Margrit closed her eyes, then nodded. "All right. I'll take anything. I'm lost." She laughed without humor. "What is he?"

"A gargoyle, as he said. But you mean that question in a larger sense, I think. The answer to the question you really mean is, he is one of the Old Races."

"The old races. And I thought that was like the lost tribes

of Israel, or something." Margrit shook her head. "What the f—" She cleared her throat, censoring herself. "What are the old races?"

"They were the children of a different evolutionary path, from before this world settled on what direction it would take. There are four or five left, now. Five, if the selkies still survive. They were so terribly few, and then..." Her thin eyebrows arched and she shrugged. "There used to be more. Creatures you know the names of. Yeti and siryns."

"And then?" Margrit put the question off in favor of a second: "Sirens?" She glanced toward the door, half expecting to hear police cars wailing.

Chelsea's mouth pursed in amusement. "Siryns," she corrected. "Mermaids, you'd probably call them. Sea-born creatures, whose shape could be changed to let them leave the oceans, only at great cost. Once transformed, they could never return to their home."

"Isn't that a fairy tale?" Margrit smiled crookedly, meaning to tease, but Chelsea's eyebrows flitted up.

"Many of humanity's oldest legends stem from creatures that were once real. And a few of them still are, but not the siryns. They're dead now, or so depleted they can no longer breed. The selkies had countable numbers a few generations ago, but the siryn pods disappeared in the seventeenth century. A shame," she murmured. "Their music was enchanting."

"Literally?" Margrit asked, humor infusing the word. Then her eyebrows dipped. "How do you know?"

Chelsea's eyes disappeared into a smile and she gestured with her teacup. "I collect knowledge of the Old Races. My records are desperately incomplete—only the gargoyles truly record their histories—but there is information to be found, if that's what you desire." She swirled the tea in her cup thoughtfully. "If you have only the gargoyles to deal with, you'll be fortunate. They're the least changeable of the remaining Races, and perhaps the most trustworthy."

"Chelsea," Margrit said as steadily as she could, "the only gargoyle I know is suspected of murder. You're not inspiring a lot of confidence here. What are the others? How can I recognize them?"

The woman looked up, her lips pursed in a wrinkled smile. "Dragons and djinn, selkies and—" She broke off, distracted. "'Dragons and djinn' go together so nicely in the mouth. It's a pity none of the others are so tasty to say."

"Selkies and...?" Margrit prompted, a little desperately.

"Oh." Chelsea's thin eyebrows shot up. "And vampires, of course."

"Vampires." Margrit wrenched herself from a blank-eyed stare filled with nothing but Chelsea's pleasant expression and a phantom thrum in her own ears. She felt nailed to the chair, grounded in a way that mocked the soaring freedom she'd felt in the Blue Room. Instead of being on the verge of breaking free, the earth itself seemed to have set hooks into her muscles and skin, binding her down with malicious intent. "Vampires and dragons and... They don't exist."

Neither did gargoyles. She could all but see her own thought reflected in Chelsea's gaze. A chill made her shiver, and Margrit wrapped her hands around the teacup, lowering her eyes to study it. "I don't want to believe this."

"Not believing won't make it any less real."

"I know." Beneath the emptiness in her stomach lay a

kernel of acceptance—and an edge of excitement. Rationality told her this was all nonsense; her own experience told her otherwise. "I know," she repeated with more strength. "Am I too far in it to back out?"

Chelsea shrugged, a minute motion that Margrit saw through her eyelashes. "Probably not. Will you abandon Alban, then?"

The acceptance burst through in a quick explosion of recognition, fear dissipating into a familiar thrill of preparing for battle. "No." Margrit looked up, fighting back a tiny grin. "No, it's not in me. You're totally serious, aren't you. There's these old races and I've gotten dragged into them. Jesus." She got up to pace about the tiny back room, realized there wasn't enough space, and sat down again. "So what are you? Chelsea Huo, Proprietor of Huo's On First: Also, Old Races Propaganda Officer on Tuesdays and Thursdays?"

She laughed, pouring Margrit another cup of tea. "Close enough, overlooking the fact that it's Saturday morning now. There are people in most of the large cities, Margrit, who know about the Old Races. It's nearly impossible to live an entirely isolated life, even when you're trying to protect a secret identity. There are people who help. With food, with money, with shelter."

"With books," Margrit said.

Chelsea nodded, eyes disappearing once more into a smile. "I help, when I can. I wouldn't say propaganda officer. I prefer not to talk too much about them. Secrets don't stay secret if you talk a lot, and the Old Races rely on discretion." There was a warning in her words, one that made Margrit look up and spread a hand in promise.

"Who would believe me?" Margrit frowned at her tea, brushing the question aside. "If the old races—"

"Old Races," Chelsea said gently, with an emphasis Margrit hadn't used herself, a quiet resolve that bordered on reverence. "Give them the respect of years, Margrit. The Old Races are a group of peoples who have survived Saint George and Van Helsing, Odysseus and Aladdin. They have survived persecution and now eke out a living in a world so crowded with people they have no choice but to wear human forms and pretend they're something they're not. Afford them the title they give themselves. They deserve that much accord from humankind. They are the Old Races."

"Ala…they're all fictional, Chelsea. Legends."

The woman glanced toward her bookstore, the leaning stacks and golden lights suddenly seeming darker and more ponderous as Margrit followed her gaze. "Are they?" the proprietor asked, with a spark of challenge in her eyes.

Certainty fled, leaving a question where none had ever been. After a few seconds Margrit gave an unsure smile and inclined her head. "Okay. The Old Races." She said the words more carefully, making them a title in her mouth, then sighed. "If the Old Races rely on discretion, then isn't what's going on with Alban dangerous for all of them? If the police arrest him, or even just bring him in for question-ing, and dawn comes—why wouldn't the other Old Races just get rid of him first? Before that risk could come to fruition?"

"Get rid of him?" Chelsea echoed the phrase with interest.

Margrit made an abrupt motion with her hand. "Kill him.

Take him out of the picture. Whatever was necessary in order to ensure he wasn't going to betray the rest of them, whether he meant to or not?"

Humor creased Chelsea's mouth. "It's such a human response, isn't it? Destroy the source of trouble. Murder is a human weapon, Margrit. The Old Races don't stoop to it. To kill one of their own—any of the Old Races—is an exiling offense."

Doubt crept into Margrit's tone. "They wouldn't kill one of their own even to protect the rest?"

"It's not their way."

"That's—" Margrit broke off and laughed, a low sound. "Insane. Not that killing people is a good thing, but—you know what I mean." She looked up to find Chelsea's bemused smile turned on her. "It's not human behavior."

"That," she said, "may be the point."

Margrit dropped her chin, frowning at her tea. "What do they do to people who threaten the status quo? There must be something. There must be ways to find help or to get someone out of the limelight. Like witness protection." A pang knotted her heart, stealing her breath. Witness protection would mean losing Alban.

If she could lose something she'd never had. Margrit tightened her hands around her teacup, remembering the hope in his colorless eyes and wondering at her own regret.

"I'm sure there is." Chelsea shook her head. "But I'm not the person to ask that question of."

"Then who is?"

Chelsea swirled her tea again. "If I tell you, you'll act on the knowledge?"

"Yes." Margrit tempered the bluntness of the answer with

a faint smile. "I told him I'd help him, for one thing. For another, this is like Pandora's box. I can't put all this knowledge back inside where I don't know it anymore. I'm involved in this."

"Acting on what I tell you may involve you far more permanently than you wish, Margrit." Chelsea's almond eyes were serious. "You're at a place where you might still walk away from what you know, but the line is there and you verge on crossing it."

Margrit felt a smile creep over her face, the same tense, prepared smile that she felt when facing a courtroom or a new runner in the park. It spread tingles through her body, lifting hair on her arms and making her aware of every tiny sound around her: the ticking of a blunt old grandfather clock, the creak of floorboards, age and weather changes settling them rather than the pressure of footsteps. Horns and engines in the streets beyond the front door, as quiet as they ever got in the city. Amusement flashed through her as she remembered Cole's words: Russell had waved a red flag in front of her and she'd charged it. The same was happening here, the taking of a major risk. Jumping with both feet. Leaping headlong before looking. Margrit's smile grew into a full-out grin. God help anybody who tried to stop her. "I'm prepared for that."

Wryness sparked in Chelsea's expression, more vivid than speech. "Then you need to talk to a man named Janx."

Margrit flinched, straightening up so fast she spilled tea on her hand. She sucked the hot liquid off her skin, staring at her in astonishment. "Janx?"

Chelsea's feathery eyebrows lifted again. "You know him?"

"No, but somebody else said his name to me tonight, too. I've never heard of him. Who is he?"

"He runs an establishment in East Harlem called the House of Cards."

"*Oh.*" Margrit slumped back, staring into her teacup. "They say the guy who runs that place is a devil."

Chelsea cocked her head to one side, her expression unchanging. "The criminals in your world use Janx's people to do what even they won't, Margrit. He's a dangerous man."

"But he'd know about people you don't?" Margrit studied the petite woman across the table, gauging the tension in the lines of her mouth.

"Janx has informers," Chelsea murmured. "I only have gossip. This is terribly dangerous, Margrit."

"This is the part where I say, 'Yeah, well, so am I,' right?" She crooked a grin. "Okay, so I'm not. But maybe there's something I can bargain with. Something he might want?"

"Your life would be a pretty trinket," Chelsea said mildly. Fine hairs lifted on the back of Margrit's neck, delicate prickles that stayed awhile, then spilled down her spine and ran goose bumps over her arms.

"Are you trying to frighten me?" she asked as lightly as she could.

"Yes."

Margrit inhaled, then let it out in a little puff of breath. "It's working."

"Good." Chelsea pursed her small mouth again. "Unfortunately, I don't have another answer."

"There's always another answer." Margrit pushed her chair back and stood up again. "In this case, the other answer is 'Go directly to jail, do not pass go.' So I guess I'm going to East Harlem instead. Thank you, Chelsea. For the tea and everything."

The shopkeeper stood, smiling, and came around the table to hug Margrit, who squeaked at the unexpected embrace. "Be careful. And come back and visit, if you can. We can exchange stories about Alban. I'm sure you'll know him quite well by then."

Margrit grinned, flipping her hair over her shoulder. "That sounds fun. Thanks again. For everything. Especially for taking the risk of trusting me and telling me some of what's going on."

Chelsea made a dismissive moue and flicked her fingers. "It's not that much of a risk, my dear."

Margrit pushed her way through the beaded curtain that separated the little back room from the main area of the bookstore, then turned around to wave. Chelsea nodded, reaching for Margrit's teacup as rattling beads fell into place. She rubbed her fingers around the inside of the cup, smearing a thin film from the tea between her fingertips, and touched her fingers against her tongue. Bitterness stung her, a potent mixture disguised from Margrit by the tea's strength and unfamiliar flavor.

Doorbells jangled, announcing Margrit's departure. Chelsea smiled after her, wiping the substance away on her shirt as she climbed to her feet and went to wash the dishes. "I'm afraid it's not that much of a risk at all."

⊕NLY N⊕W—too late—did questions rise up in Margrit's mind. A dozen things she could've asked Chelsea about the man she was going to see now warred within her. Which of the Old Races he was, for example. A devil, Chelsea had said. Margrit pressed her lips together, scowling. Which of the Old Races most seemed like a devil? The djinn, maybe; Margrit had a vague idea from Scherezade—or Disney's *Aladdin*—that djinns were horned, demonic creatures. None of the other races seemed to have that connotation, though she had no idea what a selkie was.

Weaknesses—that would have been another good question to ask. Favorites or passions or hatreds. Excitement had driven her forward, when intellect should have held her back, gathering information. She was better than that, a better lawyer and a better investigator, though she'd never been faced with a situation so extraordinary. That, if anything, was her excuse, and now it was too late to do the research she should have. The cabbie—a different one—was getting impatient with her sitting frozen in the taxi, staring at the unmarked warehouse that supposedly held the House of Cards, all but on the banks of the Harlem River. Randall's Island was a shapeless blob in the distance. Margrit transferred her gaze back to the warehouse, then clenched her teeth and paid the cabbie.

"You want me to wait?"

Margrit gnawed her lower lip. "I don't know how long I'm going to be. You might as well go."

The man shrugged as she climbed out. "Your funeral."

"Thanks a lot." She slammed the door and stalked across the street, wondering how in God's name she was going to get into the place. Surely there was some kind of necessary password. Either that or she'd been watching far too many movies.

"How unusual. A woman we don't already own." The voice came from her left, from a doorway she hadn't even seen until someone spoke. The darkness of the city night swirled in a cocktail of black fog, and a man stepped forward, a glass-headed cane in his left hand and a slight limp in his right leg. "And who might she be?" His voice was full of oily amusement, entirely, Margrit was sure, at her expense. She glanced around, despite being certain there was no one else there.

"If she's me, you could address me directly." At least her antagonistic tone didn't betray her nerves.

His mouth curved sardonically. "Who are you?"

Antagonism vanished with the unpleasant discovery he was indeed addressing her. "Margrit." She swallowed, trying to bring her voice back. "Margrit Knight."

"Margrit Knight. Being here tonight suggests you keep interesting company, Ms. Knight. I am Ebul Alima Malik al-Shareef di Nazmi al-Massri." He bowed elegantly. "My friends call me Malik."

"Mr. al-Massri." Margrit managed a faint smile, not foolish enough to play on the assumption he meant to indicate she was his friend. "It's nice to meet you."

Malik chuckled, a thin sound that cut the air. "You will of course come in." He gestured to the entrance. Footsteps echoed quietly around her, men appearing out of the door and from down the street to move closer, surrounding her.

"That's not necessary," Margrit said, pleased with the steadiness of her voice. "I didn't come for trouble and I don't need to be herded like a cow."

Malik's eyebrows went up fractionally. "A young woman who speaks her mind. How nouveau."

"Welcome to the twenty-first century," Margrit muttered as she stepped past him. Malik laid a hand on her arm, very gently. She stopped as if he'd dropped a wall in front of her, the hair rising at the back of her neck. His touch was light, but it bespoke possession, as if Margrit were a thing, not a person. Anger and fear washed through her, giving her the edge she needed to turn her head and look up at him. He was no more than three inches taller than she, with dark eyes and lashes that any woman would envy. He wore a goatee, tight and neatly trimmed to accentuate a full mouth. His hair was long and pulled back in a glossy ponytail, and his shirt, colorless from a distance, was of melded grays that looked like running water.

"I assure you," he breathed, "I know which century we're

in, and I know which century I come from. There are advantages to this one, but there are traditions from my childhood that I'm eager to uphold."

Margrit's fear drained away, leaving her as buoyant and cheerful as if she'd just been on a late-night run through the park. "Mr. al-Massri," she murmured back, "Malik. I'm a lawyer, and I've seen a hundred guys like you. You think you're the shit because you're carrying around a gun and a history of being the top dog. Let me tell you two things. First, you're the doorman, which means not in charge here, so you probably ought to get over the superiority complex. Second, while there are things that scare me, little men with little dicks aren't one of them. You want to try me, someday you'll get your chance. But not tonight, so you might as well get over yourself and let go of me."

Color leeched from Malik's face until his cheekbones stood out as ugly blue shadows in the city night, rage compressing his lips and taking the blood from them. He removed his hand from Margrit's arm, gesturing sharply to two of the four men who'd joined them. They jogged forward, taking up the lead and the back, with Margrit between them as they went through the shadowed door Malik had appeared from. The sharp-featured man stayed behind, his rage palpable and directed at Margrit, as if he could shred her with his will alone.

That, she thought, was very possibly the most supremely stupid challenge she'd ever made.

She grinned, falling into step with her escort, cold spilling down her scalp with a tingle like mint shampoo. Supremely stupid, but a lot of fun.

The House was not, and had never been, a home. Margrit was led up two flights of stairs before entering the occupied area of the warehouse, concrete stairs turning to cast-iron grating that creaked beneath her feet. A windowed alcove overlooked a room that ran the length of the building, glaring with dark neon lights and the desperation of an off-Boardwalk Atlantic City casino. Men and women lingered around poker tables and pool sharks, losing cash and hope. The air felt dirty, as if it had absorbed too much grease and needed to be taken out for a wash. High windows were boarded over in places and let streetlight through in others, though it didn't permeate the gloom.

Margrit followed her escort, her knees feeling weak and loose, each step a cocky swagger. Hands in her pockets, she sauntered through the alcove door as one of Janx's men held it for her, and walked into a room where the air was too thin to breathe.

Everything stilled, as if the lack of air had preserved the place in a time capsule. Margrit's last breath lingered in her lungs, the waiting exhalation promising to be a cough, as if she'd somehow stepped from sea level to a mountaintop.

The single table in the room had more to do with elementary school cafeterias than power-lunch offices, and the seats were metal folding chairs without cushioning. The back wall, of semi-mirrored steel, gleamed with faint reflections of neon from the space it overlooked, and the floor shook with raucous music playing in a room beneath the casino.

A slender, handsome man with green eyes and a shock of dark red hair sat alone at the table. His feet, clad in expensive, dull-leather shoes, were crossed at the ankle and propped lazily on the table; he held a cigarette in one hand, smoke curling idly around his head. He smiled when they entered, eyes crinkling in the same way Chelsea's had, but what looked wizened on her appeared ageless on him. He gestured easily, indicating the seats. Margrit's feet felt heavy, and an inexplicable panic thrust her shoulders back, as if she was preparing to escape the room and the man by running. She took a sharp breath, trying to fill her lungs, and was grateful it didn't send her into spasms of coughing.

The man smiled again. "Malik told me we had a visitor."

To her shock, Margrit saw Malik standing against the reflective wall, his mouth still pressed in a thin line. She was certain he hadn't come up the stairs with her, and her bewilderment brought a nasty smile to his face.

The other man's gaze raked over Margrit—undressing her, she thought uncomfortably. "He spoke quite eloquently of you, Margrit Knight. Welcome to the House of Cards. I am, of course, Janx. Please, sit down."

"Of course." Margrit shuffled toward one of the chairs, wondering where the looseness she'd felt a moment before had gone. She felt earthbound for the second time that evening, as clumsy as she had in the interrogation cell. Janx smiled again, this time revealing teeth that looked pointed. Margrit sat down heavily, wetting her lips. "It's nice to meet you."

"Nice!" He sat back, spreading his hands expansively. "Not terrifying? Not alarming? Not frightening?" He flipped his cigarette, holding it between his index finger and thumb, and took a slow drag, watching Margrit intently.

She wet her lips again and swallowed dryly. "Those things'll kill you." Her voice was too hoarse, her confidence gone, but Janx flung his head back and laughed out loud. Smoke sailed from his nostrils in thin streams as he stubbed out the cigarette, then smiled merrily.

"No, my dear young woman, I don't believe they will, but I do give you credit for having balls." His eyebrows shot up challengingly. "Please don't tell me you object to the phrase. I would be so disappointed."

"No." Margrit cleared her throat and pulled her shoulders straighter. "No, it doesn't bother me."

"Excellent." Janx grinned and unfolded his legs, swinging them down and leaning across the table. "A lovely woman, out without her gargoyle protector, even with dawn being so many hours away. One hardly expects a gargoyle—particularly Korund—to take risks, and the sunrise is so terribly dangerous. Still." Janx clucked, mocking dismay. "How disappointing, don't you think? A wonderful treat like you, all alone. It's been a long time since a woman's been here." His eyes lit up, glittering hard and gemlike.

Margrit glanced out the windows, down at the casino. "What about them?"

Janx gestured dismissively. "Old, used, desperate goods. They've paid everything they can pay, and all that's left is a carcass that refuses to die. But you, mmm, yes. You're much tastier."

A thin trickle of outrage slid through her belly, lending her strength. "I'm not a snack."

"Oh, but you are. With spice, at that." Janx flicked a hand out and curled a lock of Margrit's hair around his finger, letting go again too quickly for her to react. "Creole, perhaps. Something old and slow-roasted. Am I right?"

Margrit straightened her spine with a deliberate breath that returned strength and the sense of freedom, both emotionally and physically. She smoothed her hair back with both hands, pushing it over her shoulders, and offered a polite smile that went nowhere near her eyes. "My people are from Virginia."

"Such a pity." Janx clucked again. "Ah well. Not even I can be right all the time. Now." He laid his hands on the table, palms down, fingers spread. His fingernails were perfect, smooth rounded arcs with delicate half-moons at the base. "Tell me, Margrit Knight, whose people are from Virginia, what *is* it that you think I can do for you?"

"Three things." Margrit kept her eyes on Janx's face, more than half afraid he would strike like a poisonous reptile if she stopped watching him. Her voice was steady, though, even challenging. He shouldn't have fondled her as if she were to be assessed as an investment. It made him too fallible in her eyes, relegated him from something worth fearing to someone whose interests could be bought and sold, just like anyone else. From that perspective, he was no more than another lawyer across another courtroom table, negotiating a deal. Her actual life wouldn't be hanging in the balance if that was true, but the silent reminder was enough to keep her calm.

Janx's eyebrows shot up again. His eyes were very green and full of mirth.

"Three. Either you have no idea what you're asking for, or you are far, far braver than your people are generally given credit for." He examined her judgmentally, and amended, "Perhaps a bit of both. Three things. You understand there is a price for anything you ask."

"And it can't be settled ahead of time." It was an educated guess, but the faintest smile quirked the corner of Janx's mouth. "I know. I understand." Margrit lifted a hand, stopping his speech, and went on. "But they'll be of equal value. The price of a question answered will be another question answered, not an action or an inaction. That much I insist on."

Janx pursed his lips. Thin blue smoke swirled around him and faded again before he leaned forward a fraction of an inch. "You insist."

Margrit nodded, lifting her chin.

"What," he asked, "makes you think you can insist, young lady?"

"Because I've met men like you," she answered with quiet determination. Behind Janx, Malik hissed in a breath. Margrit let herself smile a little, but otherwise ignored him and met Janx's vivid gaze. "Being a criminal isn't the same as being without honor. I think your honor is of more worth to you than a bad bargain."

"The bargain," Janx pointed out, "would be bad on your side, not mine."

Margrit shook her head. "Still. I want your word, Janx. Equal value, or I walk out of here now."

Astonishment darkened his eyes to jade. "And what," he asked, fascinated, "makes you think you could do *that?*"

She leaned back in her chair, suddenly confident. "Because if I do, I'll owe you something."

Janx sat back in turn, his chair scraping against the hard floor, and clapped his hands together once, a sharp sound echoed by a bright laugh of delight. The smoky air swirled again, trails lingering around his shoulders as he beamed at her. "My God. No wonder Korund chose you to break centuries of silence with. Very well, Margrit Knight. Your bargain is struck. Three things, with payments of equal value to be rendered at a later time. Name the first."

Margrit exhaled, letting her eyes close briefly. "First," she said, looking at Janx again, "first I want to know why you're talking to me at all." It was a weak question and she knew it, but she squelched the impulse to shake her head, and kept her gaze steady. Weak, but necessary. Without understanding why Janx was willing to play her game, she wasn't going to survive.

He blinked once, then smiled a snake's smile, the expression slithering across his mouth and away again. "Fascinating. Perhaps I sense a kindred spirit in you. A certain pleasure in laying cards on the table, mano a mano, yes? Perhaps it's that you put Malik in his place, something that needs doing more often than he might care to remember. Perhaps it's merely a rare occasion that I speak with a young woman of such temporary and fragile beauty and so little fear. Why *are* you not afraid of me?"

Margrit tilted her head to the side. "Is that your exchange question, Janx? I'll answer, but it'll bring me down to two payments owed."

Admiration slid through his green gaze. "Balls of solid gold. Fair enough. For you, my worthy adversary, I think the price is worthwhile. Why are you not afraid of me?"

"There's no point." She slid her hands into her jeans pockets to keep from folding her arms over her chest defensively. "You could kill me before I blinked, and there's not a damn thing I could do to stop you, so why be afraid?"

Janx's eyebrows rose until his pale forehead was wrinkled with laughter. "How fatalistic. But do go on, Ms. Knight. My answer came in three parts. I expect the same of you."

The corner of Margrit's mouth turned up in a little grin. "Fair enough." She dipped her chin, acknowledging that she'd stolen his words even as she considered the answer. "Part of it is my job. I'm a lawyer, Janx. If I crumpled every time I had to face down a powerful man, I'd be useless. So even if I was afraid of you, my training is to not let it show." The impulse to flee rather than admit to being afraid made her feet itch, and she swallowed on a dry throat. Janx's pupils dilated as if he sensed and responded to the physical changes in her body. He was a formidable enemy, but Margrit found her grin widening. A formidable enemy, but God, what fun! "Mostly, I trust your honor even if I don't trust you."

"Not many people would see a difference."

"Not many people are me." Margrit pulled a hand out of her pocket to put two fingertips against the cafeteria-style table, her wrist arched high. "Second. I want to know what you know about Alban's enemies, including whether he and I have any in common." Her heart rate accelerated, betraying her uncertainty about whether Janx would accept the two-part question as one.

His pupils dilated a second time, a tell as clear as anything a human might reveal. Margrit drew in a slow, deliberate breath, working to slow her heartbeat. Amusement curved Janx's mouth again and he nodded very slightly, confirming her suspicion: he could *hear* her heart. It jumped in her throat, making her next swallow thick.

"And if I say I know nothing?"

"Then find out."

Janx's eyebrows rose, comically surprised. "Are you delivering me an ultimatum, my dear?"

"You promised me three things, Janx. You have a network I don't have access to." Margrit lifted her own eyebrows innocently. "Of course, if you're telling me you're incapable of finding anything…"

His eyes narrowed, darkening to jade. "You tread on dangerous ground."

"I've been on dangerous ground since I walked in here. I need answers. People are dying."

"That," Janx said icily, "is not my concern."

"It is if you want to be able to hold the second and third prices over my head."

Janx bared his teeth. They *were* pointed, slightly curved in. Margrit swallowed the impulse to ask how he kept from biting his own tongue. "And your third request?"

"I never said I was going to ask for all three tonight."

Anger lit Janx's eyes, green paling to the color of new leaves. "That wasn't established at the beginning of the game."

Margrit made a moue, shaking her head. "Not my fault."

"The third price will be high," he warned her. Margrit felt the pulse thud in her throat, a sick and slow beat, but she inclined her head in a nod.

"I'll pay it. You have my word."

"Remarkable," Janx murmured, then flattened his hands on the table again. "Very well. I can give you three names right now. Perhaps more later, but for now, these three. Grace O'Malley. Biali." A youthful, impish grin brightened his face. "And the one you have in common—Eliseo Daisani."

"I haven't even served the injunction yet." The words came out numb and foolish, but Margrit couldn't stop them.

Janx laughed and leaned in confidentially. "My dear girl, I don't believe he intends for you to do so at all. I believe his words were, 'incapacitate her.'" Janx smiled beatifically at her.

"*What?*"

"The problem with handing things off to underlings," Janx said, full of mocking sympathy, "a little term like 'incapacitate' turns into a hit-and-run. Such a pity."

Margrit's gaze snapped to Malik. The word *irrational* whispered through her mind, but she seized on the hunch anyway, her voice sharpening with accusation. "*You* were driving that car!"

Malik smiled and spread his hands.

"You sent him after me." Margrit turned back to Janx, her voice low and shaking with anger and fear. Janx chuckled and leaned forward, taking one of her curls in his fingers again. The gesture was possessive, even more so than earlier, as if her coolness had no effect at all. Icy rage splashed through her, the angry need to make an impression of autonomy on Janx and all his ilk.

"I'm not your enemy, Margrit. Don't damn the messenger."

She wrapped her hand around Janx's wrist. His skin was cool, his pulse fluttering fast as a bird's beneath her fingers, and his eyes widened fractionally. Not many women—not many *people,* she thought—would have touched him.

"Don't push it, Janx." The accusation bled from her voice, leaving cold dislike in its place. She moved Janx's hand away from her hair, slowly and deliberately, then released him. His eyebrows lifted as she stood, putting her fingertips against the table. "I'll be back tomorrow night to see if you have any more information for me." Cold with fury, she turned her back on him and stalked from the room, feeling his gaze follow her out.

HE'D L⊕S+ HER, afraid—wisely afraid—to stay near her building, with the police investigating her so closely. And the cryptic message may have been too cryptic, but Alban hadn't wanted to risk the others understanding and warning the police where he or Margrit might be in another twenty-four hours.

Surely a day would be enough time for Margrit to extract herself from police proceedings. Especially when she shared a connection with the officer who had called her. Alban had seen it in the way her body language shifted, in the change of her scent, guilt mixing with surprise. Guilt was an emotion that belonged to humans, not the Old Races, but its toll was easy to recognize. Anyone seen with a suspected murderer might feel it, but it had run deeper in Margrit while she'd spoken to the detective below.

And yet she hadn't betrayed Alban's own secret. Partly out of self-preservation, almost certainly. No one would believe the truth. But she'd told him to go, more than once. Had warned him away, and created chaos with her arguments and her friends, to give him the time necessary to escape.

Was that trust? Alban made a fist and knocked it against a roofing tile, snarling without sound. He hadn't been able to read the answer to his question in her dark eyes, in the frantic moments before he took off. She'd drawn breath to speak, and for an instant he'd considered throwing caution to the wind. Snatching her up and taking to the rooftops without hearing her answer.

He breathed a laugh that wasn't, closing his eyes against the cityscape. For a fraction of a second he'd debated doing that. But it was no more in his nature than…Alban lifted his gaze again to the eastern horizon, graying with the coming sun. No more in his nature than facing the dawn.

A day. He could remain hidden for another day. After two centuries, another few hours could hardly matter. Just so long as Margrit trusted him, so long as she came to Chelsea's after sunset. She would, Alban promised himself. There'd been trust in her eyes. He was almost sure of it. She would come.

She would come, so long as no one else died.

Alban curled his hand into a fist again, then launched himself into the air, racing the sunrise home.

Irrational fought with *don't panic, don't panic, don't panic,* not just back to the street, with Malik's malicious escort, but back to the West Side and her apartment building. Margrit made it up two flights of stairs before her knees gave out and she sat heavily, fingers pushed into her hair. Tiredness made her hands shaky, and the muscles of her legs feel weak. "Get up, Grit." She spoke the words wearily, wrapping her hand around the banister and pulling herself to her feet. "You're in it now, sister." It took a long time to climb the final three flights of stairs, and she had to concentrate to slide the key into the apartment's lock.

Dim morning light spilled down the apartment hallway, shadows picking out more shadows. Margrit leaned back against the door, staring blankly through the darkness toward the balcony. She could hear Cole or Cam rolling over in bed, disturbed but not alarmed by her arrival. That was the only movement in the apartment; there were no shifting shadows on the balcony to say that Alban had returned. Or if he had, the rising sun had driven him away again, unable to withstand its light. She shuffled into the kitchen, hesitating at the balcony door, searching the coloring skyline without success. Regret lanced through her, and she watched a few minutes longer, until the sunrise became bright enough that she couldn't pretend it wasn't there. Alban was gone, wisely. It would be night before she saw him again.

There were things to do. The case to study, an injunction to prepare for Monday morning. Margrit pulled a cup of yogurt from the fridge, squinting against the brightness of the refrigerator light, and sat down at the dining room table with a yawn.

The clatter of her yogurt cup against the floor woke her up hours later, nestled against Cole's chest. "She's fine," he murmured over her head. "Fell asleep working. She must've come in late." Margrit heard Cam's near-soundless laughter as Cole bumped a door open with his hip. A moment later he put her onto her bed between piles of laundry, and drew a blanket up over her, murmuring, "Go back to sleep, Grit."

He kissed her forehead as if she were a child, making her smile drowsily before sleep claimed her again.

Headlights haunted her dreams, round white flashes of brilliance that cast impossible shadows on the street in the seconds before impact. Shadows of monsters: winged and enormous, with snarling teeth and curved claws, and Chinese dragons with whiskers like pale smoke streaming past their heads. Rasping sands whisked around her, scraping at her skin and roughening her throat, only to be washed off by a deluge of salty water that pulled her under in its deadly tow. Hard light swept by again, illuminating swirling fiends as tires squealed. Faceless devils surrounded her, tightening their circle with every pass, until fine silver threads began to appear, tying her to each of them in a sticky web. Margrit twisted and thrashed and finally jolted upright, tangled in the covers, her heart hammering.

City noises filtered through the drumming of her heart: horns beeping and engines running, airplanes roaring overhead and voices calling back and forth, an endless cacophony of white noise. It blotted out the memory of the dream long enough for Margrit to stare at the bedside clock, then stagger out to the kitchen. She pulled a carton of orange juice from the fridge and downed same without getting a glass, wiping the mouth of the carton perfunctorily with her sleeve. "Don't tell," she whispered to it, and went to stand at the balcony, staring down at the street. The juice carton felt unreasonably heavy in her fingers. She sloshed the liquid around, watching the flow of traffic with unfocused eyes.

Vampires and dragons and gargoyles. "Oh my." Margrit sat on the doorframe's edge, swirling the juice and taking absent sips.

There were critical moments in cases when she knew she'd come across the piece of information that would win the day or damn the defendant. Moments when the law hit critical mass, and nothing would stop justice—or injustice—from being done. Those rare seconds took her breath away, filling her with bright enthusiasm that seemed to stream from her fingertips and her eyes when she moved. Even if the news was bad, the realization of hitting a point of no return was stimulating. It was one of dozens of reasons Margrit practiced law; those moments stood out of time in ways that defined her.

Luka Johnson's case had been one from the beginning. From the moment the case was handed to her, Margrit had been filled with conviction—irrational conviction, she'd often teased herself with a smile—that they would win, no matter how long it took. The bone-deep belief had kept her going, kept Luka going, through the girls' birthdays and through the Christmases spent apart. It would just be a matter of time, Margrit had promised Luka repeatedly. They'd been in it together, neither of them straying from the path to clemency, until they could both walk out free women. Margrit had taken on the case knowing she'd be in it for the long haul.

A part of her had already accepted that she was in it with Alban for the long haul. Had been, maybe, since he'd appeared in the park, tall and absurdly polite, striking up a conversation in the middle of the night as if it was normal. Had been, certainly, since he'd revealed his true nature, the massive stony shoulders and delicate-looking wings a draw she wouldn't be able to resist in the long run. How could anyone? Margrit wondered. Introduced to an element of the world that she'd never known existed, how could she go back to the way things had been? She'd tried—not long, and not hard, she admitted, but for a few hours she'd insisted to herself that she couldn't champion the gargoyle, and that his world couldn't mesh with hers.

And her subconscious had told her otherwise. Even now, if she closed her eyes, his image played in her darkened vision. His was a hard picture to hold on to, sliding between the man and the monster, though both had the same gentle hope in their expressions. He'd expected rejection, and who could blame him? She was human, and he was…

"Beautiful." Margrit dropped her head against her knees, the juice carton dangling from her fingers as she remembered immeasurable grace and the strong lines of his face and body in either form. He was breathtaking.

Which didn't make him innocent. She lifted her head again, staring at the buildings across the street. It was a fair bet that simply knowing the Old Races existed was detrimental to her health. There would be no protection offered humans by Old Race covenants, which meant for her own safety the only way to go was forward, gathering as much information as she could.

Margrit gave another breathy laugh. Information, the one really priceless commodity. She finished the juice and crushed the carton. Even if she hadn't gone to see Janx— which, by the light of day, seemed ever more stupid—she'd become irrevocably involved. Anything she learned, the *more* she learned, would be her weapons against Janx and any other Old Race individuals who wanted to work with her or use her.

But Alban had come to her first, with a case. It was the

easiest place to begin. Prove his innocence or guilt in her own mind. Find a way to help him if he was innocent, or turn him over to the Old Races if he was guilty.

A chill ran over her skin, brought on by more than the thin winter sunlight and still air. A lawyer was not supposed to play the role of judge, jury and executioner, but with a man who couldn't be brought before human authorities, Margrit could see no choice.

She threw the juice carton away en route to the shower, her lips pressed together. God, she hoped he was innocent.

Garish headlines stood out from the faded microfilm, the print old-fashioned to Margrit's eye. She sat back in her chair, pressing her fingertips against her eyelids. Reverse-color images danced against them: Monster Haunts Debutante.

Six headlines over a time period of a hundred and fifty years. A scattering of others, with less dramatic fonts and less prominent displays, said things like Stalker in Central Park? and Woman Feels Protective Presence. Two of those described a tall blond man with pale eyes and broad shoulders. Alban.

Margrit dropped her hand from her eyes and shuffled papers she'd printed out, pushing the top few aside to expose the first of four whose headlines were damning.

Murder In The Park!

Four murders in almost two centuries. All of them were women featured in other articles, complaining of monsters and stalkers in the dark. Margrit sighed and sat forward again, spinning through the reel in search of marriage records.

Four deaths, stretched over decades. The thread was there only if you knew to see it. "Or if you know to make it up," Margrit muttered. The man in the nearest booth to her leaned back and gave her a sharp look. She scowled and went back to her microfilm.

The debutante married shortly after her "monster" headline appeared. A photograph in the society section showed a petite, dark-haired woman on the arm of her new husband, her curls worn unfashionably long for the twenties. Tricia Sanger, née Perry, soon to move to Philadelphia, where her husband would pursue his career in the oil industry. She was one of the two who'd survived an encounter with Alban.

Margrit growled under her breath and slapped the microfilm light off, pulling her lip in frustration. She was thinking like Alban was guilty.

But the equation added up. What were the odds someone else was stalking the same women Alban had encountered, over more than fifteen decades? Margrit shook her head almost before she thought the question, dismissing the possibility. Humans didn't live that long.

Did gargoyles? She blinked and straightened her spine, staring at the dark microfilm reader screen. She was taking Janx's word for it, and found herself grunting with irritation.

The man down the aisle cleared his throat disapprovingly. Margrit gritted her teeth and muttered, "Asshole." The disapproving man didn't hear that, and she found herself flashing a smug grin at the screen before becoming lost in thought once more. "You're taking Janx's word," she repeated aloud, trying to keep it under her breath.

Do you trust me? She could hear Alban's deep voice shivering through her bones, the quiet hope and desperation in the question.

Did she? Margrit slumped in the chair, fingers finding their way to her forehead to press there. Did she trust him, or was it just the romance and excitement of learning there were people, not-human people, living secret lives in the world she'd thought she'd known? Did she trust Janx's word over Alban's? Margrit snorted quietly. "Only if you're suicidal, girlfriend. Dammit." The guy in the booth down the row from her frowned again. She frowned back and printed out Tricia Sanger's wedding announcement, adding it to the pile of papers on her table.

If it was Alban killing these women—Margrit shook her head abruptly and turned the reader back on. It wasn't. Not now, at least. Maybe over the past two centuries, but not now. She would be his target now, not random women in the city. He—or someone—killed one at a time, over two hundred years. Not two in five days.

"Not guilty, your honor. Not this time, anyway," she breathed. "Or I hope not." She'd deal with the past later. For now… Margrit turned her wrist, glancing at her watch. Sunset wasn't for hours, and she had three names. Biali meant absolutely nothing to her; she would have to ask Alban if it had meaning for him. The others…

Eliseo Daisani was the easy one, and she was sure she wouldn't find a history of his grievances with Alban in the microfilm archives. But the third…

Margrit abandoned the microfilm archives and jogged upstairs to the public computers, logging into the *New York Times* Web site to punch "Grace O'Malley" into the search function.

The most recent headline dated from a few months earlier, bold letters declaring *Pirate Queen Reveals Treasure!* Margrit clicked through, flicking her finger against the mouse button impatiently while the page loaded.

Local legend Grace O'Malley came forward yesterday to reveal an archaeological find off an abandoned subway line beneath the streets of New York. Evidently used as a speakeasy in the 1920s, the room she discovered has been closed up since at least 1925, when a wall collapsed, cutting off a section of the subway line. The route was never reopened, and the speakeasy has remained untouched for eighty years. Bottles of gin still line the counters, and cigarettes lie in ashtrays, undisturbed for nearly a century. At least three decorative Tiffany windows are intact.

O'Malley herself has a notorious reputation as a vigilante and thief, allegations she has denied in the past. Despite repeated efforts, no prosecution has ever been brought against her, suggesting that there are those within City Hall who are on O'Malley's side. Named for the legendary Irish pirate Grace O'Malley, who ruled the high seas during the 1500's, the modern-day O'Malley's mission statement is to help young people who don't otherwise have a chance. As usual, she was not available for comment.

City officials are pleased that she brought her discovery to their attention, and say her revelation of the site was prompted by the hopes of improving her perceived status in New York, a move away from the piratical nature she's been dubbed with. The city hopes to open the site to the public within three months as part of a New York history tour.

Margrit fumbled her phone out of her bag, tapping it against her mouth for a moment before beeping out a number. No one glared this time; the computer room was considerably louder than the microfilm archives. "Cam? This is Grit. Want to go play tourist with me?"

"Places like this always make me want to chop all my hair off and start wearing fringy dresses."

"Cole would burst into tears if you cut all your hair off." Margrit grinned up at her tall blond friend as they shuffled forward in line. "So much for New Yorkers being blasé and bored, huh?"

The historic subway site teemed with visitors, many of them with city-bred accents. Cam laughed and shook her head, claiming, "They're all from out of state. New Yorkers are too cool to come poking around like this on opening day."

"So what's our excuse?"

"You're up to something." Cam lifted her eyebrows challengingly, making Margrit grin again.

"You'd look great in flapper dresses. C'mon, I want to get inside."

"See! I knew it!" Cam followed on Margrit's heels like an oversized, smug puppy. "You *are* up to something. You're changing the subject."

"What?" Margrit looked over her shoulder, eyes wide with innocence. "You *would* look great in flapper dresses. You're tall and slender. I've got the wrong shape."

Cam made an hourglass in the air, saying, "Va-va-va-voom is not the wrong shape."

"It is for a flapper." Margrit slid past a pair of men, each carrying a three-year-old on his shoulders. "It's—wow."

The speakeasy reminded her of Daisani's offices, filled with lush fabrics undamaged by time, thanks to the sealed-off air of the abandoned subway. The newspaper article had been misleading: the club was built into the tunnel itself, with rich woods curved along the walls, polished until they gleamed. Electric light fixtures were set in so neatly they seemed to be part of the wood's golden glow.

The back wall of the room was one of the Tiffany windows, abstract patterns of brilliant reds and greens edged by dune gold and gray. Somehow light filtered through it, no one point of brightness suggesting a single source of illumination.

Cam let out a low whistle. "This was rich people territory."

"No kidding. God, look at that window!" Margrit dug her cell phone out of her purse, snapping pictures and peering at the photos to judge their quality. "Can I have this in my bedroom?"

"Which part?"

Margrit waved an expansive hand. "All of it!"

Two aisles ran the length of the room, their red carpet barely worn with time. Margrit felt guilty stepping on it, and one of the attendants gave her a rueful, acknowledging smile. "It's all right. We're going to keep it open like this for about a week, and then the whole viewing area is going to be changed so the carpets aren't damaged. Take advantage while you can."

Margrit nodded, still feeling guilty as she moved forward. The pile was thick beneath her boots, shifting with her weight, as if the rug were brand-new. The sitting areas were cordoned off with velvet ropes, but a glance at the carpeting there told Margrit the furniture hadn't been moved to accommodate tourists. The club was laid out the same way it had been for eighty years or more. Couches and chairs covered in leather and velvet were set around teak and redwood tables, close enough for easy talking, without drinks being out of reach.

"A chaise longue," Margrit said with a giggle. "A real chaise longue. Cool."

"You just reverted to being about twelve," Cam said, grinning.

"Well, it *is* cool!" she protested. "Isn't it?"

Her friend held up a hand in agreement, still grinning. "It is. You're just not supposed to let it show."

"Bah. Wow!" Margrit stopped in front of the left-hand window, which curved the entire height of the subway tube wall. "That's, wow." The astounding golds and reds that were part of the back wall's glass mural were more muted in this window, the gray more pronounced, and mixed with rich sea-blues.

"This is more of that expensive lawyer-school talk, right?" Cam stepped past Margrit to nod at a chess set laid out on one of the tables. "I want *that*. I think that's real ivory."

"And obsidian," another of the attendants volunteered. "The chess pieces are extremely fanciful, clearly hand-carved. It's more than six hundred years old, and is believed to come from Saudi Arabia. The white pieces appear to be mermaids and the black are traditional Middle Eastern warriors. Please be careful, ma'am," he added as Cameron leaned as far over the velvet cordon as she could.

"I am," she promised. "They're just beautiful. And it looks like somebody was in the middle of a game."

The attendant smiled. "The pieces' locations were written down immediately, so they could be returned to the proper place once we were done looking over the room. It's amazing it hadn't been looted. Especially considering who found it."

"Everybody's got something they respect," Margrit said. "Maybe history is Grace O'Malley's thing."

"Whatever the reason, we're greatly appreciative." A deep voice broke over Margrit's and she turned to find herself shaking hands with the mayor. "Ms. Knight. It's a pleasure to see you again. Congratulations on the Johnson case."

"Mayor Leighton." Margrit smiled up at the man, her hand enveloped in his. "Thank you. It's nice to see you again, too. This is my friend Cameron Dugan."

"Mayor." Cam shook hands, looking slightly starstruck as Leighton turned back to Margrit.

"I hear you're about to take on our city's greatest benefactor, Ms. Knight."

Margrit let another smile flash across her face, hoping it buried the feeling of dismay that swept her. "I know squatters rights are an unpopular issue, Mayor, but I hope I'll have your support on this case. Mr. Daisani owns the building and certainly has the right to bring it down, but the haste he's approaching it with will put literally hundreds of people on the street again, and it's the dead of winter. I'll be serving the injunction to halt the proceedings first thing Monday morning."

"If Ms. Dugan doesn't mind, I'd like to steal you away for a few moments to discuss just that, Ms. Knight." Leighton arched carefully groomed eyebrows at the blond woman.

Cam spread her hands. "Of course. Go ahead. I'll meet you outside, Margrit."

"Sure." Margrit pressed her teeth together as she smiled, allowing Leighton to guide her away from the tour.

SIXTEEN

"ANYTHING YOU CAN think of." Margrit sat on the front edge of a couch whose springs had seen better days, her fingers folded together in an attempt to keep herself from pouncing on the girl across from her. The memory of Mayor Leighton's genial, steely-toned warnings made her entire body feel alight, unnaturally aware of the heat of her own blood. The list of city projects Mr. Daisani was funding—and of the officials he likely had in his pocket—was longer than Margrit could remember with outrage still flaming through her.

She felt as if seconds were being counted off in heartbeats, every one of them pulsing life through her extremities, until her fingers tingled and her feet itched to run. She'd known—intellectually—that strong-arm tactics were often used, that politicians belonged to other, wealthier men. New York's own Tammany Hall history came to her in bursts of anger, but she'd never quite imagined she'd run up against the same behavior herself.

Forthright fury had flung her in the other direction, more

determined than ever to not let Daisani or the city administration he seemed to control win the battle over the decrepit building. Pure temper had brought her to Cara's home, and the girl was wide-eyed and silent under the barrage of Margrit's emotional intensity.

"Anything." Margrit tried to gentle her expression to mere earnestness. It felt as effective as trying to stop a charging bull.

Cara Delaney shook her head, twisting her hair over a thin shoulder. "I'm sorry. There was no talk of developers, nobody coming around or anything, not until a few days ago. The day I met you. They put up signs...." Cara gestured in a small circle, indicating the signs Margrit had seen on her way in. Typical yellow-and-white notices of public interest, indicating that the building was condemned and would be knocked down seven days from the time of posting.

And, at a glance, it was clear the building would be better off razed. The stairs to Cara's fourth-floor apartment had creaked ominously with Margrit's weight as she'd climbed them, avoiding broken boards and gaps in the railing. The walls didn't remember the last time they'd been painted, and the pipes, half exposed in the ruined halls, looked to be held together with rust. Light fixtures held bare bulbs, and windows were cracked with age, paint on the sills peeled back to reveal old, dry wood. It had the air of a place that people went to die, alone and forgotten.

Margrit exhaled. "Tuesday. Yes, I read them. I should be able to get an injunction in place first thing Monday morning, which will give us more time." They'd covered that more than once. "But seven days is awfully fast. There's got to be something about this building specifically that's important." She didn't want to frighten the girl by mentioning the conversation she'd had with the mayor. Cara had the look of a woman who might give up in the face of such resistance.

"You can't think of—" Margrit broke off, then sat forward as guilt and fear darted across Cara's face. "What? What was that thought, Cara?"

The girl shook her head, a stiff motion full of violence. "Nothing."

"Cara." She slid off the couch and crouched in front of the younger woman, taking her hands. "Look. I'm your lawyer, all right? That means anything you tell me is absolutely confidential. If there's anything at all that might help me figure out why Daisani wants this building down, you need to let me know. You won't get in trouble for it. I haven't been able to find any information about new developments for this area, not in any of the city filings— I'll look more on Monday, when things are open again—but not online, either. I'm working blind here, Cara. If you can shed any light…" Margrit managed a crooked smile and loosened her grip on Cara's cold hands. "I need your help."

The young mother wet her lips twice, her eyes fixed on the floor, before she whispered, "S-something of mine is missing. Mine and Deirdre's. Something important."

"Something that might have to do with the building?" Margrit tightened her hands around Cara's again. "Whatever it is, you can tell me. It's all right. Trust me," she added with a wry chuckle. "After the last few days I've had, nothing can surprise me."

"The workmen came through," Cara whispered. "They put up the signs and banged on all the doors and herded us out, to make sure we all heard and understood what was going on. When I came back here, my—our—" She took a sharp breath, as if trying to ward off hyperventilating, then squared her shoulders. Her voice was stronger as she said, "They're the only thing of value that we owned. Two furs. A small one for Deirdre and a larger one that was mine. They were in a basket beneath the bed. I thought they'd be safe."

"Furs?" A dozen questions flashed through Margrit's mind, and some must have come out in her tone, because Cara lifted her head, eyes suddenly dark and defiant.

"They were ours honestly, Miss Knight. I didn't take them, if that's what you're thinking. They weren't stolen. They're ours, honest and true."

"I believe you." Margrit met her defensive gaze with a calm, steady one of her own, and squeezed the young woman's hands. "I believe you. But…" She shook her head. "I don't understand why that might have something to do with the building being knocked down."

Cara's shoulders slumped. "Maybe it doesn't." Her tone belied her words, however, although Margrit didn't understand why. Cara looked up again, misery darkening her eyes to black. "But we've got to have them back, Miss Knight. We can't live without them." The despair in her voice bordered on strange, but a penny dropped at the back of Margrit's mind, providing her with a visual so intense she actually focused beyond Cara, on the image. Daisani's private office, by the bookcases. Two furs, pinned to the wall next to the window, where sunlight wouldn't damage them.

One large and one small, both unexpectedly soft and lush to look at.

"*The Secret of Roan Inish*," she blurted. "Oh, my God. I saw that movie. I remember now. That's what a selkie is, I knew that. Seal people. Oh, my God. You're a selkie." She sat back on her heels, gaping at the girl, whose face lit with panic and confusion. "No! No, it's okay, it's—oh, my God. He's got your sealskins. You're a *selkie*."

Margrit jumped to her feet, pacing the little apartment in a few long strides, then swung back to face the stricken mother. The air seemed sharper, clearer suddenly, and it sang in her lungs like the promise of a hunt. This was the high of running, the excitement of never knowing what danger lay ahead. Lifeblood. Margrit's words spilled out, tumbling together in her haste. "It's all right. I know about you, about the Old Races. I've even met Janx—"

Cara blanched and scrambled backward in her chair.

"No! No, I'm not friends with him, I'm not—but God, no wonder, are there other selkies here? Is that what Daisani wants with this place? Does he know about you? Oh, my God." The need to run throbbed through Margrit's body, impatience driving her to pace the room again. "Jesus, God, this makes more sense now, I mean, it would if he knows, if…" She shoved both hands back through her hair, raking her ponytail out and tying it up again in swift movements. "Okay, Margrit. Think, Grit! No, screw thinking, just tell me what's going on. Cara. Cara, it's all right." She strode back to the girl, kneeling again in a deliberate effort to make herself smaller and less threatening.

"I'm sorry," Margrit said. She modulated her voice until it was calmer and more reassuring. "That was like being outed by a complete stranger, wasn't it. I'm sorry," she repeated. "But am I right, Cara? Are you one of the selkies?"

The disbelief and fear written across her face answered the question without words. "How—?"

Margrit crooked a little smile. "I made friends with a gargoyle a few days ago. Alban Korund."

Cara's eyes darkened again. "The outcast." She looked down at her lap, lips pressed together. "I didn't know you knew about us."

Margrit's eyebrows shot up. "Outcast? Alban's an outcast? Why? What'd he do?" White horror coursed over her vision, making everything too bright and dreadful to contemplate. "Did he kill someone? Isn't that the exiling offense?" Had she been wrong after all? If Alban possessed the ability to kill, the doubt she'd begun with on his behalf became far harder to hold on to. A seemingly gentle manner could hide danger. Margrit had to remember that.

Cara stared at her, wide-eyed with surprise. "There are other offenses," she whispered. "Telling humans we exist is one." It was nearly a question, but Cara shook her head, dismissing any need for answering. "Please, Miss Knight. I'm an adult and can go for a long time without wearing my other skin, but Deirdre—"

Cold worry filled Margrit's core, replacing the excitement of discovery. "How long?"

"A week," Cara whispered. "Maybe two. I don't know, Miss Knight. We don't keep our children apart from their skins. They get sick."

"I will do everything I can," Margrit promised in a harsh whisper. "I'll go beard the lion in his den, if I have to. Cara, *are* there other selkies here? Is that what Daisani wants with this place? Does he know about the Old Races? About selkies? I thought—I'd been told there weren't many of you left. Maybe even none at all."

Cara jerked her eyes up to Margrit's, surprise swallowing brown irises to black. "There are. Please, Miss Knight, you can't tell—"

Margrit chuckled and dropped her head. "I know. I know. Even if you weren't protected by the lawyer-client confidentiality—I know. God, what a mess. All right." She lifted her head, lips pursed. "Does Daisani know about the Old Races? Has he got some kind of grudge against your people? Something that would prompt him to do this?"

Cara laughed, a quiet bitter sound that seemed at odds with the dark innocence in her eyes. "They all think we're mongrels, Miss Knight. They don't need any other reason to hate us."

"They? Mongrels?"

"The others. The gargoyles, the djinn." Cara made a short hard gesture, as if cutting herself away from them. "The other Old Races. We bred with humans," she said flatly. "To survive. There was no other way."

"You can do that?" Margrit's voice soared with surprise, and she cleared her throat. Cara sent her a look as flat as her words.

"It's the third exiling offense. We're careful about the bloodlines, to keep as true as we can so we don't lose ourselves to humanity, but they wouldn't care. As far as they're concerned, if any of us are left we're contaminated." The girl sounded older than her years, as if an ugly memory learned by rote had come alive to haunt her. Then vulnerability washed back in, her gaze going dark as she dropped her eyes. "It's just how it is."

Sympathy surged up in Margrit, and she offered her hand. "So we're cousins."

Cara hesitated, then put her pale fingers in Margrit's café latte ones, eyebrows drawn down with uncertainty. "Cousins?"

Margrit smiled. "Sure. If your people bred with humans to stay alive, then we're cousins, right? Not close, maybe, but cousins." The smile turned into something near a laugh. "There are six billion of us, right? Strength in numbers, Cara. Who cares what the other Old Races think." Margrit squeezed her hand, nodding. "It'll be okay. I'll figure out a way to make it all work."

She burst out of the apartment building at a run, despite her jeans and heavy boots. She couldn't think, being too excited and full of revelation to put coherent thoughts together. She needed the clarity of motion, the purity of thought that developed as her strides lengthened. It was miles to the nearest park she knew, miles to get home or to the office, and she wasn't sure where she needed to go, anyway.

Run. That was what she needed most. To run. Lose herself in physical action and let it work its magic, clearing her mind and tiring her body until she could make sense of the unexpected, chaotic layer of the world she'd been introduced to.

The rational mind wanted to discard the proof she'd been handed: Alban's impossible transformations; the manifest panic in Cara's eyes as she'd realized Margrit knew her secret. The thinness of the air around Janx, as if she stood in the presence of something that took up all the oxygen in the room, rather than the cheerful redheaded devil she'd met. An entire world under her nose her whole life, and Margrit had never suspected.

Unmitigated disbelief seemed in order. Margrit huffed a smile. Unmitigated disbelief in the sky or gravity made about as much sense. The only thing to do now was run with it.

Run, and ignore the blisters from the boots, she thought ruefully, collapsing onto a park bench half an island later. "Ow." She bent forward, pulling a boot off to examine her foot as it steamed in the cold air. Red spots graced her heel and instep, and a blister had already burst on the side of her big toe. "That was dumb." She pulled her sock and boot back on and flung herself against the back of the bench, arms spread wide as she stared at the sky. A mounted policeman clopped by and she nodded without seeing him, gaze fixed on the darkening dome high above. It was too early for stars, too much blue left above the city, but Margrit searched for one anyway, trying to settle on a wish.

The fruitless one that came to mind was wishing she understood the world she'd found herself involved in, but even without wishes, she knew she was beginning to. The pieces didn't fit yet, but they would, and when they did a murderer would be caught and Alban's name would be cleared. And Margrit would have some bad enemies. Eliseo Daisani already wanted her incapacitated or working for him. Either would make certain she was under control.

A grin slid across her face. Daisani would have to learn to live with disappointment. Margrit laughed. In five days she'd gone from knowing nothing of the Old Races to spitting in the face of a powerful man who wanted to harm a selkie girl. The world had changed, and she was ready to take it on in all its new glory. An impulse rose up in her, delight over telling—Tony. Only there'd be no sharing this with him, and the realization filled her with regret. Margrit shifted restlessly. Out of everyone she might tell, he was the first and last who should be told. Catching killers was his job, and Margrit wasn't equipped to do it, but there was no way to explain the situation to him without betraying confidences. Not just Alban's, but those of whole races who relied on discretion for survival. As much as she'd promised Tony they'd talk, that they'd try to make it work, there were larger factors in place. She couldn't share with him what she'd learned any more than he could talk to her about the intimate details of his investigations. The inevitable wall was one they'd have to learn to scale together.

Or not at all. The thought whispered through Margrit's mind and she pushed it away with a shake of her head. There would be a way to make it work, as long as they were willing to try. As long as they could find enough common ground to keep them together through the rough patches. She scanned the streets and pathways near where she sat, suddenly have the sensation of being watched.

But no one was skulking nearby, there was no sign of her sometimes lover, and who else would be watching? Sunset was still more than an hour off, Alban imprisoned in stone until then. A bus lumbered up, belching and groaning, and Margrit limped up its steps, watching shadows gather in the park as it pulled away from the stop.

"Ow ow ow ow ow." Margrit slid down the inside of the apartment's front door, untying her boots and peeling her socks off carefully. She crawled into the bathroom to find astringent and bandages, while Cole came to frown at her.

"Cops rough you up?" He was only half kidding; Margrit looked up at his tone and cracked a smile.

"Yeah. Friction burns to the feet. It's a new torture—eeeyow, that stings!—device." She wrinkled her face and waved her feet in the air, hissing as hydrogen peroxide worked into blisters and raw spots, clearing potential infections away.

"That why you decided to take a nap at the dining room table this morning?" Cole's voice was brusque to hide worry, and Margrit gave him another fond smile.

"No, not really. They let me go around 1:00 a.m., I guess. I had some stuff to do after that. Thanks for picking me up this morning, Cole. I thought I could just tough it out, but the last thing I remember was putting the yogurt down. My stupid feet are from going running in dumb shoes."

"Something happened with the case." Cole walked back down the hallway to the kitchen, making his words a statement instead of a question.

"Yeah. I think I found out why Daisani wants that building knocked down. It looks like it might be some kind of long-term personal thing for him." Cara, she realized, had never verified that Daisani was a member of the Old Races. Margrit muttered under her breath, wondering if the girl had avoided answering because it wasn't true, because she didn't know or out of misplaced loyalty to discretion in the face of discovery. Bandages in place, Margrit abandoned her socks on the bathroom floor and hobbled down the hall after Cole, still mumbling.

"Is there any point at all in suggesting you should think about dropping this case, Grit?" Cole stood over the stove, intently watching a pan of oil heat. Margrit peered around his shoulder hopefully.

"Is that going to be fried chicken?"

"I don't know how you can tell it's fried chicken from a sauté pan full of oil. Don't avoid the question."

"Possibly the chicken in the fridge this morning tipped her off," Cam said from her perch on the dining room table. She'd cleared several inches of space, piling Margrit's paperwork even more precariously than it had been. Every time her weight shifted, so did the stacks of files. Margrit came over to extract a portable file box holding folders labeled Important, Really Important and Russell Will Kill You If You Don't Finish This. The last was stuffed to bursting, and Margrit shuffled through more papers from the table, sliding them into the appropriate folders.

"Hello, how are you, it's nice to see you, too, and what'd you tell him, anyway, Cam?"

"Just that the mayor came looking for you personally to head you off on the Delaney case. You know—" Cam looked over her shoulder with a grin "—the truth, and that sort of thing."

"We lawyers try to stay away from that," Margrit said, mock severely. "Anyway, you're the one who told me I was bullish in my acquisition and destruction of targets, Cole. If you want me off it, you should probably be telling me to go for it gung ho. Do not," she added, "suggest that path to my parents. It'd probably fool me if they tried pulling it."

"Eliseo Daisani and Mayor Leighton and who knows who else…" her friend murmured. "Are you sure you're not in over your head, Grit?"

"Not at all. Fortunately, it's my head. Besides." Margrit leaned on the table, making it wobble threateningly. Cam put a hand out for balance, looking alarmed. "Besides,"

Margrit repeated, "for one, it's just starting to get interesting. For two, there's no way to see if I'm in over my head without going for it, right? And for three, if I win this case I am going to be like unto God."

"Or dead." Cole turned to face her worriedly, while the oil gave a sudden pop. "Margrit, I'm wondering if you being hit by that car wasn't an accident."

"Dear Lord," she exclaimed. Her pulse accelerated and she grinned faintly, oddly relieved to be talking with a mere human and not to Janx. Then she almost laughed at herself. A mere human. How quickly she'd become accustomed to the impossible. "Now I've got hit men after me? Cole, are you sure you're not turning into my mother?"

"God, I hope not," Cam said fervently. Margrit laughed and Cole cracked a grin that faded quickly.

"I'm just worried, Grit. Eliseo Daisani is big guns."

"Ah, but I'm faster than a speeding bullet." Margrit looked at her abused feet. "Well, usually, anyway. And chicken's almost the only thing you actually fry. Usually you bake stuff. If I peel potatoes will you make homemade french fries?"

"I'm not getting across my sense of urgency to her, am I," Cole said to Cam.

She laughed. "Try again after dinner. You know how she is about food."

Margrit glanced out the kitchen window. "Better hurry, if you're trying again after dinner. I've got a date."

"With Tony?" Cam and Cole chorused the question, both turning to gawk at her.

Margrit blinked. "Yeah. Because things are going really smoothly with us right now, what with him picking me up for murder and all." She pressed her lips together, then muttered, "Shit. The Superbowl's tomorrow."

Cole and Cameron exchanged guilty looks. Margrit snorted. "You guys should go. I just don't know that I'll be joining you, under the circumstances."

"The circumstances might be exactly why it would be good to go," Cam suggested.

Margrit shook her head. "I don't know. Maybe if I talk to Tony. I don't know if I bend that far. Besides, I've got a lot of work to do, especially with missing Friday because of the concussion." She lifted a hand to press her palm over her goose egg, wincing mildly. "So don't worry about it."

"Mmm. Who's the date with, then?" Cole turned back to his oil, rolling flour-breaded chicken into it.

"Oh, you know." Margrit sighed. "The usual. Alban Korund with the knife in the bookstore."

CAMER⊕N, LAUGHING, DUG out the Deluxe Edition Clue game, and between fried chicken and home fries they determined it was really Miss Scarlett in the library with the rope. Margrit slipped away to her date—coffee with a coworker, she'd finally ended up claiming, since neither of her apartmentmates would believe the truth—a couple of hours after sunset.

Huo's On First was startlingly busy, with a book signing and reading going on in its crowded foyer. The bells on the door rang as Margrit pushed her way in, apologizing in murmurs to both the author and the people there to see her. Chelsea waved from atop a bookshelf—apparently it was her natural habitat—and nodded toward the back room. Margrit edged her way through the stacks and brushed the beaded curtain aside as quietly as she could.

In the prosaic yellow light of reading lamps, Alban seemed larger than she remembered him. He sat in an armchair meant for someone smaller, his shoulders overflowing it as he leaned to one side, head braced against his fingertips. He looked, Margrit thought, exhausted and terribly human. Suddenly at a loss, she hung back in the doorway, watching him. It was long moments before he lifted his head, and she saw his eyes dilate with surprise before she smiled crookedly. "Hey."

"You came." Relief filled the gargoyle's rumbling voice. "I thought—"

"I might not have, if I hadn't found a cabbie who knew what Huo's On First was. I was thinking, *What's on second?* But I'm here. I'm here, and I've got an awful lot of questions, Alban."

"Yes." He closed his eyes again, sinking into the chair. "I'm sure you do. This—might not be the best place for us to stay, though."

"Somebody might've followed me?" Margrit teased. Alban lifted his gaze again, no humor meeting her question. She swallowed, remembering her own cynical thought that Tony might've let her go just for that purpose. "Yeah. Okay."

"There's rooftop access from here. If…" Alban hesitated, lifting his pale eyes to her. "If you trust me."

Margrit let go a breath of laughter, averting her gaze. "I'm here, aren't I? Maybe it's good I didn't get a chance to say so last night. Running off with you would've convinced Tony I was guilty, and now he just thinks I'm a victim." She winced as she glanced back at Alban. "A potential victim." She winced again. "That's not coming out right."

"But you," he said. "You don't think so?"

Margrit held her breath and the gargoyle's gaze before letting both go with an explosive sigh. "I think you're not the one killing women in the park, anyway. It's not your style."

"My—" Alban broke off, staring at her with dismay. "Do I want to know why you think I have a style?"

"Probably not, but if we're going to get through this, you're going to have to hear it. For what it's worth, Alban, I'm on your side."

He came to his feet slowly, with the massive grace Margrit was beginning to recognize in him. "It's worth a great deal," he murmured. "Thank you."

"You're welcome. Who's Biali?" Soften him up, Margrit thought, and then hit him when he's not prepared.

Alban gave a start, like a cat being jolted out of sleep. "Biali is—where did you hear that name? He's an old...acquaintance."

"To be forgot?" Margrit asked, her tone deliberately light, though it did little to mask the sharpness. "I got the name from Janx."

What color there was leeched from Alban's skin, leaving him paler than new ivory. "Janx?" He barely whispered the name.

"I've been busy since you saw me." Margrit pursed her lips, judgmental and not hiding it as she studied Alban's pallor and the surprise in his eyes. *Now or never, Grit.* She pulled her gaze away once more and looked around the room, taking the calm beat of her heart as the Richter scale to judge her fear by. "So where's this rooftop access?"

"This way." Alban offered a hand and Margrit slid hers into it, momentarily struck by the size and strength of the fingers enveloping hers. Aside from dancing together, it was the first time he'd really touched her, and that...hardly counted. She hadn't known his secrets then; hadn't known what manner of man held her. She hadn't known how his appearance would change her life.

Alban led her through a back door in Chelsea's tiny apartment, both of them silent as they climbed the stairs to the roof. Once there, he drew her close, so gently she realized how easy it would be for him to injure her through carelessness. A surge of dangerous warmth swept over her. It was foolish to be drawn to things that could harm her, but she trusted the gargoyle. Trusted him far more than she trusted the New York City nights that she ran through every evening. Any man could be dangerous the way Alban was: strong, certain of himself, sensual. And the city where she jogged nightly had none of the gargoyle's gentle side, no need or desire to protect without possessing.

Possessing. The word lingered in her mind, bringing color to her cheeks as Margrit curled herself against him. More than one person had treated her as a trinket in the past day, but Alban, who might have seemed the most possessive of them all, had nothing of that in his touch. His heartbeat was steady and slow beneath her cheek, making her own seem absurdly quick in counterpoint, but there was nothing inhuman about the arm he slipped around her waist. Solid, but not like stone. Simply like a man, warm muscle and sinew holding her safe.

Margrit closed her eyes, tightening her grip around Alban's neck. "I've never done this."

He chuckled, his breath stirring her hair. "I would think not."

She looked up to find a teasing smile turned down at her, and felt laughter well in response. "I meant at all." She bumped her hip against his in admonition, smiling even as the action made him draw her against him a little more solidly. "I've never flown."

Alban ducked his head toward hers. "Then this will spoil you for your people's methods of flight." He crouched, then sprang straight upward, unhindered by Margrit's weight.

Space imploded around her as he shifted forms within the circle of her arms. Blood tingled beneath her skin, pinpricks shivering over every inch of her until she was achingly aware of Alban's body pressed against hers. There was no human softness left to him, his muscles stronger and ropier than they had been moments before. His face changed, centimeters from her own, with rougher lines replacing the more familiar human form, and warm white hair washed over her forearms like heated stone. His wings spread, so close and broad they blocked out what few stars shone through city lights, though the crescent moon made a spot of brightness through the thin membrane. Not human, but his body heat and the way he cradled her told her he was still far from stone.

A thrill bordering on panic fluttered in Margrit's stomach, pulling laughter from her. Her body stung with need, a runner's high pushed to the point of ecstasy and desire. She tilted her head back, making a vulnerable line of her throat, and pressed her breasts against Alban's chest as she arched in his arms. Her breath was torn away, tears streaming from her eyes as the wind straightened her hair and slapped strands of it against her cheeks. Buildings sailed by beneath them, their familiar forms utterly changed from this new vantage. Margrit heard herself laughing and pulled herself up against Alban again, burying her face in his shoulder. "This is fantastic."

Given the rush of wind in her own ears, she was uncertain he could hear her, but he laughed, a deep sound of delight that seemed to shiver through Margrit's body. "I thought it would suit you."

"It does." The impulse to curl her leg over his hip to hold herself closer to him sent a deep jolt of desire through her groin. The impulse was as alarming as it was appealing, and Margrit shoved it away, stretching into the wind.

As if it was less dangerous to trust the gargoyle with her life than to find him desirable. Margrit let go her hold around Alban's neck with first one arm, then the other. She curved back, making a rainbow arch, until only the gargoyle's grip around her waist kept her from falling hundreds of feet through the air. Delight and fear shivered through her like a drug, heightening her awareness of tactile sensations. The wind against her face cut like ice shards, tasting clean and cold so far above the city. Exquisite counterpoint came from Alban's warmth where her hips pressed into his. Heat surged through her again, this time mingled with laughter that she didn't dare release. Arching into the wind had not been the way to escape her growing awareness of the intimacy offered by sharing the sky with a gargoyle. Another blush and shiver seized her, sheer curiosity making her wonder if a winged creature could make love to an unwinged one in the air.

"Margrit?" Alban's voice, always low, seemed to carry more question in it than usual. Perhaps she wasn't the only one becoming ever more aware of the familiarity of their pose. Margrit caught her lower lip between her teeth, deliberately twisting to look down on the city beneath them.

The lights were bright and stationary despite the wind that flattened her hair into her eyes. Flight, to her modern mind, was a method of rapid travel, leaving things behind in an instant, but with Alban it was different. For him it was a thing of nature, not languid, but not mechanically quick. Wholly natural, yet completely unnatural to human expectations.

"Aren't you afraid you'll be seen?" Even as she asked the question a pang of regret slipped through the heat building in her core. It wasn't the response the gargoyle had looked for when he'd spoken her name. For an instant she wished she could take it back.

"I do not do this…often," Alban rumbled after a moment, the deep granite of his voice cutting easily through the wind. "When I do, I try to stay above the towers, so no one simply looks out and notices me. It helps that I can only come out at night. City lights help block curious eyes looking up, and the sheer improbability of my existence helps people doubt what they see, if they do catch a glimpse of me. And," he added prosaically, "I'm usually very, very careful."

"Usually." Margrit tilted her head back again, looking down at the streets gliding below. "This isn't being careful."

"No," Alban agreed, "but I thought you might enjoy the scenic route. Hold on," he advised. He cupped his hand behind her head, pulling her out of her arch and against his body again. Margrit slid an arm around his neck, closing her eyes and inhaling his scent in the instant before the wind ripped it away. He smelled like raw broken stone, newly shattered, an outdoors smell that Margrit was surprised she recognized, having been raised in the city. Alban banked, slowing, then rolled her in his arms, making her yelp as her eyes popped open with surprise.

The city was right side up. Alban still held her firmly around her waist, but instead of being pressed chest to chest with him, her hip fitted against his, her ribs stretched along his side and her arm wrapped securely behind his shoulder. The intimacy was gone. "You've done this before," Margrit said into the wind.

"Not recently. What would you like to see?"

"The Chrysler Building," Margrit said. Alban flashed a smile, no distress evident in his expression. Maybe the surge of want had been only on her part, she thought, but shook her head even as Alban banked again, climbing higher into the sky. Human or not, the gargoyle was male, and Margrit had felt evidence of his attraction when their hips had been pressed together. He might have been as uncertain as she of the right steps to take to address that interest.

Powerful muscle worked beneath her arm, Alban's wings gathering air and pushing them higher as they angled through the city toward the glittering steel-peaked building. Triangular windows in the massive arches glowed yellow, blazing with friendly light. As they neared the skyscraper, Alban caught an updraft and soared on it, his great wings suddenly all but still. Margrit laughed breathlessly, reaching out as if she could touch the building.

"I must've seen this in a hundred movies," she said. "I've been looking at this building from the ground my whole life. It didn't seem so big." She found herself counting the steel-framed stories that narrowed toward the spire, even though she knew there were seven of them. "Did you know they put that up in an hour and a half?"

"The spire?" Alban asked. A heavy shifting of muscle brought spread wings back into play, and he climbed the up- draft to circle lazily around the top. The red light at its tip spilled down over them, a faint discoloration.

Margrit nodded. "So it could be the tallest structure in

the world. They built the spire in the elevator shaft and mounted it without telling anybody they were going to. But the Chrysler Building only got to be the tallest for four months, before they finished the other one." She nodded toward the distant Empire State Building, an embarrassed smile playing at her mouth. "I always felt a little sorry for it because of that. I like it more than the Empire State Building."

"People seem to. Do you want to look at the eagles?"

"Yes!" Margrit laughed, then shrieked with panicked delight as Alban tucked his wings and went into a dive, plunging thirty stories. Wind ripped through her hair and she hid her face against his shoulder, trying to protect herself from the speed. His arms tightened around her reassuringly, and then with a jolt his wings flared again, catching the air and reversing the downward rush. An instant later he landed on the outstretched head of an eagle, setting her down on toe tip, then releasing her.

Paralyzing vertigo swept over her. The eagle's head lurched under her feet, and she stumbled without having moved. The ground, sixty stories below, plunged upward, threatening to dash itself against her. Margrit swayed, sickness rising up in her stomach and overwhelming her with dizziness. Raw terror turned her skin to ice, sweat leaping out in cold beads. Safety seemed only as far away as dropping to her hands and knees, but fear held her frozen, certain she would miss the broad steel head entirely and fall six hundred feet to the ground. Words failed her, a thin keening cry breaking from her throat instead, a sound of panic.

"Margrit—?" Alban barely finished the word before he understood. The eagle's head fell away from beneath her feet as he scooped her into a bride's carry and leaped into the air, catching another updraft that let him wheel away from the building. Margrit flung her arms around his neck, burying her face in his shoulder, unable to move or speak until she felt him backwing again, and they came to land with a gentle thump. Even then it wasn't until he knelt, cautiously setting her on her feet, with his hands large and supportive at her waist, that she managed to pry her eyes open.

"We're on the ground," Alban murmured. "Are you all right?"

Margrit knotted her arms around her ribs, jaw still locked in fear. It took long moments to unclench her teeth, her gaze never straying from Alban's steady, calm eyes. "I'm…" She shuddered, a violent little motion, and forced herself to drag in a deep breath as she glanced away. The inhalation brought with it the scent of winter-dead earth, hints of old rot and new life both entangled in it. It gave her something to cling to, and her eyebrows drew down as she glanced about. Graves and old headstones, ranging from the elaborate to the very simple, were scattered around her, and a cast-iron fence stood some yards away. "This is Trinity Church. What are we doing here?"

"I live here. Are you all right, Margrit?"

She shivered again, scrutinizing the yard, and nodded stiffly. "Yeah. I'm okay." With fear receding, embarrassment came to take its place, heating her cheeks as she further tightened her arms around her ribs. "I was all right while we were flying, but when there was something under my feet and I was that high up I felt like I was falling." She gave a wan smile and cast a sideways glance at the gargoyle. "Some tough New Yorker I am, huh?"

"I'm sorry," Alban said quietly. "One tends to forget a fear of heights when one cannot fall." He took his hands from her waist slowly, as if uncertain that she would remain standing without his support.

"I'm okay." Her promise had no heart to it, Alban's words striking unexpectedly deep. *One forgets the fear of heights when one cannot fall.*

Handsome. Gentle. Kind. Observant.

Alban flexed his shoulders, wings widening, then folded them down as if deliberately making himself smaller.

All the romantic terms that described Alban left one thing unsaid: *Not human.*

Margrit swallowed and took a small step backward, voice scratching as she reached for something to say. "You live here? In a church?"

"For just over two centuries."

Margrit turned her face away, eyes closed as she exhaled a breath bordering on unhappy laughter. "Two centuries." Janx had told her the truth, then, about at least one thing. *Not human,* she thought again, and made herself look at the gargoyle. "How old are you?"

"I was born in the year 1533, by your calendar. The same year Elizabeth I was born. Margrit, are you certain you're all right?"

Margrit's gaze slid off him again and she turned it to the nighttime shadows of the Gothic church. "You really live here?"

Momentary silence met the question, as clear as the gargoyle confessing that he noticed her avoidance. "I do."

"Isn't that sort of stereotypical?"

Alban laughed, a deep warm sound in the cool graveyard.

His lack of reservation caught her unexpectedly, and Margrit looked back to find his smile genuine and tinged with hope. "It is," he said, unrepentant amusement in his answer. "There are reasons for it, not the least of which is that your people expect it. No one thinks anything of a gargoyle hunched in an old churchyard. Would you like to go in?" He offered his arm.

"Alban," Margrit said quietly, "no one thinks anything of gargoyles at all." She pushed her hands into her pockets, trying not to see him slowly lower his arm, and followed him as he led her through the graves. "Doesn't the local priest notice somebody lives here?" The question came too loudly, a staccato burst to break the silence. Alban glanced over his shoulder.

"Some of them suspect. Or, I should say, some of them seem to know someone lives here, although I don't think any of them suspect the truth. It's something of a game."

Margrit looked toward the church. "What about the others? If you've been here two hundred years, haven't other priests noticed you?"

"Some. Some have been friends. Some of them have never noticed me at all. Your people, Margrit, are very good at closing their eyes to what's before them. This way." He stepped past her, over a mossy green grave marker. Margrit lurched to the side, avoiding stepping on the stone, trying to make out the words in the dim light.

"Atkinson, 1799," she murmured.

"John," Alban rumbled. "The Ludlums, to the right, there in the middle, and the Waldens, here." He nodded toward his feet, and the lichen-stained stone almost below them. "I knew John. I like to think he and his family wouldn't mind that to hide I must step over them." He pressed his palm against a square of brownstone. It slid back with a scrape, opening a small door in the wall. Alban ducked through, his form shimmering and shifting, the man fitting through the narrow opening more easily than the gargoyle could. "Be careful. The passage leads downward."

"Did someone build a secret passageway just for you?" Margrit turned to take a final look over the graveyard, peeking from behind the wall that neatly concealed Alban's hidden door.

Several yards away, at the church's front corner, a bemused Episcopalian priest with an erratic white beard and elevated eyebrows stood watching her.

Sweat sprang up on Margrit's forehead and palms, the sheer panic of youthful guilt clenching her stomach. For long seconds counted off by the wild hammering of her heart, she and the priest looked at one another through the dark night. Then he inclined his head graciously and walked around the corner of the church, leaving Margrit alone. She finally blinked, tears ducts flooding as a reminder of how long she'd stood there, eyes wide. Then she giggled nervously, whispered, "Son of a *bitch,*" and bolted through the doorway, feeling like a child who'd won a reprieve from detention.

"Margrit?"

"I'm fine." Her voice squeaked, making her blush and fight off another giggle. "Um, so someone built this place just for you, or something?" she repeated, trying to shake off her nervous laughter at being discovered.

Alban looked over his shoulder. "Yes." The door swung closed again behind Margrit, almost silently. A familiar snick sounded, a lighter making a small spot of brightness in the dark. "Richard Upjohn, who built this church, was a friend. It was constructed in 1846. I'd been living here almost forty years before it was built."

Margrit tucked her hair behind her ears, watching the steps carefully as she trotted down them. "What were you living in before they built this?"

"The old church. This is the third on this site. Richard was a romantic, very much in love with the strange and beautiful. I thought it was safe to introduce myself."

"And he built you a chamber?"

"Deep below the vaults." Alban nodded, pausing to lift a torch from a wire basket on the wall and putting the lighter to it. Flame faltered, then flared, sending a warm glow through a black-walled room.

Margrit touched a finger to the wall; it came away sooty. "Not much for housecleaning, hmm?"

Alban echoed the gesture, examining his fingertip. "Black walls seem natural to a night dweller. I never thought of cleaning them," he admitted.

Margrit smiled and stepped past him into the room. It was almost twenty feet on a side, enormous for a single room, but small for a dwelling. A cot like the one she'd slept in at the apartment above the bar was set in one corner; shelves stood against the wall at the head of the cot. Leather-bound books overflowed the shelves and lay in stacks on the floor. A small wooden table was pressed against a wall, a single chair pushed beneath it. Books and candles sat on the table. There was nowhere to cook, nor any obvious ventilation. Margrit turned, taking in the room as a whole. "Is there a back way out?"

Alban paused in the act of lighting another torch, examining her. "You don't look like someone who would think of foxholes," he said after a moment's consideration.

Margrit shook her head. "I'm not. It's just that if I were...like you...I wouldn't want to live in a room with only one exit."

Alban inclined his head, then finished lighting the second torch. "Under the bed. A trapdoor that leads into storm tunnels beneath the city. The passage to the tunnels is unpleasant, and the tunnels even more so, but both are superior to being burned alive."

"Or broken to shards," Margrit said. Alban lit another torch, nodding. The glitter of plastic wrapped around a book caught Margrit's eye, and she picked it up, looking at the tagged spine. "You have a library card?"

"I do. Getting money can be difficult, so I take my pleasures where they're most affordable."

"I'd think Chelsea would lend you books. Why don't you get a night job, if money is tight? I mean, if you have no money, what do you eat?"

"Small children."

Margrit blanched and looked up, the book sliding from nerveless fingers. It hit the floor with a hard crack, and Alban threw his head back, laughing out loud. Margrit picked the volume up, color heating her cheeks. "That wasn't funny."

"Yes, it was." Laughter echoed around the room again, deep and rich. "Oh, forgive me, but that was very funny." He cleared his throat, still grinning, the open expression bringing human vitality to chiseled features. Margrit's shoulders shook with laughter, her shock at his answer fading to rueful humor that she tried to hide with a stern look. Alban shrugged with the fluid motion of a pleased cat. In repose he was austere and beautiful, but with laughter creasing his features, he seemed approachable, almost ordinary, despite the wings that wrapped around his shoulders.

"Some of my people do take night jobs, security positions or the like. I…have chosen to remain outside of that. I prefer to have no part in your social security system, or anything that's a means of identifying myself. I used to leave the city to hunt, but these days I volunteer at homeless shelters and have soup or sandwiches when I need to eat." Alban's expression turned serious and he put forth a hand, though he didn't seem to expect her to take it. "Thank you for trusting me, Margrit."

The attempt at looking stern ceased to be a struggle. Margrit wrapped her arms around her ribs as she studied him. "You're welcome," she said after a few seconds. "But you're not out of the woods yet. Tell me about Tricia Sanger."

EIGHTEEN

A GOGGLE-EYED LOOK of astonishment, Margrit reflected a moment later, was no more attractive on a stone face than a human one. Alban's jaw actually dropped and he took a step back, blinking in astonishment. "Patricia…Perry. She married, I remember that. Margrit, what—?"

"Ann Boudreaux," Margrit said very quietly. "Rachel Ward. Julia Patterson. Christina Lee."

Alban flinched with every name, backing away until he bumped into a wall and sank down into the crouch that looked so natural to him. "Susannah Albright," he murmured. "I only learned their names from the papers. From stories of monsters haunting women in the dark." A smile with no joy in it passed over his face before he lifted his hand to hide all expression. "Susannah married, as well. You wouldn't have found her in the list of dead women."

"No." Margrit's voice cracked as she shook her head. "She and Tricia Sanger survived your watch. Alban, what happened to them?"

"I don't know." The gargoyle's voice dropped low in frustration. "Margrit, I swear to you, I don't know. I never spoke to any of them. I never harmed any of them." He ran his hand over his face again, lips compressed. "They were a little like you," he murmured eventually. "Brave, perhaps braver than they were wise. I watched over them, when I could."

"And?" Margrit could hear the hardness in her voice and made no attempt to gentle it. "One woman dying under your watch I could dismiss, maybe. Even two might be coincidence. But not four, Alban. Not four."

"More than four." Reluctant dread colored Alban's voice and he shook his head. "There've been…a dozen, over the years."

"Jesus, Alban." It took conscious effort to hold herself still. Margrit wet her lips, refusing to let herself fold her arms defensively as she stared at the gargoyle. The itch she'd felt in her feet while facing down Janx was back, making her want to bolt for the door. She could have—may very well have—misjudged. For a fleeting moment she regretted not being able to tell Tony he'd been right, before she drew in a breath so sharp it made her lungs ache. She was hardly dead yet, and—maybe—Alban wouldn't have confessed the secret if he was guilty.

Or maybe he just didn't intend to let her go. Margrit flared her nostrils in defiance, denying her own thought. "So tell me what's going on." Her voice cracked and she swallowed, fear making her want to rise on her toes, ready to run.

"I have never killed a human." Alban turned his head to the side, a swift and guilty motion. "A woman," he amended. "And never outside of a battle for my own life. Margrit." He lifted his gaze, challenging and desperate. "When did they die?"

Margrit glared at him. "June 18, 187—"

"No! The *hours,* not the days."

"Julia Patterson…" Margrit's chin came up, surprise and relief making her suddenly cold. She reached for the blanket on Alban's bed, dragging it around her shoulders and reveling in the scratchy gray wool. "Julia Patterson was found an hour past noon, still warm." Margrit sat down, the strength that had pushed her to run deserting her without warning. She barely heard her own whisper. "It couldn't have been you."

Alban lowered his head, curled knuckles scraping against the floor as he swung his arm down, a gesture of relief. "I can't prove the hours on all of them, Margrit. Some of them—most of them—were women so unimportant the police never took notice. But I swear to you, I do not know what happened to them. I stopped—" He broke off, then heaved a breath that bespoke exhaustion. "I stopped watching them so closely. For eighty years I've been…"

"Alone?" Margrit's murmured question seemed loud in her own ears, as if unnoticed voices had fallen silent just as she spoke. Alban's forehead wrinkled and she looked away before he could catch her gaze again.

"Alone," he agreed after a few seconds. "More alone than usual. That this has begun again…" He straightened, turning away from her to idly straighten books in the dark wooden shelves. "I didn't think I had enemies."

"What about Biali?"

Alban stilled, then faced her again. "What were you doing talking to Janx?"

She held up her hand, palm out. "Right now you're the one answering questions. What about Biali?"

Exasperation crossed his stony face, making heavy lines that seemed more etched than temporary, though they smoothed away again in a moment's time. "Biali and I were rivals when we were young. It means nothing now."

"Janx listed him among your enemies. Biali, Eliseo Daisani and Grace O'Malley."

Befuddlement colored Alban's features. "The pirate? She died centuries ago."

Margrit smiled briefly. "I guess it's her ghost, then. Don't you read the papers?"

"I find them depressing."

Margrit lifted her eyebrows and pulled the blanket tighter. "I guess they can be. O'Malley is this eccentric who's trying to change the world from the bottom up. I don't know what her connection to you might be. What was Biali your rival over?"

Alban curled his fingers in a loose fist, offering a smile that had more to do with loss than joy. "A woman. Isn't that always it?"

"Not in my experience. What happened?"

"We fought bitterly over her. I won, and nearly lost her for it." Alban shook his head. "Biali came too close to dying. Our people aren't so many that we can afford that kind of rivalry. Hajnal was furious." A smile, crooked and ashamed, curled Alban's mouth and slowly turned into a grin. "She didn't speak to me for six months. She didn't leave, just refused to speak. Women of every race seem to think silence is a terrible punishment."

"That's because women talk a lot. You're supposed to

miss the sound of our voices." Margrit smiled in return. "Maybe it doesn't work very well."

"Stone," Alban pointed out, "doesn't usually have a lot to say. Threatening it with silence is a peculiar form of punishment." His smile returned briefly, then faded again. "She forgave me, in time. Biali never did."

"What happened to her?" Margrit put the question out cautiously, and was unsurprised when all the humor left Alban's expression and he looked away, as if studying memories.

"She died." He was quiet a few seconds, then went on, seeming to sense that Margrit hesitated to ask more. "The French Revolution was surprisingly bad for my people. I think we had become complacent, Hajnal and I. We'd lived in Paris for decades by then." He gestured around his dark quarters, the movements graceful. "This place doesn't show it, but we're as fond of luxury as anyone, and the elite of Paris could and did adopt the most extraordinary habits. A couple who only came out at night was hardly notable."

Margrit glanced around the dark-walled chamber. "I'd think you could do that today, too."

"Perhaps," Alban admitted. "I haven't wanted to try for a long time. Not until—" He broke off, looking at her. She frowned, then ducked her head in understanding. Alban waited a beat before continuing. "When there were successes in the revolution, we weren't prepared. It had been tried so many times, so poorly. We knew the threat, but like everyone, we thought it would fail, as it had half a dozen times before. And in the end, it did, but…" He shook his head. "We were wealthy. They caught us just before dawn." He lifted his chin, looking away again. "We are not easy to kill," he said softly, "particularly in our natural form. We fought. Many men died. I have never, before or since, tested myself against a man. I hope I never will. It rained that night." He closed his eyes.

The chill of rain washed over Margrit, sending trickles of icy water down her back. An unfamiliar sound, like thunder, rolled, broken by distant retorts. "Gunfire," she heard Alban say. "We knew about guns, of course. I had even fired one. But the idea that they could be used against us…"

Light blasted, inverting darkness into sharp illuminated shapes, like a dance floor on drugs. Pain ripped through Margrit's shoulder and she fell back against the wall with a cry, trying to staunch a wound that wasn't there. Under her fingers, blood flowed, thick and gritty, not with dirt, but with its inherent being. A second burst of pain slammed through her gut and she doubled over, gasping, staring blindly at cobblestones and mud, water streaming just beyond the tip of her nose. Her hair, long and white, fell past her shoulders, dragging in the dirty water. "I had never imagined we were vulnerable to humanity's noisy tools. I was shot."

Margrit planted a hand, heavy fingers with dangerously taloned nails, against the ground. She shoved herself to her knees, ignoring the burning agony that pulsed through her shoulder. Wrapping her arm around her belly, afraid to look and see that her insides might be spilling out, she roared, a deep sound like a jungle animal, and staggered to her feet.

All around her, men screamed. Her wings flared, widening, making her larger, the unfamiliar play of muscles in her back seeming natural. Through the rain, through bedraggled hair, she saw a man lift a rifle, and panic flared. A bullet through the wing would cripple her for life, would assure that she couldn't escape the humans' insane revolution.

She roared again, wings folding back in. It made her feel vulnerable, too small, although she towered over even the tallest of these men. Her own voice called, "Hajnal! *Hajnal!*" in sonic bellows as she swung her fist in a wide circle. Two men fell, their necks snapped with the force of the blow; neither would rise again. She snatched the rifle from another's hands and bent it, mangling it before she dropped it into the mud, crying her lover's name.

"She had been there only moments before," Alban said, voice still filled with confusion. Margrit, half doubled with pain, stumbled forward, slamming her fists against bodies indiscriminately, shouting for Hajnal. She took no more than a dozen steps before collapsing to her knees again, heaving for breath around the agony in her belly and shoulder.

An iron bar smashed into the back of her head. She fell again into the wet. Under the sounds of rain and gunfire, the rod whistled through the air again. Margrit grunted and rolled, catching the bar in a fist and heaving. The eyes of the man grasping the other end widened as his feet left the ground, and Margrit heard a solid thunk as he hit a building and slid down it. Bracing herself with the bar, she got to her feet again and began to swing.

The light changed, bringing the glimmer of dawn as men died beneath her hands. She heard Hajnal scream, and twisted toward the sound, running heavily, every step jarring pain through her injured body. What she would give for a dragon's fire, or the blinding speed of a vampire!

Nearly all the mob were dead when Margrit/Alban fell to her knees at Hajnal's side, but so was Hajnal. Her wings were shattered, torn by gunshots, and an oozing hole above her heart pulsed with the black blood of her life.

"The sun is rising." Hajnal's voice was like Alban's, rough and gravelly, though not as deep. "You have to go, Alban. You must go."

"No. No, Hajnal, I won't. I can't."

Hajnal laughed, and coughed up blood. "We will both die if you stay. Remember my name. Tell my story. And *go!*" The effort to speak shook another rattling cough from her. "Go, before the sun rises."

"I can carry you," Alban/Margrit said stubbornly. Pain exploded through Margrit's shoulder as she tried to lift the fallen gargoyle. Hajnal closed a hand around her arm, weakly.

"You can't. Perhaps the stone will save me. Go. Go, Alban. Come back with sunset, if you must, but go now." Fire reflected in Hajnal's eyes and she surged upward, a last burst of strength, to catch the flaming torch a man swung down toward Alban's shoulders. Hajnal screamed, the smell of burning stone thickening the rain-filled air. *"Go!"*

Margrit launched herself into the sky. Every wingbeat seared, muscles protesting and failing. Every lurch higher into the air felt closer to the rising sun. She fled, afraid to even look back.

"I returned the next morning." Words penetrated Margrit's hearing again and she glanced up, the blanket clutched around her shoulders, the pain in her belly and shoulder receding. "I fell in an alley when the sun broke the horizon, and stayed the day, frozen in stone. The stone…heals. My injuries were greatly reduced by nightfall. I went back. I searched. She was gone. There was…" Alban opened a hand and scooped it against the floor, then lifted it, fingers spread as if something might fall through them. "Only rubble. I waited—searched—a long time, but finally hope seemed to be gone. I came here and have never returned." Ancient sorrow and loss colored his voice.

Margrit sat silent for long minutes, watching him, then closed her fingers over her aching shoulder. "What did you do to me?"

Consternation wrinkled Alban's forehead. "Memory rode you?"

She laughed weakly. "That's a perfect way to put it. Like I was there."

His eyes clouded. "I apologize. I had no idea humans were sensitive to it."

"What is it?"

"Our way of sharing history."

Margrit rubbed her shoulder again, then pressed a palm to her stomach. "God, Alban, why didn't you use it against them?"

The gargoyle looked at her without comprehension. She spread her hands, deliberately stopping herself from prodding the sore spots where memory suggested she'd been shot. "The men in the revolution. Why didn't you put nightmares into their minds to send them running?"

Alban's chin lifted. "I would never have imagined such a use for the sharing."

"Yeah." Margrit pressed her lips together. "Welcome to why we're the dominant species. You thought of dragon fire.

You thought of vampire speed. But you couldn't think of your own telepathy?"

"It seems not," Alban said slowly. "My people are very strong, Margrit. We don't have to look beyond that strength for ways to protect ourselves in battle."

"You might want to rethink that attitude." She bit her lip, then pushed her hands through her hair, tangling her fingers in curls. "I'm sorry about Hajnal. You—God, you haven't been alone since then, have you?" Alban's faint, sad smile curled a fist of sorrow around her heart on his behalf. "That's terrible."

"Watching over women like you eases the ache a little." He shrugged, then folded his arms over his chest, frowning. "What sent you to Janx? You're lucky you survived."

"Chelsea told me about him. And Tony had just mentio— shit." Margrit stared at Alban, irritation heating her cheeks. "Shit. He set me up. He set me up!"

"The police detective?" Alban's eyebrows drew down. "How?"

"Janx. He mentioned Janx. He said—shit! *Shit!* We've got to get out of here. Shit!" Margrit scrambled from the bed, throwing the blanket off her shoulders. "Come on. We've got to leave." She darted across the room, taking the stairs three at a time and talking over her shoulder as Alban followed her. "He said they'd gotten an anonymous tip. That's how he knew you were at my apartment. And then right before he let me go he asked if the name Janx meant anything to me." She slapped the inside of the soot-stained door, looking for the catch to open it. "He set me up!"

"I do not," Alban said with great precision, as if doing so would force Margrit to suddenly make sense, "understand."

She hit the door again. "Janx tipped him off, the son of a bitch. I don't know," she snapped, before Alban asked. "I don't know how he knew it was Janx, but I will sure as hell find out. He gave me the name to see if I'd go to Janx. He's fucking following me, I know it. I thought I was being silly and paranoid, but now I think he hopes I'll lead him to you, and dammit, I might have. If he *did* follow me tonight... How the hell do I open this thing?"

Alban put one hand against the door and lifted his other one, palm out, to calm her. "He couldn't have followed you beyond the bookstore, Margrit," he said gently. "Unless he's grown wings." He offered a brief smile, pointing upward. "Remember?"

Margrit sagged against the wall as anger and panic bled out of her. "Right." Lips pressed together, she took a deep breath, then straightened before making a mewl of dismay. "My shirt." Tugging it over her shoulder to see the back proved what she'd suspected: soot was smeared across it, blackening the fabric into oily streaks. "Crap. Well, crap. This is dry-clean only, too."

Alban chuckled. "Better a sooty shirt than a betrayed hideaway, I think." He edged her aside and put his hand against the door, tilting his head as he listened. "The mechanism is here." He touched a shallow groove in the stone, light gleaming dully off a black iron catch now that Margrit knew where to look. She reached for it, but he stayed her hand, shaking his head.

"You may be right, after all."

Margrit's fingers clenched into a fist. "What? You just said—"

"I know. But the voices I hear—I believe your detective

friend is just on the other side of the door." Alban hesitated. "Your people make use of tracking devices, don't they?"

Margrit snorted, then winced at the sound, fearful it might carry through the stone walls. "I don't think the NYPD has that kind of money, Alban." She found herself patting her hands over her body regardless, searching for anything that didn't belong. "Shit. Will they be able to open the door?"

Alban shrugged, liquid motion. "The mechanism is well hidden, but I don't think it'll stand up to a thorough search."

"Well, they can't catch you," Margrit said flatly. "There's no way you'd get out of there by dawn, and I'm not letting them turn you into a freak show."

"I can hide in stone," he reminded her. "They could find only you."

"Can you? Can you turn all the way to stone before sunrise?"

Alban nodded. "It's not usually necessary, but yes."

"Okay." Margrit bolted down the stairs, then stopped, turning to look up at the gargoyle. *"Shit."* Alban's wings flared, a sudden sharp motion that scraped them along the narrow walls as he avoided crashing into her.

"What?"

"The club…" Margrit grimaced. "You hid in the Goth Room. I sort of identified you in the security video. Tony saw your other shape. I'm sorry."

"He saw it?"

"Well, he thought it was a mask. He thought you were incredibly clever, actually," she added, then shook her head, pushing curls behind her ears. "But if he sees the same face here—"

"Then he'll think the mask I used was modeled after it," Alban said. "Believe me, Margrit, nothing else would make sense to him." He cocked his head, listening. "They're searching the wall now, Margrit. Maybe they won't find the opening mechanism, but—"

"The storm tunnels," Margrit blurted.

Alban's eyebrows rose. "Not a pleasant option."

"Better than abandoning you here," she said.

Alban studied her briefly, then touched her cheek. "There isn't much time." He turned her around and nudged her down the stairs; Margrit jumped the last three and skidded across the stone floor. Alban shouldered past her, seven feet tall and winged, to lift the cot with easy strength and set it aside. A leather satchel was crushed against the wall by the cedar chest, which Alban pushed aside with a scraping noise. Beneath it, one of the flagstones had grooves in its shorter sides. Margrit stared down at them.

"Gimme a lever and I can move the world, Alban, but how the hell are you going to move that?"

He glanced at her, amused, and crouched, sliding massive fingers into the grooves and gripping. Smooth muscles in his arms and back bunched, and he straightened from the legs, lifting the stone so easily it might have weighed no more than a few pounds. A two-by-three-foot hole gaped in the floor, leading into blackness.

"Good," Margrit said in a strangled voice. "Good, lifting with your legs. Good for you. Jesus Christ!"

Alban rumbled with laughter, propping the stone on his shoulder and gesturing. "The tunnel is broad enough to fit me. You should be able to make it easily, but it will be dark. The torches won't last in the water."

Margrit laughed, a soft high sound of alarm. "Is there a light at the end of it?"

"There's ankle-deep water and muck at the end of it," Alban said. "Are you sure you want to do this?"

"You could've lied," she muttered, but nodded.

"Go, then," he said. "I'll be behind you."

Margrit sat down, swung her legs into the hole and, mumbling reassurance to herself, dropped into the pit.

NINETEEN

STALE AIR MET her, the scents of rot and dankness growing stronger as the tunnel angled deeper. Margrit moved with her head down and eyes closed, trying to convince herself that she was breaking the blackness around her like a wave, letting it wash over her, and leaving it behind. She breathed carefully, each exhalation deliberate, as if her lungs carried light and she was trying to stir it into the air.

The exit couldn't be too much farther. Margrit tried not to think of Alban behind her, his head and shoulders bumping against the tunnel walls. Her slight form touched the walls only when the tunnel curved, and then she jerked away from them, distressed at the closeness.

"I'm not claustrophobic," she mumbled.

"Good," Alban said out of the silence behind her. She shrieked and collapsed against the tunnel floor, muscles gone watery. "Margrit?" he asked in alarm.

"I'm okay," she said shakily, pushing back up to her

hands and knees. "It's just so dark I didn't think I could hear anything."

The blackness seemed friendly for a moment, filled with Alban's amusement. "I understand. It isn't too much farther."

"How can you tell?"

"Would you have an escape route like this without knowing how far you had to go to get out?"

"No," Margrit admitted, and then the ground disappeared from beneath her hands and she fell forward, screaming.

She hit the bottom hands first, elbows bending to take her weight. She rolled, still screaming, through thick, murky water that splashed sluggishly into her mouth and eyes. She swallowed convulsively, then surged to her knees, gagging and choking. Seconds later, heaving breaths in through her nose, tears streaming down her face, she heard Alban land behind her, a delicate splash that rippled the water around her.

"Margrit? Are you all right?"

"No." She spat, then swallowed again, trying to hold back tears. She snuffled, wiped her hand across her nose and gagged once more, biting her tongue to keep from sobbing. "I mean, I'm not hurt." She choked on the words and stumbled to her feet, shivering. "But I'm not okay."

"It's safe now to light a torch—"

"No!" Margrit nearly collapsed back into the water, her own wailing sapping her strength. "No, don't, I'm all disgusting and horrible and…" The words turned into a snivel and her face crumpled in the darkness, tears making hot streaks down her cold cheeks. "You didn't tell me the end was that close," she said miserably.

Alban came closer, water splashing as he moved through the darkness. "That wasn't the end of my tunnel," he said. "Someone dug up there. Mine ends a few hundred feet away, in a dry place. I'm sorry, Margrit."

"Grit." She sniffled. "You could call me Grit. But not Peggy or Peg or Meg or Maggie or Madge or Marge or any of the other nicknames you can think of that go with Margrit."

"Grit." Alban paused. "Isn't that a food?" he asked eventually, then repeated, "Grit," and seemed to be shaking his head. "No," he said with a note of finality. "I don't think I can."

Despite herself, Margrit giggled, a painful little burst of sound that came out through her nose. "Yeah, Grit, like the food, but singular. Why can't you?" She shuffled through the cold water toward his voice.

"It's painfully lacking in formality. Could you call me Al?"

She giggled again, then sneezed and coughed, bending over to hack water from her lungs. "You're not an Al."

Alban's fingers found her spine, a light comforting touch. "You see?" he asked. "Grit and Al are a different pair entirely. You and I are Margrit and Alban."

"Margrit and Alban sounds nicer, doesn't it?" She straightened, coughing once more. Alban's hand remained at the small of her back a moment longer, warm and gentle enough to drive away her cold misery. The shiver that ran over her had nothing to do with the chilly glop sliding down her skin, but instead brought heightened awareness of the closeness of bodies and the possibilities illuminated by shadow. There was nothing inhuman about his touch when darkness cloaked the hand on her spine, nothing alarming or strange that should be backed away from.

The line he traced up her body lit trembling sparks inside her, until he found her shoulder and followed her arm back down, to wrap his fingers around hers. His hand, stony and solid, dwarfed her own. The sparks were quenched as Alban's alien form came to the forefront of Margrit's thoughts once more. Confusion rushed in to replace the heat she'd felt, leaving her frighteningly alone in the dark tunnel.

"Yes," he murmured. "It does. Are you all right?" he asked again.

Margrit nodded in the darkness. "I'm okay now. Thanks."

"You're sure you don't want a light?"

She ran her free hand over her sodden shirt and filthy jeans. "It'd probably be easier to walk," she said reluctantly. "Just don't look at me, okay?"

"I'll try not to," Alban said, amused.

"You're making fun of me."

"Yes." He let her hand go and rummaged through something, then said, "Put your hands out," and deposited a leather bag in them when she did.

"What is this?" she asked.

"Things I might want in the event of a quick escape. I keep it under the bed."

"Oh! I saw it, yeah. I didn't know you'd grabbed it."

A match flared and Alban's smile came out of the darkness. "I did. There, this will help." The flame grew brighter as he put it to a torch, waiting for the wood to catch.

"Have you ever heard of flashlights, Alban?" Margrit

looked down at herself as the light increased. Her clothes and hair were wet and dirty, but not as appalling as she'd imagined. The cold water around her ankles was littered with floating debris and yellow scum. Margrit shuddered and lifted her eyes.

"It could be worse," Alban offered, looking her over.

Margrit smiled briefly. "You said you weren't going to look."

"I forgot," he said easily. "I've heard of flashlights. I've just never managed to buy one, for some reason."

"Probably because torches are a lot more dramatic and well suited to the whole creature-of-the-night thing."

Alban's jaw worked, as if he was trying to come up with a protest. "I very much would like to say that I'm not a creature of the night," he finally grumbled.

Margrit felt a smile slide into place and grow. "Yeah, and I'd like to say I'm not covered in slime, but neither of us is going to get what we'd like. How do we get out of here? I want a shower." Her voice rose in a whine and she scowled.

"This way." Alban gestured with the torch. Margrit shouldered the leather bag and slogged after him, staring fixedly at his back instead of at the murky water. His wings fell like a cloak, easier to see from behind than in front. The membrane was so thin that torchlight glowed through it, warming the ivory skin to a more human color. It looked soft and delicate, though it was capable of offering Alban the capability of flight, so had to be less fragile than it appeared. The impulse to touch the cascade of pale skin gripped her, and Margrit moved closer, reaching out without thinking how intrusive the action would be.

At the first touch of her fingertips she could feel both extraordinary strength and impossible softness. The sensation wasn't an unfamiliar one, though Margrit associated it with far more intimate parts of a man's anatomy. Heat flushed her cheeks as Alban's breath caught, wings fluttering at her touch, and she realized the comparison might be closer than she'd known. He turned toward her, his tight features highlighted by the torch's flame. Margrit dropped her hand, fighting not to twist it behind her back guiltily, and found herself without words as she stared up at his angular, alien face.

He was so vividly male, and so completely not human. It created a divide that Margrit could almost see a bridge over, but didn't know how to cross. Didn't know if she could. Didn't know if she wanted to. Male, but not a man… His eyes were wide and watchful in the torchlight, dark pupils eating the colorless irises, as he waited for her to choose.

"You're beautiful," Margrit said awkwardly. Alban's eyelashes fluttered, so subtle a motion that it might have meant nothing, but inside that instant possibilities shattered once more, leaving him with a brief smile and shuttered gaze.

"Thank you." He glanced down the tunnel, breaking the moment for good. "Not much farther. You're doing all right?"

Margrit bobbed her head, managing a faint smile of her own, painfully aware of how meaningless it felt. Alban offered her his hand again, and she took it, walking beside him. "So can you magically find the tunnel that comes out beneath my apartment building? Isn't that how it works in the stories?"

Alban's quiet laughter echoed off the walls. "Maybe if I lived beneath the streets, but my preferred paths are over the rooftops. The best I can do is get us to street level. Which should be…" He slowed, then stopped, lifting the torch. Several yards away, the tunnel dead-ended. Frowning, Alban looked at the ceiling, then walked back a few feet, studying the top of the tunnel rather than the path they'd taken.

"There aren't any wrong turns," he said under his breath.

"Don't tell me the end of your tunnel comes out on the other side of that wall."

Alban's mouth twisted. "What would you like me to tell you?"

"That you know a way out of here and we're not going to freeze to death in a sewer? No, wait." Margrit's voice rose. "That *I'm* not going to freeze to death in a sewer, because *you* can just turn to stone and sit it out. That's what I'd like you to tell me!"

"We're not going to freeze to death in a sewer," Alban said, so calmly that it made Margrit hear the edge of hysteria in her own voice. She let out a breath of relief. "It's a storm drain," he added.

She closed her eyes, setting her teeth as she counted to ten. When she trusted her voice, she lifted her chin. "All right. I'm better now. I'm not usually like this, you know."

"Not usually cold, wet, hungry and stomping around in sewers with a gargoyle? I'm surprised." Humor glinted in Alban's colorless eyes. "You're handling it very well for an amateur."

"You're making fun of me," Margrit accused again.

He shook his head. "Not this time. You show amazing fortitude." Margrit ducked her head, absurdly pleased, and Alban smiled enough for her to hear it in his voice. "I can think of two options—go back the other way and see where the far end of this drain leads, or take the tunnel back up to my room."

"Where Tony and half the NYPD are probably pulling your books apart."

Alban growled, deep and low enough to lift hairs on Margrit's arms. She raised a hand in apology. "Hey. Hey, sorry. I hope they're not." He growled again, and Margrit dropped her hand, sighing. "Going back doesn't seem like a great idea, is my point."

Stone scraped against stone, sending reverberations bouncing through the tunnel, the sounds so deep Margrit's ears itched. Alban lifted the torch again, his expression becoming wary as he looked beyond Margrit toward the dead end. He flashed into human form as she spun to face the wall, which shifted with slow deliberation. Brick dust shivered into the air, hanging there before drifting down to the dank water. Alban's torch threw soft shadows into the darkness beyond the opening, then caught reflections from eyes and teeth as figures began to creep forward into the light.

Margrit backed up until she stood beside Alban, gripping the leather bag with both hands as if it was a weapon. He rolled his shoulders, dropping into a slight crouch, and growled through bared teeth, as though he forgot which form he wore.

A blond woman with short-cropped hair came out of the darkness, splashing without concern through stagnant water, firelit drops rolling down her leather boots. "Got the coppers after you, do you," she said, then let go a sarcastic snort when Alban and Margrit's stiffening shoulders answered the question against their wills. "This tunnel dead-ends on this side, too, so it looks like you've got two choices, loves. You can come with the lady, or you can go back and face the tiger."

* * *

"Alban," Margrit said through her teeth, "what is she?"

The blonde stepped forward with the confidence of a cat and took Margrit's jaw in her hand. Margrit jerked away, wondering if the woman ever slipped, and if she did, if she washed herself as if to say, *I meant to do that.*

"What am I? Is it blind you are, girl? I'm the lady. The coppers back there, they're the tiger. Get it?"

"I get it. Alban?"

"Just a woman," Alban said cautiously. "Just the lady."

"Just!" Mock offense filled the woman's voice. "I'm a hell of a lot more than *just,* love."

"What are you doing down here?" Margrit asked. She didn't look as if she belonged in a sewer, not that Margrit knew what someone who did belong in a sewer looked like. The woman's pants and coat were leather, too, as water-treated as the boots, and the collar of the coat came up to her chin, fitting snugly. She looked like she barely needed an excuse to shoot someone.

"Oh no," she said. "I get to ask the questions—these are my tunnels, see. But I already know what you're doing. So. Make your choice. We can close the door back up and you can rot, or you can come with us."

"We'll come with you."

The woman smiled. "Smart girl. C'mon, kids." She turned on a heel and strode back toward the opening.

"Did she mean us?" Margrit asked quietly. Alban spread his hands without answering, and followed the blonde.

A dozen teenagers closed in around them as they stepped through the opening. One pushed a switch on the wall and the door swung closed, subsonic rumblings making Margrit's ears itch again. "I think she meant them," Margrit muttered.

Alban murmured an unintelligible curse to the ceiling. Margrit looked up to see a boarded-over square in the concrete.

"Your exit?" she asked. He nodded.

"Been wondering," Grace said. "Found that a good six or seven years ago. Closed it right up and dug the other hole. Took weeks to build this door." She thumped the tunnel end with a fist. "Nice to know that years of paranoia pay off. Come on, now. Keep an eye on them, kids." She strode off again, the teens gathering around Alban and Margrit and, by force of numbers, ushering them forward.

They walked through concrete tunnels and slushy, thick water until Margrit's feet were numb and Alban's torch burned low. Occasionally they dropped down a level, or came up one, but Margrit had the sense they stayed largely on a single plane. Other than that, she had no feeling at all of where they were or where they were going. Questions to the teens—all of them dressed similarly to the blonde, in waterproofed, warm leather or denim—earned her skeptical looks and no responses. After a while she stopped trying.

Eventually the air cleared, and one of the teens yanked a heavy steel door open, gesturing them all up a rickety wooden staircase into the basement of a building. Another dozen young people, all of them clean and wary, climbed to their feet, watching the newcomers arrive. The blonde barked an order and the teens scattered, two returning minutes later with tea and towels. Margrit took a towel gratefully and sat on the floor, pulling her shoes off to rub life back into her feet.

"Thank you," she said, when blood began to tingle painfully in her toes.

"You're welcome," the blond woman said. "There'll be food soon. While we're waiting, why not explain to me why I shouldn't kill you?"

"Why would you have waited this long if you were going to kill us?" Alban asked.

The woman's smile went bright and sharp. "There's a bigger audience here."

"That gun you mentioned the first time I met you," Alban said to Margrit.

"Yeah?"

"You don't really have one, do you?"

She let out a humorless laugh. "No."

"It wouldn't matter if you did." The woman lifted two fingers, dollars held between them. "I'd have taken it from you. Your pockets," she said to Margrit, who stuffed a hand into her jeans, coming up empty.

"That's my money!" She looked around at the silent teens, then back at their ringleader. "Jesus, what are you, some kind of Fagin's Morlocks?"

"You don't seem like the literary type, love. I'm in awe." The woman crouched in front of Margrit, still holding her money aloft. "It's not even a bad description."

Margrit stared at her, then tossed her head in a gesture of futility and frustration. "You're Grace O'Malley. The vigilante. I should have recognized you."

"Why?" she said easily. "Ever seen a picture, love?"

Margrit caught her breath, startled. "No. Nobody ever posts a picture of you. Why not?"

"Grace doesn't like having her picture taken." The

woman curled her fingers around Margrit's cash, then slowly lowered her hand. "Compromises safety, it does. And so do you, love. You want to live, I need a guarantee that our little secret down here isn't going to be spilled."

"Why'd you rescue us? Wouldn't it have been easier to just let us rot?"

Grace's eyes deepened with a sad smile. "Because it's what I do, love. I take a risk on the ones who got left behind. But you think I'm one of the bad guys, don't you?"

"She ain't," a boy mumbled into his knees. "All of us, we're off the street 'cause of her. We'd die for her."

"An army of children?" Margrit asked, disapproval coloring her voice.

Grace curled her lip. "Not for me. For each other. It doesn't always work." Her eyes grew dark and sad again. "Kids die out here. Stray bullets destroy dreams. Drugs do it slower, but just as certain. The ones who stay with me usually get out, and that's about all anybody can do. But the thing about me is people don't know how I get around."

"Rooftops," Margrit guessed.

Grace snorted, unladylike. "I prefer belowground. It's hard to fall off a tunnel." She studied Grace, then Alban. "I can't afford to let people who can't keep a secret go."

Margrit glanced at Alban. "We can keep a secret."

"Talk is cheap, love. Try again." Grace stood up and pulled a gun from the small of her back, cocking it so casually that Margrit felt no sense of danger until the warm metal pressed against her forehead.

"Wait," Alban said.

"Alban, no." The words were out before Margrit considered how foolish it was to protest an action that might save her life. Ignoring her, Alban slowly came to his feet.

"Send the children out," he said. Grace's eyebrows arched. "Send them out," he repeated. "You've got the gun. I offer an exchange of secrets, but not in front of the children."

Grace studied him a fraction of a second longer, then jerked her chin. The teens filed from the room, a few looking back over their shoulders. Margrit, shivering from trying to hold still, whispered, "Don't they have any curiosity?"

"They trust me," Grace said. "I trust them. It's all we've got down here. I'll shoot your pretty girlfriend, love, if you make one move toward me."

"I believe you," Alban said. "I would like to ask that you not shoot *me* when the secret has been exchanged."

Grace laughed, a sharp clap of sound like a gunshot. "That's not a promise I'm willing to make, love."

"Alban, *don't*," Margrit whispered.

"I have to." With the words, he shifted, the ripple in space tearing at the corner of Margrit's eye. Inches from her face, Margrit saw Grace's finger tighten against the trigger as she took in the gargoyle's height and breadth, the wings that half opened, then closed again to make him smaller.

Very slowly, Grace lifted the gun away from Margrit's forehead, cupping the butt in both hands, muzzle pointed at the ceiling. Alban stood motionless, Margrit on the floor beside them, heart hammering in her throat.

"All right," Grace said, after seconds stretched until they felt like minutes. "All right, then, love." She nodded once and uncocked the gun, sliding it back into her pants beneath the hem of her coat. "There's dinner in the making. Are you hungry?"

TWENTY

"THAT'S IT?" MARGRIT asked with a dry throat as Alban shimmered back into his human form. Grace whistled sharply and the doors opened again, children filing back in and settling into their places.

"That's it, love," she replied. "Miriah cooks up a good pot of chili. You're welcome to eat with us, and you can tell me why you're running from the coppers. Here." She fanned out the money she'd taken from Margrit's pocket. "Suppose you'll be needing this, if you're not going to be dead."

Margrit exhaled a shaky laugh and took the cash. "Thanks. I'll tell you about the cops if you tell us why Janx put you on Alban's list of enemies."

The blonde blanched, waving one of her kids away as her voice dropped. "Janx?"

"He's a…" Margrit threw a glance at Alban, who shook his head minutely. "A gangster."

Grace shook her head. "I'm not asking who he is, love. I know that already. Bad business, is what he is, and more trouble than me and my little gang are worth." She shifted her shoulders uncomfortably, moving a few steps farther away from the children. "There's a hundred stories about me, and none of them are true, but I'm not in that league and I don't want to be."

Margrit smiled. "The tabloids—"

"I'm not," Grace said sharply. "The things the tabloids make me out to be, I'm not. They want me to be some kind of superhero, but I'm a long way from it."

"Then what about all the amazing stuff you're supposed to do?" Margrit couldn't keep the crooked smile off her face. She felt Alban turn to her, examining her, but didn't look back, afraid he'd see a light of glee in her eyes that she neither could nor wanted to hide.

Grace made a swift dismissive motion. "Once," she said. "Once, four years ago, a bloke grabbed one of my girls. Not even mine, yet. I'd been trying to talk her into coming here. Her brother was running with a gang and she had nobody else. This johnny comes out of nowhere, down on the street. I pick up a tire iron and crack his skull, and a week later I'm looking in the paper and there's three men apprehended by Grace O'Malley what've been arrested and put in jail. Inside a year, whenever somebody's left broken in a place the coppers can find him? It's me. On one hand, it's grand. The boys on the street don't play hardball with me and mine as long as we keep a low profile. On the other? The cops are always itching to bust me. They're not much for vigilantes."

She waved her hand dismissively, and a note of fear entered her voice, invading the brash confidence. "But Janx. That's a man I'll not tangle with for life and limb. What's he doing, waving my name about?" Her hand drifted to her waistband. "This place I've got here, it's fragile, you understand? I'm not afraid for me. Grace is harder to hurt than she looks."

Alban rumbled, a soft sound of curiosity that brought Grace's attention back to him. "Used to hearing a bit of stuff say that, are you, big man? It's true. I wouldn't survive down here if it weren't. I think you know a thing or two about that, don't you."

"I do. It is—" The gargoyle broke off, a smile so faint it might have been imagined creasing the clean lines of his face. "It's good to see people surviving. Doing more than surviving." He gestured, encompassing the room, and Grace gave him an open smile that made Margrit's spine stiffen.

At a glance, Grace fit into Alban's world in a way she never would. The underground vigilante belonged to dark places and hard living, a life eked out beneath the streets. Alban's world might lie above them, but it was as much enclosed in darkness as Grace's. For an instant Margrit saw them from the outside, both tall and pale, Grace's platinum hair nearly as pure a white as Alban's. They might have been made to fit together.

And Margrit had no claim on Alban.

She twisted a hand behind her back, closing it into a slow fist as she tried to bring Tony's image to mind. The pairing of Grace and Alban overwhelmed it, and Margrit looked away, making herself focus on the contained anger that came into Grace's voice as she answered the gargoyle. "I'll survive. It's the kids I worry for. Maybe it don't look like much, but they're off the street here. It's a chance to find a way into the world."

"It's a strange place to do it from." Margrit's voice was soft but easy, the calm she needed in the courtroom serving her well in Grace's home.

The blond woman spread one hand, the other staying near the gun at the small of her back. The confidence in her tone was back, but her eyes were still too dark, concern coloring them. "Mostly they try to fix problems from the top, love, but you've got to get to the root. I don't have a church or a lot of money to back me up. The only way I can see to do it is to climb into the guts of the thing and start lifting people out." She made a stirrup with her hands and jerked upward, as if boosting a rider, then broke her fingers apart with a shrug. "Janx is everything these kids need to stay away from. And he could destroy this with a word." She turned to survey the boys and girls, some sleeping already, others gathered into quiet groups, studying or reading. "I've got books and dreams for them. Janx has got video games and flash. Most days I wouldn't blame them for taking the glitter. But we hold together with what we've got."

"Like great outfits," Margrit said with a tentative grin.

Grace turned a wry smile back at her. "All the cool kids dress in leather. Besides, it wears well, love."

"We have no quarrel," Alban said, making it a question.

Grace's eyebrows, much darker than her hair, shot up. "I've never seen you before. I've got nothing against you, though…" She looked him up and down, ending with an appreciative leer. "Now that you mention it, I wouldn't mind having a bit of something against you, at that."

Margrit felt her shoulders rise again, the hairs on her neck bristle. She put her hands in her pockets and bit the inside of her cheek, dropping her gaze to the floor. Grace noticed the reaction and threw her head back in a startlingly rich laugh. "Prancing on claimed territory, am I? No offense meant, love. Just having a bit of a flirt."

Margrit mumbled a disclaimer, then lifted her eyes again, avoiding Alban's gaze. She could feel him watching her, curious, perhaps even hopeful. *Just like a man,* she thought. Maybe a little more sensitive than the average human male.

She tensed her biceps and forearms to shake away the thoughts. "On the one hand, it's good you haven't got a problem with Alban. On the other—" she hissed out a breath through her teeth "—it means Janx played me. I'm getting tired of that."

Grace gave another laugh, this one short and incredulous. "You've dealt enough with Janx to get tired of him playing with you? You've got the luck of the Irish in you, girl."

"Probably somewhere." Margrit pushed her hands through her hair, ending up pulling her ponytail out as she turned, aimlessly examining the room and the young people in it. "Lost New York. All the places that got built over and forgotten about, but maintained some infrastructure."

"What about it?"

"It's your territory, isn't it?" Margrit turned back to Grace. "Does Janx know you operate down here? Below the streets?"

She shrugged one shoulder eloquently. "Not so's I've told him, no, but there's not much Janx doesn't know, especially what with him owning half the police force."

A thin slice of cold cut its way along Margrit's nervous system, Tony's stolid expression leaping to her mind. Why had he pointed her at Janx? Why had he known the name— worse, perhaps, the voice? Could it be—

She cut off that line of thought, aching with unhappiness. They'd been together on and off for over three years. Anthony Pulcella was a good man and a good cop, if unlikely to stick it out through the rough times. But that was her fault every bit as much as his, and it certainly didn't point to him being bought and paid for. His anger over her involvement with a murder suspect was justified, even if there was simple human jealousy compounding the problem. Margrit didn't believe she could be that wrong about him, not after all the time they'd spent together.

"You're a lawyer, Grit," she muttered, not meaning the words for anyone but herself. "You're supposed to be a good judge of character. Stop with the second-guessing."

"Oh, hell." Margrit looked up to see a combination of disgust and frustration in Grace's eyes. "That's where I've seen you. Knight. Margrit bleeding Knight, wandering right into my bloody den. Bloody hell."

Margrit blinked. "You know me?"

"Of course I do." *Course* came out with more of an accent than Grace had used before, dragged out into *caarse*. "You're the lawyer knocking down my building."

Margrit's jaw dropped. "Me? I'm trying to keep a buil—*your* building?"

"Not mine." Grace took a few long-legged strides away, covering as much territory at a walk as Margrit would have running. "Of course it's not bloody mine, for all I wish it was. For five years, six, we've had a bloody base right beneath it, as close to a center of operations as I've got. We can get all over the city from there, fast. That building coming down is like dropping a bloody bomb on my work. These are good kids." Defeat sharpened her tone. "Most of them are, whether they're mine or not. It's just the choices they've got are so damn bad. If I have to start over again—"

"Then you will," Margrit said. "Because you know it makes a difference."

Grace let out an explosive sigh. "And that's why you do it, too, isn't it, love?"

Margrit shared a rueful smile with the blond woman. "Some days, yeah." She tucked hair behind her ear, chin lifting in thought. "Does Janx know about your place? Beneath the Daisani building?"

"Like I said, love, there's not much he wants to know that he can't find out. We try to keep quiet, but maybe somebody noticed us. We've used that space a long time." Grace hooked her thumbs in her belt, rocking back on her heels as she studied Margrit. "If he knows…"

"I'll find out," Margrit said flatly.

Grace laughed again, more quietly, as if she knew without looking that some of the kids were sleeping. "And how'll you do that, I'm wondering?"

"He owes me a favor, if nothing else. Maybe I can get the truth out of him."

"He owes *you*?" Grace kept her voice low, mindful of the nearby teens, but the tone changed to reflect disbelief. "How'd you manage *that*?"

"By promising three unconditional favors in return." Margrit made a face.

Grace rocked back. "That was a bad idea."

"You don't say." Bad idea or not, thinking about it sent tingles of adrenaline through her system. "It'll turn out all right. I hope."

"I hope God himself will come down and give me the kiss of angels," Grace said. "Hoping won't make it happen."

Margrit smiled curiously. "Kiss of angels. I've never heard that expression before. Sounds like a blessing."

"Or a curse," Alban murmured.

Margrit and Grace gave him equally sharp looks, Grace ending hers with, "You're a quiet one, aren't you? And I would be, too, if I were you. Look, I'm no enemy of yours and I hope you're none of mine, but if you've brought Janx down on my head…" She shifted her weight, her hand drifting to her waistband. Alban rumbled deep in his throat, and Grace swaggered forward, challenging him.

"For God's sake." Margrit stepped between them, scowling up at Grace. "You wouldn't really have shot me."

Grace's lips curled. "That'd be telling, love."

"Janx scares you," Margrit said, keeping her voice low even as Grace stiffened in offense. "He scares you, and I'm not surprised. He could ruin you. That's enough to frighten anyone, even if they're running a more legit business than yours. I will figure out what's going on here and make it stop." Determination hardened her voice and she found herself curling her hands into fists. "People are trying to bulldoze me every way I turn, and I am not going to let them do it. Even if I didn't like what you're doing here, you're de facto on my side right now, so I'll be your advocate." A smirk fell across her face at the unintentional play on words. Grace snorted in approval, falling back a step.

"I will find a way to stop this." Margrit shoved her fingers through her hair again, relaxing marginally as some of the tension ebbed. She was making that promise a lot recently, she reflected, and then sighed as she glanced around at the labyrinth of doors and tunnels leading from the basement chamber. "I'll find a way to stop it," she repeated. "As soon as somebody tells me how to get out of this room."

Margrit was only half certain Grace had made the exit route more complex than necessary. Half certain; for all she could tell, every twist and bend they'd taken had been part of the shortest route to the street. They'd surfaced closer to Trinity than she'd expected, Grace leaving them with a nod. Margrit watched the platinum-blond woman disappear through a storm gate, then shook her head. "I hardly even thought she existed."

"You said there were stories in the papers about her," Alban pointed out.

Margrit shrugged and turned back to him with a smile. "There are stories in the papers about Elvis sightings, too. All right. Let's go."

Suspicion darkened the gargoyle's expression. "Where?"

"To see Janx. I'm going to kick his butt." Margrit almost believed herself, and grinned toward the sky.

"I am not bringing you to the House of Cards." Alban's tone was flat, his gaze fixed on the disappearing point of the city streets. Margrit's grin faded and she shrugged, turning to cut down a side street. Silence followed her, then Alban's footsteps, and his wary question: "Where are you going?"

"To a subway station."

"Margrit…"

"Why does everyone have to sound like my father?"

Margrit wondered out loud, turning back to the gargoyle. "Look. Fine. I don't care. Don't bring me there. I'm going anyway, so you may as well just suck that up, all right? It's late, I'm tired and I want to find out what the fuck is going on and why my life is getting jerked around." She stepped forward, putting her fingertips against his chest, almost a shove. "Maybe you can afford to spend fifty years lying low and hiding from the cops, but know what? I can't. In fifty years I'll have used up my allotted three score and ten, and frankly, I can think of better ways to spend it."

Alban put his hand over hers, the warmth of his fingers making her suddenly aware of his heartbeat beneath her palm. "Can you," he murmured.

Margrit's breath hitched and she went still, caught not by his touch, but by his words. There was hope in them, running deeper than she knew how to respond to, though she found herself fighting the urge to step forward into his arms. The visceral memory of his body against hers in flight took her by surprise, of the way his strength and surety had kept her safe as they soared above the city.

Soared above the city. The man before her could take wing and fly, a creature wholly unlike herself, a mere mortal bound to walk the earth.

Margrit took a step back. "I'm going to see Janx. Are you coming or not?"

Alban sighed. "Does it have to be the subway?"

"You lied to me." Margrit leaned over the lunchroom table, aggressively facing her opponent. "You lied to me, and I found you out, Janx. You owe me."

Janx gave her a lazy grin and let his focus flicker to where

Alban stood behind her, arms folded across his chest to make himself a living wall. The gargoyle wore his human form, hair so white it reflected in the burnished steel walls, but even without his stone breadth, he was wider across the shoulders than any of Janx's men.

"Alban," Janx said cordially.

Alban dropped his chin a fraction of an inch, the barest acknowledgment he could make.

Janx snorted thin blue smoke and swung his feet off the table, standing with liquid grace. "You don't keep very polite company, Margrit Knight."

"Especially these days." She kept her gaze on him, deliberately including him in the bad company. Then, to her dismay, she found herself struggling against an answering smile as Janx turned an amused look on her. He *enjoyed* being himself, so much it was nearly impossible for her not to like him. Worse, he knew it: deeper amusement flickered through his eyes, turning them from the green of new leaves to jade.

He came around the table with long, fluid steps and lifted a hand as if to touch her chin. Margrit's smile fell away abruptly, and Janx froze as if she'd caught his wrist in an icy grip. Neither of them looked at Alban, though Margrit was sure Janx was as aware as she was that the gargoyle had tensed.

"Ah, yes." Janx dropped his arm, eyes shifting color with the changing shadows as he moved. "My lady prefers not to be touched. I remember now. So." He stepped back, just out of Margrit's personal space, his gaze narrowed on her. Goose bumps stood up on her arms, making her fully aware that Janx's motions, his choice of distance, were deliberate.

He was giving her the space she needed for comfort, the dancing amusement in his eyes hidden now as he studied her and ran his tongue over one of his curved eyeteeth. "What lie have you caught me in, and why are you so certain of it that you're willing to come to my territory and accuse me?"

"Grace O'Malley is not Alban's enemy."

Janx's eyebrows shot up so fast they seemed like a streak of flame crossing his forehead. "Don't tell me you found the notorious pirate queen and asked her!"

Margrit flicked her fingers in dismissal, then found herself rubbing her thumb against her index and middle fingers, as if pantomiming a sign for cash. Janx turned his head a fraction of a degree, studying her action. Disappointment slid through his gaze before he lowered his eyelashes and gave her an unexpectedly sly look. "I suppose how you learned it doesn't matter that much, since you've managed to find me out. But do you really think that means I owe you something new and fresh, my dear?"

"Yeah." Margrit took the step forward that Janx had taken back, putting him once more into her personal space. He was taller than she was—everyone was—but she looked up at him with all the challenge she could muster.

He quirked an eyebrow, good humor restored by her audacity. "And if I disagree?"

"Then I think I don't owe you anything else. Come on, Janx. You sent me on a wild-goose chase, and I want to know why. And I want any other names you've come up with since I was here last night. Don't tell me you're going to disappoint me."

Janx glanced over her head at Alban. "You really don't

deserve her, Korund." He returned his gaze to Margrit, lips pursed with hopeful curiosity. "I don't suppose you'd abandon the good and true Stoneheart to live a life of decadence and depravity with an aging gambler?"

Alban's warning growl made a deep counterpoint to Margrit's astonished laugh. "I'm not a gambling woman, Janx. I try to play games I can win."

"And yet here you are," the red-haired man murmured. "Who does that say something about, I wonder." He turned away from her abruptly, moving with the loose-jointed fluidity that marked Alban's actions, as well. "O'Malley is less of a goose chase than you think. Look deeper, Ms. Knight, if you want the heart of that matter. As to the rest of it." Janx produced a shot glass so quickly Margrit blinked, certain it hadn't been up his sleeve. A second swift motion brought forth a clear flask, from which he poured rich amber liquid into the glass. The smoky aroma of whiskey spun through the air for a moment before he drank it in one swift swallow, then turned back to her. "You have canceled no debt. I owe you nothing more. Go." He curled his lip in a snarl and gestured with the shot glass. "Go, before I test djinn against gargoyle and take you as the prize."

"You owe me a name." Margrit's voice was steadier than she expected it to be, low with confidence. "You promised me more information tonight, Janx. Don't jerk me around."

He looked at her without expression, then gestured again with the glass and turned away. Margrit stood motionless, studying his silk-clad shoulders as she let out a near-silent sigh. Malik coalesced in the corner nearest the picture windows, fingers curving, as if he was drawing Margrit nearer. Instead she turned away, touching Alban's elbow to bring him with her. He held the door for her, one arm stretched over her head as she paused in the frame and looked back over her shoulder.

"Ausra," Janx said, without turning. "The name you want is Ausra."

TWENTY-ONE

"WHAT WAS THAT?" Alban managed to hold his tongue until they reached the street, leaving Janx's...*alcove,* Margrit thought, deliberately wiping the word *lair* from her mind...behind.

"That was his honor getting the better of him. I set out an expectation last night. He couldn't not fulfill it."

Alban looked down at her, full mouth set in a thin line. "Why not?"

"Because men like him have nothing but their honor." Margrit shook her head. "I've defended guys like him. You might not agree with their moral code, but they've got one. Without honor he's just another two-bit criminal. He's got too much pride to let himself go that far. He'd sell you out for a nickel, but if he makes a promise he'll keep it."

"He's not a man at all, Margrit." Alban spoke quietly.

Margrit frowned at the river across the street, black and smooth, reflecting the city lights. The comment resonated too sharply with her own thoughts, with the rising conflict of emotions she felt when she looked at Alban.

"I don't know," she murmured, more to herself than the gargoyle at her side. "He isn't human." She folded her arms around herself, still watching the water. "But he's a person."

"Be cautious, Margrit." Alban's voice rumbled with warning. "Janx is not human."

She turned toward him, spreading hands whose café latte skin was soured to yellow beneath the streetlights. "A hundred years ago people your color wouldn't have thought someone of mine was human." Intensity filled the words, their importance enough that she felt her hands trembling as she held them out.

"My color." Alban sounded startled, spreading his own pale hand above hers.

She nodded shortly. "Don't kid yourself, Alban. In this form, you're a white man. Politically advantageous, economically powerful, socially acceptable. A hundred years ago if someone saw you and me standing here like this, you'd be the human and I'd be something less. A century before that, you and I standing here would have been master and slave. Or I might've been lucky. Two hundred years ago I might've been a free black, a placée. Know what that is? It's a rich white man's dark-skinned mistress. Somebody my color would've been a quadroon, very exotic. Light enough to be almost acceptable." Her heart hammered in her throat, thick and choking. "So forgive me if I'm having a hard time with what makes someone *human* or not."

"Margrit, we're different *races*. Different—"

"They call it racism, Alban." Her voice rose, growing sharp. "All the shades humans come in are defined as races, like we're alien from one another. It doesn't matter that we can all interbreed and make pretty brown babies." She clenched her hands, emphasizing their color, then turned away, shoving them into her pockets. "I don't like the word *race,*" she added to the street. "If we have to be defined in smaller groups than just the human race, it should be by ethnicity."

"What are you, ethnically?"

She swung around on her heel, snapping, "American. On both sides, my people have been in the United States since the seventeen hundreds. I don't know what else it takes to be just an American. What do you see when you look at me?"

"A human woman." Alban sounded surprised.

Margrit grunted, surprised herself. "Not a black woman? Not just a woman? A *human* woman? I couldn't pass for one of your people?"

Amusement flickered over Alban's face. "You lack the grace. Forgive me. I don't mean it as an insult. But humans are more solid, more grounded in their movements, than the Old Races usually are. Even your greatest athletes are so very—" He broke off, struggling for a word, and opened his hands helplessly. "Human. In their grace. So connected to one form, to one way of being. There's breathtaking magic in it, but it is not the magic of the Old Races. It's wholly your own. What do you see when you look at me?"

"A white man," Margrit said, but even as she spoke Alban changed form, trusting the alley shadows to hide him from passersby. Margrit stared up at his heavy-shouldered figure, the wings folded against his back to make him smaller than he actually was, and hesitated. Alban smiled again, barely creasing the stony crags of his face.

"Am I a person?" At Margrit's nod, he added, "Are the

gorillas your people have taught to communicate also people?" She nodded a second time and he shimmered back into his human form, looking down at her. "And are they human?"

Margrit looked away. "No."

"Neither is Janx, Margrit. Tread lightly."

"It shouldn't matter." She spoke quietly, recognizing too clearly echoes of the conversation with her mother.

"It should." The disagreement was startling enough to jog Margrit out of her thoughts, making her glance up at the gargoyle again. His expression was unreadable, cast— Margrit flashed a brief, frustrated smile at her choice of phrase—cast in stone.

She lifted her hands, pulling her hair free and remaking her ponytail before sighing. "This isn't the time to argue about it, one way or another." The statement had a familiar ring, familiar enough to make her cringe internally when she recognized it. It was the same kind of phrase she and Tony often used before taking a break from one another. For an instant Margrit wanted to take back the words and pursue the conversation, argue the semantics of humanity and racism. Instead she dropped her shoulders and stared at the ground a few seconds before choosing her course. "It's getting late. Janx said something yesterday about it being dangerous for you to be out near sunrise."

Alban's nostrils flared with dislike. "Dawn is a long way off at this time of year."

Margrit huffed a humorless laugh. "Which doesn't answer the implied question, Alban. What was he talking about?"

Alban bared his teeth, then shook his head and stepped back into the alley. "Physically, my people are not easily damaged. But we have times of vulnerability. Dawn, most particularly." He was silent, his jaw thrust out as he stared across the alley. "If we are chained at dawn, in the moments of transformation…iron binds us."

Margrit stared up at him. "Seriously? How?"

He dropped a hand, opening his fingers. "It becomes part of the stone when we transform. Once it's been absorbed, we can't rid ourselves of it. The chains can be unlocked, but not broken." He glanced down at her. "I believe gargoyles are the only of the Old Races to have ever been enslaved."

"But—"

Alban shifted his shoulders. "Margrit, it can wait."

"But what about the other Races? Don't they have—"

"Margrit." He shook his head once more. "Dawn comes late this time of year, but it still comes. If you want to talk to Biali before tomorrow night we need to do it now."

Margrit closed her eyes. "All right. And what about the other one? Ausra. Who is she?"

"I don't know her. The name—" Alban broke off, silent for a moment or two. "It means dawn. Just as Hajnal does." He sighed. "She's probably another gargoyle. We tend to have a rather limited number of names we choose. We're fond of words that mean dawn and sunset. Our hours of transformation."

"What does Alban mean?"

Sheepishness crept over Alban's face. "Dawn."

Margrit laughed. "I see." Her good humor faded and she gnawed the inside of her cheek. "So she's another gargoyle."

"Probably. Although if Janx is giving out her name, she may work with Daisani, which means she could be a vampire, as he is."

"A vampire?" Margrit's voice rose and broke.

"Yes." Alban arched an eyebrow, looking down at her.

"Eliseo Daisani is a *vampire?*"

"Yes." Open amusement creased the gargoyle's face.

"Vampires don't come out during the *day*, Alban!"

"Oh," he asked mockingly, "they don't?"

"No, they don't! Everybody knows that! Vamp—" Margrit bit the word off, staring up at him.

Alban spread his hands, smiling. "I don't know how the legends got mixed up, but vampires have never been night-bound, Margrit. Only my people. You are not so safe from the monsters as you think you are. You're pale," he added in surprise. "A few days ago you didn't believe in vampires at all. Is it so bad to hear your myths are wrong?"

"Apparently," Margrit said in a thin voice, "there was some part of me that believed. Yes. It's that bad. A vampire? I went and talked to a vampire? In an office building?"

Alban tilted his head, eyebrows wrinkled in curiosity. "You just faced down a dragon. Why would a vampire worry you?"

"Dragon." Margrit closed her eyes, remembering the way blue smoke had clung around Janx long after the cigarette was out. "Of course he was a dragon. What else could he be. Fine."

Alban, very mildly, asked, "You made a plea on his status as a man without even knowing what race he came from?"

Margrit thrust her jaw out. "Does it really matter?"

"Yes," Alban said again, more sharply. "It does."

She ground her teeth, then relaxed her jaw deliberately, though she couldn't keep rancor from her words. "All right. Fine. Biali, then. Where do we find him?"

Alban shimmered into gargoyle form, again trusting the

darkness of the alley to hide him from any watching eyes, and nodded toward the sky. "Up there." He offered her an arm in an oddly submissive gesture.

Margrit stepped into the embrace with an anticipatory grin, curling her arms around his neck. "What's wrong? You're kowtowing."

He laughed, the sound low and rumbly by her ear. "You would kowtow, too, to a woman who looked like she'd bite a dragon's hand off at the wrist when he touched her without permission." Alban crouched, power surging through his muscular legs to send them into the sky, his wings snapping open without the slightest jarring.

Margrit laughed breathlessly, partly in response to the gargoyle's words and partly in response to the thrill of leaving the earth behind. "I didn't know he was a dragon."

"Would it have mattered?"

She twisted to watch the House of Cards recede below them. "I'm going to be cocky and say no." She grinned as buildings below began to blur into one another as the two of them gained height. "I could get used to this."

"I wonder if you could," Alban said, more to himself than her. An ache of sympathetic loneliness ran through Margrit's heart, weakening her arms, and she slipped a little. Alban's grip tightened, solid and safe. She drew herself up again, nose buried against his neck, but she remained silent.

"She's a pretty little bit. For sale?" Biali squatted on an eagle's head at the Chrysler Building, hunched and broken. Like Alban, he had nearly white hair even in his human form, which he wore now, but the resemblance ended there. He was short and thick, muscles on his muscles, like an aging prizefighter. His left eye was scarred over. Margrit wondered what that damage looked like on his gargoyle face. In the moments between his landing and his transformation, she hadn't been able to tell.

"No," Alban said before Margrit could squawk a protest. "She's my attorney."

"The law." Biali growled in revulsion and spat to the side. "You're better letting me dump her off the building, Korund."

"I think not right now," Alban said, then left English behind, speaking a guttural language that sounded like stones scraping. Biali shifted backward on the eagle's head, eyeing Margrit suspiciously, then snarled and squinted his one good eye at Alban.

"Last time, Korund. This is the last time." He waited for Alban's faint acknowledging nod before continuing. "I saw your face all over their news, but I'm not the one who put it there. You're not worth the trouble."

"You thought I was, once."

"Pah!" Biali tossed a hand in disgust. "You were a warrior then. Good enough to give me this." Heavy fingers indicated his face. "Good enough to kill me."

"I didn't, though."

"Mercy is a strength." He almost sang the words, his voice full of ridicule. "Mercy has brought you low, Alban. You could have led us."

"To what? A glorious sunrise defeat at the hands of the humans? By the time we thought of it there were too few of us to wage war, even among ourselves. I had no wish to see another of our kind die."

"Mercy," Biali said again, scathingly. "Go away, Korund.

I'm not the one murdering women in the park, and if I were, I wouldn't be trying to make it look like it was you. I choose my fights in alleyways, with men who stand a chance."

"No single man could defeat one of us, not without weapons. Is this what you are now? One of Janx's thugs?"

Biali smiled, an ugly one that wrinkled his scar. "We're all of us thugs and killers. You've just forgotten your nature in your long years of isolation."

"We don't have to be." Alban turned to Margrit. "He's telling the truth. We can go." He slid an arm around her waist as she looked back toward the other gargoyle.

"Biali?"

"It speaks!" He rose from his crouch, stretching his thick shoulders. "What?"

"Who is Ausra?"

Surprise flickered across the scarred gargoyle's face, his eyebrows drawing down before he shook his head, one short abrupt movement. "Never heard of her. Sorry." He stepped back, then lifted his arms above his head and fell, graceful for all his width, off the eagle's head into darkness.

"I don't believe him. He knows Ausra."

"You speak," Alban murmured dryly. Margrit shot him a sharp look, then pulled away to see him better. She'd held her silence for long minutes after they'd returned to earth, watching the city begin to come to life around them.

"At least I'm a *you* instead of an *it*. He's a real charmer, isn't he?"

"We Old Races rarely have reason to charm humans, Margrit."

"Tell that to Janx and Daisani."

"Janx and Daisani are not usual."

"Are you?" Margrit asked sharply, then dismissed the question with a short brush of her hand. "What makes you think he was telling the truth?"

"We don't lie."

Margrit laughed out loud. "Oh. So you're all thugs and killers, then? He was telling the truth?"

"Margrit," Alban said with exasperation.

"No! Don't *Margrit* me, Alban. Either he never lies or there's a possibility I'm right. Which is it?"

"Exaggeration and lies aren't the same thing."

"You're not answering the question." She stalked a few yards ahead of the gargoyle. "Do you exaggerate?"

She heard Alban's hesitation in his intake of breath. "I don't eat small children," he finally said.

"Still not an answer. That was a joke. It's a different realm of communication entirely. If he's lying, Alban, how would we make him tell the truth?"

"Gargoyles don't lie," Alban repeated, frustration replacing hesitation. "It's not in our nature, Margrit. No more than growing wings and flying is in yours."

"I think you've been alone too long." Margrit turned to face him again, scowling. "Nothing stays the same forever, Alban, not even stone. The weather wears away at it, if nothing else. I think living night to night in a human world for centuries on end probably changes you more than you know. I think you're stuck in a way of life that ended decades ago."

Alban stepped closer, his size suddenly evident as he frowned down at her. Margrit's temper flared again, giving her the nerve to hold her ground, hands on her hips, as she glowered back at him.

"In less than a week, you think you know the Old Races so well?" he asked.

"I think I know people pretty well, Alban, and I think people adapt to survive in the environment they're forced to live in."

"We're not—"

"Don't!" Margrit snapped a hand up, cutting off his argument. "So you're not human." The words sent a shudder through her, a sudden acknowledgment of Alban's alien nature that lifted goose bumps on her skin. "You're still *people,*" she muttered. "And people do what they have to. They change."

"I haven't."

"Maybe that's what you thought you had to do." Margrit turned away, irritation still in full bloom, and stared down the city block toward the lightening sky. "And I think Biali's lying. I just don't know how to make him tell the truth. Short of an iron collar around his neck," she added, only half joking.

"Margrit!"

She looked over her shoulder at Alban. "I'm kidding. I wouldn't do it, but that's what I'm saying. Welcome to the human race." Margrit extended a hand, its color changing with streetlights fading and sunrise coming. "I think I'm basically a pretty good person, but there's still a part of me that *thinks* that way, even if I wouldn't act on it. Maybe it's human nature, maybe its society, but you don't have to go far to see how fast people turn to the concept of might makes right." She shrugged, dropping her hands as her annoyance faded. "You really think somebody living among us for centuries wouldn't learn to think that way? To take whatever advantage they had or could make in order to protect and survive?"

"Margrit…" Alban made a slow fist in the shadows. She watched the light shift, then jerked her head up, heart rate accelerating as she realized what she saw.

"Alban! The sun's coming up!"

"Yes." The word was hardly more than a whisper, his acknowledging nod just as faint. Acceptance filled the single word, no fight to it, sparking anger in Margrit's breast. It sent her running toward him, shoving him with her momentum.

"Go! Get somewhere safe!"

"Margrit," he repeated, and she pushed him again.

"We can argue later! Go! *Go!*"

Alban inclined his head and turned, a few long-legged strides taking him down an alley. The last step became a leap, air and light imploding around him as his form shifted. Crimson light colored alabaster skin as he reached the rooftop and disappeared from Margrit's sight.

TWENTY-TWO

SOMEONE, SOMEWHERE, WAS playing the *William Tell* overture very, very badly. It echoed in flat tonal beeps around the curved walls of the hidden speakeasy, bouncing off the stained glass windows until they bled together and shattered into a cacophony of falling glass.

The chess pieces, ebony and ivory, swelled into life, facing off against each other with drawn-back lips and clawed hands, hissing silently at one another with the increasing pace of the music. Margrit shrank back from them, trying to hear her own labored breathing, feeling as if she were caught in a test tube. The light bent around her, making a fishbowl of the speakeasy. A rook on the ebony side ballooned larger, solid and misty at the same time. He slid forward, reaching for an ivory pawn, which was small, delicate, wide-eyed with fear. Margrit pounded on the wall of her glass cage, shouting a soundless warning that went unheeded. The pawn shrank in on herself, arms wrapped around a tiny bundle as she cowered.

An ivory knight crashed forward, blocking the rook's progress. For an instant the chessboard went still, rook and knight facing off against one another, against all the rules of chess. The rook flashed a malicious smile and leaped toward its opponent, sending them both tumbling across the floor. A knife rose and fell in a flash, and the rook shrieked, a silent cry that shook the walls of Margrit's glass prison.

The ivory king stood above the wrestling pair, his shimmering blue staff thrust through the rook's back. The rook convulsed a final time and collapsed on top of the knight, who panted out a thanks and shoved the corpse away. The rest of the chess figures were strewn about the speakeasy lounge amid shattered glass and broken furniture. Both sides, ivory and ebony alike, were watching the ivory king, who made a gesture of fluid, weary grace. Without argument, the pieces turned away from him and began picking up pieces of the ruined stained glass windows. They fit shards together without paying heed to which window they'd come from. Margrit found herself pounding against her prison walls again, in time to the beep of the overture. She felt her mouth forming words, felt the vibrations of her shouts in her throat, but heard nothing. *You're doing it wrong!* she yelled silently. *You're—*

"—doing it wrong!"

She jolted awake, throat raw from shouting, one hand clenched around her cell phone, which was repeating the overture tones yet again. Margrit flung it away violently, then winced and scrambled after it, looking for the right button to turn the alarm off. The beeps finally silenced, she dropped her head to the floor and made a fist, smacking the wood. "Shit. Shit, shit, shit. And good morning to you, too, Margrit Elizabeth." She rolled onto her back, staring up at the bumps and lines of her bedroom ceiling, until a knock intruded. Margrit pushed up on an elbow. "Yeah?"

"It's Cam. Are you okay?"

"Damn, and I thought it'd be Jude Law come to take me away from all this." Margrit lay back down, staring at the ceiling again. "C'mon in."

The door creaked open, Cam peeking her head in. "I heard swearing. *Are* you okay?" The door opened farther as curiosity got the better of her. "You're on the floor."

Margrit nodded.

Silence reigned. Then Cam said, "You smell like a sewer."

Margrit nodded again. "I fell in one."

"You *what?*"

"Actually, it was a storm drain. Still didn't smell good." She wondered if Janx's nose was more sensitive than hers, and if her visit had offended him. The idea was both alarming and amusing. She grinned at the ceiling.

"How? No." Cam cut off Margrit's answer before she began it. "Shower first. Cole's already at work, so you'll have to suffer through my breakfast while you tell me what's going on."

"I can't, Cam."

"You didn't come in until dawn, Margrit."

Margrit closed her eyes. "I know. And what you're thinking is—probably right. But I can't tell you."

"Nobody *else* can, either, Grit."

"I know." Margrit sat up, wrapping her arms around her knees and dropping her head against them. "But I can't."

Cam stood silent for a moment, leaning heavily on the doorknob. "Can you tell me why you can't?"

She lifted her head, but closed her eyes. "Because somebody's life depends on me not telling."

"People like the women who've died?"

Margrit winced, shaking her head. "Someone else."

"Alban," Cam said. Margrit nodded. "His life is more important than the people who are dying?"

She opened her eyes again reluctantly. "All I can say is it's complicated, and I know that's not a good enough answer. But it's the only one I've got. We're trying to find the real killer, but I can't tell you anything else. I promise that if I ever can, I will tell you. Okay? I'm sorry I can't do better."

Cam sighed and came into the room, to crouch at Margrit's side before pulling her into a hug. "I guess it'll do. Are you okay, Grit? For real?"

Margrit wrapped her arms around her housemate gratefully, returning the hug. "I'm all right. I'm in way over my head and I have no idea how this is going to end and I smell like a sewer, but I'm basically all right."

"You have a weird definition of all right, Grit." Cam tightened the hug briefly, then let her go. "All right. Go shower. I'll fix you breakfast. You look like you need it."

"Yeah." Margrit turned her cell phone over, staring thoughtfully at the screen. "Okay." She clambered to her feet and followed Cam out of the room, earning a raised eyebrow when her friend realized she was being followed.

"Shower that way, Grit. Kitchen this way. Remember?"

"Uh-huh." She edged past the taller woman to the dining room table and dug her laptop out of a briefcase.

"Margrit, what are you doing?"

"They put the pictures together wrong," Margrit said absently. "Hang on, I'll shower in a minute." She got a cup of yogurt out of the fridge while the computer booted up, and dialed her e-mail address with her cell phone, paying no attention to Cam's bewildered expression.

"Do you still want breakfast?"

"Breakfast?" Margrit spoke around the spoon, then smiled as Cameron's question registered. "That'd be great. You just know me and yogurt. Oh, they turned out. Good."

"What?" Cam came to stand over her, resigned to her behavior.

"The pictures I took at the speakeasy. The windows." Margrit saved photos from her e-mail to the desktop as she spoke. "They put them together wrong."

"Stop talking and do your thing here, Grit. You're not making any sense."

"Watch." Margrit amalgamated the three photos, setting different transparencies and adjusting their placement. Cam drew in a sharp breath and leaned down to get a better look at the screen.

"Holy cow. Lookit that."

"I dreamed the windows got broken and they put them back together wrong," Margrit said quietly.

Set correctly, the abstract colors of the three speakeasy windows made a whole and complete picture, each photo giving depth and structure to the other layers. Grays no longer made random splotches in the brilliant shades of crimsons and teals; sand dune yellows built clear shapes, none of them complete without the others.

"That looks like a dragon." Cam pointed to the dominant crimson, coiling around the combined frames into a sinuous whiskered creature of power and grace.

"Gargoyles," Margrit whispered, touching the grays on

the screen. The gargoyle pictured seemed more delicate than Alban, as if it was perhaps female, but the breadth of wing and the comfortable crouch were unmistakable. She traced blues in the picture, picking out the graceful outlines of a half human, half seal creature.

"Mermaids," Cam offered. Margrit nodded, not wanting to admit how she knew otherwise.

"Like the chess set. There was a set with mermaids and desert creatures in the club."

Cam traced another shape with her fingernail. "Like this? It's the right color, all sandy, for the desert. It looks wispy, though. Like a genie. Want to make a wish?"

"I wish I could figure out what the hell was going on," Margrit said. "And then there's this." She touched the one human-looking figure among the others, picked out in blacks, a cloak flaring behind it like the gargoyle's wings. "I wonder what it is."

Cam grinned. "Man conquering the monsters, obviously."

"Obviously." Margrit slid down in her seat, staring at her screen. Not man, she thought. The fifth figure's cloak was subtly segmented, more insectoid than Alban's wings, or the representational gargoyle in the picture.

Five. The Old Races.

Her wish had come true. Staring at the consolidated photographs, Margrit understood at least another part of what was going on. The selkie living in Eliseo Daisani's building was happenstance, a bonus to gild his real goal with. He didn't care about destroying a rival member of the Old Races. It was pettiness that drove him, sheer childish pettiness. He was taking the building down in revenge.

Because Grace O'Malley had discovered and exposed his hidden speakeasy.

Margrit stood on the spot Her Majesty Queen Elizabeth II had stood upon the occasion of her visit in 1976. Tourists and congregation members came and went, never leaving the Trinity courtyard quiet. The noon service had become a two o'clock tour, and there hadn't been a long enough break in activity for Margrit to make a dash to Alban's hidden chamber. Not so hidden anymore; the door was closed, but yellow police tape cordoned off that corner of the church, warning Do Not Cross.

Frustration had driven her to come lurk around his daytime refuge. Even if he wouldn't be awake—or there, for that matter; he was unlikely to have snuck across police lines just before sunrise—it was possible she might find a hint somewhere in his room as to where he might be when his first home was compromised. Maybe nowhere, maybe hidden on a rooftop somewhere. The memory of his headlong flight into sunrise sent a wave of worry sweeping through her. He'd risked too much by being with her. Risked exposure.

Risked more than that. Risked exile, for telling her the Old Races existed. Though he was outcast already, according to Cara. Not, Margrit thought, the most reliable source of information, if her own people were considered anathema among the Old Races. But the selkie girl had been as casually dismissive of Alban's status as she'd implied others might be of hers.

It was a topic that could wait. Would have to wait. Margrit bounced on her toes again, impatient with the need to deduce where Alban might have hidden. The room he'd brought her to when the car had nearly hit her, maybe; even now she couldn't clearly remember where it had been. That she'd been almost too dizzy to walk when she'd left seemed irrelevant.

It was also unavoidable. She rocked back on her heels, glaring futilely around at the congregation. If she could get into Alban's chamber, it'd be the work of a few minutes to look, and then she could use up some of the energy building in her by running to the new location. Alban still wouldn't be awake, but at least it would be action. Forward motion. Margrit felt as if she hadn't moved forward in days. She knew intellectually that she was wrong. New information kept coming to light, but for a woman whose greatest joy was plunging headlong through park pathways at an all-out run, inching toward resolution felt irritatingly slow.

A smile flashed over her mouth as she recalled Luka Johnson's disbelieving joy at clemency being granted. There was something to be said for the snail's pace, even if Margrit preferred the hundred yard dash. She just had to keep that in mind.

"May I help you?" someone asked at her elbow. Margrit jumped off the plaque guiltily and shook her head.

"No, I'm just—" She broke off to gape at her questioner, whose beard was as erratic in daylight as it had been the night before.

"Just waiting for an opportunity to slip into the bowels of our church?" he asked with the slightest of smiles.

Caught, Margrit gaped another moment, then ducked her head. "Something like that."

He nodded, then tilted his head in an invitation to walk, waiting until they were away from the church to say, "I had an active imagination as a child. I loved the idea of good conquering evil, of God conquering the devil. I thought churches were more than just houses of worship. I imagined them as so strong in faith that they might pin down dragons and demons, evil captured and imprisoned by goodness. I grew up in this parish. Trinity was my church. It was stained black, you know. From the pollution. I thought it was from the evil it kept from the world, that it had become tarnished in order to protect its people. I heard my calling and spent years abroad, all around the country and the world, until I finally came home to New York and to Trinity." He paused, turning back to look up at the graying sandstone. "They cleaned it while I was gone. My black, Gothic church proved to be pink."

"It's still beautiful," Margrit said.

"Oh, yes," he agreed. "But different. A great evil might be kept below a black church, but beneath a pink one?" He chuckled. "So the first time I saw Alban, I understood what I wouldn't have understood as a child."

Margrit swallowed on a dry throat. "What's that?"

"That God and his creations are more wonderful and mysterious than I could hope to comprehend. That for a creature such as he, the safest home possible would be in a church. Did you know, Ms. Knight, that once upon a time, men could claim sanctuary against the world inside a church? A sort of religious non-extradition treaty."

Margrit gave a start, then grinned with embarrassment at her shoes. "I kind of knew," she admitted, "but only because I saw Disney's *Hunchback*." She looked up again. "You know my name."

The priest laughed. "Knowledge is where we find it. Even

in Disney." Laughter tempered to a smile and he shrugged one shoulder, a somehow cheery gesture. "You made a splash on the news the other night. I like to think I pay enough attention that a pretty young woman's name wouldn't fall out of my head in a matter of days."

Margrit's forehead wrinkled with amusement. "Are you flirting with me, Father?"

The priest waggled his eyebrows, good humor in his eyes, then shot a glance at the cordoned-off corner of the church. "I've never spoken to him, Ms. Knight, but I believe he is our protector. Church sanctuaries are no longer recognized as such, so I helped the police as best I could. But tell me." He turned to face her, blue eyes bright in the afternoon light. "Am I right?"

Tears stung the backs of Margrit's eyes, prickling her nose and making her sniffle. She smiled around them and nodded, clearing her throat. "You are. I think he's been kind of a quiet guardian, but…" She paused, turning to look at the empty space in the sky where the towers had once stood. "But he's one of the good guys, Father. Sorry if that's not the right word to call you. I'm Catholic."

The priest grinned through his beard. "Everyone has their flaws." He glanced at the church, then nodded toward it. "Good luck in finding the truth, Ms. Knight." He walked away, his purposeful strides calling attention to himself. Margrit slipped through the hidden door under cover of his dramatic departure, and let it close behind her.

The chamber below still glowed with torchlight, dim but steady. Margrit jogged down the steps, afraid to see a disaster left by the police force. A dull thud echoed as she came down the stairs, and she startled. "Alban?"

"Not exactly."

Margrit rounded the corner at the base of the stairs. Detective Anthony Pulcella sat in the chamber's single chair, elbows on his knees, a leather-bound book open in his hands. Beyond him, the books stood in tidier rows than they'd been left, straight in the shelves and piled neatly on top of each other. The cot was back in its corner, the cedar chest at its foot rather than under it. Books that hadn't been on the floor before were now, although the stacks were orderly, and the wardrobe stood several inches away from the soot-blackened walls. The patch behind the wardrobe was pale, the same color stone as the church above. Tony, still in uniform, looked as out of place in Alban's home as Margrit imagined she must: both of them modern pieces in a refuge meant for classics.

"So no Superbowl this afternoon?" The casual question came at a price, sorrow draining into Margrit's chest as if a faucet had been opened. Tony looked up sharply, eyebrows drawn down over dark eyes. He looked, Margrit thought, like a policeman ought to, his strong jaw set with concern and maybe a little righteous anger. She felt as if she were watching him through a window, a distance that allowed her to see the world he lived in without being able to step through and rejoin it herself.

Heat flashed over her at the thought that she might not want to belong to that world anymore. Margrit shivered despite the warmth she felt, pushing the idea away. It was too large and too uncertain to wrestle with just then, especially with Tony literally in the picture.

"I won't be able to get the afternoon off," he said after several long moments, his voice steady. "Even if I could—"

"I wouldn't be there," Margrit agreed. A smile played across her mouth, more pointed than she wanted it to be. "I mean, really, Tony. Is there any way for us to get through this?"

"I don't know." The detective's voice dropped. "Grit, none of this was supposed to go this way. I really wanted to make it work. I wanted us to be together."

"I know. But then I started harboring a murderer, and you started arresting me, and things just really get out of control when incidents like that are part of your everyday life."

"I didn't arrest you."

"This probably isn't the time to get hung up on the details, Tony. I didn't harbor a murderer, either, but what fun is a fight without sweeping statements?"

"I'm sorry, Grit. I don't have time for a fight right now." Tony sounded weary, closing the book he held and hefting it a little. "*Great Expectations.* First edition, just like almost everything in here. Signed by Dickens himself. This is the first of three volumes." He offered the book to Margrit. She opened it, looking at the author's signature, black ink browned with age, then closed it again gently. "Who is this guy, Grit?"

"He's an author," Margrit said, smiling with an unkind pleasure at irritating the detective. "Very famous. Wrote a lot of long books—"

"Margrit."

She looked up, still smiling. "Sorry. What do you want me to say, Tony? He's not a killer. That's all I can tell you."

"Tell me how you got out of here last night. The bed was still warm from body heat when we came down the stairs. Tell me how you left my man behind at Huo's, for that matter."

Margrit's smile thinned. "Tell me how you found this place if I lost your man."

"I got another tip."

"From Janx." Margrit watched the skin around Tony's eyes tighten, and nodded slightly at scoring a hit. "You working for him, Anthony?" The question was intended to get a rise, Margrit no more believing Tony was dirty than he believed she was involved in the murders.

Anger flashed across the detective's face, her ploy successful. Margrit waited for a pang of regret and felt none, her own anger keeping more delicate emotions at bay. "I said I wasn't looking for a fight, Grit. I've been after Janx for years. I'm looking for something to pin on him."

"So you used me as bait? Tony, you might not be looking for a fight, but I'm spoiling for one, and don't you think setting your girlfriend out as bait is a little shady? Or did you think I was guilty enough to see if setting me up gave me the rope to hang myself with?"

"You're right." Tony got to his feet, words driving him to action. Stacks of books made pacing difficult, but he moved around them with grace that belied exhaustion. Ponderous grace, Margrit thought; human grace.

"Setting you up sucked," Tony said abruptly. "And I'd do it again, Grit, because you were the only goddamn lead I had. I'm sorry that it fucks with us, but if it helped me catch a murderer I'd just have to find a way to live with it."

Margrit rolled her tongue around the inside of her mouth, looking away and studying Alban's room as she worked to hide her displeasure. The tidiness did something to loosen the knot of anger within her, and she sighed. "I'm surprised you didn't destroy the place."

"You know me better than that." Hurt, more tangible than offense, filled Tony's voice. "A B.A. might not be as impressive as a law degree, but I know when I'm dealing with priceless material. We took the place apart, but I wasn't sending books like that one up in flames."

"Thank you."

Tony nodded. "As a favor, answer my question. We found the stone beneath the bed, but one person can't lift that thing. Not even one person and you. And there's no other way out."

"Then I guess we weren't here. Look." Margrit held up a hand. "There's nothing here, Tony. You didn't find anything, and I'm not going to volunteer any more information. For one thing, my attorney told me not to. For another—"

"You're protecting him."

Margrit pressed the novel against her chest. "I'm sorry."

"Are you?" Tony rubbed a hand tiredly over his hair. "You're going to a lot of trouble to be a pain in the ass for somebody who's sorry."

"It's not really any trouble at all," Margrit mumbled, then raised her voice a little. "I really am sorry. I didn't mean to get mixed up in this, and I'm sorry I can't be more help."

"I could arrest you for obstruction of justice."

"But you're not going to, or we wouldn't be talking about it. Believe it or not, the reason I'm stuck in this is because I'm trying to do my job, just like you're trying to do yours. I don't know how, but somehow these murders have got to be tangled up with Eliseo Daisani and that building he wants taken down."

Color leeched from Tony's eyes. "Is that an educated guess, or do you know something?"

Margrit frowned up at him, shaking her head. "Just a guess. I— Why? What's happened, Tony?" When he didn't answer, she took a step forward. "Tony?"

"Eliseo Daisani's personal assistant, Vanessa Gray, was murdered this morning, a couple of hours before sunrise." He met her eyes. "I don't suppose you know anything about that."

Horror pounded in cold spurts through Margrit's body, tingling and prickling. She shook her head, a jerky, numb movement. Tony sucked on his teeth. "You were one of the last people to see her alive, you know."

"I only met her Thursday," Margrit whispered scratchily. "She didn't like me."

"From what I've heard so far, she didn't like anybody except Daisani, and maybe not even him. She had no social life outside the office." Tony gave a sharp nod. "Which is why you were one of the last to see her. Unfriendly or not, she was good at her job. And she fit the profile."

"Nobody else was that high-profile, though." Margrit shuffled to the chair Tony had abandoned, sitting down hard and clutching the book against her chest.

"No, and this time he made a mistake."

"I was with Alban all night, until just before sunrise." And not until after sunrise had it struck her that Alban's daytime refuge had been compromised. Irritation welled in her breast again, this time at the simple lack of foresight that gave her no way to contact the gargoyle. "It wasn't him."

"I know."

Margrit wrenched her gaze up. "You know?"

"Gray's building has security cameras on the doors and in the elevators. We've got an unidentified male assaulting the doorman and getting off the elevator on her floor. Nine minutes later he gets back on. It's not your man."

Margrit sagged, putting the book in her lap and covering her face with her hands. "He's not mine," she said quietly, though voicing the statement made her heart tighten. "Does that mean this is over now?"

"For you, yeah. For me, no. I still gotta find this guy. He's an expert." Tony made his way through books to the stairwell, lifting his hand to put it against the wall, then dropping it before he touched soot. "And I still want to talk to Korund. There's something off about that guy."

"This guy in the elevator's killed three people and you think *Alban's* off?" Margrit looked up through her fingers to see Tony's faint smile.

"All a matter of taste, I guess. Look, Grit. I'm sorry. For what it's worth, I'm sorry."

"Me, too."

"Yeah." Tony stayed silent a few seconds, then turned back to look at her from the stairwell. "I'll call you?"

"I guess." Margrit lowered her eyes, keeping her gaze fixed on the floor until he left. She let go a rough laugh once she heard the door click shut, and collapsed onto her back on Alban's cot, staring up at the depthless, soot-covered ceiling. It had been a coincidence that pulled her into this mess. A coincidence, and now she was eyeball-deep in debt to a gangster dragon, and had a job offer from a corporate bloodsucker.

"At least it isn't boring." Her voice sounded hoarse in her own ears, and she put a hand over her throat, giving a rough laugh. "Jesus, Grit. You're so fucked."

And there was nowhere to go but straight through it. It

didn't require thinking about; neither Janx nor Daisani would let her slide off their radar simply because there'd been a misunderstanding. Nor was there any point in breaking down. Margrit had gone into the situation with her eyes open. She'd taken on the risks knowing what Alban was.

"Just one *little* breakdown?" she asked no one in particular, and sat up again, scrubbing her hands over her face. "All right, girl. Time to go see Daisani."

TWENTY-THREE

"I WANT HIM dead."

Margrit stood with her palms stiff against her thighs, shoulders hunched. This was not how she'd anticipated the interview with Daisani beginning. After long moments she swallowed, trying to wiggle life into her fingers. "Are you talking to me, Mr. Daisani?"

Daisani whipped around to face her, afternoon sunlight glowing white through the tall windows directly behind him, a blinding aura. "Of course I am. To who else would I be speaking?"

Margrit squinted and turned her head, trying to focus.

"I don't—I don't understand." The speech she'd prepared fled from her mind, leaving her feeling unexpectedly fragile and very alone. "I don't kill people, Mr. Daisani."

"Neither do I, Miss Knight. I'll let the criminal justice system do it for me. But they must catch him."

Margrit shook her head. "I don't understand what that has to do with me."

"Everything." The vampire clipped the syllables. "You have

walked into the House of Cards not once, but twice, and come out not just whole, but with information you wanted. You are involved with Alban Korund. Cara Delaney has turned to you for help. Unless you are a tremendous fool, which I doubt, you are clearly aware of factions that the police and legal forces in this city are not. I cannot and will not further compromise my position by allowing another party to be privy to information you already hold. Find him, Margrit."

A knot of tension snapped in her shoulders and she exhaled, turning to lean heavily on one of the overstuffed leather chairs. She folded her arms beneath her breasts, knowing that the action signaled closing herself off, and shut her eyes for a few moments. Daisani went still, so still that even in the silence of his office she couldn't hear him breathing. "I'll want something from you in exchange."

His silence became incredulous. Margrit looked up, her fear drained away. Not even excitement was left to chill her; this was the deal moment, too important to color with emotion.

Daisani's mouth worked, as if he was searching for words. His teeth were perfectly normal and flat, unlike Janx's.

"Vanessa was with me longer than you can imagine. She was indispensable to me. I will not allow her killer to go free and I require you to obtain the information I need. You have the audacity to demand something from me in return?"

"You need me, Mr. Daisani. You've just said so. You can't go to Janx and his people for this because you think they're responsible, and you're not willing to bring another player into the game. So you need me."

Daisani hissed, stepping toward her, sunlight trailing after him like a golden cloak. The walls of the office seemed to constrict, trapping her. "Of course Janx is behind it, but I cannot touch *him*."

"Why not?"

Daisani snarled, turning away with another hiss. "He and I have an understanding. If I remove him, someone who doesn't know the rules will take his place. I have no wish to begin the game anew."

"You mean, when you need someone butchered, you go to Janx, and when he needs someone financially ruined, he comes to you. It's a nice setup, Mr. Daisani. I imagine you've been doing it for a long, long time. And in the meantime you just take out each other's pawns? A game of one-upman-ship?"

"Vanessa was far more than a pawn," Daisani snapped. "She was with me for decades. I will extract real revenge at a later date. For the moment, the killer himself must be exterminated. You will find this man!"

"Then you'll give me the selkie skins." Margrit nodded toward the displayed furs without taking her gaze from Daisani.

Fury lit his eyes, and for all that she was watching him, Margrit didn't see him cross the space. He was simply beside her inside a breath, lividity raging in his expression. "You dare. You dare negotiate with me. That is a very bad idea, Miss Knight."

"People keep telling me that." The vampire's proximity sent waves of alarm through her body, painful tingles and an impulse to run. Margrit held herself still, meeting Daisani's eyes, and saw surprise reflected there.

"People." He spoke the word despite himself, in a low and warning growl. "Is that what we are?"

Exasperation flooded Margrit. "For Christ's sake. What is it with you and Alban? Yes! You're people. You're not human, but you're certainly people. What do you expect me to call you? Bogeymen? Things that go bump in the night? Hell, you don't go bump in the night at all, which is just wrong."

Daisani stood close enough that she could feel anger and grief retreating in him, replaced momentarily by interest. "You're taking this in very good stride, Miss Knight."

"Yeah, well, I'm a runner." Margrit fiddled with her pony-tail, betraying nerves with the action, but unable to stop herself. "I'm a lawyer. I meet people every day who are on the surface considerably worse than you are. You, Janx, Alban, you're really all so…*normal*. You can do stuff I can't, but so can Michael Jordan." Dismay hit her palpably enough to make her want to step back, though she held her ground even as she groaned. "Please don't tell me he's one of you."

Daisani's shoulders rose and fell, a single admission of silent laughter. "I believe Mr. Jordan is as human as you are, Miss Knight."

Margrit's stomach twisted and unknotted again with the astonished realization that she'd defused the vampire, at least briefly. "Thank God." A wave of tiredness swept over her and she stepped out of Daisani's space, planting her hands on his desk and letting her head hang. "I'll find your pawn for you, Mr. Daisani, but under the terms I've stated."

He was there again, in her space, brushing his hand over her hair so lightly she barely felt the pressure. "I'm surprised you're not bargaining for the building."

Margrit looked over her shoulder at him, wetting her lips. "I can deal with that in a courtroom. You have just as much reason as I do to keep selkie skins out of the press."

"More," he murmured. Anger stung his expression again and he stepped away, nostrils flaring. "The bargain's made. Deliver the assassin to the police and you'll have your skins."

Margrit let go a sharp breath and let her head droop farther for an instant, before straightening up. "Work with me here, Mr. Daisani. The baby can't survive long without her skin."

Daisani's lips actually parted in astonishment before he laughed, a surprisingly deep note tainted with grief. "You are audacious, Miss Knight."

"I'm also serious, Mr. Daisani."

"Of course you are. Are you sure you won't take a job with me?" His gaze swept her, a mix of criticism and admiration. "I'm always looking for new blood."

Margrit's breath caught in her throat, neither an inhalation nor exhalation, simply frozen as her mouth went dry and her eyes began to burn, unable to blink or water. Running in the park, even dealing with Janx, had nothing on the tightness of her chest now, as she stood face-to-face with a vampire. One part of her mind screamed to her to run; the rest held her in place, stiff with terror, hoping that the predator wouldn't notice the prey if it didn't move.

Daisani's eyes half closed as he inhaled deeply. "I wondered. You do know," he purred.

"I know." Margrit forced out the words, her voice hoarse. "And I was doing so well."

"You were. But now." Daisani spread his hands, eyes still

half-lidded. "Now I think we truly understand one another." He turned away, walking to the far end of his office with the liquid grace Margrit was coming to recognize as a hallmark of the Old Races, and took the smaller of the two sealskins down from the wall. "A gesture of good faith," he murmured as he returned to her, offering the skin. Margrit put her hands out for it and he folded it between them, then put his hands over hers. They were hot and dry, the pulse shockingly fast.

"A gesture of good faith," he repeated. "But if you fail me, Miss Knight, you had best remember I have more than one use for new blood."

Margrit made it all the way to the lobby before she threw up.

Evening sunlight shone a brilliant gold, making Margrit's eyes ache as she squinted against it. The bitter aftertaste of bile hung at the back of her throat and her stomach churned, making her eyes water at the acidity. She clutched the soft sealskin against her chest, running before she was even aware she was moving. Escape seemed paramount, anything to put distance between herself and the man she'd left behind.

Man. The word haunted her even as she ran, Daisani's sheer unnerving presence upsetting her definition of the concept. She'd met frightening men before, killers who looked at her as if she were something meant to be dominated and consumed. She'd never felt so much like a morsel on a plate as she had standing inside Eliseo Daisani's personal space.

Part of it was the terrifying way he moved, with no pretense of humanity in the impossibly quick flow from one place to another. Alban, by comparison, was as ponderous as a human, the weight that stone lent him binding him to the earth as surely as Margrit herself was. But then, she'd ridden memory with Alban, she reminded herself forcefully, and in that shared history he had wished for a vampire's unearthly speed.

And there was that in itself: the gift of sharing memory, so she'd been a part of it, thinking herself there until she could barely distinguish herself from Alban. It was not a human talent. Not something a man could do.

She didn't want the gargoyle to be right. Didn't want the differences between them to be as broad as *human* and *inhuman*. She knew the marks racism left.

Alban belonged to another race.

Margrit drew breath through her teeth. It didn't matter right now. What mattered was whether she'd played it right in her meeting with Daisani. She'd never had so much as a chance to mention Grace O'Malley or the real reasons he wanted Cara's building taken down. It *was* something Margrit could argue in court. Not the real whys and wherefores, but a plea for an injunction against the speed with which Daisani's corporation was moving would stand up. It would cause a delay, giving her time to deal with the real issues.

The warmth of seal fur against her skin told her everything she really needed to know. Margrit burst into Cara's building as the sun slid past the horizon.

Waking up outdoors was startlingly cold.

Despite not being particularly susceptible to cold, winter seemed to have settled deeply into his skin, stone chilled all the way through. Alban opened his eyes slowly, searching memory for the last time he'd slept outdoors with no protection from the elements. It had been decades, perhaps bordering on centuries. If it could be said that stone softened, he was clearly getting soft.

He left his eyes half-lidded as he glanced around the rooftop. There was no frost built up on his skin; sunset was barely past, the western sky still bleeding gold and red. Margrit's building was just two blocks away, as far as he'd needed—or dared—to fly in the moments before sunrise that morning. That, too, had been a sign of softness: he had sensed dawn coming, but lingered too long with Margrit, arguing about Biali's trustworthiness.

Alban made a fist against his knee, a slow action that belied the depth of frustration that surged through him. He hadn't made her understand. The Old Races had nothing but their trust in one another. Without it, they were all dead, exposed to humanity as freaks and curiosities.

The sky had been bright with daybreak when they'd finally ended the discussion, gratifying alarm sweeping Margrit's face as she realized the hour. She'd pushed him away, hurrying him to safer grounds. Not as safe as his home beneath Trinity, perhaps, but quiet rooftops were less risky by far than city alleys.

There were no sounds of activity on the roof now, nothing to betray him as he straightened from his protective crouch to his full height, shaking off the gargoyle for the man.

"I couldn't stand it, love."

Alban whipped around, hands curved to mimic the talons he didn't have in this form. Grace O'Malley sat on top of one of the roof's heat vents, a leather-clad leg cocked up so she could wrap her arms around it. Alban flexed his fingers again, willing himself not to flash into the more dangerous gargoyle form. "How long have you been there?"

Grace lifted her chin, nodding toward the sunset. "Long enough to freeze my pretty tush. I followed you."

Alban snarled, discomfited, and deliberately stepped back, trying to regain his equilibrium. "How?"

"Now, that'd be telling, love. Just know I been keepin' watch. You can thank me for it later." She gave a wink that made Alban shift his shoulders with unease.

"Couldn't stand it," Grace said a second time. "It's been a long time since I've seen a gargoyle."

"You…" Alban curled his lip, weighing his words before he spoke. "You know about gargoyles." He exhaled, finding he was relieved. "No wonder you didn't panic."

"I know lots I shouldn't, love." Grace hopped off the heater and landed as silently as a cat, sauntering up to him. "There's not lots I can offer that you'd have a need for, I'd wager, but there might be a thing, at that. A thing or even two."

"What?" Alban's shoulders rose defensively, and Grace grinned at him.

"The coppers found your lair, didn't they? And you'll be needing a place to stay now. Somewhere safe in the daylight hours. I can give you that."

"At what cost?"

Grace's expression hardened, making her beauty seem old and dangerous. "Help me protect the children, love. That's all." The hardness faded from her expression and she lifted a fingertip to Alban's chin. "Well, maybe another thing or even two, at that."

Alban wrapped his hand around hers, dwarfing her fingers even in his human form. "And if I don't?"

She shrugged. "You're Alban Korund, love. There are plenty who'd pay to wrap that fine throat of yours in irons. Korund the Outcast. What else do they call you? 'The Breach?' What's that one mean, Korund? I've wondered awhile, I have."

Disbelief and fear rose in his breast, mixing together to create fury inside an instant. Alban tightened his hand around her wrist, keeping to his less powerful human form with conscious effort. "How—?"

Grace gave a dismissive laugh. "Don't bother, gargoyle. I told you, Grace knows more than she should."

"How?" He didn't loosen his grip, his heartbeat a stony thud that rarely came to his notice, but now rang loud and heavy in his ears. "Who are you?"

"Grace O'Malley, love." She made her fingers thin and slid her hand from Alban's grasp, so easily his own fingers crushed together. "Only Grace O'Malley. Have we got a deal?"

Alban snarled again, hands knotted so tightly he felt the ache to his bones, as deep as the cold that had settled in them. "A gargoyle does not need coercing to protect the helpless, Grace O'Malley. But I wonder if Janx wasn't right, after all."

"I'm not your enemy, Korund. Opportunistic, is all. I like to make sure everyone understands the rules when we play the game. Will you watch the children?"

Alban pulled his lips back from his teeth, once more keeping his human form with effort. "I do not play games, Grace."

Her eyes narrowed. "So I'm told. And I'm told you hold the pieces to bring it together, as well. It's an enigma that you are, isn't it, love? Grace likes a mystery." She reached out to brush a finger down Alban's chest, a featherlight touch that felt as if it slipped beneath his skin instead of pressing against it. Alban caught her wrist again and she froze, not out of fear, but with amusement dancing around her mouth.

"Who tells you these things?"

Grace shrugged loosely. "Another gargoyle, a long time ago. Her name was Ausra."

"Cara?" Margrit pounded on the door, then tried the knob, aware she was intruding but too breathless and hopeful to care. She'd taken four flights of stairs two steps at a time, Deirdre's sealskin warm against her belly, *safe,* her only thought the baby girl's sweet, tired smile. "Cara, it's Margrit. Can I come—in?"

Cara sat in the midst of shambles, the worn apartment rendered far worse than it had been the first time Margrit was in it. The sofa had been upended, cushions cut open, with stuffing strewn across the room. Deirdre, oblivious to her mother's distress, lay in a mat of the stuff, cooing and pulling white batting apart with determined baby fingers.

Crockery lay shattered, chunks of porcelain spraying out of the kitchen. Scars marked the walls where they'd been hit by shards of dishes, the pieces of a jug lying next to the window. Blankets had been torn to strips and were flung about the room in wanton destruction. The building had no heat; without blankets to bundle in, Cara and Deirdre could easily die of exposure.

"Daisani?" Margrit dropped to her knees, taking the girl's cold hands in her own. "Cara, did Daisani do this?"

She laughed, a soft, bitter sound. "My neighbors."

"Why?" Margrit's voice rose and broke, incredulous. "Why would they do something like this?"

Cara turned her gaze on Margrit, hopelessness in her brown eyes. "Because I talked to you. Because I asked for help. They think if we keep our heads down we'll be forgotten, just like we always are. They think the building won't come down if they stay quiet."

"They need a scapegoat." Comprehension wasn't the same as understanding, not on an emotional level. A chill ran over Margrit's skin, leaving sorrow in its wake. "Someone they can actually attack, somebody closer to their level than Daisani's corporation. Oh, Cara. I'm so sorry. You and Deirdre should come back to my apartment. It's warm, and you'll be safer."

She drew herself up, straightening her thin shoulders. "No, thank you."

"Cara, this could just be the first wave. It could get a lot worse. For your own safety—"

"Miss Knight," she whispered, "I'm stronger than I look." Her fragile bone structure belied the words, but Margrit found herself drawing back, stomach knotting.

Not human. It was hard to remember. Hateful to remember, Margrit thought, but she set her jaw and asked, "What about Deirdre? Are you strong enough to keep her safe, too?"

Despair slumped Cara's shoulders. "I thought I was. But without her skin—"

It was Margrit's turn to straighten, shock and embarrassment coursing through her. "I forgot. That's why I came. Here." She withdrew the fur from beneath her shirt, missing its warmth as soon as it left her. But Cara gasped and snatched it up, clutching it against her chest. Joy illuminated her, making her seem fully alive for the first time since Margrit had met her. It enhanced her color, bringing warmth to her cheeks and brightening her dark eyes to amber. Her pupils were still enormous in their golden bed, making her waifish and vulnerable, but strength shone from them now. Determination, and beneath that a core of something wild, as if the girl had been transformed into a creature raised by wolves.

Not human, Margrit remembered again, but unmistakably beautiful. It hadn't been, until that moment, a word she'd have chosen to describe Cara. Now she wondered how she'd missed it.

"Miss Knight! You—how did you—?"

Margrit smiled quickly, wryly. "Believe it or not, Daisani needs something from me. I got this in return. I'll get yours back, too, Cara, so just hold tight, okay?"

Wariness crept into the wolf-colored eyes. "What did he need from you? You have to be careful, Miss Knight. You don't understand the dangers."

"He needs me to find someone," Margrit answered quietly. "Cara, I need to understand the danger I'm in." She managed another quick smile. "I know I'm in trouble, so anything you can tell me, anything at all, might help me."

"Do you know what he is?" Cara's voice dropped to a whisper, as if she didn't want Deirdre overhearing the conversation. Margrit nodded, and relief let Cara change positions, sitting Indian-style with Deirdre's skin still held tight in her hands. "There are five of us left," she whispered. "Five Old Races."

Margrit nodded again. "Dragons and djinn, selkies and gargoyles and vampires." Chelsea was right, she realized. "Dragons and djinn" was delicious to say. The other pairing lacked the music, and vampires stood uncomfortably alone.

"Selkies from the sea," Cara explained, still whispering. "Gargoyles from stone, dragons from fire, and djinn from the air. We all have our places in the world. Djinn are desert-dwellers. Gargoyles like the mountains. Dragons came from the hot places near volcanoes, but they can't stand one another and have spread far and wide so they don't have to share territory. We all know where we come from."

"Water, earth, air and fire," Margrit said. "But what about the vampires?"

Earnestness faded from Cara's eyes. "The vampires say they're not from this world at all."

Cold sprang up over Margrit's skin. "Is that even possible?"

Cara studied her for long moments, then got to her feet and climbed over the ruined remains of her sofa to pick Deirdre up. Margrit stood, watching, as the baby squealed indignantly, then cooed when Cara wrapped the sealskin around her.

The fur squirmed, writhing, suddenly full of life as it snuggled and wrapped itself around the child in Cara's arms. It distorted space more violently than Alban's transformation, an external element to it that he hadn't shared. Then Cara held a mottled tan-and-white baby seal, its brown eyes as bright and interested as Deirdre's had been. For the first time Margrit saw strength in Cara's thin body, as she held her child and leveled her gaze in blatant challenge. "You tell me, Miss Knight."

At Margrit's hard swallow, the girl knew she'd won, and spoke with authority. "Janx would use you up and cast you aside, Miss Knight. That's what dragons do, when their treasures lose their luster. Alban Korund would crush you and it'd be over in an instant. But Daisani will make you his creature, until you can't live without him, yet you have no life with him." Cara ran her fingernails over her daughter's seal belly, splitting an invisible seam until the skin fell away and a wriggling, happy baby girl emerged.

"I owe you," Cara said, "and I can survive without my skin if I have to. If you get a chance to break free of Eliseo Daisani, Miss Knight, don't hesitate. Everything you do for him, even making a bargain to help someone like me, will pull you down until the deeps are stained and the shallows run red with blood."

Denim was lousy material for running pants. Margrit jogged anyway, arms loose and her strides long as she darted around other people, brushing shoulders and elbows with them. The cadence of *ir-rah-shun-al* was gone, leaving her mind clear to think about other things.

Like how to trace a hired killer. Margrit let out a breath through her nose, almost a laugh. Finding a hired killer was even further outside her arena of expertise than housing lawsuits. Nice girls didn't know about that kind of thing.

The key, though, had to be the *hired* part of the equation. Whoever had killed Vanessa Gray had done it for Janx, so the money would lead back to him. Should lead back to him. Whether it could be traced was another question entirely.

With Daisani's help, overt or otherwise, the money could lead back to the dragonlord. But Daisani *wouldn't* help. Margrit shook her head and rounded a corner, strides lengthening. She understood on a surface level why he wouldn't touch Janx, but the subtleties of their interactions were beyond her.

If she thought much about it, that fact was a relief. She grinned briefly, shaking her hands to loosen them as she cantered through the city. The pavement sent sharp jolts into her knees with each impact, comforting and always the same. Someone whistled as she jumped a curb, the impersonal admiration helping to restore Margrit's sense of freedom in running.

Fingering Janx wasn't the answer. There had to be another way to find the killer through him. Margrit skidded to a halt at a crosswalk, jogging in place to keep her heart rate up while she waited for the walk signal.

He'd promised her one more favor. Margrit broke into a run again, flashing a smile at a passerby, then huffing in discontent. One more favor, but she didn't want to call it in yet. She owed him already. When she made the third request, she wanted it to be huge.

Margrit wondered when protecting her own life had become something less than huge and laughed, a breathy burst of sound that interrupted her run. She stopped to catch her breath, saying, "Okay," out loud. A passerby averted his eyes and Margrit flashed a grin after him, trying to keep her thoughts to herself.

She had to find Alban, first. Janx could wait. If she were a gargoyle caught outside at sunrise, she would… Well, *she* would go back home again come sunset, or as close to home as she could get. His hideaway under Trinity had been compromised, so her apartment might be the next safest place. Margrit dug her cell phone out of her pocket and dialed her home, propping one foot on the building behind her.

After four rings, the answering machine picked up. "This is Grit. If Alban comes by, can you ask him to give me a call? He doesn't know it, but they—well, they didn't find the real killer yet, but they know it's not him. Tell him…nevermind, just have him call. Thanks. Bye." She hung up and tapped the phone against her lips, then punched up the received-calls screen, a thought striking her.

Alban's number wasn't there. She scowled at the screen, remembering he'd called her on the house line, not her cell. "Crap!" She dialed the house back and added, "Me, again. Could you also check the answering machine and see if there's a record of Alban's cell phone number on it? Thank you. I owe you. Bye again."

Follow the money. Margrit pushed away from the wall and began running once more, phone back in her pocket. Follow the money without implicating Janx. "You don't ask much, do you," she muttered under her breath, as if Daisani might hear her.

Janx. That son of a bitch. Her thoughts came around full circle again and Margrit shook her head in time with her stride.

A car, moving more slowly than she was, poked its nose into the walkway against a light change. Margrit hit it with her elbow and forearm, rolling across the hood, and stopped to pound her fist against the metal, denting it. "Watch where you're going!" She came to her feet, continuing on, leaving the woman in the car gazing after her with panicked eyes.

A moment later Margrit slid to a halt at another intersection, smacking her palm against the street lamp. "How do I do it?" she asked out loud, distant stoplights steaming and fading behind the white of her breath in the misty air. She closed her fist and whacked the lamppost again. "You got caught up in some kind of huge freaking game, Grit, and you don't even know the rules. Dammit!" Her palm made a hollow clang as she hit the post again, harder, then ducked her head, laughing with frustration. "Son of a bitch. Margrit, you idiot. Go on. Waltz in. Demand some favors. Negotiate a deal." She rotated her head, looking up at the streetlight. "I am in so far over my head I don't even know what game I'm playing."

"Janx does," a voice growled behind her ear, and a hand clapped over her mouth.

TWENTY-FOUR

MARGRIT SCREAMED, A constricted squeak behind the hand over her mouth. An arm slammed around her waist, pinning her own arms against her sides, and she twisted with panic, throat loosening enough to scream again, the sound muffled by the man's hand.

"You think you're good, don't you?" he breathed in her ear, his voice too soft to be recognized. "Too good to get caught. You're just another piece of meat, girl. Just another piece of mortal meat. You're coming with me."

The city turned to mist around her.

Her lungs burned, vision swimming red: the mist was unbreathable, and it went on forever. Streetlights left oily yellow trails of fog through the scarlet, like blood on butter. Cars driving by tore black jagged streaks through her belly, pulling Margrit's insides out and stretching them until they snapped back and tangled around her feet. She stumbled, her heartbeat crashing in her ears, each thump slower than the last.

The crimson dimmed, her misty vision narrowing to pinpricks. Margrit's panic faded into exhausted relief, contentment rising up in slow waves through her body, to burst behind her eyes in white and blue spots. They said drowning wasn't a bad way to die, in the end. Maybe she was drowning. Sound receded, hollow and distant, and she closed her eyes, waiting to drift out of consciousness and out of life. She tried for a last breath without expectation, like a drowning man facing the inevitable.

Air flooded back into her lungs, so real and heavy it made her cough. With her arms still pinned at her sides, she clawed at her thighs, inhaling frantically through her nose and choking until tears spilled over the hand covering her mouth. The man holding her swore in a language she didn't know, yanking his hand away. Margrit gasped in a lungful of thick, palpable air, choking again, then lifted her foot and brought her heel down on the man's instep as hard as she could.

He howled and let go of her waist, careening back a step. Half blinded by tears, Margrit spun around and jabbed hooked fingers at his eyes.

Her hand went through his head and she slammed her stiffened fingers into a steel wall. A horrible pop sounded. Margrit screamed, pinching her fingers with her other hand as she fell forward and leaned against the wall, panting.

"Well played," a familiar voice said with admiration. Margrit, gritting her teeth, lifted her head to see Janx, feet propped on his table, applauding her lazily. "Not wisely played, but well played. Did something break?"

"I'm afraid to look," Margrit said through short breaths.

Malik appeared beside her, coalescing from the smoke and shadows in the room. His smile was pained, one part pleased to have frightened her and one part furious she'd gotten in a hit. Margrit bared her teeth at him, as much in defiance as to hold back gasps of pain from the throbbing in her hand.

"Let me see." Janx stood and came around the table with more grace than Margrit thought humanly possible. Then she laughed, a rough sound of distress, because it *was* more grace than humanly possible. His hands were cool and his touch delicate, soothing. He smoothed his palm over her aching fingers, then caught them and pulled them straight. Margrit gagged, sweat standing out in cold drops on her forehead and neck. Janx held her hand between both of his while she breathed raggedly through her nose, waiting for the pain to subside. "Not broken," he reported. "Badly jammed, but not broken. They'll hurt for a few days. That was remarkable, Margrit Knight. Foolish, but remarkable. A show of bravado goes so far in making my day."

"Don't. Ever." Margrit closed her eyes, trying to get her breathing under control. "Don't ever send him for me again, Janx. Not like that." She looked beyond the dragon at the smoky room. "Alban isn't here."

"Have you lost your gargoyle?" Janx asked, full of good humor. "I will send who I want, how I want, for you, when I need you."

Margrit folded her injured fingers under her arm, the pressure alleviating the pain a little. "Just remember it's a level playing field."

Janx smiled curiously. "Do you really think so?"

"I think we humans are good at leveling it at any cost. I haven't lost him, I just thought he might've come by here."

"You might come here, Margrit. I don't believe Alban would unless you gave him no choice." Janx looked stern,

shaking his head. "And instead of either his or your volun-
tary company, I have another murder. Whatever is the world
coming to?"

"Another—*another* one?" Margrit set her teeth together.
"You set your killer loose on somebody else? How many
does it take to make a point, Janx?"

"I did no such thing. Let me be perfectly clear, Margrit
Knight. When I want someone killed, I don't take half a
dozen innocents along with her." Janx pursed his lips,
looking thoughtful, then amended, "Not usually, at least.
It's messy, and while you may think me brutal, I'm not
stupid. Collateral damage means trouble for me and my
people. That's not what I'm looking for."

"Daisani's convinced you were behind Vanessa's death,
and you haven't given me anything that convinces me you're
not responsible for the rest of them." Margrit spat the words
as much to distract herself from the pulse in her fingers as in
genuine fury and frustration. *Air*. Cara had warned her that
djinn were creatures of air. That Malik could appear and disappear at will seemed obvious, in retrospect.

"There was a situation to take advantage of, with regards
to Daisani's woman. The rest—you're hardly worth lying to.
And I do have information."

"You're full of shit." Margrit elbowed past Malik, heading
for the door.

"Margrit." Janx's voice came down like a net, sending
spasms through her neck and thighs, so she couldn't move
forward. Her injured fingers wouldn't allow her to clench
a fist, sapping her ability to struggle against the dragon's
command. Only when she eased back a step did her body
relax. She turned to face Janx again.

He dipped his hand into a pocket and came up with a polished, egg-shaped stone, which he held balanced on all five fingertips. It was translucent blue, with a fragile spot of lilac at the larger end, just above his fingers. Through the center, a nearly colorless slash of blue blended to half a dozen white streaks of varying widths that wrapped halfway around the stone, then ended abruptly. Janx rotated the object in his fingers, sending a six-pointed star glittering over its surface.

"It's a rock," Margrit said. "So what?"

"Not a rock. Sapphire," Janx stated. "Corundum."

"Corundum." Her gaze went back to the stone, a chill settling in her stomach. "Corundum," she repeated. "Korund. Alban?"

"It was found this evening at the most recent murder scene."

"Jesus Christ." Margrit came forward, reaching for the stone. "How did you end up with it?"

Janx winked, lifting the object a little higher so her fingers closed on air. "It belonged to Hajnal."

"What?" Her arm fell.

"Alban gifted it to her, three centuries since. The stone is unique," Janx said dryly. "I am not mistaken in this."

Margrit reached for it again, her expression steady, and Janx smiled, placing it in her hand with a graceful twist that again brought out the star across its surface. She lifted it to the light from the casino, watching the star dance. "Has there been anything else like this?"

Janx smiled. "Is that your third request, Ms. Knight?"

Margrit folded her fingers around the sapphire—it filled her palm, egg-size as well as egg-shaped—and scowled. "No. This is part and parcel of the second request, and you know it. I asked for information. You've been withholding."

"Are you so confident of that?"

"Actually, yeah." The question inspired confidence in her and Margrit moved away to lean against the solitary table, folding her injured hand under her arm again, the jewel still held in her other palm. "Yeah." Knowledge came as she spoke, slowly and thoughtfully.

"Two women died before I came to see you, and you eked another night out of me by not giving me Ausra's name. By that time a third woman was dead. Three's enough for a pattern, isn't it? Brown-eyed brunettes, twenty-five to thirty-five years old. Vanessa Gray was a little old, but close enough. You hired a copycat." Margrit closed her eyes, tilting her chin toward the ceiling for a moment. "Son of a bitch," she murmured. "You hired a copycat killer."

"I deny that most strenuously," Janx said mildly.

Margrit opened her eyes. "Give me a break, Janx. I'm not interested in busting you. You could confess your sins to me back to the beginning of time and there's nothing I could do about it. God, how much did it cost? How do you hire a killer that fast?" Margrit shook her head before he answered, and unfolded her arms, turning the stone in her palm. "I don't really want to know. What I do want to know is how you ended up with this."

"You call in an old debt," Janx murmured. "From far away, if you must, but that's why I love to bargain, Ms. Knight." He flicked his fingers in a throwaway motion, adding in a more normal tone, "I have people who work for me. You don't need to know anything more than that."

"People who gave you details about the murders," Margrit guessed. "So your copycat could get it right. God, you're a smooth son of a bitch."

Janx, eyes laughing, bowed from the waist. "Thank you."

"Is she alive, Janx? Is Hajnal alive?" A mix of hope and dismay ran through Margrit as she voiced the question.

"I haven't heard Hajnal's name in centuries, Ms. Knight. A week ago I'd have said with certainty that she was dead. But now…?" He nodded to the jewel Margrit still held. "Now I'm not certain of anything about her."

"Now you owe me, Janx. You got what you wanted. You sent me on a goose chase after Grace O'Malley—" it hadn't been a goose chase, but Janx didn't need to know Margrit had realized that "—to earn time to set up your copycat, and now Vanessa Gray is dead. So pay up. Is this the first thing that's been left at the crime scenes?" She held the sapphire up between two fingers.

"It's the only thing that's been reported to me, Ms. Knight. The only thing that's been delivered to me from those crime scenes." Janx inclined his head.

"I have to call Alban." Margrit put the stone on the table and dug her cell phone out of her pocket, beeping the numbers to her home phone automatically.

The screen popped, graphics winking into a thin line as the phone gave a high-pitched whine. Margrit stared at it, then looked at Janx, who turned to Malik, tsking. "You've ruined another phone, Malik. It's the method of travel," he explained to Margrit. "The dissipation wreaks havoc on electronics. It makes talking with the djinn who are in the field difficult."

Margrit puffed her cheeks in exasperation. "Yeah, well, it makes talking to Alban difficult, too. Can I borrow your phone?"

Janx's eyebrows shot up.

"Oh, come on," Margrit said. "You just ruined my seventy dollar phone. The least you can do is lend me yours."

The dragon shrugged and slipped a phone from his pocket, tossing it to her. Margrit caught it with her hurt hand, unwilling to let the sapphire go, and swore as the plastic knocked against her fingers. Amusement colored Janx's eyes and Margrit tightened her hand around the sapphire as if she might crush it out of sheer frustration. Trying to keep from cursing again, she turned the phone over, scowling at its red-and-gold-streaked cover plate. "Very nice. All fiery and stuff." The words were muttered under her breath, but Janx grinned as she dialed home.

"Cole, Cam, somebody, please be home. Pick up. I need Alban to call me right away, at—" Margrit turned Janx's phone over, checking for a number on the back. There wasn't one, and she sighed. "Nevermind, I'm not going to be at this number for long anyway. I just…"

A prickly awareness made her arms itch suddenly, chills racing down her spine. Margrit cancelled the call with a shiver, mumbling, "Something happened. Lost the connection," as she scrolled through to the recently-called list. Her home phone number was highlighted, a question mark blinking next to it. Four more numbers, all local, were listed below it.

"Ms. Knight? Are you well?"

"I'm just afraid something happened," Margrit whispered. She hit the screen-down button once, then a second time, watching the numbers that had been called scroll by. Her hands shook and she fumbled, sending an extra screenful rolling by, too quickly to be read. Five blips of sound resulted from the buttons she'd inadvertently pushed. It would take three to get back to the main screen, return to the called list, and dial her home number again. She didn't know if Janx could hear the tiny beeps.

You call in old debts from far away. She shook her head, a savage motion. Three more screens of numbers flashed by.

The second-to-last number on the screen came up with an international calling code. Margrit stared at it, a block of ice forming in her stomach and spreading throughout her body.

"Ms. Knight?"

Margrit jerked her gaze up, feeling as if the phone number must be imprinted across her eyes. She shivered again, then smiled as if embarrassed. "Couldn't remember my own number for a minute." She cleared the screen, returned to the called list and let the phone redial the number.

Eleven blips. The number needed to call a New York City number. Janx couldn't know she'd searched his calls. Margrit met his eyes as her home answering machine picked up again. "Sorry, I got cut off. I hope this is recording. Look, if you see Alban, just tell him to be careful. Really careful. I'll talk to you later." Margrit turned the phone off and handed it back to Janx, the European number rattling in the back of her mind. "Thanks. I've got to go."

"What are you going to do?"

Margrit picked up the sapphire. "I'm going to find Hajnal."

"With that?" Janx's eyebrows arched with amusement and he nodded toward the gleaming stone.

"I wasn't planning on using it as a homing device, but I'm taking it with me, yeah."

"Why ever would I let you do that? Do you have any concept of the value of that stone?"

Margrit opened her hand and looked at it, then shrugged. "Honestly, not a clue." Curiosity welled up and she glanced at the redheaded dragon. "Do you really have a hoard?"

Janx laughed aloud, his pleasure so obvious it brought a smile to Margrit's mouth, as well. "If I did, Ms. Knight, I wouldn't answer that."

"Worth asking." She curled her fingers around the sapphire. "I need the stone, Janx. Alban's not going to believe this without it. He thinks she's dead."

"She's been gone for over two centuries, Ms. Knight. Odds of her survival are not good. I may not be certain, but I wouldn't place a bet on her survival without further evidence."

"And you're a betting man."

Janx flashed a brilliant grin. "Yes, I am."

"Right now I'm inclined to bet on almost anything. A week ago I didn't even know any of you existed. A missing gargoyle turning up after two hundred years of being presumed dead isn't that hard to believe." Margrit lifted her eyebrows. "You going to let me take it?"

"You and a priceless sapphire alone in East Harlem at night?"

"Looks like it, because there's no way in hell I'm letting *him* take me anywhere again." Margrit shot Malik a glare.

"I will allow you to take the sapphire," Janx murmured, "because I am curious as to how this passion play of yours will turn out, Margrit Knight."

"Passion plays are morality stories, Janx."

"And so might this yet prove to be," he agreed smoothly.

"You'll return the stone to me when the performance is done. And in the meantime, permit me to arrange a car," he said, his pleasant tone cushioning the iron in his voice.

Margrit set her jaw and leaned against the table, folding her arms under her breasts. Her fingers protested, but the pain had faded. Like it or not, Janx's ministrations had probably done the injury some good.

"Do what you have to do." She bit her lip, repeating the international phone number in her brain, a soundless recitation. Janx spoke in the background, then broke into her silent litany.

"Malik will walk you down to the street."

"I'd rather you did," Margrit blurted.

Surprise darted across Janx's face. "Very well," he said after a moment, and offered his arm. Margrit put the sapphire in her pocket, hissing as she bumped her fingers against the denim seam, then took the dragon's elbow. "Not many people would prefer my escort to Malik's," he murmured as he ushered her down a set of stairs.

"I told you before," Margrit said. "I trust your honor. I wouldn't trust him as far as I could throw him."

"Djinn are difficult to throw." Janx smiled. "They tend to dissipate. It's hard to get momentum from fog."

"See?" Margrit grimaced at her toes. "Honor among thieves."

"I'm not sure if I should be flattered or not," Janx said dryly, pushing open an exit. In the alley outside, a PT Cruiser idled, its red paint like drying blood in the darkness. One of the men who'd walked Alban and Margrit into Janx's office a few nights earlier leaned against the hood like a displaced mountain, arms folded. "Patrick will drive you."

"I don't think so," Margrit said. Janx's eyebrows lifted.

"You'll be perfectly safe," he assured her.

She shook her head. "*I'll* drive me. You can send somebody for the car in the morning."

"What about honor among thieves, Ms. Knight?"

Margrit shook her head again, looking up with a little smile. "There are limits, Janx. If somebody goes against your orders, it might be bad for him, but it's going to be a lot worse for me. I'll drive. Thanks for the car."

Janx hesitated a moment. "You do know how?"

She snorted and walked around the vehicle, pulling the driver's door open. "I know how. Just because I'm a New Yorker doesn't mean I can't drive." She ducked inside, watching out of the corner of her eye as Janx and Patrick exchanged glances. Janx nodded almost imperceptibly, and Patrick pushed away from the vehicle.

Margrit let out a breath she hadn't realized she was holding, and drove away.

"Tony, this is Margrit. Dammit, why aren't you picking up? I've got something for you." Margrit closed her eyes, repeating the European phone number slowly. "I'm pretty sure that's right. Don't ask where I got it, but it might help you track down the guy in the security video, the one who killed Vanessa Gray." Margrit thumped her hand against the inside of the phone booth, swearing when renewed pain flared in her swollen fingers.

"The guy's a copycat, Tony. Please don't ask me how I know. I'm calling from a pay phone because my cell phone's screwed up, so don't bother trying to call me back. I hope that number's good, Tony. I hope..." She sighed. "I don't know what I hope anymore," she said quietly. "Maybe we're back where we started, needing to talk. I hope we get a chance to. Bye, Tony." She hung up, staring blindly through the glass walls. If the number led to Janx's hired assassin, she'd have done what Daisani wanted.

"If," she whispered, dropping her hand into her pocket. The sapphire there felt like a dead weight, holding her in place with unanswered questions. She smoothed her thumb over its satin surface, warm now from her body heat, and looked without focus at the PT Cruiser outside the phone booth.

What happened to somebody who disappointed a vampire? Cara's warning had been vague. Creepy, but vague. Margrit's laugh sounded brittle within the phone booth walls. She pushed the door open and crawled back into the car, curling her arms around herself for warmth and comfort. Alban would know. Alban would tell her.

If she could find him.

He had to be safe. Almost any building top would have proved a haven against the rising sun. *Your kind,* she remembered him telling her, *don't see what's in front of them.* A newly arrived gargoyle on a rooftop might go unnoticed. Even if it didn't, calling someone to remove it would be more than a day's work. Margrit bit her lower lip, then straightened up. Alban could take care of himself. She had to find Hajnal, prove her theory. Margrit would bring Alban the mate he'd mourned for so long.

A cord of dismay knotted around her heart, creating a cutting sensation she could barely force herself to acknowledge. Finding Hajnal meant losing Alban.

And it was better that way. He wasn't human, not a man

at all, according to his warnings and admonishments. Better to finish this and rebuild her life with Tony, memories of murders and fantastic Old Races left behind.

The idea left a dry and bitter taste in her mouth as she pulled away from the phone booth to find the one person who might know where Hajnal was now.

TWENTY-FIVE

"BIALI! GODDAMMIT, BIALI, I know you can hear me!"

Margrit knew nothing of the sort, but she stood on her apartment rooftop anyway, bellowing into the wind. "Biali!" She'd gone home hoping Alban would be waiting, and, failing that, hoping that shouting from *any* rooftop would earn a gargoyle's attention. So far neither hope had proven true. She folded her arms around herself and stomped in a circle, frustration helping to keep her warm, but not enough. "Biali!" Wind rushed through Margrit's hair, chilled her face. "Biali, dammit, answer me!"

"Have you lost your little mortal mind?" Biali's rough voice cut through the wind as he landed on the concrete behind her with a thump. Margrit spun around, hair blowing into her mouth and eyes. She clawed it out of the way, wrapping her hands around it and wincing at how the wind stiffened her injured fingers. Biali crouched before her, already in his human form, weight forward on his toes.

"Do you not like people to see your other face?" Margrit asked without thinking.

Surprise creased the scar that ran across Biali's right eye. "Insightful little bint, aren't you? What do you want?"

"Tell me what you know about Hajnal."

Biali came to his feet in a movement that bespoke anger and grace all at once. "Hajnal's dead. Has been for centuries. Don't tell me you're up here crowing your throat dry to be told that. What are you trying to do, lawyer? Call every Old Race in the city to your doorstep? They're not all as friendly as I am, and Korund's not here to watch over you."

Margrit let go of her hair with one hand, strands of it instantly snapping into her face, and pulled the sapphire out of her pocket, letting it rest in her palm. Biali snarled with recognition, pouncing forward to snatch it from her. Margrit flinched back faster than she thought she could move, closing her fingers around the stone.

"You've got no right to that," Biali growled. "It belonged to Hajnal."

"I've got at least as much right to it as Janx," Margrit said. "That's who I got it from. Know where *he* got it?"

The gargoyle dropped into a crouch. "Tell me."

"He got it from the latest murder scene, Biali. Now, want to try again? Tell me what you know about Hajnal. I don't think she's dead."

Anger reflected in Biali's eyes. "Where's she been for two hundred years, if she's not dead? You want to know what I know? The women who are dying? They all look like her."

Margrit took a step back, startled. "They do?"

Biali smirked, dropping his chin. "Korund didn't tell you, did he. Maybe he doesn't even realize, though I'd think he would. Two centuries alone with nothing but memories of the one he lost. I'd think he'd recognize her anywhere. She was little, not like most of us, and dark, and that's really not like us."

"Dark? They're all white, the women who've been killed."

Biali snorted. "Dark hair, dark eyes. Some color to her skin." He looked Margrit over, curling a lip. "Less than a darkie like you, but compared to the rest of us she might've been black as midnight." Faint pleasure creased his face when Margrit tightened her fingers around the sapphire, warmth flushing her cheeks as she fought not to rise to the insult. Satisfied with the barb, Biali went on, flicking a broad hand toward his nearly white hair, close in color to Alban's. "We mostly come in pale, but her family name was Dunstan for a reason."

Margrit shook her head. "I don't know what that means."

"Dark stone." Biali seemed to get peculiar satisfaction from translating the name, as if it was another jibe at Margrit herself. "Her family bred true, but not often. Hajnal was a rare one. That stone isn't yours to keep."

"I'll give it to Alban," Margrit said. Biali pushed his lips out, but nodded.

"She's dead, lawyer. You're just digging up old graves."

"But what if she's not? Could she do something like this?"

"Could a gargoyle rip apart a few human women?" Biali snorted again, sarcastically. "One of our children could kill a mob of unarmed adult humans. If we'd done that a long time ago we might not be so few, and you so many."

"Is that what you think should have happened?"

Biali studied her, then set his jaw and looked away. "I think your people would've outbred us and the war would've been lost in time anyway. It wasn't only Hajnal's family that bred rarely. Korund's right, not that I'd say it to his face. There aren't enough of us. There never have been."

"Will your people die out?" Margrit let her hair go and wrapped her arms around herself, frowning at the gargoyle as curls whipped her face again.

Biali barked laughter. "We live a long time, lawyer. Maybe when your folk have destroyed themselves, we'll have a chance to try again. There aren't many of us, but don't nail the coffin closed yet."

"I don't want to." Margrit tightened her arms, surprised at her own ferocity. "You think she could do this."

"Any gargoyle is physically capable of it. But if she were alive, I don't know why she'd kill women who looked like her. We don't kill for fun."

Margrit's eyebrows rose a little. "I thought you worked for Janx. Beating people up."

Biali shrugged. "Gotta make a living, lawyer. It's survival, not entertainment." He grinned suddenly, toothily. "Can't say that I don't enjoy it, though. Kind of a chance to get—" He broke off. Margrit's chin came up.

"To get back at us for not knowing you even exist," she guessed. Biali's scar creased as he grimaced and shifted his gaze away. "I'm not even sure I can blame you," Margrit said. "You all live in a shadow world, don't you? You gargoyles especially. The rest of them can at least participate during daylight. You never even see the sun rise."

"Don't feel too sorry for us," Biali spat. "Our world is something you'll never know."

"I've seen a little bit of it," Margrit said. "I'm beginning to understand why you do what you do. Why Alban's made the choices he's made. I don't think I'd want to put myself through two hundred years of solitude, but maybe it seemed like there wasn't anything else."

"There wasn't."

"There's always something else," Margrit argued. "There's always a choice. Maybe not a good one, but there's always a choice. Alban says your people don't change their names."

Biali's eyebrows drew down. "That's for dragons and djinns," he said derisively. "We gargoyles know what we are."

"But what if you had to make a choice?" Margrit asked. "What if you had to change?"

"I got no idea what you're talking about, lawyer."

"My name's Margrit. Margrit Knight."

"Knight," Biali said after a few long moments. Margrit ducked her head, savoring the small triumph. "I got no idea what you're talking about, Knight."

"Alban said Ausra means dawn. Just like Hajnal does."

Wariness came into Biali's eyes. "So?"

"So I think two hundred years ago, Ausra was Hajnal. And I think you know where she is."

"I told you before," Biali grated. "I never heard of Ausra."

A woman, bedraggled with travel but carrying herself with pride, stepped into Margrit's line of vision. Her hair was black with rain, the water pulling curls out of shape, and her skin was amber-tinted, translucent. She was lovely, delicate in facial structure and body, but there was a coldness in her dark eyes, an absolute lack of empathy that made Margrit feel uncomfortably like prey. Not until the woman shifted her shoulders, half spreading graceful wings, did she recognize her as a gargoyle.

Shock coursed through Margrit, the crash of her heartbeat suddenly noticeable. It felt wrong, too slow, and at the same time as if it had suddenly leaped to a rabbit's pace. Then Biali's rough voice came from within Margrit's own throat, filled with astonishment. "You're dead."

A sharp smile cut the gargoyle woman's face and she moved, so quickly Margrit flinched, trying to avoid her.

Memory shattered with the movement, leaving her alone on the rooftop facing Biali. Margrit held a hand to her head, blinking from the echoes scraping around in her skull, then lifted her gaze to the gargoyle. Nothing had changed in his sour expression; no hint remained of what had transpired between them. Alban hadn't known humans were capable of hearing the telepathic link that allowed gargoyles to share their memories. Neither, it seemed, did Biali.

A faint smile curved Margrit's mouth, telltale admission of having won a round. "You're lying." The confidence in her own voice fed on itself and she stepped forward, challenging the blunt-featured gargoyle. "I don't know if your kind go crazy or not, but—"

"We don't."

Margrit's smile faded and she rubbed her temple again, as if doing so would push away the memory of the gargoyle woman's cold eyes. "Well, that means Hajnal, or Ausra, or whatever you want to call her, is killing people deliberately and with malicious forethought. That doesn't really make me feel any better. I know that the human justice system can't deal with this, Biali. We're not equipped to, even if it's humans who are dying. Is there— Do the Old Races have a justice system? You must," she said, the realization striking her even as she spoke. "Cara called Alban an outcast. Why? How did that happen?"

Biali laughed, a sharp sound. "Cara? That's not a name belonging to one of ours. Who is she?"

Margrit hesitated, remembering the young mother's reticence in naming which races others of the Old Races belonged to, even when it proved clear that Margrit already knew they existed. "A woman I'm helping. A new case."

"Oh." Biali's lip curled, turning his scar into an angry wrinkled slash in the nighttime shadows. "That selkie girl in the vampire's building. Her people are dead, lawyer. Don't listen to stories told by the last of a dying race. It's superstition and lies. Our justice system is nothing like what you're talking about. War tribunals, maybe, but even those aren't something you'd recognize."

"I know what a war tribunal is," Margrit said dryly.

Biali turned his head and spat to the side, his disgust palpable. Margrit watched him, not yet finished with the conversation, but curious about his anger.

"You know what *your* war tribunals are. Ours are different. We can't afford the kind of battles you people pick."

Margrit shook her head, letting the subject of Alban go. "You can't afford a renegade gargoyle, either. You loved her once, Biali. I need your help to stop her, to locate her and find a way to get her out of sight, now." *The guy's a copycat, Tony.* Margrit wished she hadn't said those words. "Doesn't she understand what will happen, if my people catch her?"

Biali put his weight on his knuckles, shifting and

frowning one-eyed up at Margrit. She waited a moment, then stepped closer to him. "Do you know where she is, Biali?"

"No. And if I did, I wouldn't tell you. Whatever's between her and Alban is their business, not mine." He scowled at her. "Korund took my eye and gave me my life. We don't owe each other anything."

"Not even the survival of your species?"

Biali shook his head. "Not even that." He turned, loping a few strides away, the space around him imploding as he shifted from human to gargoyle form.

"Biali!"

The scarred gargoyle turned back to her. The right side of his face was shattered, raw stone with edges smoothed by time. What was left had once been handsome, in the massive way of the gargoyles, though he'd never been as chiseled as Alban. How much of that played into the ancient antagonism that stood between the two, Margrit wondered. "You loved her once, Biali," she said. "Would she have wanted you to walk away from this?"

He smiled, a ghostly expression that rent the craggy ruin of his face. "No," he rumbled, "but she didn't choose me."

Margrit closed her hand uselessly around the sapphire as the gargoyle pitched himself from the building and disappeared into the sky.

Evasive answers and half-truths. Margrit left with an unfocused destination in mind, not wholly surprised to find herself climbing the stairs to Cara's apartment not too much later. She had questions she wanted to ask Alban, but with no way to contact him, Cara or Chelsea Huo seemed the best people to talk to, and Cara's apartment was closer than the bookstore.

For the second time that day, there was no response at her knock. "Cara, are you home?" Margrit tried the knob again, startled when it turned under her hand. She cautiously pushed the door open. "Cara? The door was—*shit!*"

The apartment was empty. Even the bedraggled furniture was missing, the rugs picked up from the floor and posters gone. The floor had been swept clean and the walls seemed to have been scrubbed, as if someone was trying to erase all signs of recent habitation. Margrit took a few steps inside the door, looking around in dismay. "Cara?"

The girl's name echoed through the empty rooms, frighteningly loud. Only that afternoon Cara had promised she could handle her neighbors, and now she had disappeared, so utterly that Margrit could hardly believe she'd ever been there.

Margrit took the stairs down in leaps, breaking into a flat-out run once she hit pavement, to find a pay phone and dial Tony's number. His answer was composed mostly of silence, before he made a tight promise to be there as quickly as he could. Margrit paced outside the building, keeping warm through movement, until the detective arrived, looking as if he hadn't slept.

"I'm only on my way back to the station, Grit. I can't stay. I'll take a look, but…" He shrugged, a movement of exhaustion and anger. "You know we can't file a missing person's report until she's been gone twenty-four hours. Come on. Show me the place." He brushed by her without further greeting, frustration in his movements.

Margrit hung back a few steps, eyebrows drawn down. "Tony?"

He stopped just inside the building, shoulders pulled back and full of tension. Margrit reached out to touch him, then stayed her hand, unsure how the gesture would be taken.

"There's been another murder, after the two last night. One of those was Gray. The other happened in the park, over on the east side."

Margrit slid her hand into her pocket, tightening her bruised fingers around the sapphire Janx had given her. "I'm sorry, Tony. Another?"

"In the last hour. Down on the park's southern end." He swung to face her, defeat clearly written on his features. "This guy's going to disappear, Grit. He's got one on each side of the park now. He's done. I can feel it. He's going to get away with murder, and there's nothing I can do to stop it."

"Maybe you'll get lucky," Margrit offered hollowly. "I'm sorry," she repeated. "I know I said thanks for coming here, but thank you again. I didn't know there'd been another murder. I'm surprised you could come."

Tony pulled a thin smile. "It lets me put off going back to the station and getting busted for letting the city go to hell in the past week. Let's go upstairs. I'll see if there's anything left that might be helpful."

"Thanks," Margrit repeated quietly, and took the lead. Guilt was assuaged by anger as she pushed the door open, the room's emptiness echoing back at her. "She's gone."

Tony sighed, looking around. "So's everything she

owned. It doesn't look like a kidnapping to me, Grit. It looks like she packed up and moved away."

"Inside a few hours, without telling me?"

"Margrit." Tony reached for her hands, then stopped, unsure of his welcome. The distance between them she thought suddenly seemed uncrossable, with too many sharp words lying there, waiting to cut again.

Too many secrets. Only a handful of days ago they'd stood on the edge of trying to build a life together. More had changed in that time than Margrit could wholly fathom. *She* had changed more in that span of days than she could explain.

She put her hand out abruptly, bridging the space Tony had hesitated to breach. He took it carefully, his grip warm and strong, and stepped a little closer, ducking his head toward hers. "Maybe she's just found a better place and hasn't had time to tell you yet."

"In two *hours?*"

Hope slid out of the detective's eyes. "Grit, I know you're upset, but yelling isn't going to help."

She sighed and manifested a brief smile. "I thought you boys from big Italian families solved everything by yelling."

"Well, you know," Tony said with a deadpan shrug. "It's all that NYPD sensitivity training."

Surprise caught Margrit out and she laughed. "That must be it." The laughter faded away as she glanced around the apartment again. "Tony, I'm worried about her. I'm afraid the neighbors who tore up her apartment came back to finish the job. If I'm going to pursue this injunction, I'm going to need her as the plaintiff, and to be there looking fragile and pathetic. Her and Deirdre. Dammit. Dammit!"

Margrit pulled away and stalked to the window, frustration and anger reasserting themselves as she spoke. "Russell may not even agree to go forward with this if we don't have her. Cara's a great victim." *Hypocrite,* she told herself. Even hating to have her own physical aspects played on, she would still use Cara's for every advantage they could provide. "Things are totally out of control."

"It can't be that bad." Tony followed her, stopping just far enough away to not be intrusive. "Look. I'll put out an APB on her, okay?"

"Yeah. Shit." Margrit turned to slide down the wall, lacing her fingers behind her lowered head. Her fingers protested and she flexed them cautiously, trying to work some of the ache out. "This just feels like a last straw. You wouldn't believe some of this shit, Tony."

The detective slid down beside her. "Try me."

"I would if I could." She lifted her head enough to stare at her own feet. "Janx tipped you off about Alban being at my place the other night, didn't he? That's why you asked me about him."

Tony didn't answer. Margrit glanced at him, discovering his expression was tight. She lifted an eyebrow and he wet his lips, evading answering with a question of his own: "Why'd you go to him?"

"A friend of Alban's said he might know something about the murders." Margrit huffed a laugh at her fast and loose version of the truth, but shrugged it off. "It was the first time I'd heard of him, except when you'd asked me who he was. Your turn."

"It was him." Tony sighed. "We've always got somebody on him. He made a pay-phone call the same time the tip came in. Besides, I've listened in on enough of his conversations to know that voice. Sounds like a used-car salesman. Oily."

Alarm clustered in Margrit's stomach, making hairs stand up on her arms despite her sweater. "You've got him bugged?"

"No. We try, but the bugs never last for more than a couple hours. Something always fritzes 'em out, even in public places. It's like he's got some kind of antibug aura."

Malik, Margrit thought, though aloud she said, "Great. Just what you need. An unbuggable bad guy. Is that how you found the room beneath Trinity Church? A helpful tip from the friendly neighborhood crime lord?"

Tony slid another glance at her, then looked away. "I lost you outside Huo's on Saturday night."

"Dammit! I knew it! You were following me!"

"You were my only lead, Grit," he said without apology. "When we lost you I…" He exhaled a deep sigh. "I went to see Janx myself."

"You *what?* Jesus, Tony, you don't know what you're dealing with there." Margrit clenched her teeth, torn between wanting to protect her erstwhile lover and being unable to betray Alban and the Old Races' secrets. Worry bubbled in her stomach and she wrapped her arms around herself. "You've got to be careful."

He gave her another sideways look, a smile playing at his mouth. "You're saying this to me? Janx and I go back a ways, Grit. I've been on him for years and he knows it. Cat and mouse game." He shrugged. "Maybe he figures giving me a heads-up on a guy who might be killing women all over the city will commute some of his sentence when I finally make the arrest. So did he know anything?"

Margrit pulled her head down until her upper spine

cracked. She sighed, feeling tension release with the popping nitrogen. "I wish."

"You telling me the truth?"

Margrit smiled. "I thought you believed people were basically honest, Tony."

"I do. I also know you've been keeping things from me all along with this goddamn investigation." There was no heat in the detective's voice, just weariness.

"You haven't been exactly forthcoming yourself," Margrit said, but nodded against her knees.

"I want this thing over with. I want our lives back, Grit. Just you and me and our breakups. Like it used to be, without your new friend in the picture."

"Alban's not…" She had no words for what Alban was or wasn't. *Not human* whispered through her mind again, and she sighed. "It shouldn't matter."

"It does matter, Grit. I don't know who the guy is and I don't like that you've been covering for him. If there's something going on, don't I deserve to know?"

Margrit released her head, turning to look at the dark-haired man by her side. "Nothing's going on." It was as much an untruth as anything Janx or Daisani had said to her. "Nothing like you're thinking." Warmth crept up her body and she lowered her head again, hiding any telltale blush that might color her cheeks. "We'll see what happens. Right now I'm going to see if I can find anything out about where Cara might have gone. I'll talk to Daisani if I have to."

"You think Eliseo Daisani disappeared your client?"

"Under the circumstances, I think it's not beyond the realm of possibility, although I wouldn't say it in a court of law just yet. If you'll put out that APB…"

"Yeah." Tony got to his feet and offered her a hand. "I will. It might take awhile. There's a lot of shit to clean up after this murder. I'll do my best, Grit, okay?"

"Thank you." Margrit hesitated, then let him pull her to her feet. "I owe you one, Tony."

"Yeah." He crooked a faint, uncertain smile, still holding her hand. "We better?"

"Better than what, Tony? We're not together. I mean, you can't think we are. Not with…" She trailed off, unwilling to discuss recriminations and recognizing too clearly their same old pattern in her reluctance. "This still isn't the time to talk about it. I've got to find Cara, and you…"

Tony whitened his lips, then nodded, expression unreadable. "I have to go explain to my boss why there's another dead woman in the park." He let her go without trying for a kiss, his face still drawn and serious. "Be careful, Margrit."

"Yeah. You, too." Margrit turned back to face the empty apartment so she didn't have to watch him go.

TWENTY-SIX

AFTER A LIFETIME of not knowing gargoyles hid in the city's shadows, Margrit's irritation at being unable to find the one she sought was blown out of proportion. Having Janx's Cruiser made both her irritation and her inability greater: convenient as a car was, she couldn't watch the sky while she drove. Fingers tapping against the wheel, Margrit guided the vehicle toward downtown, wondering if she might find somewhere to park it at or near the Legal Aid building on Water Street.

Work. A wince tweaked her. The weekend was gone and she hadn't been near the office, much less spent the hours putting together supporting documents for the injunction that she'd promised she would. She thought of the *Russell will kill you* file folder and let a deep breath turn into a sigh. He'd have to kill her. There was no way to turn back the weekend and be in two places at once.

Besides, with Cara missing, there might be no case for the injunction anyway. Margrit swore under her breath and pushed away thought in favor of concentrating on driving.

Minutes later she pulled into a downtown parking garage and took the ticket, trying not to think of how much the fee would be for overnight parking. Maybe she could deliver the stub to Janx and let him pick the car up himself.

The idea brought a grin to her face and she left the garage cheerfully, stretching her legs into a jog. Huo's on First was close, and if anyone had a sense of where Alban might have hidden in the moments before sunrise, Chelsea seemed a likely candidate. Margrit came up the steps to the bookstore two at a time, cheeks pink from exertion. Chelsea appeared from the stacks with a look of amusement. "There you are. Who's after you?"

"Nobody, I hope." Margrit folded her arms over her chest. "I can't find Alban. He suggested meeting here before, so I hoped…have you seen him?"

Chelsea tilted her head toward the beaded curtain at the back of her store, smile warming. "He's waiting for you."

Margrit jolted, a few quick steps sending her through the rattling curtain. Alban stood in time to catch her as she flung her arms around his neck. Even in human form, his scent was cold stone, the clean smell of earth after rain. Margrit inhaled deeply, tightening her arms around him and trying not to let herself think beyond the warmth and safety she found in his embrace. "Where the hell have you been? I've been trying to find you all night. I thought maybe something'd gone wrong this morning, at sunrise."

He closed his arms around her carefully, as if she might be fragile. "I landed a few blocks from your building just before dawn. Perhaps I should have just gone to the top of yours, but I thought if anyone knew where you lived…I was careless," he admitted. "I haven't been that incautious in centuries. I won't do it again." He shifted his weight back so he could look down at her. "After I checked your home and saw you weren't there, I came here. I hoped you'd think to. I'd have called your cell phone if I'd known the number."

"It doesn't work anymore. Malik phased it into oblivion."

"Malik?" Alban's voice rose with alarm. "You've seen Janx?"

"I've been busy since I saw you." The words seemed so inadequate she laughed and cast a helpless glance upward. "I haven't done my laundry, though. It's Sunday, right?"

"It is," Alban said, bemused. "Laundry?"

"That was my big plan for Sunday. Laundry and cleaning the bathroom. Maybe watch the Superbowl. I wonder who won." She breathed a laugh and ducked her head. "How did I end up chasing down murderers and gargoyles instead?" She held up a hand to stop his reply, wincing at her purpling fingers. "Rhetorical question. Lawyers like those. Janx set us up, Alban. He sent us after Grace O'Malley so he'd have time to hire a copycat killer. Vanessa Gray was murdered last night."

Alban's eyes widened, palpable shock rolling off him. "Daisani's assistant? That Vanessa Gray?"

"That one."

Alban whistled, a long high sound of wind howling through stone, and Margrit looked at him in surprise. "You can whistle?"

His eyebrows wrinkled. "Can't you?"

"Of course, but it's so frivolous. You're sort of stolid. I wouldn't have thought whistling was in a gargoyle's nature."

Alban chuckled. "I don't do it often." Laughter faded into concern. "Do you understand what Gray's death means, Margrit?"

"That Daisani's schedule will be messed up for a week?" Margrit lifted her hand again, dismissing her own flippancy. "I know that Daisani hauled me in this afternoon to tell me I was personally responsible for apprehending the killer. He knows Janx is behind it, but he won't go after him."

"Personally responsible." Alban's voice became quiet. "Had he said that to me, Margrit, my inclination would be to run."

"I did," Margrit admitted in a mumble. "After I threw up." She stepped out of the gargoyle's embrace, shrugging. "But not far, because can you imagine any place on earth that he couldn't find me, if I ran? I can't, and I'm pretty damn sure if there was somewhere, it wouldn't be an island paradise in the Bahamas."

"Mmm. It may be worth considering, regardless."

"I'm not going to run, Alban. Besides, I might've gotten a lead. I had to borrow Janx's cell phone after Malik zotted mine, and I found an overseas number. Maybe it's a place to start. I called Tony with it."

"Tony. Your detective." The words were half a question, and Margrit felt her shoulders go stiff and uncomfortable.

"Not exactly mine. It's complicated." She lifted both hands, index fingers pointed upward, and ducked her head toward them, bringing her thoughts under control. "Not the point. Gray's death was the point. I thought I knew what it meant. Is it more than a thorn in Daisani's side?"

"Far more." Alban's voice dropped and he turned to lean on the table. It creaked beneath his weight, and Margrit winced, taking an inadvertent step backward. "Gray had been with Daisani since the eighteen eighties."

Margrit tilted her head, scrubbing a finger against her

ear. "I'm sorry, what did you say? The early eighties? She must've started working for him when she was about fourteen, then."

Alban looked down at her. "The *eighteen* eighties."

Incredulous laughter broke from Margrit's throat. "The woman was only forty years old."

"Vanessa Gray has been Eliseo Daisani's assistant— among other things—since eighteen eighty-three. Some of the stories about vampires are true."

A cold wave ran through Margrit, numbing her fingers. "What, he made her a vampire?"

Alban shook his head. "No more than I could be made human. But a taste of a vampire's blood can bring long life, Margrit. Very long life. I'm sure the records claim a line of descent, family working for family for generations, but it's the same woman. She was well over a hundred years old."

"People don't live that long," Margrit whispered. The memory of a photograph, an austere bob-haired Vanessa Gray standing beside Dominic Daisani, flashed through her mind. "Jesus. That picture at Daisani's office. It's them, isn't it? Not their grandparents."

Alban inclined his head marginally. "Eliseo Daisani's blood could turn New York into the City of Youth for three generations. Vanessa Gray might have been expected to live centuries, if she'd been allowed to—age naturally, for lack of a better phrase. The blood of vampires is potent stuff."

"So Janx really won this round," Margrit whispered. "Does this kind of thing happen a lot?"

"No. It precipitates a kind of war, Margrit. Brief and violent and destructive. Perhaps a battle more than a war," he said with a quick wave of his hand. "We can't afford wars."

"There aren't enough of you," Margrit murmured.

"And wars tend to be noticed. Especially when fought in the streets of human urban centers."

Margrit nodded, only half listening. "Who's Janx's second? Malik? Does that mean his life is on the line now?"

"That…is a difficult question. Yes," Alban said abruptly. "Very probably. The difficulty is in how. We do not kill our own."

"Malik's not one of Daisani's own."

"We all are, in a way. We Old Races."

"You have to hang together, or you'll most surely hang separately?"

"As your founding fathers aptly said, yes."

"Is that why Janx and Daisani haven't killed each other?"

"I'm not certain they would anyway. They're in the habit of one another, as well. They've been playing this game for a long time." Alban lifted broad shoulders and let them fall again. "But Eliseo may make an example of Malik, despite convention."

"Good," Margrit said viciously, and lifted her chin in defiance as Alban's eyebrows rose. "I don't like him. He scares me."

"Malik scares you."

Margrit's chin rose higher. "Yeah."

"You bargain with Eliseo Daisani, Janx has gained three favors from you and *Malik* frightens you?" Humor colored Alban's voice.

Margrit wrapped her arms around herself defensively. "Janx has his own kind of honor, and Daisani…I don't think

I'm even worth killing. Unless that number doesn't pan out and the guy who killed Vanessa disappears for good. Then I'll probably get to be a six-o'clock-news object lesson. But Malik would hurt me just because he could. What happens if Daisani takes Malik out?"

"In my youth he would have been exiled for such an action," Alban said slowly. "But he held less power in the human world then. Exile from the Old Races would mean comparatively little to him, and those of us who have to deal with him would find ourselves doing so regardless of his status. I don't know, Margrit. Perhaps something like war, after all."

Exile. The word echoed in Margrit's thoughts as she looked up at the gargoyle. "Exile. You mean he'd be an outcast?" She remembered clearly the curl of Cara's lip, the sneer in her voice as she labeled Alban that outcast. The arrogance seemed all the more out of place knowing the selkies were considered mongrels among the Old Races, but the dichotomy hadn't bothered the thin-boned young woman at all.

Alban's eyes glittered as he glanced at her. "Yes." Weight burdened the word, a weight Margrit was certain she wasn't meant to hear or understand. She put her hand out, gripping the table before she spoke.

"Is that what happened to you?"

The gargoyle went still, more profoundly still than any human Margrit had ever seen. Even his hair seemed too heavy to be moved, and his breath seemed as if it might never come again. "I shouldn't be surprised," he said finally. "In a matter of days you've become more conversant with our people than I have been in centuries."

"What happened, Alban?"

"As you surmise," he said after long seconds. "Nothing more and nothing less, Margrit. It isn't something I care to dwell on. Hajnal died and I fled the Old World for the new, with only memories to live with."

"That's all? That's all you're going to tell me?" Margrit leaned forward, as if her intensity might draw more information from the gargoyle. A whisper of presence made itself felt in her mind, alien and familiar all at once, and she curled her fingers, as if she could hook them into shared memory. Her injured hand protested the action, and Alban shifted away, placing a subtle distance between them. Margrit's eyebrows drew down. "What aren't you telling me?"

He turned toward her with a faint smile. "Why do you think there's something I'm not telling you?"

"Because you're not letting memory ride me," Margrit said, suddenly sure of herself. "You're making certain it doesn't."

"I chose long ago not to share memory again, Margrit. I'd have been more cautious earlier if I'd known humans were sensitive to it."

"Why?" she asked, mystified. "Why would you deny yourself that? The memories I got weren't nice ones, but I'd think being alone after sharing a telepathic link with someone would be incredibly depressing." The gargoyle shifted at the accusation, and Margrit caught her breath in recognition of his unintentional admission. "It is, isn't it? How much of being an outcast is self-imposed? Why would you do that to yourself? Are you on a two-century sulk?"

Alban growled deep in his throat, and Margrit smiled, triumphant at forcing a client to acknowledge something he didn't want to see. He wasn't exactly a client, she reminded herself, but the principle remained the same. It was time to back away now, leaving him to stew over her words, making him wrestle with their truth. The tactic proved much more useful than continuing to push, in her experience.

"All right. Okay. I'll let it go this time. We've got enough to deal with right now. What's Janx doing, upsetting the balance like this?"

Alban looked past her, into the bookstore's yellow light beyond the bead curtain. "Making a play I don't understand," he said after a moment. "To make a blow as direct as this one, whatever he's doing, he must be very confident of his position."

"Is Janx ever not confident?" Margrit asked wryly.

Alban blinked, then smiled at her. "No," he admitted. "None of us tend to lack confidence. We've paid the price, though. There aren't many of us left."

"Maybe one more than you think."

"I know," Alban agreed. "The woman Ausra. Grace O'Malley knows her. Knew her," he corrected. "She disappeared years ago."

Margrit stared up at him. "When did you talk to Grace?"

"Just after sunset. She followed us yesterday and found the building I slept on. She was waiting when I woke up."

A chill of irrational jealousy and concern swept over Margrit, lifting the hairs on her arms. "I spent all day worried about you," she muttered childishly. "And she knew where you were?"

"Margrit." Alban tipped her chin up, smiling down at her. "She offered me a daytime haven, nothing more."

Margrit snorted. "So what'd she say about Ausra?"

His smile faded. "Very little. Grace knew what she was, not much more. She was dark-haired and small."

"Like Hajnal," Margrit said.

Alban's eyebrows rose. "How did you know that?"

She looked down, feeling his gaze on her. "I've had a busy evening." The events of the night suddenly overwhelmed her, the list of them leaving her without a place to start. She finally said, "Janx gave me this," and took the sapphire from her pocket. It rolled in her palm, lamps making a bright star on its side, before she met the gargoyle's eyes.

Alban took the stone with thick fingers, the least graceful move she'd ever seen him make. "Where did you—" He broke off, squeezing his eyes closed, and rephrased the question. "Where did he get this?"

"There was another murder tonight," Margrit whispered. "The real killer this time, not Janx's copycat. She left this at the scene."

Alban jerked his head up, meeting Margrit's eyes. "She?"

"Doesn't it have to be? Someone's trying to draw you out, blame you for the deaths of women who looked like Hajnal."

Alban went gray, a bleaching of color that left him less human than before. "How do you know that?" he asked indistinctly. "I didn't want to tell you—to frighten you."

Margrit ducked her head. "I'm not easily frightened, remember?" The reminder of his words brought a brief smile to Alban's face, and she exhaled. "Honestly, I'm already scared, Alban. I'm in way over my head. Anyway, Biali told me. More than told me," she added, remembering the too-vivid shock in Biali's memory at the gargoyle woman's arrival. "I talked to him earlier tonight."

"Biali. Janx. Daisani. Malik. Are there any of the Old Races you haven't had truck with since I last saw you? Biali," Alban repeated, then pressed his mouth in a thin line as he curled his hand around the sapphire. "I suppose I could've guessed. Tell me what it is you think," he said without looking back at her. "Tell me what you've deduced, Margrit. I have no heart for speculation." He seemed to age with the words, until Margrit bit back tears and took a tentative step toward him.

"She didn't die. She got away somehow, and it's taken her this long to find you again. Or maybe she's been waiting for you to expose yourself and talk to somebody. All those other women who died—"

"Daylight hours, Margrit," Alban reminded her heavily. "Hajnal, had she survived that night, could not have killed any of those women. They died during daylight hours."

Margrit bared her teeth, frustrated at the reminder. "All right. Still, you've said you live alone, privately. Maybe you're hard to find."

"I have been so deliberately, though if someone…haunts me…then perhaps I haven't been circumspect enough. Margrit, I saw—"

"You saw her dying. But dawn was close, and you said the stone heals you. Maybe she got away, Alban. Maybe she was too hurt to find you again. Ausra is Hajnal, Alban. I saw it in Biali's memories. She was small and had black hair and amber skin and—"

"What?" Alban's voice went hoarse. "You—what? Rode memory with *Biali?*"

"I didn't mean to. He didn't mean to let me. I was asking him about Ausra and he said he didn't know her, but this time a memory caught me. She walked right up to him and he said, 'You're dead.' I saw it. They're the same person. I think Hajnal must've gone crazy." Insistence lost the battle to sympathy as Margrit concluded her argument.

Alban stared down at her, sightless. "We don't—" he began.

Margrit shook her head. "Somebody who knows about gargoyles is out there killing people, Alban. Somebody who knows about you. Somebody who's willing to risk exposing you all, just to hurt you. If the Old Races are so circumspect, isn't what she's doing insane?"

"It can't be," Alban said, but without conviction. "You… saw her?"

Margrit edged another step forward and wrapped her hands around his, around the sapphire in his palm. "I'm sorry. I know it shouldn't be, but that doesn't mean it can't be. All kinds of things that shouldn't be, are. Like us."

"Us." He looked down at her with weary, questioning eyes. Margrit's heart skipped a beat and she wet her lips, trying for a smile.

"Us," she said again. "I mean, a gargoyle and a lawyer? That can't be written in the book of things that should be."

"Is it wrong?" Alban wondered, without moving. "This thing that shouldn't be?"

"No," she whispered. "No, it's not wrong."

He straightened away from the table, making it creak again, and brushed a taloned finger against her cheek, pushing an errant curl back from her face. "It has been a very long time since someone said my name with hers, and meant us."

Margrit gazed up into his eyes, unable to take a deep breath. "Maybe it's time to start living again, Alban."

' "Perhaps it is." He cupped her cheek in his palm, his hand dwarfing her skull. Smiling, Margrit turned her face into the touch as Alban lowered his head.

Beads rattled, a soft precursor to Chelsea's voice. "Forgive me." She shifted the curtain a few centimeters, enough to look into the back room. "Forgive me, but I thought you needed to know. There are police on the way."

"P⊕LICE?" SH⊕CK +IGH+ENED Margrit's stomach
even as Alban took a few quick steps toward the stairway
leading to the roof. "How did they—"

"Someone must have seen me come in," he growled. "I
should have used the roof."

"But I told Tony that—" Margrit broke off with a soft curse.
"I told him Vanessa's killer was a copycat. There'd be no
reason to retract the APB on you, Alban. You're still their
primary suspect. We've got to get out of here." A sense of the
absurd rose in her as she echoed the words of a hundred bad
movies. "Who knew people actually said things like that?" she
breathed, then followed Alban across the room, stopping at
the foot of the stairs, where he blocked the way. "Go," she said
impatiently. "It's not like I can fly out of here without you.
We've got to find Hajnal, Alban. We've got to stop her. Go!
Move!" She pushed him, which was as effective as trying to
shift a wall.

Beads rattled as Chelsea disappeared back into her bookstore. Alban glanced at the swinging curtain, then slowly

uncurled his palm, where the sapphire rested. "When we were very young, we made a foolish promise to each other."

"What was it?" Margrit squeezed past the gargoyle, taking the stairs two at a time. Alban followed ponderously, stopping again at the first landing while Margrit searched fruitlessly for something to block the door with.

"That if we were ever endangered and separated, we would find the highest place in the city or countryside where we were, and wait every night for a month for the other to come."

"Great." Margrit caught his hand, tugging him up the stairs. Alban followed, as if the only thing keeping him in action was her momentum. "We'll go to the Empire State Building. It's tallest now."

He made a low sound in his throat, loosening his hand and slowing to a stop. Margrit turned back, impatient, to catch a distant look in the blond man's eyes, as if he no longer saw her or the stairs where they stood. "In Paris, it was Notre-Dame. We loved the cathedral and its gargoyles. Once in a while we'd settle there for a day, to be among our human-made brethren. Every night, Margrit." He refocused on her, his expression drawn. "I waited every night for a year. She didn't come. She cannot be alive. Biali's memories must be wrong."

Margrit groaned and took Alban's hand in both of hers, putting her whole weight into pulling him, without effect. "We'll never know if we don't try. Come on, Alban."

"Margrit, it was centuries ago, and she never came."

Exasperation overtook her. "Do you have a better idea? You could go back downstairs and let the police arrest you, for example. I'm sure they'd be very understanding at seven-thirty when the sun comes up and you turn into a block of rock, which you've already got for brains. Come *on*, Alban!"

Irritation flooded his face, the first real expression since she'd suggested Hajnal was alive. He looked up the circling stairway, then flexed his shoulders. "Do you insist on climbing all of these on foot?"

"I wouldn't mind a faster route if you'd like to give me a hand. Are you with me now?"

Another grumble sounded low in his throat, but Alban offered a hand, a slow, graceful movement. Margrit plucked the sapphire out of his other hand and put it back in her pocket, shrugging when he looked askance at her. "So it won't get dropped."

"I wouldn't drop it." He closed his fingers around hers, pulling her into his embrace, and she heard words that went unspoken: *no more than I would drop you.* "Hold on," he said above her ear. "There isn't room here for my wings, and leaping requires both hands."

"I'm a runner, Alban," Margrit muttered against his chest. "My strength's in my thighs, not my arms."

After a tension-charged moment, he replied with humor, "Remember this was your idea."

He slid his hands under her bottom and lifted her as if she weighed nothing, wrapping her thighs around his waist. Margrit barely contained a shriek of laughter, ducking her face against his shoulder to smother a shout that would bring the police to the stairwell in seconds. She locked her ankles behind him, then leaned back, grinning as heat colored her face. Her heartbeat scampered faster when she met Alban's cautious eyes, inches from her own. She ducked her head forward, bumping her nose against his, and Alban responded to the intimate invitation.

Margrit's breath disappeared; awareness of his strength and closeness superseding all else. Clarity descended, making her hands tingle with knowledge of the thing that lay between them, as yet unbreached. It would remain that way unless Margrit acted, Alban's nature precluding such a thing.

Should and *ought to* were washed aside in favor of the hunger she'd been trying to ignore. For an instant they were simply two people sharing desire, Alban's mouth as soft as any man's, Margrit's fingers tight at his nape. They were both wordless, breathless, when they broke apart, Margrit's eyes wide until a broad grin overtook her.

"This was my idea?"

He arched pale eyebrows, smiling. "I wouldn't want you to fall." He cupped a hand at the back of her head, drawing her nearer. "You'll still need to hold on, Margrit. Hold close."

She put her cheek against his neck, nodding. "I am. Don't let go."

"Never." Muscle bunched under her thighs as he crouched, then uncoiled in a burst of power, leaping upward with dizzying strength. She squeaked, a constricted sound as much of laughter-filled panic as fresh desire, the play of Alban's body against hers feeling far more personal than even the kiss they'd shared. Her bottom brushed his thighs again as he landed against the edge of a stair, the abrupt stop lasting only a few seconds before he leaped again. Eyes closed, Margrit felt the strength of his arms as he darted toward the roof. It seemed as though the power in his hands must dent the railings he clung to for brief moments, but there was no sound of rent metal, only her own near-silent laughter, muffled against his shoulder.

The landing at the top of the stairs was different, more solid. Margrit dared lift her head for a moment, wide-eyed. "Are we still alive?"

Alban tucked his hand against her bottom to lodge her more firmly around his waist as he pushed the roof access door open and stepped through. "Quite." The door banged behind them and Alban broke into a loping run. "Hold on."

"I am!" The words turned into a helpless shriek as he planted a hand on the waist-high roof wall and vaulted it with ease, flinging them into the air. Wind rushed, screaming past her ears and snapping hair into her face, and then Alban, wrapped in her embrace, transformed.

The soft implosion shot through her at every contact point, an erotic charge that weakened her muscles more thoroughly than any lover's touch ever had. For an instant she was falling, unable to cling to the gargoyle any longer.

As if he expected it, Alban took her weight and pulled her close again. Margrit whimpered, rescue too close at hand for fear to prompt the tiny sound. Instead it was born of desire powerful enough to make her languid and needy, cradled in Alban's arms. She nuzzled his neck, making another senseless little noise as she tasted desire sharp enough to be tears in the back of her own throat. The faintest thought intruded, that soaring above the streets of New York in search of a killer was a wildly inappropriate time to give in to need.

Irrational, she thought, and it brought her back enough to prod muscle into responding. She hugged Alban closer, and he turned his mouth against her hair, murmuring, "Don't worry. I will never let you fall."

"I know." Margrit pressed her lips against his throat, her eyes closed. "I know."

"She's not here, Margrit." Alban came up to her side, hands in his pockets, shoulders tense, the intimacy of their flight lost as they renewed their search for Hajnal.

Margrit leaned against the concrete barrier, fingers laced in the latticework wire that prevented jumpers. "Doesn't it look peaceful down there?" Headlights and taillights streaked, eighty-six stories below, the sounds of the city faint when they could be heard at all. "I used to love coming up here when I was a kid. I'd scare the hell out of my Mom. Dad would put me up on the wall—" she bumped her elbow against the barrier "—and I'd hang on to the wire with both hands and look out. Once I tried climbing up to the bars." She nodded upward at the curving steel spikes above her head. "Mom nearly had a heart attack. There's a picture of me doing that, like a baby Spider-Man."

"Margrit." Impatience filled his voice. "She's not here. Why stay?"

Margrit tilted her head to the side, looking up at him. "Because we paid twelve dollars each to ride up the elevator, and I want to look around?"

Alban's expression soured. Margrit smiled, lowering her voice. "We couldn't just land here, Alban. The observation deck's open till midnight."

"There are very few people around," he muttered back. "It would've been safe."

"Maybe." She leaned against the wires again. "But I like the elevator. I used to think that being this high would show me how to fly. Anything that can get this high should be able to fly, shouldn't it?" She spread her arms, spinning slowly. "But I never learned how."

"You can fly now," Alban murmured. Margrit bumped her hip against his, smiling as she looked up at him.

"I can," she agreed in a whisper. "It's like magic." She curled her arms around his neck, leaning her head back to look up at the floors above the observation deck, then let go with a start. "This isn't the top floor, Alban."

He glanced up. "I know."

"So it's not the highest point in the city." Margrit gestured upward. "There used to be rooftop access below the tower. A gargoyle could still get up there."

Alban's jaw tightened and he stepped back. "Wait here." With a perfunctory look around, he sprang upward, shifting into gargoyle form midaction.

Margrit watched him climb toward the upper floors. "Where would I go?" she murmured to herself before turning back to the view. She was half-asleep on her feet, supporting herself with throbbing fingers wrapped through the wires, when Alban touched her shoulder. Margrit yelped, yanking her hands free, then swore and stuffed them under her arms while she blinked tears away and scowled at Alban.

"My apologies."

"It's okay," she muttered. "Did you find anything?"

He opened his hand silently. A tiny model of a Gothic cathedral sat in his palm, with a tower, complete with miniature scaffolding, at one end.

"That's Saint John the Unfinished. It's right next to my apartment."

Alban, despite the tight line of his mouth, chuckled. "I believe it's Saint John the Divine."

Margrit widened her eyes with innocence. "Isn't that what I said?" She left humor behind, squinting up at the tower. "She must have put it there. Why Saint John?"

"It's Episcopalian," Alban said. "Like Trinity. Perhaps it's a warning. Telling me she knows my daytime hiding spot."

Margrit's shoulders straightened as she caught her breath. "You believe me now?"

He folded his hand over the miniature, his hesitation clear. "I don't see how it's possible, Margrit."

She touched his closed fingers. "I know, but we don't have anything better to go on. Isn't moving forward and exploring the chance better than holding still and not knowing?"

"My people are made of stone," Alban said, a whisper of wryness in his voice. "To remain still is natural."

"Yeah, well, it's killing people. *My* people. How do I convince you? If the sapphire isn't enough, if the carving isn't enough, if me seeing Biali's memory isn't enough, then what does it take?"

"Memory…" Alban's colorless eyes lost focus, his gaze looking through Margrit instead of at her. Then his shoulders grew tense and he shook his head. "No."

"What?" She tightened her hands over his. "What was that thought, Alban? Come on. You said—you said your telepathy was your people's way of sharing memories. Does that mean you can—" She caught her breath, taking half a step back so she could see him more clearly. "It means you can access other gargoyles' memories, doesn't it?"

"I have not shared memory in two centuries, Margrit. Even if they let me back in I may not be able to sift through the memories to find the truth of Biali's recollections."

"Let you back in? How could they stop you?"

"Those nearby can sense it when we step into memory. With focus, someone can be driven out."

"Why would they do that?"

His gaze flickered to hers, then away again. "Outcast," Margrit said after a moment. "Exile. That's how you're punished, by not being allowed to join the memories. What'd you do, Alban?"

"That," he said, "is not my story to tell. No," he added more sharply, as Margrit drew a breath to protest. "No. Let it be enough for you to know that my people do not refuse to share memory. At most we will exclude a specific memory, and even that returns to the whole when we die."

Margrit made a fist of her hand, clenching her teeth when her fingers ached. "All right, fine." She pushed away the questions she wanted to ask, finding another facet to focus on. "If Hajnal is dead her memories ought to be part of the whole. You know her better than anybody. Better than you know Biali. Look for *her* memories in the gestalt. If she's there, we'll know what happened and we'll know Ausra is someone else."

"Gestalt," Alban echoed quietly. "Is there nothing you humans do not have a word for?" He dismissed the question by following at once with another, his expression bleak as he looked down at Margrit. "Do you insist on this?"

"Yeah." She heard herself draw the word out incredulously, sounding like a teenager. "Yes. You've got to try, Alban. If they won't let you back in, we'll cross that bridge, but this is the best way to be sure of who we're dealing with. Besides, how many of them are there around here to play watchdog?"

A corner of Alban's mouth curled up, so slowly it was obviously against his will. "Gargoyles are very good watchdogs, Margrit. There are not many nearby, but there may be enough. I'll try," he added before she could work up another argument. "I'll try, but this is not a good place to do so from. Entering memory is usually best done in private."

"We could go back to my place." The offer sounded so natural and so absurd Margrit laughed, clapping a hand over her mouth at Alban's quizzical glance. "Sorry," she said through her fingers. "Just, you know, that's sort of a stereotypical invitation to…" Heat built in her cheeks when his expression grew more curious. "Nothing. Nevermind. We can go somewhere else."

All her humor fled and she turned an inappropriate glower toward the streets below. "Maybe to the safe house Grace offered you."

Alban slipped a finger beneath her chin, not quite touching her, but encouraging her to look up. "I would be honored," he said quietly, "to accept your offer of your home as a haven."

Margrit puffed her cheeks out and exhaled noisily, feeling chagrin slip away into embarrassment. "Oh. Okay. We could stop by the cathedral on the way. It's just up the street from my apartment."

"A glide-over," Alban agreed. "Perhaps she's waiting for us there."

A note of suppressed hope rang through his voice, making Margrit's heart tighten. "You really don't want to do this, do you."

"No." He slipped an arm around her waist and curled one of her arms up around his neck, turning his head as he checked for spectators on the observation deck. A young couple rounded the corner and disappeared from sight. Alban shifted in Margrit's arms, clearing the safety mesh with an easy leap. "But I will do it for you."

TWENTY-EIGHT

THE DISTANT STREETS seemed as serene as they had from the building, New York's frenetic pace left behind. Margrit turned her face against Alban's shoulder, trusting him to hear even as the wind ripped her question away. "Is it always like this?"

Above her, Alban shook his head. "It's not always so calm. These last few days have been unusually so." He paused, then added judiciously, "At least, as far as the wind is concerned."

"The calm before the storm? I wonder what's coming, then." Margrit lifted a hand to block wind from her eyes, watching Central Park increase in size as they soared closer to it, banking to the west. "It doesn't look like there's anything but peace down there. Maybe that's why you've been able to stay out of it for so long. Because you see the world from above."

"You are too generous." Alban's voice was a basso rumble by her ear before he nodded below. "The cathedral."

Margrit twisted, looking down. "Huh. It really is a cross."

"Cathedrals usually are."

Margrit tried to elbow him without unwinding her arms

from around him, then merely wrinkled her nose. "I'm not used to seeing them from above. Some of us don't get the bird's-eye view as a matter of course, you know." She studied the cathedral as they soared over it, Alban keeping high in the sky as he made slow loops through the air. "I live at the other end of the street and haven't even been here since the fire," Margrit admitted guiltily. "I used to do the vertical tours, but you can't anymore."

"I've never been on one."

"You could climb to the top of the cathedral on the spiral staircases. I loved it." Margrit paused. "If she was here, where would she be?"

"*I* would be at the tower," Alban replied after a moment's hesitation of his own. "The highest point. Hold tight." He dropped into a dive tempered by the flutter of wind against partially folded wings.

Margrit swallowed a yelp, knotting her arms around his neck and struggling with laughter that was half terrified, half gleeful. Their plummet ended with a snap of his wings, catching air again to bring them up in a swoosh only a few dozen feet above the cathedral tower. Margrit's heart hammered against Alban's chest, giggles running through her.

"I can't decide if that's the best thing ever or tantamount to suicide," she said against his collarbone.

He tightened an arm around her briefly, solid and comforting. "I've been doing this a long time. You're in no danger."

Margrit nodded, then loosened one arm to look down as Alban circled the tower. "I don't see anyone. Should we land?"

Alban rumbled disapproval. "I'd prefer not to endanger you in that way. It may be that I can't fall, but you don't share that advantage. I see no one, either. Perhaps the carving is nothing more than a warning." His wings pumped as he spoke, bringing them higher into the city night.

"Maybe. But why would she bother? It seems more like a game of cat and mouse to me. Like it's a clue." Margrit twisted to look back at the receding cathedral. "I think we should look more carefully."

"I will," Alban promised. "But not with you so vulnerable. Do you have a rooftop access key?" He wheeled again, bringing them down on top of Margrit's apartment building.

"Uh. Yeah, I think so." She stepped out of the gargoyle's arms to gingerly slide her hand into a pocket. It came out with keys dangling from her fingertips. "Here we go."

"All right. I'll check the tower and come to your balcony in a few minutes."

Margrit laughed. "That's going to be kind of hard to explain if either Cam or Cole are home, Alban. I can wait here."

A furrow appeared between his eyebrows. "I don't like the idea of leaving you alone."

Margrit's laughter faded to a crooked smile. "I've gotten along without you for this long, Alban. Look, if you don't want to leave me, we can walk down to the cathedral after you try the gestalt for information. All right?"

He tilted his head, birdlike for all his size, and murmured, "You've gotten along with me guarding you for this long," before nodding. "All right. I hadn't thought of the balcony being a problem," he admitted as she unlocked the rooftop door. "Too accustomed to flight, I suppose."

"Isn't that a sort of dangerous habit?" Margrit's question echoed in the stairwell, the fire door clanging shut behind them. "Wouldn't it be safer to walk places instead of risking a fire escape or an alley for changing your form?"

"Yes." A note of strain came into Alban's voice and Margrit glanced over her shoulder at him, curious. He'd returned to his human form while she wasn't watching, his expression dark, eyebrows drawn down and his mouth thin. "It would be much safer. There would be no chance of being noticed in the skies, or caught unawares by a deal going on in the dark."

"So why risk it?"

"Margrit." His voice altered, deepened even more, and she turned again in time to see his wings snap out, flaring in the narrow stairwell. He looked barely contained, all raw earthy power, with one taloned hand turned up in supplication. The other curved around the railing, less for support than to show the dangerous strength in those hands: beneath his grip, steel buckled, all too ready to give way to his demand.

Embarrassment and desire crept up by degrees, heating Margrit's cheeks as she stared at the unearthly being on the stairs above her. His chest rose and fell in tight breaths, as if the air wasn't enough to sustain him, and his gaze, usually so colorless, was dark and demanding. Margrit took one step toward him, reaching out to put her fingertips against his diaphragm. He shuddered under the touch, and his upturned hand slowly closed in a fist. "I have lost much to your people." Gentleness was gone from his voice, leaving granite to scrape across Margrit's ears. "I will not let you take the skies."

"I'm sorry." The words were a blurted whisper on the edge of a rising tide of overwhelming sorrow. Margrit slid her fingers up his chest, marveling at the smoothness of his skin, like polished stone. She pulled herself onto the stair with him, then onto the one above, where she was tall enough to sink her hands into his hair. "I'm sorry," she whispered again, and found his mouth with her own, driven by a desperation she'd never known.

He made a small sound, surprise coupled with urgency, and lifted her as easily as he had earlier. Margrit wrapped her legs around his waist, fingers knotted in his hair, her tongue seeking his insistently. Her heartbeat took the air from her lungs, turning it into heat that spilled through her body. She laughed, breathless soft noise that bounced against concrete walls, and shimmied out of her jacket, letting it fall to the steps.

"Margrit." Alban rasped her name, breaking the kiss long enough to put his forehead against hers, his breath coming in quick gasps. "Margrit, we're in a stairwell."

She leaned back, looking down nine floors to the bottom of the shaft, then turned a sly smile on the pale creature who held her. "Yeah. We are."

"You can't…" His protest trailed off as she deliberately undid the buttons of her blouse and let it slip from her shoulders with a whisper of silk. Alban's gaze slid from the curve of her breasts within her bra, to her eyes, then back again, astonishment warring with prudence and want.

"Yeah. I can. I really can." Margrit laced her fingers into his hair again, teasing his earlobe with her lips and tongue. "If I take your pants off you now, will they be gone in your other form?"

Alban laughed, a throaty sound of amazement. "No. You'll have to do it all over again."

"That," Margrit breathed, "has promise. But not right now. Sit."

"What?" He sank down even as he asked the question, wings folding behind him. Margrit unwound her legs from around his waist, settling on his lap as she slipped her hand over his shoulder and traced one of the delicate-looking tarsals. Alban caught his breath, arching under the touch, and Margrit laughed, a quiet sound of delight.

"Sensitive," she whispered. "Very nice. Now change."

"What?" he asked again.

She leaned back, laughter dancing on her lips. "Change. I don't want to have to undress you twice, but more to the point, I'm sorry, Alban, but you're almost two feet taller than me and I've seen you naked in this form. I'm just not that brave."

His brows furrowed, injury clear in his expression. "Am I that...oh," he said with dawning clarity. "*Oh.* Oh. Yes." The last word was accompanied by an implosion of space, Margrit squealing a laugh as his lap shifted and became human in size. "Margrit..."

She arched an eyebrow playfully. "Don't tell me you're too staid and proper for horsing around in the stairwell."

"No," Alban said hastily, then hesitated and amended ruefully, "Yes, probably." Despite herself, Margrit laughed again, the bright sound reverberating down the stairs. Still rueful, he murmured, "But I was thinking more that while I may not feel cold the way humans do, concrete steps are still far from comfortable."

"Humph. I thought men were supposed to be willing to

forgo creature comforts at any time for the sake of a little nookie." She couldn't put censure into her teasing, instead dropping her mouth to kiss his throat again.

Alban ducked his head over hers, curling her against his chest. "Perhaps," he whispered. "But I am not a man."

"So you keep reminding me." Margrit slid her hand down his stomach and beneath his waistband. He drew in a sharp breath, lifting his head as his eyes dilated. She glanced up, putting her lips against his mouth before whispering, "But I think you'll do." Then she scooped her blouse from the floor and slipped it on without buttoning it, before putting her jacket back on.

"All right, Alban 'Mr. Propriety' Korund. We'll go downstairs to the apartment. But if my housemates are awake, you're just going to have to suffer through a concrete-numbed butt." She leaned in for another lingering kiss, then climbed off his lap and offered a hand, which he took as he stood.

"You make a compelling argument."

"Of course I do. It's my job." Margrit wound her fingers through his to lead him down the stairs.

"*Margrit.* We've been trying to call you back all—shit!" The door swung open before Margrit had time to turn the key in the lock, Cole's worried expression turning to outright alarm as he took in the man behind her. The heat of desire fled as Margrit lifted her hands guiltily.

"It's okay, Cole. Cole. It's all right. You heard my messages, right? That the cops know it wasn't Alban?" She delivered the reminder with all the cool certainty she'd learned to project in law school, utterly ignoring the minor detail that she skirted the truth so widely it might as well have been an outright lie.

"Yeah." Cole's jaw set as he stared at Alban. "He can't come in, Margrit."

"That only works on vampires, Cole," Margrit muttered beneath her breath, then shot a look over her shoulder at Alban. The corner of his mouth twisted upward and he shook his head, a tiny motion. Margrit felt herself bare her teeth, aware that it was a very human and aggressive response to yet another myth shattered. "Cole, you've got to trust me. Alban needs a quiet spot to—to meditate—for a while, and this is the only place I can think of to go."

"Excuse me," Cole said through his teeth to Alban, and wrapped a hand around Margrit's biceps, pulling her into the apartment. He closed the door on the gargoyle as she jerked away, offended at the manhandling, and glowered up at him with a temper only slightly offset by knowing his behavior was born of concern for her.

"What the hell do you think you're doing, Grit?" Cole demanded quietly. "It's eleven at night and you're running around New York with a suspected murderer? You're bringing him to your *house*? Cam's and my house? You're— Margrit, your *shirt* is undone!"

She looked down to where her blouse fell open beneath her coat, her lacy bra clearly visible. She knotted a hand in the silk, closing it again. "I need you to trust me, Cole."

"What about *Tony*? I thought you two—"

"Cole!" Margrit let go of her shirt, her hand cramping from tension. "Cole, I don't have time for recriminations right now. We won't be here long. We've just got to do something—"

"Yeah." He sneered, shooting a too-obvious look at Margrit's open blouse. "I bet you do."

Rage surged through her, so hot she didn't know she'd moved until her hand cracked across Cole's face, leaving a palm print that first bleached white, then curdled red. It took a will of iron to not follow with another blow, this time with a closed fist. "How dare you." Her voice was so low it sounded distorted to her own ears. "How *dare* you."

Unable to trust herself, she turned away and opened the door, noting Alban's distressed expression in one glimpse before carefully, so carefully, closing the door quietly behind her. She was afraid to give in and slam it, afraid the release of fury would shatter the tenuous control she held on herself. She couldn't remember hitting anyone since she was a child, and had now struck two men inside a week. An accusation hung on her lips: *What have you done to me?* as she stared up at Alban, hardly able to see him for the white rage still dancing through her vision.

"We're leaving." Margrit began walking toward the staircase, a blind, automatic action that had no purpose beyond getting them somewhere else. She went up, not down, an unconscious choice in deference to the gargoyle with her, though as they approached the rooftop door she asked, "Is this what happens? Is this what happens to people—humans—who get involved with the Old Races? Their ordinary lives just fall apart?"

The accusation was unfair and she knew it; she'd chosen to take Alban's part. *Fair,* though, didn't hold weight against her anger.

"Margrit, I'm sorry." The words seemed to take all of Alban's strength. "I shouldn't have involved you. I *am* sorry.

I'll leave you. Whoever is behind this, it's not your affair, and I shouldn't have turned to you for help."

"Oh, no." She stopped a few feet from the access door, turning to look down the steps at the gargoyle. It seemed hardly possible that only minutes ago they had been entangled in passion on these same stairs. "I don't think so, Alban. If my normal life is going to fall apart, I'm goddamned good and sure going to see through to the end what's sending it to hell. This is not…" She reached for the railing, curling her injured fingers around it for support as she gritted her teeth. "This is not your fault. I'm sorry. I'm completely fucking furious at Cole right now, and you're here, so I'm taking it out on you." Her speech was too careful, the vestiges of anger still coloring it, but it was the best she could do. "This is my way of not bursting into tears because I'm so pissed off," she added with a thin smile. "Sorry. Look." She tightened her fingers on the railing until the ache in them began to overwhelm the boiling anger that seemed to make up her insides. "Look, I don't know where else to go for privacy. What about your apartment, the one you took me to when the car hit me?"

"It is my fault," Alban disagreed quietly, but passed a hand through the air as irritation distorted Margrit's features again. "I thank you," he murmured. "For choosing my path despite the cost to yourself. I am sorry for that cost, Margrit. I…didn't think." He exhaled then, glancing down the stairwell. "If I'd only thought of that apartment first," he said a bit dryly.

Unexpected even to herself, Margrit released a short staccato laugh that helped shatter some of the discord within her. "If you had, we'd be having a lot more fun right now. Should we go there?"

Alban's gaze flickered to hers, wry as he understood too clearly that she was not making a proposition. "If you wish. It's likely here is as good a place as any, though." He indicated the stairwell with a graceful sweep of his hand. "Unless many people use the stairs this late at night."

"Most people use the elevator at any hour. If the stairs are quiet and private enough, why didn't you just say so in the first place?"

"Margrit." Alban turned a steady look on her. "When a beautiful woman invites you to her apartment, only a fool says no. I may not be a man, but I'm also not a fool."

Another laugh broke free, a choked sound of surprise and confused pleasure. Margrit took one step down and Alban slipped his arms around her, sighing against her hair. "I am sorry," he said once more. "The darkness and quiet of a private room would have been pleasant, but this will do. Better here than outside, where the cold would harm you, or wasting the time to return to my other apartment. Keep watch, Margrit, and I'll see what memory can tell me."

TWENTY-NINE

IT WAS NOT as he remembered it.

He recalled a peak thrusting toward the stars in a clear, midnight blue sky. Now that peak was hidden by dark clouds that roiled with the movement of his wings. Fog stirred around him, a fine mist against his skin, almost rain. There was no easy passage, no welcoming sense of being a small part of a greater whole. He'd given that up centuries earlier, yet still found the lack unexpected.

No matter. Memory could be clouded, but never forgotten. He knew his own path there, and for over a century, Hajnal's had run beside it. They were intertwined, and no mere fog could keep him away from her.

He banked and rolled in the air, closing his eyes against wind and spitting water, letting old familiarity guide him where vision could not. Shadows closed around him, mountains of memory belonging to those whom he had grown up among. Those peaks were to be trusted, no more changeable than the sun's path in the sky.

But there was a bleakness to them that he didn't

remember. A sense, unfamiliar to him, of being worn down by time. Too many of those mountains no longer grew, he realized, their reaching peaks stunted by their creators' deaths.

How many? The question lanced through him, a pang of regret. Deliberately avoiding his own people for so long had left him less knowledgeable about their numbers. Aside from the recent meeting with Biali, Alban could not clearly remember the last time he'd spoken with one of his own.

Which had been the point of exile. "The Breach," Grace had said accusingly. Alban drifted in memory, tasting the wound of that word. It, too, was something he couldn't clearly remember last hearing, though that may have been due more to a deliberate reluctance on his part. Biali was not above throwing cutting words, working to provoke a fight wherever he could.

Blackness boiled up in the clouds, a wall forming out of the fog. Nearby memory-mountains darkened, seeming to move closer, until the space in which he unfurled his wings felt tight and constricting. Alban inhaled, filling his lungs and broadening his chest, an act of defiance against claustrophobia.

"You don't belong here, Korund." The voice should not have surprised him, though it did: Biali's gravely tones. The one gargoyle with whom he'd had contact was now the one to stand in his way. For the first time Alban wondered if the scarred gargoyle had been asked to stay near him, in order to provide just this kind of barrier from the memories. Certainly no one else of their people would be as enthusiastic about the prospect of thwarting him. It was not the nature of gargoyles to hold grudges, but then, neither did stone forget easily.

Clouds whirled in circles, black and gray streaming together with the beat of wings, and Biali's thick form came out of the mist, his scarred face curled in a sneer. Weight came behind him, the ponderous weight of time and memory; of disapproval, as heavy as mountains. As the closest to him physically, Biali stood guardian against Alban's intrusion into the memory of their people, but he carried the support of others with him. All around him, mist dripped and formed into solid streaks, building a granite wall between Alban and his destination.

"She was my mate, Biali. Don't I have the right to visit her memories?"

"No." The gargoyle gave no quarter, the sound of rock slides thundering in his voice. "No longer."

Alban flexed his wings, feeling dampness catch and trickle down the membranes. "I defeated you once before."

"Centuries ago. You were young. You had passion. You have nothing now, Korund. Turn back. You're not welcome among us any longer." Biali's wings flickered, keeping him aloft in the memory of mind as the wall grew higher behind him.

"I would walk the path my mate knew," Alban whispered. "I would see her last moments."

"You could've done that two hundred years ago. Instead you made yourself something we had no word for. Your chance is lost. Leave this place." Biali's massive chest flexed, his hands curving into dangerous talons, every action a prelude to battle. "Leave, or make me force you out." Dark hope infused the last words, so raw Alban backwinged, moving a short distance away.

The scarred gargoyle was right. Three hundred years ago he'd had passion and youth on his side. Two centuries of exile now made him a poor match against a gargoyle whose employ for the past fifty years had been thuggery. For a few seconds Alban hesitated, caught in the swirling mists and watching the wall betwixt himself and his goal grow taller. Easier, surely, to let it go.

And let Margrit die.

There was no surety in the thought; Margrit had not been threatened. Other women, yes, but not even women Alban had watched, making the connection tenuous at best. Tenuous, and yet they'd had a look about them… Dark hair, often marked with curls; flawless skin, pale to olive in tone. Vanessa Gray, with her straight brown hair, had been the least like the others, and she'd died for the game between Janx and Daisani. But more, she'd died because the killer who haunted Alban's steps had created a circumstance in which Vanessa might be removed. For the one, Alban could have let it slip by. But for the other, and for the determination in Margrit's gaze, he raised his eyes to look across heavy fog at his rival.

"I will pass." Simply spoken, the phrase had the weight of ritual to it. Pleasure glittered in Biali's gaze, the only acknowledgment that battle had been agreed upon.

He exploded forward, leaving behind the protective wall. Alban folded his wings and dropped, not a dive, simply a plummet that took him out of Biali's space inside an instant. Wind and the weight of his falling body made his wings scream in protest when he snapped them open again, climbing below Biali, his goal the foreboding wall.

Biali slammed into him from behind, driving them both

into the black barrier. It gave with the impact, shuddering around them. Memory, the stuff of its being, fragmented, shards flying loose to embed themselves in Alban's being.

A woman's presence shattered through his mind. Worn with travel, but proud, she had translucent skin, tinted gold and delicate features half-hidden by hair blackened and heavy with rain. Beautiful, delicate, she was a creature of obsidian and amber, carved by a master.

"Hajnal." Alban's voice broke even in the depths of memory. The woman lifted her eyes, meeting his with a dark gaze cold and empty as a winter night. There was no recognizable music to her memory, no hint that her path had lain with his for over a century. Only rage and betrayal shimmered in her eyes. She lifted a hand to strike, and Alban waited for the blow, too astounded at the bleakness within her to resist.

Memory shredded and tore away with Biali's howl of anger. Wakefulness came back to Alban, rain lashing his skin as the fog seemed to respond to Biali's cry, intensifying into a storm. Alban reached for the wall, clawing at it as if doing so would grant him access to the recollections that had been torn away. Biali's weight hit him in the back and he roared, snapping into a ball—a vulnerable, dangerous position. He dropped again, skidding and bouncing against the wall of memory. On the third bounce he acted, straightening his legs as he hit. Momentum shoved him upward, hands clawed to sink into Biali's shoulders as the other gargoyle dived toward him. Flesh gave more easily than he expected, Biali bellowing with pain as Alban tore skin and sinew, releasing not blood, but a flood of memory.

Amber skin and pale, locked together in the sky.

Rage and betrayal exploded in Alban's breast, fury at the inconceivable. The laughter of pleasure rode on the wind, and for an instant Alban saw through memory to recognize a vivid sneer of triumph smeared across Biali's scarred face. Then remembrance swept over him again, a barrage of impossible truths.

They stood on a precipice, circling one another warily, no longer the men they could pretend to be, but primal creatures of earth and stone. The sky above was the same slate-gray, nighttime clouds lit from behind by a determined moon. The embattled gargoyles stood out, slashes of blinding white against duller tones. Others gathered to watch; foremost among them stood Hajnal, her delicate features creased with concern and anger. Her skin beneath the diffuse moonlight was milkier than in Biali's more recent memories, both creatures now coloring history with their own perspectives.

Three centuries on from that fight, Alban still felt the talon-ripping horror of stone shattering beneath his blow, Biali's face half torn away. Alban shuddered, old pain remembered anew, and Biali leaped forward again, landing a blow as crippling as that one had been, hundreds of years earlier.

It was difficult to remember that the battle was not in truth physical, but fought in the corridors of memory, with strength of the mind instead of strength of the body. Alban shouted in pain, feeling moments of his own, hoarded close, torn loose from him. There was no telling, from his side, what slipped free; no way to know what exploded from his close-kept secrets into Biali's consciousness, and from there, when the sharing came, to the greater memory banks.

So many things. Regret lanced through him, a pain as real as bodily harm. So many secrets kept, to risk being lost here and now. Alban pulled his lips back from his teeth, snarling as he bent to the attack again. They'd lost flight somehow, rolling and sliding across the surface of the memory wall, as if it had come to encompass the two of them in a sphere safely away from the stony mountains that made up the greater gargoyle memory.

He did not remember landing the blow that opened a new wave of memories for him to sift through. His own hands—Biali's hands—covering smaller ones, the golden tint to her skin played up brightly against the near white of his own. Carving soft stone together, making tiny figures that settled into a peg-holed board. His hands guided hers, a sense of proprietary pride in each small cut of the knife. First gargoyles, carved to perch on the high places of a city built onto the board, then human figures. Women, all of them, as frail in reality as the figures seemed in massive gargoyle hands. Then wings through the air, the creak of scaffolding, and the carvings left behind to brave cold New York nights.

He felt his head crack to the side, his cheek split open to release another smattering of recollections. Even in the midst of battle he curled his fingers, as if doing so would call memory back to him, keep it safe and protected within him. It couldn't, didn't, happen that way, and a howl of protest broke free from his throat. Biali's laugh, rough and sour, cut through it, as if the other gargoyle considered Alban's cry a weakness.

Outside of memory, outside, it seemed, of time, Alban saw Biali lift his hands, doubled together to make a stony hammer, and swing them toward his skull.

* * *

Silent as stone, still as stone. Margrit watched the gargoyle and the stairs, one more than the other; footsteps would echo if anyone used the stairwell, and Alban's immobility was fascinating. He breathed, if only just. Margrit held her own breath in order to be still enough to see the incremental lift and fall of his chest.

Mist floated around her and swirled away again, the experience clearly not her own. There were glimpses, nothing more, of what Alban saw: a mountain range wreathed in fog, each peak carved into a rugged, stony gargoyle form. She struggled among the frozen statues, trying to find her way. A surge of determination rose up through the struggle, pushing her back: Alban, rejecting her from the gargoyle gestalt as surely as he thought he himself might be rejected. There would be no shared memory between them if he had his way, and as the gray walls of the stairwell reasserted themselves, it seemed he would.

A vivid pulse of color broke through fog and gray walls alike: a slender redheaded man with laughing jade eyes, his gaudy crimson cloak thrown back to show a high-collared shirt with a ruff at the throat. A second man, smaller and swarthy, with his black hair tied back in a ponytail, made a dour counterpoint to the redhead, his own clothes dark and well-fitted, a long black coat worn over them. Both were dwarfed by the size and power of Alban's human form, almost as pale as his gargoyle shape. He, too, wore fashionable clothing from another era, his own long hair held by a sapphire ribbon matching a cloak that only emphasized the breadth of his shoulders. The three stood facing one another, an agreeable standoff that ended with a sweep of crimson cloak as the redhead bowed sardonically to the other two.

A woman stalked through the gathering, turning the figures to wisps of fog. Her skin was copper, her black hair fell in lush waves around her shoulders, and her gaze, dark and forthright, looked through memory directly at Margrit. She slid a hand over her belly, a gesture old as man itself that told Margrit the woman carried a child, for all that there was no hint of it yet in her form.

Then, with a savage wrench, that image was ripped apart, exposing a gargoyle woman bent in the rain. She appeared sallow in the dull light, her hair tangled and dripping in midnight curls. Her wings flared and she cried out, a sound Margrit echoed aloud, clapping her hands over her mouth.

Bullet holes riddled the gargoyle's wings, blackened her skin in places; pain and rage were made manifest in the play of powerful muscles beneath torn skin. She shoved herself upward, kneeling in the rain, and threw her head back to howl defiance to the rising sun.

Stone swept over her, catching her in all her tattered agony. Margrit flinched, biting the ball of her palm to keep from crying out again as the memory fled.

Alban caught his breath, sharp and unexpected after so many minutes of stillness. As if the sound released her, Margrit's knees buckled and she knelt beside him, dizzy. Alban put a hand out, steadying her, then met her gaze with his own.

"She lives." His voice, always gravelly, was even rougher than usual. Once certain Margrit was steady, he released her, bringing a hand to his head and grimacing. "Biali defeated me in the memories. I…could not follow them into the

heart of it, to see how she survived, but I saw her. Through
his eyes. They have…" a note of bewildered hurt came into
his voice "mated. She seemed so cold. As if I didn't know
her at all, Margrit. As if she'd become someone else."

"Ausra," Margrit whispered. "She did become somebody
else. People, humans, do it all the time, Alban. They do
whatever they have to, to survive. If that means finding a
new persona and wearing it until you can't remember who
you used to be, then that's what we'll do. Maybe even gargoyles will, if they're pushed far enough."

"Perhaps." Alban's hand fell away from his forehead,
heavy and graceless. "She's left a carving for us—for me—
at the cathedral. That much I saw, in Biali's memories. I
should go alone, Margrit."

Her eyebrows shot up. "You and what army are keeping
me from going?"

"If she's trying to draw me there to wreak some sort of
vengeance—"

"Then you're sure as hell not going alone," Margrit
finished.

"It could be—is likely to be—dangerous. You humans are
so fragile." Alban brushed her cheek. "I don't want to see
you hurt, trying to help me."

Margrit released a humorless breath. "You should've
thought of that before you got me mixed up with Daisani
and Janx. It's too late to keep me safe, and I'm not letting
you go alone."

Alban's mouth curved as he glanced toward the top of the
stairs. "I could just leave you."

"The cathedral's a block away. Leave me behind and I'll
just run over there and kick your ass up and down the

sidewalk when I catch you." She stepped closer, putting herself firmly in Alban's space. "I'm going where you're going, buddy."

"Buddy." Alban tilted his head, the graceful action of a winged creature. "Does the use of nicknames suggest a new level in our relationship, Margrit?"

"Yeah. It suggests the level where I feel free to kick your butt if you leave me behind." Margrit turned a suddenly cheerful smile on the gargoyle. "So which will it be?"

Alban tipped his head again, bringing it closer to Margrit's. Her smile grew, her heartbeat thundering at the intimacy of his approach. With his mouth very nearly against hers, he murmured, "Forgive me."

In the same breath he gathered himself and leaped, clearing Margrit and the steps above her easily. She shrieked and ducked out of instinct, realizing his intent too late. She whipped around and scrambled up the stairs, tripping over her own feet in her haste. Fumbling with fallible, human grace.

Alban shot her one apologetic look over his shoulder before shoving open the rooftop door and disappearing into the night.

THIRTY

ALBAN IMAGINED HE could hear Margrit's outraged gasp cutting through the air behind him; imagined he could hear her curse, and her footsteps echoing in the stairwell as she bolted down them. Imagined, too, that there would be a moment when she looked down the hollow shaft made by the circling stairs, and thought she might jump to the bottom as easily as Alban himself could have. Rash impulse defined her, in many ways; the willingness to act boldly, consequences be damned. That sense of infallibility sent her running through the park each night, challenging the darkness. It would send her after him to do the same, even if she had to take the mundane route of dashing down the stairs.

Reaching the cathedral was a matter of seconds. He winged a tight circle above the unfinished southern tower, searching the shadows for Hajnal's form. There was no one there; he hadn't truly expected her to be. Biali might lead him to her, but memory told Alban she'd left deliberate clues.

Faster to follow them, and try Biali only if this route proved fruitless.

Faster. The thought came back to him so unexpectedly he chuckled. Margrit's impatience was compelling. Less than a week had passed since he'd first spoken to her, and already the human need to get things done *now* seemed to be wearing off on him.

Laughter faded as he landed atop the tower, falling into a habitual crouch. If Margrit's idea of the appropriate speed at which to do things could be so easily learned, perhaps she was more right than he'd given her credit for. Perhaps his people had changed more through their interactions with humans than he could have thought. Exiled from his own kind, he had deliberately held himself apart from humanity as well, seeking no solace in companionship. It was possible the gargoyles had passed by him in their social evolution, and that he, now, was a relic from a time gone by. *The Breach.* He formed the words without speaking them aloud. Maybe the inherent accusation went deeper than he knew.

The quandary could wait. Alban pushed to his feet, eyes half-closed as he turned his head, listening for the bang of a door and footsteps slapping on the sidewalk. Margrit would be there soon. Better if he was gone, drawing danger away, before she arrived.

It took a handful of moments to find the carving among the partially finished blocks of the tower. The board, several inches long, was spiked with carved ivory pieces: the Empire State Building at midpoint, Trinity Church near the bottom, tiny carved trees littering the space that was Central Park. Carefully carved figurines were fitted into peg holes in the board; a miniature Alban sat hunched by Trinity, and beautifully carved, tiny women fitted into holes punched around the edges of Central Park—four of them, making a diamond. A fifth hole lay next to the first—first because it was the location where the first woman had died, no other reason. The figurine that belonged in that hole rolled on the miniature's surface.

Alban picked it up, studying it without truly seeing. The color, old ivory, brown with age, told him all he needed to know. Lying in his palm, it was the same color as Margrit's skin, café latte, warm, lovely.

Margrit's scream tore up from below.

She'd stood gaping after Alban for what felt like an impossibly long time. In a handful of days she'd come to think of him as someone who didn't make decisions quickly, bound as he was by the element that was his essence. But beneath that, more profound even than the stillness of stone, was the nature of a gargoyle: to protect. She'd stood there, swaying in astonishment, wondering if others of the Old Races also had fundamental streaks in their being. If dragons lived to hoard, or vampires to feed. She couldn't think what the selkies or djinn might inherently embody. Maybe renewal, for the selkies; they came from the water, where all life began. Their choice to breed with humans made sense, in that light.

That was as much time as Margrit wasted in thought. She'd taken the stairs down four and five at a time, swinging on the railing to give her feet wings. Her injured hand yowled in protest every time she wrapped it around a bar, that only gave her more reason to reach the bottom faster.

She burst from her apartment building at a flat-out run, swearing aloud when forced to hurdle an icy patch at the foot of the steps. There was no sign of Alban in the skies above. Margrit hurled herself down the sidewalk toward the cathedral, forthright anger driving her even as logic told her there'd be no way to catch the winged creature, nor any way to learn what Hajnal's next step might be.

A minute later Margrit ran up the cathedral steps, pounding a fist on the door and shouting uselessly. No one answered, though even if they had she could hardly imagine being allowed inside. She danced back again, turning her gaze upward, hands lifted to block the streetlights and help her see into the dark more clearly. "Alban! Alban, Goddammit, I know you're up there! You can't do this to me! You can't—"

A blow like a sledgehammer caught her in the ribs, knocking her breath away. An instant later she rose skyward, thrown ignominiously over a slender shoulder. Wings smaller than Alban's, more delicate, strained against the air, as if Margrit's weight was dangerously heavy.

Margrit caught her breath and let it out in a scream.

A snarl, higher in pitch but no more human than Alban's growl, answered her. Wings slammed back, buffeting Margrit's skull between them, and for a moment disorientation took over. She drew breath for another scream as her head cleared, but the sound was cut off in her throat as the female gargoyle banked in a dangerously sharp turn, bringing them down among the trees of Central Park. A uniformed police officer lay crumpled near a footpath. Margrit shook her head, trying to clear her vision, then shrieked again as the gargoyle dumped her to the earth, a dozen feet below.

A swallowed scream erupted from her throat as she hit the ground badly, her left arm snapping audibly with the impact. White pain lanced through her, and she lay facedown, panting in agony, too stunned to move.

"Margrit!" Alban's voice came from above, just before another impact: the gargoyle woman landing with a thud, her feet on either side of Margrit's ribs. She crouched, taking Margrit's hair in her hand and pulling her head back.

"One more step and she dies."

Margrit whimpered, pushing herself up a few inches with her right arm. The weight on her shifted, and she was helped onto her back by a foot to the ribs. Stars swam behind her eyes and she gritted her teeth against nausea, trying to focus. "Hajnal?"

The woman standing above her was barely taller than Margrit herself, with large eyes and beautifully arranged flat, shining curls that spiraled around her face. Carefully shaped eyebrows rose at Margrit's question, and she laughed, a sweet rich sound that was nothing like the granite of Alban's laugh.

"Hajnal? Oh, that's even better than I hoped. No, I'm Ausra." She turned her head in a snaky motion, to smile at Alban. "Don't tell me you don't recognize your own little girl, Papa."

Adrenaline ricocheted through Margrit's body, a vicious swell of energy numbing her hands and deepening the nausea in her belly. But it gave her the strength to stagger clumsily to her feet, clutching her left arm.

Alban stared at Ausra, his expression too blank to register shock or disbelief. Then he closed his eyes, in one brief moment of defeat. "You look very like her," he said. "Even

Biali thought you were she, in that first instant he saw you."
His voice dropped to a whisper. "And I couldn't go far
enough into the memories to find the truth. He taught you
to carve. The memories are clearer now." Alban opened his
eyes again, barely seeming to see Ausra. "I knew she
couldn't be alive. Not after so long, not without me
knowing."

"Alive?" Ausra gave him a hard-edged smile of anger. "Not
for two centuries, Father. Not since you abandoned her."

"I didn't," he whispered. Ausra hissed, flashing a hand
out. Long fingernails caught Margrit's cheek, laying it open.
She cried out, clapping her palm to her face and leaving her
broken arm to dangle.

"Every time you lie," Ausra purred, "she hurts."

"I'm not—!"

Ausra's arm flashed up again, warningly. Margrit made a
little sound of fear, stumbling back a step. "No," Alban
blurted. "No. Don't hurt her."

"How precious," Ausra murmured. "Concerned for the
mortal girl. Did you care about all the other pretty toys,
Father? The ones I left broken in the park for you? That was
the best part," she said with wide-eyed glee. "Destroying
them in daylight, so all you knew was that they died, never
how. And the guilt kept you hidden for so long, Father. I've
been waiting to play again. They break easily, but they can
last a surprisingly long time if you're careful."

"Father..." Alban shook his head. "How can I be your
father?"

"Oh, the traditional way." Ausra walked around Margrit
with lanky strides. "Mommy and daddy gargoyle loved each
other very much, you see, and one day they had a little

gargoyle." Her voice slid to ice. "Only Daddy had abandoned Mommy and baby by then."

"No!"

Ausra's hand flashed again. This time Margrit brought her forearm up, blocking Ausra's next attack. The impact made her stumble to one side, Ausra's size belying tremendous strength. Margrit's whole body ached from stopping the blow.

Her assailant tilted her head slightly, acknowledging Margrit's attempt to save herself. "It won't help," she assured her, "but it's more fun if you fight back. Too bad about your arm. Not that the odds were even to begin with, but now you don't even stand a sporting chance."

"Ausra." Alban's voice was strangled. "This can't be true. I would never have left Hajnal if she were pregnant."

"No, of course not," Ausra cooed. "Not even to save your own stony skin, Papa. Of course not." The mocking gentleness left her voice, turning it back to ice. "She died because of you, and it's long past time you paid for it."

"How?" Margrit wrapped her hand around her left arm again, holding it against her body. "How can you be his daughter?"

Ausra clicked her tongue. "Didn't we just go through this? Mommy and Da—"

"You're the first witness." Shocked recognition flooded Margrit, washing pain away for a moment. "You're the one who reported Alban at the scene of the crime."

Ausra smiled. "And you jumped right on my bandwagon, didn't you? Faster than I'd even hoped. I thought I'd have to go round and round, waiting for you to join the game. I didn't count on the Gray woman dying, though. I was afraid you'd lose the scent. I had to go to certain extremes. You do have my mother's stone, don't you?" she inquired politely. "I'll want that back before you die."

"Janx has it." Margrit's lie sounded thick to her own ears. "Why don't you go get it from him?"

Acidic laughter cut the cold air. "Janx? The dragonlord? How would he get it? Your detective should have brought it to you."

Margrit managed a laugh of her own, edging back half a step. She hardly imagined she'd escape, but the longer a guilty client talked, the more likely she was to say something damning, or for the circumstances to change. "Tony wouldn't have shown it to me, Ausra. You think I'm important to this case. He didn't. He'd have had no reason to. Anyway, somebody working for Janx took it from the scene before Tony ever saw it. Janx showed it to me last night. That's why I thought you were Hajnal. I thought she'd lost her mind and was killing people. I didn't count on a crazy daughter." Flippancy helped keep Margrit's mind off the white-hot pain in her arm, and she'd pulled back a few steps without Ausra stopping her. Maybe she could run.

Outrun a gargoyle. The thought was ludicrous enough to make her smile.

"She wasn't pregnant," Alban whispered. "She never told me."

"Do you want to know?" Ausra demanded. "Do you really want to know? Shall I share the memory, Father?"

"No…" Margrit lifted her good hand, as if she could hold off the wall of memory that rose up and threatened to drown her.

Bleeding from a dozen gunshot wounds, her wings in

tatters, she crawled toward the east, leaving blood and water smeared together on the cobblestones. She shoved herself upward as rain-heavy clouds lightened in color, and howled out her life to the rising sun. Dawn, when it came, brought a blissful recession of agony, healing stone offering a last chance at life.

She woke weak, her breathing difficult. A man sat beside her, a human, his eyes dark and thoughtful. She snarled, lunging for him, but chains brought her up short, manacles bound into her very flesh at wrist and ankle, around her throat. He didn't move, only sat there, utterly without fear.

Memory blurred. She grew stronger, testing her chains the same way at each sunset. He left her food, starting with raw meat, then finer items, experimental. She slept, even during the nights, during the hours that were normally hers to live. She broke a chain, if not the iron bound to her skin, and he began drugging her food. She could smell it, but had no choice: it was eat what he gave her or starve, and her body was too weak to go for days and weeks without meals.

Her wings didn't heal. He stitched them together, and the skin slowly grew back, but they were thick and heavy, and when she moved them, they barely responded.

Worse than the thickness of her wings was the growing thickness of her belly. A burning anger coiled above the child growing inside her, waiting for the chance to break free and destroy the man who had captured her.

Waiting, with desperate hope, for Alban to find her.

Outside of the memory, Alban cried out, agonizing shout that brought Margrit to her knees, sobbing.

She knew it wouldn't happen. She had told him to run, had been glad when he did. She knew he would wait, too, longer than they'd agreed. She would have. If she could only escape, even into the memories, she could find him; find *help*.

But iron bound her, and nothing in the gestalt had warned her that in binding, it cut away her natural ability to reach the shared history that was her people's greatest legacy. In six hundred years of living, she had never felt so alone. Waking every night to the bone-throbbing cold of the iron chains was bad; waking unable to find her way into the comfort of mental touch drove her slowly mad. At first she knew it, and fought it, but as weeks turned to months exhaustion defeated her strength, burned away her anger, and left her raw-voiced with shrieking out her solitude. Reason failed; worse still, the reason to retain sanity failed. Once, she'd known that a gargoyle's death passed memories to the next nearest of her kind, making certain that no history was lost forever. A baby's mind wasn't meant to take that kind of influx of experience, even from a composed elder who could control the sharing. A child burdened with the chaos that had become Hajnal's mind could be scarred beyond repair.

She rarely recalled that, toward the end. Sparks of panic rose up with no explanation behind them, making her fear and weariness that much worse. And then new life came forth, screaming, frightened, cold, entering the world with the last of her mother's strength and all of her mother's madness.

The memories became Ausra's own, a solemn child playing before the fireplace. "Tell me about Mama, Papa," she begged, and Hajnal's captor smiled tolerantly and told her a story that gave lie to the little girl's nightmares.

"I thought everyone played all night and turned to stone in the day," Ausra whispered beneath the rush of memory. "I was seven when I learned otherwise."

Taunting laughter, edged with fear, and a blue-eyed boy at church hissing "Nightwalker!" to her during the evening service.

"You aren't like the other children, no," her father told her later that night. "You're different, but you're strong because of those differences. When you're older, we'll try to help you seem more like the others, but remember, my girl." He crouched, smiling at her. Ausra's reflection shone in his eyes, dark-eyed child looking back with equal parts trust and hope. "Remember your strength.

"It's dawn," he murmured to her years later. "Hold yourself, daughter. Face the sunlight. It is in you."

And Ausra, leaning into the dawn, did. Watched the sun break the horizon, coloring the sky gold and red, its light searing her eyes. She flung her hands up, crying with pain, and stone swept over her.

But the next morning she did it again.

Alban made a strangled noise, stretching out his hands as if he could touch the sunrise himself. "It isn't possible," he whispered into memory. Ausra laughed, bitter sharp sound.

"Maybe not for you, but I have strength, Father. More than you. More than my mother."

Her father, dying, caught her hand, surprising strength in the old man's hands. "I've never known," he told her, "what your mother was. All I have of hers is her name, and this." His hands shaking suddenly, he dug out the sapphire stone, dropping it into her hands. "Find your heritage," he whispered. "Go with a mortal father's love."

"I searched," Ausra said, voice brittle. "I searched for decades, Father, before I learned about the gargoyles."

"You should have been able to enter the memories," Alban murmured, sorrow and bewilderment mixed in his voice. Margrit shivered with the sound of it: centuries of regret seemed to wash through his words, as if he yearned to heal the younger gargoyle's scars any way he could.

"Mother couldn't. The iron crippled her, and I was born cut off from your precious histories. I was alone until I finally found someone like me. Another gargoyle, who told me my father's name. Alban Korund, too yellow to face death with my mother, too feeble to protect her."

"Who?" Alban's voice was soft with expectation.

Ausra curled a smile and spat the name with cold pride: "Biali. I went with him to the new world, following rumor that said you'd fled there."

Alban rocked back as if he'd taken a blow, solid stony form suddenly seeming fragile, though no surprise marked his features. "I had not thought he hated me so much. He did you a disservice, my daughter. He should have brought you to our people, where you would have been welcomed."

Ausra sneered, contorting any trace of beauty out of her face. "He did what I wanted. I've been waiting since then. Hunting the women you watched, and waiting."

"Oh, God." Margrit's voice sounded thin and pitiful in the cold air, clutching her arm to her side, memory no longer a distraction from pain. "You killed all those women over the last two hundred years. The ones who'd seen Alban.

Jesus. What were you waiting for, if you were already killing them?" Ausra turned and smiled at her.

"On your knees already. I like that. Waiting for you, Margrit. Waiting for Father to risk himself in conversation with a perfectly ordinary woman. He never did that before you. I wanted to make sure he cared before I took it all away. I've been *very* patient," she said petulantly.

"But why?" Margrit lurched to her feet, gasping for air through spikes of pain in her arm. "What good will it do? There must be easier ways to destroy somebody."

"Mother died from exposure," Ausra snarled. "She died from discovery. I would have it the same way for him."

"Are you *crazy?* That was two hundred *years* ago, Ausra! There wasn't CNN on the spot then! This won't just ruin him, it'll destroy all of you!"

"It's all right," Alban said quietly.

Margrit's head snapped around. "What the hell does that mean? Of course it's not all right!"

"It is. If nothing else, I can do this for my child."

"What, *die* for her?"

Alban turned a gentle smile on Margrit, solid determination in his eyes contributing to the fear rising in her. "The sacrifice is more than worthwhile."

"You're both nuts!" Margrit shouted. Yelling distracted her from the pain, she realized, so she kept doing it, desperately relieved for anything that pushed the sick throbbing in her arm away. "You really think one dead gargoyle's going to be the end of it? Know what humans like more than almost anything? Finding stuff out! Whether you're dead or just exposed, Alban, it's not going to stop there!"

She whirled on Ausra, eyes crossing as she banged her

arm against her torso. "You think destroying him's the answer to your problems? Chickee, I'd be looking at serious *therapy,* if I were you! Look at me! Look at *me,* Ausra!" Margrit thrust her bruised right hand out, unable to move the left to do the same. "Humans are still killing each other over shit like this! Over the color of somebody's skin! Do you *really* think we're just going to shrug and look the other way if a gargoyle turns up in the middle of New York City? You're committing suicide! *Genocide!* And I'm not going to let you!"

"How are you going to stop me?"

"You can't, Margrit." Alban smiled again, distant and kind. "Ausra doesn't want all of us, only me, and I'm not one who'll be missed by our people." Weariness colored his words, his shoulders dropping, and Margrit barely heard the next words: "And some kind of peace will be welcome. I've been alone long enough." His gaze shifted to Ausra. "What matters is that my daughter will survive."

"At the cost of your life?" Margrit shouted. "That's not good enough, Alban!"

"It is." Alban took a step forward, his wings flexing gracefully. "We breed so rarely, and I have so much to atone for. I'm sorry," he said to Ausra. "I'm sorry I wasn't there, Ausra. I truly believed Hajnal to be dead. I would never have given up hope if I'd known about you. If the price for that failure is to die in your place, then I pay it gladly."

Margrit jerked herself between the two gargoyles, bellowing at Alban. "Who the hell says that's the price? One psycho gargoyle chick? I don't think so. She's not judge and jury, goddamn it, Alban!"

"She is if I accept her as such." Alban touched Margrit's

cheek. "It has been an honor to know you, Margrit Knight." He smiled a little wryly. "I only wish we'd had more time."

"If you'd stop being such a fucking idiot, we would!"

"No, Margrit," Ausra said pleasantly, behind her. "You wouldn't."

"What!" Margrit whirled around, falling a step to the side. "What?"

"You wouldn't have more time, even if Father wasn't throwing himself on his sword."

"Why the hell not?"

Ausra's fist slammed out, knuckles cracking against Margrit's cheekbone. White pain crashed through Margrit's eyes and she collapsed, trying to catch herself with her left arm. The broken bone gave further under her weight and she screamed, a thick animal sound that turned to choked sickness. Ausra pounced after her, glee written across her delicate features. "Because I'm going to kill you." She took a fistful of Margrit's shirt and pulled her up, hand lifted again.

Margrit stared up at her, muscles locked with pain and disbelief. She tried to close her eyes, filled with the irrational conviction that it would somehow hurt less if she didn't see it coming. Her eyelids wouldn't respond, any more than she could convince her legs to get up and carry her away as fast as she could run. An inhuman roar tore against her eardrums, and she thought, so that's what dying sounds like.

Alban appeared above Ausra, behind her, jaw dropped to let his roars escape, and his massive hands closed on Ausra's head. He twisted, one violent motion that turned her head around the wrong way, the sound of fireworks popping off accompanying the action. Ausra's body turned to jelly, her own weight pulling her head from Alban's hands.

Police sirens wailed in the distance.

THIRTY-ONE

MARGRIT STARED UP at Alban, her chest heaving. He stood above her, hands cupped loosely, as if he still held Ausra's head. The sirens grew louder, and Margrit shook herself, swallowing against bile. "You've got to go," she whispered hoarsely. He blinked at her without expression.

"Alban!" she said again. "You've got to get out of here. You'll still be at the station at dawn if you don't. Go. Go! I'll be…" She laughed, a funny, high sound of pain. "I'll be okay," she promised. "Go."

Memory, exhausting, washed over her: Hajnal's voice, saying the same words that she herself spoke now. Margrit laughed again, thinly. "I'm not Hajnal. Go, or it's all for nothing. Go!"

Alban nodded once, jerkily, wheeled and ran. Margrit's eyes finally closed, and she didn't see him disappear into the sky. Lights flashed, blue and white, through her eyelids, and someone shouted, "Put your hands up!"

Margrit put her right hand up, a slow painful motion.

"Both hands!" the cop barked.

Margrit shook her head. "I can't," she whispered, and lay still.

Tony was beside her bed when Margrit opened her eyes again. Tony, and more vases of flowers than she could count in a glance. She blinked slowly, then sneezed. Every muscle clenched and she flinched, expecting agony.

There was none. She opened her eyes again, cautiously, and looked around until she found an IV drip feeding into her right arm. "Ooh. They gave me the good stuff. That's good." Her eyes drifted shut again, then she frowned. "…Tony?"

The policeman gave a quiet, nervous laugh. "Yeah. Hi, Grit. Glad to see you back among the world of the living."

Margrit absorbed that. "How long's it been?"

"About eighteen hours. They weren't real worried, said you were just sleeping. I didn't believe 'em."

She pried her eyes open. Tony had days' worth of stubble, and circles under his eyes, though the bruise she'd given him had faded to faint yellow. "So I've been sleeping and you've been watching me?"

He pursed his lips, looked around, found no escape, and nodded. "Pretty much."

Margrit nodded slowly. "You look like hell."

He spilled worried laughter. "Thanks. You should see the other guy."

"Would that be me?"

Tony nodded again. "Pretty much, yeah."

Margrit absorbed that. "Is there a mirror?"

"You think that's a good idea, Grit?"

"Do you?"

He studied her, then let out a noisy breath. "Yeah, I guess. You're tough. You're not pretty right now, though."

Margrit chortled, pleased with how it didn't hurt. "I'm insulted. What's the damage list?"

"Broken arm, broken cheekbone, hairline fractures in your right index and middle fingers, stitches across the cheekbone and, how the hell did you do that with a broken arm?"

She wet her lips. The echo of Ausra's neck breaking sounded loud in her ears, sending goose bumps over her arms, even the one bound in a cast. "I had to," she whispered. "She was going to kill me." The lie came more easily than she'd expected.

Tony's gaze weighed her. "Her head was twisted around the wrong way."

Margrit stared at him without comprehension. "Isn't that what happens when necks get broken?" Her own head seemed to be floating several inches above her body, balloonlike. Uncertainty made a bubble of illness in her stomach, compounded by the painkiller. She shuddered as Tony exhaled wearily.

"Like you were standing behind her."

Margrit's tongue thickened, filling her mouth and throat. "I don't know." The words sounded as clumsy to her ears as her tongue felt. "I don't really remember…doing it, Tony."

It was a half-truth, at best. The memory of Alban standing above her, the powerful jerk of his arms taking Ausra's life, was all too clear. Too clear, the shocking pop of bone. Even if it hadn't been her hands making the twist, she could never forget the sound or the way Ausra's body had turned boneless, slithering heavily from Alban's grip. Margrit shuddered again and swallowed against sickness.

Tony's hands came into her line of vision, palms out. "Sorry. I'm not trying to put you on the spot. You okay?"

She swallowed down bile a second time and nodded. "Under the circumstances, I'm great."

"You've got that right. You've got more structural damage than the other women, but I figure you had a chance to fight back and they didn't. I'll need to get a statement when you're feeling better."

"Sure." Margrit let her eyes close again.

"Damnedest thing," Tony added. "They packed up her body and brought it to the morgue. The boys went to work on it the next morning and it'd calcified."

Margrit's eyes popped open despite the apparent weight of her lids. "It'd what?"

"They never saw anything like it. They called it sudden something or other calcification, I forget, but I think what that means is they don't know, and they're going to try hard to forget about it. I saw it. Looked like a marble statue that'd been pounded half to dust."

Your people are good at ignoring things they don't want to see. Margrit remembered Alban saying that. She shivered again. "Remind me not to use the drugs she was on."

Tony grinned ruefully. "No kidding. Look, I'll let you get some rest. It's good to see you awake, Grit. Really good."

"It's good to be awake. I wasn't sure I was going to be."

Tony nodded somberly. "You got lucky. Real lucky."

"How'd you boys in blue manage to show up in the nick of time?" Margrit frowned, then shrugged. "Almost in the nick of time, anyway."

"Half the department was in the park, Grit, with the fourth murder down on the southern end. Even city cops come running when people start screaming."

Margrit huffed a laugh. "Thank God."

Tony reached out to touch her shoulder carefully. "I'm glad you're okay, Grit. I'll—call you?"

Margrit met his gaze a moment, then dropped her eyes. "Yeah. Give me some time to get back on my feet, Tony. I don't know what's going on in my head yet."

"Sure," he said quietly. "You take care, Grit."

"You, too." Margrit closed her eyes and listened for the door closing before she let herself slump back into the pillows.

Daisani sat by her bed the next time she opened her eyes. He looked older than he had in his offices, with lines around his mouth that she hadn't noticed before, a few silver hairs threaded through the black at his temples. He rolled up his right sleeve with tidy, small movements, entirely focused on the task at hand. Margrit watched him through a distant haze of morphine for a few seconds before rasping, "Hello."

He looked up with a faint smile, then completed the last fold of his sleeve, his arm exposed to the elbow. "Good evening, Miss Knight. I'm very pleased with you."

"Oh good. What for?" Sudden panic cramped Margrit's stomach with sickness as she remembered the copycat killer. "Oh God. Please tell me they caught him."

"In fact, they did. Getting off the plane at Heathrow. I admire your resourcefulness. I could use a woman like you."

Margrit's head went balloonlike again, floating from relief, even as the rest of her body seemed to sink through the bed from the same emotion. "I think you said that before," she managed. Daisani smiled.

"I believe I did. I still mean it. But I'm not here to talk business right now, Miss Knight. I wanted to extend my sympathies on your illness and wish you a speedy recovery. And," he added, eyebrows lifted, "to make good on my part of the bargain." He turned his head, nodding at a neatly tied package sitting on her bedside table. "You delivered. The fur is yours. I trust the first one was returned to its owner in a timely fashion."

Margrit let her eyes close again. "It was. You took it knowing she'd die, didn't you. Put it up in your office as a prize. You're just a right bastard, aren't you?" The lack of wisdom in the words hit her only after they were spoken, and she swallowed.

Daisani chuckled, his voice light with humor as he spoke. "In my defense, one of my workmen delivered the skins to me without knowing what they were. I have a standing order, you see. Bring anything that seems precious or unusual directly to me."

"It was a derelict building that people were living in, Mr. Daisani." Margrit's voice was scratchy. "Taking things from people is called stealing, even if they're not supposed to be living there in the first place."

"I like to think of it as an exchange of goods. They live in my building, I collect…rent. I suspect the difference is slight enough from your perspective that you'll think me a right bastard regardless." He laughed again. "I've been called considerably worse in my time, though rarely by a mortal woman who knew me for what I am. You amuse me, Miss Knight. I think you have no idea how rare that is."

"I do try." Margrit's voice croaked and she coughed before forcing her eyes open again. "You're about the last person I'd expect to see here. What happened with the injunction?"

Unmitigated delight crossed the vampire's face. "Your supervisor has made a positive circus out of it all. He's managed to convince half the city, without saying anything slanderous, that you've ended up in the hospital as a direct result of taking on my corporation over the building destruction. The injunction went through this morning."

"You look happy about it."

Daisani beamed. "Challenges, Miss Knight, are as rare as women like you. I'll win in the end, of course, but it's positively inspiring to have someone put up a fight. In fact, that's why I've come."

"Out of inspiration?" Margrit laughed almost silently, pleased all over that it didn't hurt. Daisani smiled broadly, showing unnervingly normal teeth again.

"Precisely. I so hate to see a worthy opponent at anything less than her peak, I'm inspired to action." He smiled once more, extending his hand. "Let me help you sit up, Margrit. I have a gift for you."

Panic seized her stomach yet again and she felt color burn

in her cheeks. Daisani laughed. "Not that sort of gift. Hasn't Alban told you? It doesn't work that way."

"Thank God," she said with feeling.

Daisani chuckled again, helping her to sit up before brushing a fingertip across his exposed inner wrist. "But you are right about one thing," he murmured. "The gift is blood." He caressed his wrist again, and a thin red line opened. Margrit stared at him in revulsion, and he clucked his tongue, waving a finger at her in gentle admonition. "One sip for healing. This is a gift, Miss Knight, not a favor to be repaid. One sip."

Margrit watched blood bead as Daisani turned his wrist up to catch it there. "And two sips?"

He smiled. "Taste, and I'll tell you." He moved his wrist to her mouth, brushing liquid across her lips. Margrit licked automatically, then startled and gagged, swallowing down blood that was sweeter than her own, tangy iron drowned by a thick sugary taste. Daisani turned his wrist up again, the cut sealing over. "One sip for healing," he said, folding his cuff back down. "Two for life." He met her eyes and smiled again. "Three to kill."

Margrit's heart rate leaped, blood rushing to her face, making her wounds and bruises ache badly enough to bring tears to her eyes, in spite of the morphine. She wet her lips again, whispering, "Yeah?" through the pounding in her head. A strengthening surge of blood poured into her left arm, making the bone and muscles there throb, too. "Is this tasting an accumulative thing, or does it start over after a while?"

"Three strikes," Daisani said, "and you're out. I do look

forward to meeting you again, Miss Knight. I'll see myself
out. Don't get up." Smiling, he rose and left Margrit behind,
pain beating at her skin as if it was trying to escape.

"Grit?" Her name was spoken softly, unlikely to disturb
her if she wasn't drifting on the wakeful side of sleep.
Margrit inhaled and opened her eyes to find Cole at the edge
of her bed, wearing a tentative smile.

"Ah." She let her eyes close again. "If it isn't my roommate
the dickhead. Hello, Cole." She flexed her toes, then her
arches and upward, carefully bringing each muscle group
into play. It only became extraordinary when she twitched
the fingers of her left hand and they moved easily, no stab of
pain where the bone had broken. "How long have I been
asleep?"

"Since yesterday afternoon. Cam, your parents and I
have been taking turns keeping an eye on you. Grit, I'm
sorry. I felt like an asshole immediately, and then with you
being attacked…"

Margrit turned her head to look at her dark-haired housemate, and sighed. "You were an asshole. Don't get me
wrong. I think you should grovel a lot, and probably fix me
gourmet meals for a few weeks. But, um." She mashed her
lips together and glanced down. "I was out of line, too. You
were worried and I…look, I'm sorry, too, okay? Maybe we
should just call it even."

"Sounds good to me." Cole leaned over to kiss her forehead, then pulled her into a careful hug. "I really am sorry,
Grit."

"I know." Margrit sighed and curled her fingers into his

sweater, eyes closing again. "Man, I'm tired. When are they letting me out of here?"

"I don't know. You look a hell of a lot better, Grit. The doctors have been muttering to each other about how fast you're healing. They keep checking your charts, like they made a mistake with the initial diagnosis."

"Maybe they did. I'm feeling pretty good." The latter part, at least, was truth. There would be no explaining the gift Daisani had shared with her, not now and not ever. "Are my parents still here?"

"Yeah. They went down to get some lunch. You want me to get them?"

"That'd be great." Margrit slid deeper into the pillows. "And tell the doctors I'd like to go home, please."

Janx came as she pulled her shoes on the next morning under a nurse's watchful glare. He leaned in the door, red hair more fiery in the sunlight that streamed through the windows, and watched her admiringly. "I didn't think you'd be up so soon."

Margrit looked up, then waved the nurse out of the room as she pushed her foot into her shoe with a thump. "Apparently I'm a very fast healer. Are any of you *not* going to come see me?"

"I thought you'd be happier if I kept Malik away," Janx said merrily. "You're looking well, Margrit. You don't mind if I just call you Margrit now, do you? I think I've earned the intimacy, since you've successfully pulled one over on me."

Margrit's heart went still for a beat. "I have?"

"Please. Who else could have managed to get access to that number? Fortunately for me, the phone I called him from is owned by some poor bastard in Ohio. I imagine he was a little dismayed when the police broke down his door at two in the morning. But I must say, well done, really. I didn't even suspect. You appear to have all the guile of an ingenue, Margrit, hiding the consummate acting skills of an old dame of the theater. Are you a very good lawyer?" he asked politely, then dismissed the question by following it with, "I've brought you a gift."

Margrit straightened up, shifting her sling against her body. "I'm not sure I need or want any more presents from you people."

Janx laughed and sauntered forward to put a cell phone in her hand. "This one is purely recompense for ruining your other one. I've even gotten you the same number. Now, aren't I splendid?"

Despite herself, despite knowing what the man was, Margrit laughed. "You are," she admitted. "Thanks."

"You're welcome." He narrowed jade-green eyes at her. "There is a point of business, I'm afraid."

Margrit sighed. "Of course there is. What is it?"

"There's still the matter of favors owed," he said. "Two from you."

"And one from you. I know, Janx. Just because it hasn't been called in yet doesn't mean it's over." Margrit arched her eyebrows at the dragon. "You should remember that, too. Someday I'll need that third request."

Janx bowed from the waist. "And I'll be delighted to

honor it. You're a worthy opponent, Margrit Knight. It's wonderful to have you in the game." He clapped his hands together, a sharp pleased sound. "Now, I believe they won't let even the most fit of persons walk out of one of these death traps under her own power. May I have the honor of wheeling your chair?"

"I don't think so," Cole said from the doorway. He came in to kiss Margrit's uninjured cheek and examine her critically. "You look almost normal. I'm afraid I'm the lady's wheels, Mr…?" He offered a hand to Janx.

The dragon arched an eyebrow, then shook it. "Janx," he said. "Just Janx. You must be Cole."

Cole cast a startled glance at Margrit. "Yeah, I am."

"A pleasure to meet you, Cole. Do us all a favor, and take good care of this young lady. She's more remarkable than she knows." Janx bowed again, then exited, leaving Cole staring after him with raised eyebrows.

"Care to tell me what that was about?"

"No," Margrit said, grinning. "Just one of my many admirers. Cole, please, *please* get me the hell out of here."

The yellow police tape was gone, the ground scraped raw, no longer muddied with blood. The park lights made sharp-edged shadows on the rough earth, sunset having come and gone. Margrit hitched her thumbs in her waistband, studying the area for signs of Ausra's death, but nothing was there. A mounted policeman rode by, nodding a greeting. Margrit nodded in return, bouncing on her toes to keep warm. Running tights and a sweatshirt would let her break directly into her workout if

Alban didn't come, but they weren't warm enough for standing around the park.

Footsteps sounded behind her, and she lifted her chin, eyes closing with relief. "I was afraid you wouldn't come."

"I almost didn't." Alban's steps stopped several feet away. Margrit lifted her chin higher, feeling the distance as a wall between them, even without seeing it. "I thought a long time about leaving New York for good," the gargoyle added after a moment.

Margrit gave a laugh that made her heart ache. "Over a woman."

"Isn't it always over a woman?" Faint humor infused Alban's voice, and she turned to him, studying the angles of his face in the blue streetlights. His hair purpled beneath the lamps, his eyes colorless and intent on her. Even the suit jacket was the same, lilac in its shadows, the cold not bothering him at all.

He inclined his head, making a small, fluid gesture that encompassed the fact she was on her feet and out of the hospital. "Yes. You're healing very quickly."

"A gift." Margrit pulled a quick, wry smile. "From Daisani."

Alban's silence was foreboding. "That..." he said eventually, and Margrit laughed.

"Was a bad idea. I know. It was his bad idea, though, and I was stuck in a hospital bed. I didn't have anywhere to run."

"Running isn't your strong suit, anyway."

"On the contrary," Margrit said, offended. "I'm a very good runner."

"Not when the direction to run is 'out of danger.'"

Another smile flickered across Margrit's face, keeping more complicated emotions at bay. "Maybe not then," she admitted, then bit her lower lip. "Alban…"

"I've searched the memories," he said abruptly, cutting her off. "Mine. Ausra's, and Hajnal's through them."

Margrit cocked her head, then shook it uncertainly. "You have their memories now? How'd that happen?"

He turned his hand palm up, and his voice held old weariness. "Each family carries a part of the Old Races' history. We gather once every century to share memories, so the history remains. If someone dies, her memories go to the nearest gargoyle, so nothing is ever lost, even when a family dies out. Ausra was the last of Hajnal's family, the Dunstal line. I am the last of the Korunds. I carry the memories of both those lines, now."

"Jesus, Alban. That's a hell of a burden."

"Made the more so for exile." Alban said the words as if they didn't matter, making Margrit's teeth grind. "Hajnal's memories are, I think, tainted by Ausra's rage. It'll take time to sort through her anger and find the truth, but what I remember from the old memories, from before I left the tribe, there have only been a few cases where a gargoyle faced daylight. In each of those, the individual was a half-breed."

Margrit knotted her hands, wanting to pursue the topic of exile, though a trace of amusement slid through her annoyance. How she expected to force a creature with Alban's weight advantage to talk when he didn't want to, she couldn't imagine. She relaxed her hands, letting irritation go, to ask another question: "A half-breed? Like half…dragon? Vampire?"

Alban nodded. "Another Old Race. We're not prone to

intermingling our bloodlines, but it happens once in a while."

"Half-human?" Margrit asked in a low voice. Alban shifted backward, putting a little more space between them. Broadening the wall that lay between them. There were so many reasons not to breach it. The words danced through her mind for the hundredth time: *alien. Inhuman. Different. Racially separate.*

"It's taboo," he finally replied. "An exiling offense, as much as killing one of our own or letting humans know we exist. Though the selkies have interbred with humans for generations, to keep their bloodline alive at all. So perhaps we're not so different."

"We don't know how long Hajnal was that man's captive."

"No." Alban said the word with brusque finality, leaving Margrit to bow her head.

"Thanks for choosing me." She let a breath out, adding, "Two out of three, Alban."

He shook his head, a slight questioning motion, and she turned her gaze away, looking into the park. "You just told me three things that were exiling offenses among the Old Races. You've done two out of three in the last week. You told me about yourself, and you killed Ausra to save me. Where does that leave you?"

"Alone." The ease in Alban's voice made Margrit look at him again, offense rising on his behalf.

"That's it? You'll just sit back and take it? You had good reasons to do what you did."

"Among the Old Races, Margrit, there is no good reason to break our laws. What few selkies may be left are hardly part of our people any longer, and no one would have truck with them if it could be avoided. I've lived half my life in exile. It does me no harm to continue this way."

"I don't think that's acceptable."

"What you think doesn't matter, Margrit. It's how our society has built its laws."

"Laws, Alban," Margrit said clearly, "are for reinterpreting, rebuilding, negotiating and discarding when they no longer make sense within the confines of a society. I'm not quitting just because the going's getting tough." Regret suddenly spiked as she thought of Tony. She had stopped when things got tough with him, too often.

Margrit set her jaw, putting the thought aside. "I owe Janx favors and Eliseo Daisani wants a piece of me. Cara Delaney went missing on my watch, and I'm going to find her. Like it or not, I'm taking on your world one race at a time, so I don't see why I shouldn't go all the way and challenge your stupid exile laws, too. Walk away if you want to, but you brought me into this thing as your advocate, and that's what I'm going to be."

Alban looked down at her across the space he'd delineated, finally shaking his head. "I've put you in danger already, Margrit. I'll do what I can to remove the onus of promises made to Janx and Daisani. You'll be able to return to your own world unfettered. The rest of it is my own problem, and I choose not to question the laws the Old Races have abided by for millennia." He hesitated, as if there might be something left to say, then opened a big hand with graceful measure, and sketched a brief bow from the waist.

"Goodbye, Margrit."

* * *

Margrit watched him go, a pale form leaping above the treetops, wings snapping open to catch the air, before she doubled over to stretch her hamstrings. Then she was running, almost without transition, pavement slapping by beneath her feet as she drew in deep breaths of cold air, savoring the sheer, exhilarating joy of exercise.

Ir. Ra. Shun. Al. Safety in long strides, freedom in exercise. Margrit sprinted around a park bench and broke into a hard run down a long straight stretch, half imagining she heard the annoyed grunt of a broad-shouldered monster in the trees. A creature bound to protect by his very nature, even if he threatened to walk away from it. A smile warmed her face as she put on speed, imagining Alban's winged jumps above her.

* * *

She would never see him, he reasoned.

Humans never looked up.

* * * * *

C.E. Murphy

A native of Alaska, C.E. (Catie) **Murphy** now lives with her husband in her ancestral homeland of Ireland. Having been there for (at the time this book is published) two years, she's still waiting for winter to arrive, and somewhat gleeful that it hasn't done so yet. She's pursuing a successful full-time writing career, the details of which can be found on her Web site, cemurphy.net.

Her idea of a down-time project is writing a comic book, which caused both her agent and editor to suggest (independently of one another) that she consider taking up a musical instrument, so she has a creative outlet that isn't writing. As a result, she can now pick out a rather shrill "Ode to Joy" on the tin whistle, and has some vague hope of conquering "Yankee Doodle Dandy" in the near future.

LUNA™

www.LUNA-Books.com   LCEMBIO07TR

LUNA™

**Powerful, magical and beautiful.
A world you can only imagine.**

The Walker Papers trilogy...
three spellbinding stories featuring
Joanne Walker, a regular Seattle
beat cop who also happens to be
a magical shaman with a penchant
for saving the world....

Available wherever books are sold!

A STRANGER IN TWO WORLDS

P.C. CAST

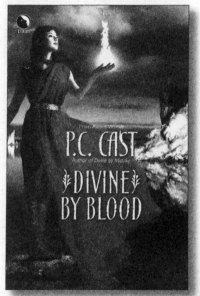

Upon discovering the truth of her heritage, Morrigan MacCallan leaves the normalcy of Oklahoma for the magical world of Partholon. Yet instead of being respected as the daughter of the goddess Incarnate, Morrigan feels like a shunned outsider. In her desperation to belong in Partholon, she confronts forces she doesn't understand or control. And soon a strange darkness draws closer....

DIVINE BY BLOOD

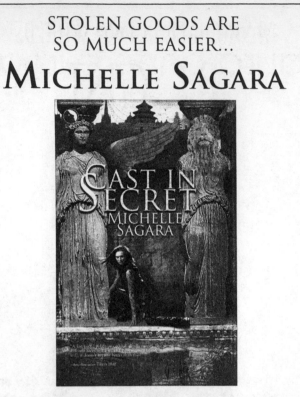